TO WIN A PRINCE

TO WIN A PRINCE

TONI SHILOH

BETHANYHOUSE
a division of Baker Publishing Group
Minneapolis, Minnesota

Published by Bethany House Publishers
11400 Hampshire Avenue South
Minneapolis, Minnesota 55438
www.bethanyhouse.com

Bethany House Publishers is a division of
Baker Publishing Group, Grand Rapids, Michigan

Library of Congress Cataloging-in-Publication Data
Names: Shiloh, Toni, author.
Title: To win a prince / Toni Shiloh.
Description: Minneapolis, Minnesota : Bethany House, a division of Baker
    Publishing Group, [2022]
Identifiers: LCCN 2022010982 | ISBN 9780764238963 (paperback) | ISBN
    9780764240881 (casebound) | ISBN 9781493439133 (ebook)
Subjects: LCGFT: Novels.
Classification: LCC PS3619.H548 T6 2022 | DDC 813/.6—dc23
LC record available at https://lccn.loc.gov/2022010982

Scripture quotations are from THE HOLY BIBLE, NEW INTERNATIONAL VERSION®, NIV® Copyright © 1973, 1978, 1984, 2011 by Biblica, Inc.® Used by permission. All rights reserved worldwide. Or from The Holy Bible, English Standard Version® (ESV®), copyright © 2001 by Crossway, a publishing ministry of Good News Publishers. Used by permission. All rights reserved. ESV Text Edition: 2016.

Emojis are from the open-source library OpenMoji (https://openmoji.org/) under the Creative Commons license CC BY-SA 4.0 (https://creativecommons.org/licenses/by-sa/4.0/legalcode)

Cover design by Dan Thornberg, Design Source Creative Services

Author is represented by the William K. Jensen Literary Agency.

Baker Publishing Group publications use paper produced from sustainable forestry practices and post-consumer waste whenever possible.

22   23   24   25   26   27   28   7   6   5   4   3   2   1

To the Author and Finisher of my faith.

Prologue

Your Majesty, do you have a recommendation on the sentencing of Prince Ekon Diallo of the Etikun tribe?"

Brielle Eesuola Adebayo, queen of Ọlọrọ Ilé Ijọba of Africa, exhaled slowly, breathing out her nerves. For days she'd prayed about Ekon's upcoming sentencing for crimes against the crown, specifically crimes of conspiracy to undermine the lawful line of succession. His half-sister, Dayo Layeni, Bri's ex-secretary, had used him in her schemes in an attempt to overthrow Bri as rightful queen.

Ekon had come clean when he realized Dayo's next step was kidnapping. Fortunately, it had not come to that, and he'd willingly shared the reasons Dayo wanted to wear the crown instead of Bri. Unfortunately, the Ọlọrọ Ilé Royal Council still found him guilty of conspiracy charges. Ekon had been willing to trick Bri into marriage. He'd knowingly colluded with Dayo to take Bri's seat to rule the kingdom. His actions deserved punishment, but did they deserve imprisonment? Or even . . . *death*?

Ọlọrọ allowed for the death penalty in crimes against the crown if the offenses were severe. Bri had quickly ruled out death, however. She'd been in no physical danger, and Dayo had been arrested, circumventing the coup. Yet their conspiracy couldn't be denied and had been confirmed by Ekon himself.

Bri had pored over the laws and judgments available in this

situation, but not one book gave a suggestion on the weight of mercy. As a Christian, didn't she owe Ekon a second chance, or was this merely a law-and-order situation? The constant questions piling up in her brain had her eating antacids in preparation for today.

"Your Majesty?"

Brielle blinked as Yemi Ladipo's raspy voice broke through her reverie. The previous council head, Jomi Oladele, had already been punished for his role in the coup attempt. He'd divulged council secrets to Dayo, among other crimes.

Bri resisted the urge to fidget and instead maintained her regal demeanor. Now was the time to decide if she'd speak on Ekon's behalf. "Yes, Mr. Ladipo. I have a recommendation."

She directed her gaze to the man in question. He stood, chin tucked to his chest. It was the same posture he'd assumed since he'd walked into the council chambers, only looking up when someone directed a question his way. He wore the Etikun colors and an *amure*—a sash—denoting his princely status.

"Prince Ekon Diallo, *omoba* of the Etikun *tribu*," she began.

His head lifted, and eyes full of contrition met hers. Her heart panged. *God would grant mercy, Brielle.*

Bri swallowed. "I have prayed over this moment. I have examined your actions and crimes against the crown of Ọlọrọ Ilé. To say I'm disappointed by your complicity in Ms. Layeni's plans would be a gross understatement, Prince Diallo. Yet I do not feel your actions are punishable by death."

His shoulders sagged.

"I also do not believe your actions warrant time in prison. Naturally, if the council decides otherwise, I will defer to their determination." She licked her dry lips. "I believe your character could benefit from community service. To spend time in our country and see the true heart of the people and what it means to serve. You do not need a title or a crown to make you worthy of serving the people of Ọlọrọ Ilé."

Ekon's eyes widened at her pronouncement, but no other signs showed surprise or shock from her recommendation. She'd already spoken to the royal council ahead of time, so she knew the punishment they'd decided upon. Her guidance was for the court's purposes, since the actual high court had deferred this case to the care of the council because of the severity of the charges. It was also to give the council an opportunity to follow her lead in doling out a sentence.

All Bri could do was pray that Ekon truly had experienced a change of heart. That serving the people would remove the privileged attitude the title of omoba—*prince*—had given him. He wasn't a bad person, per se, but he could certainly improve.

The other council members whispered amongst themselves until the acting-head of council nodded, signaling an end to the discussion.

"Thank you for that recommendation, Your Majesty," Mr. Ladipo said. "Omoba Ekon Diallo, the Ọlọrọ Ilé Royal Council has discussed the charges against you and taken the recommendation of Queen Adebayo under advisement. We are ready to give you our sentencing."

Ekon nodded, hands rigid at his sides as he met Mr. Ladipo's gaze head on.

"The council has decided to strip you of your title."

Brielle winced inwardly in sympathy. Such a harsh punishment, but she could understand the council's reasoning for the action. As much as she wanted mercy for Ekon, they could not ignore his crimes.

"You are no longer a prince within the Etikun tribe and will henceforth be forbidden to seek a seat on the royal council. You are ordered to one hundred and sixty-eight hours of community service, providing aid to the various tribes of Ọlọrọ Ilé. You will also serve three hundred and twenty hours in the position of business consultant. Your father, Prince Iseoluwa Diallo, has informed us you will no longer be working for Diallo Enterprises.

Therefore, you have the time to assist Ms. Iris Blakely in her new endeavor to help the impoverished in our country and put Ọlọrọ Ilé on the map in the fashion textile industry. Despite your current misjudgment, we believe you have the business acumen to ensure her business is a success, making Ọlọrọ a success. You will assist her in any way deemed necessary." Mr. Ladipo let silence fill the room for a moment before continuing. "Do you understand your judgment?"

"Yes, *alàgbà* tribu, I understand." His eyes flicked to Brielle. "I thank you for your leniency—especially yours, Your Majesty." He gave a bow, then stood straight.

"Then we have nothing more to say, *Mr.* Diallo. You are dismissed from council chambers." Mr. Ladipo concluded the meeting.

Brielle watched as Ekon left. She had no idea what he would face going back to Etikun, stripped of his title. How would he deal with the disappointment his tribe members would feel? She knew from previous conversations that he did not have faith to see him through this.

Lord God, please reach his heart. May choosing mercy be the right choice and not one we'll come to regret later.

ONE

Ekon

I padded out of my bedroom, stopping in the hallway to peer through the floor-to-ceiling windows overlooking the hills of Etikun. For some reason, my alarm had sounded instead of the soft voice of my personal assistant to wake me. Nazum had worked for me since I turned eighteen, and my alarm had only been a backup in case I chose to sleep in. Where could he be?

I continued toward the living area. "Nazum?"

Nothing.

The only noise reaching my ears was my slippered feet. Not a single servant ran about. The place appeared to be empty. Had something happened? I checked my mobile for any missed messages and found none. The seventy-inch TV beckoned me.

My black leather couch was perfectly positioned in front of the entertainment center. Surely the local news would explain where my servants had disappeared to. With a press of a button, I had it up and running . . . and gaped. There stood Father in his princely dress, talking to a reporter. The headline read

Prince Iseoluwa Diallo denounces son's actions. I turned up the volume.

"His mother and I are deeply ashamed. We cannot express our regret enough for his involvement with Ms. Layeni. As far as we are aware, there was no intimate relationship between them."

I shook my head. *Disgusting.* No one but the council and queen knew Ms. Layeni was my half-sister. To insinuate anything else was deplorable, but that was Father's way. Keep all misdeeds secret so he could continue the façade of the humblest prince in Etikun. But I knew the truth, the stain of his infidelity against Mother.

"Prince Diallo, do you think the punishment should have been more severe?"

Father's brow furrowed. "I do not go against my queen or the council's decisions. However, I have seen fit to add my own form of penance to their sentencing."

What? I slowly looked around my empty penthouse flat, stomach souring as realization came to me.

"What sort of reprimand will you enact?"

"I have removed all servants from Ekon's employ, transferring them to other jobs within Diallo Enterprises. They should not suffer for his gross misjudgments. I have also removed his vehicles from his ownership in order to sell them and transfer the earnings to a charity of my wife's choice."

A primal roar tore from my lips as I flipped over the coffee table. How *dare* he remove my servants! Did he expect me to do everything myself like some commoner? Simply because the council stripped me of my title did not mean I had to live like the lower class.

How was I supposed to prepare for my first day of business consulting without breakfast and clothes to wear? How would I get there? *Public transportation?*

A shudder coursed through me, and I sank onto the sofa

cushions, head in my hands as I rocked. My breath came in spurts as the implications of Father's actions sank in. I was barely cognizant of the reporter asking more questions.

Until one stood out.

"Do you still consider Mr. Ekon Diallo your son?"

My gaze rose as I held my breath.

"If he can turn his wayward ways around."

Enough of that. I turned off the news, throwing the remote to the floor. The clatter of it hitting the marble tiles made me wince. I better not have chipped them. Who knew if I had the funds to replace them, considering I was no longer a Diallo employee. Would Father cancel my bank membership as well? Could he?

I paced back and forth, chest heaving. Part of me was not surprised Father did not have the decency to explain these repercussions to my face. Learning about them on the morning news like the rest of the country was par for the course. I could only imagine the comments filling social media right now. Something I had purposely ignored since I walked out of council chambers as a nobody.

"Ahhhh!" But shouting did not make me feel better. It only made the vein in my forehead pulse all the harder.

I stomped across the room and into the kitchen. Since I apparently no longer had a personal chef, I would have to make my own breakfast. A quick glance at the stove clock showed an hour before my report time. Normally, I would eat an omelet prepared by my chef. Now I would, what . . . make it *myself*?

Unfortunately, I had no time to voice my complaints. I could not show up late and have the council's opinion of me worsen—or Father's. I shook my head and pulled up a You-Tube tutorial for making the perfect omelet. After watching the video a few times, I removed eggs, bacon, and cheese from my refrigerator. There were some *akara* balls left over from the day before the sentencing. I could heat those up to make a complete meal. It should be simple enough.

I turned the knob to start the flame as shown on the video, then moved it to the middle setting as recommended. The fire lit the stove. I smiled. Clearly cooking was not as difficult as Chef had always made it seem. I grabbed an egg and tapped it on the counter like I had seen the cook do in the video. The insides splattered on the counter, making a slimy path down the cabinet before the yolk landed on the floor.

I bit back an oath.

A quick glance located the materials to clean up the mess. The feel of the snotty yolk in the paper towel made me want to retch. Relief filled me as I managed to place the mess in the trash.

At least I had more eggs. I would simply use less force than before. A small smile shifted something inside me as I successfully cracked the egg before pushing my thumbs inside to make a hole to open the shell.

The egg exploded, sending clear and yellow liquid down my nightshirt.

The oath left my mouth this time. I glanced at my watch. How had thirty minutes passed so quickly? If I was to meet Ms. Blakely on time, breakfast would have to be postponed. I put the ingredients back in the refrigerator, then removed my shirt and tossed it into the laundry room.

That chore ranked low on my priority list. As long as I had clean clothes, I would not have to worry about learning how to operate the washing machine. I flipped through the dress shirts hanging in my walk-in closet and opted for black. It matched my growing irritation as my stomach complained about not being fed.

No servants. No cars. No title of prince. Instead, I would now answer to *mister*. What more could happen to me? The hairs on the back of my neck rose at the question, and I shook off the unnerving feeling. I needed to find a driver. My mouth curled. A taxi, even?

A few minutes later, I grabbed my wallet and stuffed it into my back pocket. A quick look in the mirror showed my smooth chocolate skin. My hair was close-cropped and freshly lined, thanks to a trip to the barber before the council sentencing. My shave this morning had maintained my clean look. The only thing I added was a black beaded necklace, interspersed with a few golden beads. I was now ready to meet Ms. Blakely and get my business consultant hours under way.

Three hundred and twenty hours!

The amount was pure ridiculousness. Yet if I worked an eight-hour day, then forty days later would see an end to my servitude. What if Ms. Blakely scheduled me for less than a full day's work? Then the torture would be endless. I had a jewelry business I was desperate to return to. But wait. Would Father allow me to return? Somehow, I needed to get back in his good graces.

Clearly, Father wanted to wash his hands of me. How could I remove the stain of conspiring against the queen from the Diallo name? Reversing such monumental damage seemed impossible.

I could still remember the rage on his face when he discovered I had been talking to my half-sister. But that was because my relationship to her was a taboo topic. No one in Etikun knew that Dayo and I shared a *màmá*, because the woman I called Mother was known as my biological mother. In reality, Dayo's mother was my biological mother, as Father had had an affair with her. I had not known this until my teens, when Dayo showed up unannounced at our house, wanting to meet me. Father forbade it, but when I turned eighteen, I reached out to her.

Now she was imprisoned. My biological mother deceased. All I had was the woman I had always known as Mother.

I shook the morose thoughts from my mind and headed toward the penthouse elevator. It led to the lobby, where everyone would see me step into a taxi instead of my chauffeured Porsche.

A taxi!

At least I would not have to drive myself around Ọlọrọ Ilé.

Fortunately, the taxi waited at the curb when I arrived on the lobby floor. I kept my eyes straight ahead, avoiding any eye contact with my neighbors and the concierge at the front desk. I could not bear to see the looks of condemnation or pity I had been receiving since first becoming headline news. There was nothing like seeing your face plastered on the screen with the words *house arrest* scrolling underneath.

The moment I stepped outdoors, reporters swarmed me, yelling my name. I pushed through the throng, ignoring the questions regarding my feelings on my father's earlier interview. I opened the back door of the taxi, slamming it shut as I slid across the cloth seats.

"Drive now," I spat.

"Yes, *ògbéni*. Where to?"

I flinched inwardly at the title of *mister*, hearing the derisive tone of Alàgbà Ladipo instead.

"Uh." I peered at the note on my phone listing the address of Ms. Blakely's business. I relayed it to the driver.

"Got it, *ògbéni*. I will get you there quick as possible."

Thank goodness Ọlọrọ was not prone to traffic jams like other parts of Africa. The island boasted a small population of less than a million.

I focused on the scenery passing by as the driver took me to Aṣọ, Ms. Blakely's business. Once I arrived, the first thing I wanted to ask was why she chose that name. Aṣọ meant *clothed* in Oninan and seemed a simplistic name for a fashion company. Granted, my experience was in the jewelry industry, but still.

Hopefully she had not submitted paperwork denoting the

name and a trademark for the logo. Certainly I could brainstorm much better options than Aṣọ. Business was in my blood and went along with the degree hanging on my home office wall. Another requirement from Father.

He had been grooming me to take over Diallo Enterprises one day, but with this setback, I wondered about my future there. Out of all the changes I had experienced this past month, not working at the family business made me the most nervous. I could not lose my position as COO of Diallo Enterprises. *I cannot.*

I would call Father this evening. Inform him how much of an asset I would be to Ms. Blakely. Father would have to reconsider stripping everything from me then. *Right?*

This was not my life, and the upsets had me shaken. Still, I had an image to protect regardless of my current infamy. I would become a prince once more, and this would all be relegated to a minor detour in my life.

"Are you okay, ògbéni? You are awfully quiet back there."

I peered at the rearview mirror. "Simply thinking, *monsieur.*" *Mister* sounded better in French. Plus, speaking the language reminded me of my superiority over the taxi driver.

I was accomplished. Held an MBA, spoke six languages, and was heir to the Diallo empire. I was no *commoner*, despite the royal council's pronouncement that I could no longer be titled. I had led a princely life, been raised in privilege from birth. I did not know how to be anything else.

Despite this, I was sure the royal council expected me to accept my new identity. The queen had even mentioned that I needed to learn what it was like to serve. Helping Ms. Blakely with all my business knowledge was a service in itself. Why must I demean myself in front of the community as well? At least that torture did not start until next week.

One thing at a time.

"I will leave you to think, then." The driver turned on the radio and began bobbing his head to the rhythm of the music.

"I appreciate that, monsieur." I glanced at my watch. I was due at Aṣọ in five minutes. "Will we arrive soon?"

"*Bééni, bééni, ògbéni.*"

His assured *yes* would not help me if he did not apply a little more pressure to the gas pedal. It would not look good if I showed up late on my first day. I sighed. This day was off to a horrible start.

The taxi driver stopped behind the vehicle in front of us and began shaking and singing at the top of his lungs.

"Ah, do you listen to this, ògbéni?" he yelled out.

"No, I have not heard this song before." Despite my obvious disdain, the driver continued his serenade. Father had always played instrumental music. Back in my university days, I had been familiar with popular songs, but that style was not something I gravitated to.

I wanted to lower myself from view in case anyone saw me with the driver exuberantly singing at full volume. Why did he have to roll his window all the way down? He looked ridiculous. Did that make me so by association?

"Monsieur." I pointed ahead when he turned to look at me. "The car has moved."

"Ah, yes. I apologize. This is my jam!"

I glanced at my watch. Two minutes to arrival and a few more miles to drive.

I was going to be late.

Eleven minutes later, security escorted me to Ms. Blakely's office. She stood behind her desk, a look of irritation on her very pretty face.

I blinked. I remembered her. She had been at the welcome ball for the queen during our Independence Day festivities. She had worn an emerald dress. I remembered because the matching jewelry had made her skin glow like a brown axinite.

"You're late," she snapped in an American accent similar to

the queen's but less cultured. No, that was not the right word. Less guarded.

I clenched my hands. If I had had my Porsche or even the Mercedes to drive, I would have been on time. Something told me the queen's best friend would not care about my plight. So I offered the truth. "My taxi driver got distracted dancing instead of driving."

Her mouth dropped open. "What?"

"It was quite embarrassing. He sang loudly—and *badly*, I might add. He would break out dancing at traffic lights only to realize traffic had commenced upon my reminder. He insisted that almost every single song that came on was *his jam*."

She folded her arms across her chest. I saw the slightest twitch of her lips.

"Fine. I'll make an allowance this time. But I expect you to be on time in the future, Mr. Diallo."

Ugh. I cannot bear that label. "That is my expectation as well, Ms. Blakely. It was my first time in a taxi, and I did not know what to expect."

Her mouth parted again, eyes wide with shock. It was quite obvious she had not been raised in a life of privilege if she thought taking a taxi a common practice. But that was none of my concern.

I slid my hands into my pockets. "I am ready to begin. Am I to work an eight-hour day?"

Her nose wrinkled as she pushed her curly mane away from her eyes. How did one woman have so much hair?

"We'll see. I'm in the early stages, but I've gotten a lot completed." She frowned, her ruby-red lips turning downward. "And unfortunately, still have too much on my plate."

"I am here to help in any way I can." And to prove to Father that I deserved the things life had afforded me, and maybe even to convince the council to rescind their decision and restore my title.

"Yes, well, have a seat." She gestured to the white chair in front of her glass desk.

I sat down and held my breath. Whatever happened in this meeting would determine my future. I could only hope Ms. Blakely would put me on a path that led me back to the top.

TWO

Iris

*E*kon Diallo.

My stomach tied itself into a million knots the moment he sauntered into my office. I tried to appear calm and in control despite the turbulence of my emotions. Ever since I'd seen a picture of the former prince, I'd been intrigued by him. Then, when I'd seen him at the Independence Day ball, my hormones had gone into overdrive like a teenager with her first crush. I wasn't sure what exactly about him made my insides flutter, but not being able to pinpoint his *je ne sais quoi* quality didn't stop the effect he had on me.

My cheeks wanted to heat at his proximity. I could only pray that he'd think my flushed face a result of anger at his tardiness and nothing more. Which I still couldn't believe. Who showed up late to their first day of court-appointed service, *then* blamed it on the taxi driver?

I didn't know what to think, but I also didn't have time to dwell on my emotions—or was that hormones? Seeing the man I'd developed a crush on in person sent a wave of longing through me, followed quickly by feelings of betrayal. How dare

21

he try to ruin Bri's ascension to the throne. She was a wonderful person and didn't deserve all the subterfuge she'd faced.

You aren't supposed to dwell on your emotions, remember? Snap to it and act like the owner of a company.

I smoothed the back of my black dress and sat. The hem matched the bodice, sporting a tribal arrangement of reds, yellows, and black. I loved the plethora of fabric available in Ọlọrọ and couldn't wait to share it with the world.

"Let me give you a little background," I said once Ekon was seated. "I started Aṣọ to give the Ọlọran women a chance to leave poverty behind and provide for their families." Purpose filled me as I remembered my first days in this country. How seeing dozens of women selling their wares for mere pennies just to feed their families pinged me with an awareness beyond myself and moved me to action. The whole country wasn't impoverished, but the wealth discrepancy between the privileged and the poor remained steep.

"Admirable."

I hid my surprise at Ekon's snooty tone. Bri had tried to tell me how he'd acted on their one and only date. The one she'd been forced to attend per the council's edict. However, the image I'd built up of Ekon in my mind hadn't believed her. Perhaps that was why his betrayal of the crown—of *Bri*—was so hard to swallow. I saw an ideal when I looked at him, not the real man. I'd do well to remember to keep my head from adding to a fantasy that could never exist.

I refocused. "You call it admirable. I call it being the hands and feet of Jesus."

He arched a smooth eyebrow. "Explain."

Did he get his brows threaded? I'd never seen a guy with such perfectly shaped eyebrows. I fought the urge to find my compact and check my own reflection. I'd looked flawless when I left my place this morning. My curls were free and out in full glory, giving me the added confidence to meet Ekon face-to-face.

And maybe, just maybe, a tiny part of me wanted to strike an impression that would make him drool. That wasn't a bad thing, was it?

Sure, wanting a man to find me attractive hedged this side of vanity, but letting Ekon know he could never have me gave me an opportunity to inflict revenge. Bri deserved my loyalty. Not only was she my best friend and the reason I was even here to begin with, but her support had secured me a working visa. Now I could turn my dreams of Aṣọ into reality.

"I'm a firm believer that the Lord wants us to be the answer to so much of the heartache in the world today. What we have is meant to be shared. No one is blessed so that only their lives can be enriched." I shrugged a shoulder. "That's my belief."

"Interesting." His tone was droll.

Okay, his superior attitude was starting to grate on my nerves. Would it be too much to have a button under my desk to press that alerted my secretary to guests who needed to be ejected from the building? Too bad I hadn't thought of that when opting for the glass desk. Instead, I chose the furniture for its fashionable design and the way the modern style projected an image of capability.

"Mr. Diallo," I intoned, "do you plan on being a help or a hindrance?"

Because I really did need help. The only thing secure was the board of directors because that had been a council requirement. The seats were filled with Ọlọrans and a few other members from countries from mainland Africa. In addition to that, I'd hired a secretary, security, and a few women to create the fashion lines Aṣọ would offer. We needed a lot more workers before we could be considered operational.

One bright spot in the sea of paperwork was my old coworker Matt. We'd worked together back in the States as fabric purchasers, only Matt had visions of grandeur and had moved steadily up in the fashion industry. When I told him about starting a business here, he jumped his old employment ship and agreed to be head of marketing. He had a wealth of expertise that would put us on the fashion world's map.

Ekon sat up. "I will help. Not merely because the council ordered me to, but because—" He clamped his lips shut.

I straightened in my seat. *Because what?* Should I ask or take his silence as cue to move on to the next topic? I batted down the Iris who wanted to know everything about Ekon and forged ahead. "I'm glad you've chosen to be an asset." I grabbed a stack of papers and plopped the ream before him. "This paperwork details the requirements the council has for the company. The board has already sent me their suggestions on how we can implement the parameters and adhere to my vision."

"Which is?" Ekon held up his hands. "Excuse me. It was not my intention to interrupt, Ms. Blakely."

Maybe he did have manners. "No problem." I'd just ignore how my last name sounded on his lips and try not to imagine how *Iris Diallo* would sound.

Foolish thoughts, yes, but it was hard to detach myself from dreams already woven. In a perfect world, Ekon wouldn't have been a potential suitor for my best friend or a traitor to the crown. Instead, we'd be married and working on our two-point-five kids. My optimistic mind had been working overtime trying to concoct sympathetic reasons for his actions.

"Tell me your vision and mission."

His demanding tone jolted me. No *please*? "My vision is to clothe the world and honor our resources."

Ekon dipped his head, motioning for me to continue.

Why did I feel like I was in the hot seat? I crossed my legs. "As for my mission, it's to clothe the world in sustainable fashion using the resources and skills of Ọlọrọ Ilé. We'll adhere to the highest standards of fashion and leave resources for future generations to thrive in the fashion industry."

"Do you not think that idealistic?"

"Are you kidding me?" I tried to study him as an employee and not a potential boyfriend. "The mission of Diallo Enterprises is to offer the world the best cut gems without stripping Ọlọrọ of its vital minerals. Are you telling me that's not idealistic?"

"Touché."

My heart panged at his cavalier attitude. "This isn't a game, Mr. Diallo."

"No, it is not." He nodded. "I merely wanted to make sure you feel strongly about your vision and mission statement. If you had faltered, I would have encouraged you to rewrite them."

"Oh." I leaned back in my seat. He'd been trying to help? I eyed him, wondering where the other shoe was.

"Are you attached to the name? Have trademark documents been submitted already?"

He didn't like Aṣọ? "I've turned in all paperwork, and the name was approved." I'd been inspired by Colossians 3:12: *Therefore, as God's chosen people, holy and dearly loved, clothe yourselves with compassion, kindness, humility, gentleness and patience.*

"Then we'll make do."

I kept my face from showing my true emotion. Or at least, I tried.

"Is there a place I can review these documents without monopolizing your office?"

The moment Ekon Diallo had walked in, his presence had taken over my office. My mind was still trying to catalogue the notes in his cologne. They were subtle, and the combination made my stomach dip as if a fainting couch were on hand.

Focus, Iris. "Per the council, you're to work in my presence. But never fear." I pointed to the table jutting out alongside the empty wall to my left. "You have your own desk that's not in the way in the least."

His lips twitched. "Very well. I assume I focus on this task until I finish reading it?"

25

"Yes. However long that takes. I put sticky notes in areas where I need your advice. Some of the government regulations on workplace requirements and insurance are particularly daunting." A snarl curled my lip as I gestured toward the papers he held.

I hated that stack of documents. Thankfully, some of the board members had very helpful ideas for building capital and seeking investors. Still, that was nowhere near the extent of the regulations we had to weed through.

"I will get to work, then." Ekon stood and held out a hand.

Oh no! Shaking hands was such a bad idea. What if when we touched, the chemistry between us went through the roof? How would I keep my composure? On the other hand, what if there was *no* spark? I'd be crushed and forced to get rid of this stupid infatuation.

Which might not be a bad thing.

I thrust my hand forward, remembering my dad's rules on presenting a firm handshake. The crease between my thumb and index finger slid right into Ekon's. Warmth enveloped my palm as I schooled my features to reveal nothing.

My face could be very expressive, so maintaining a poker face around others in the business world took every ounce of energy I possessed. Right now, I concentrated on standing upright in my black stilettos and ignoring the tingles that had erupted.

"Are you cold?" Ekon asked. He pointed to the goose bumps on my arm.

I broke contact. "When the AC kicks on, it blows right on me." I pointed upward, thankful the unit had just turned on, because now I hadn't lied. The cold air was the reason I had a wrap draped over the back of my chair. *But not the reason for your current chills.*

"Ah, I see. Perhaps you should set the temperature higher in your office." He looked around. "Do you have your own thermostat?"

I shook my head. "Maintenance is still working on that. Until they get it changed, we share the same temp as the rest of the building."

He sniffed. "Pity."

Pity how high in the air your nose is! I huffed and sank into my chair.

His snobbery nettled the part of me that wanted to believe in his potential good. Besides that, *I* was the boss, so he needed to take a hint and mosey on over to his side of the room. I stared at my desk, ignoring him. Securing a spot in a Paris fashion show was next on my agenda, not mooning over a man who was no good for me.

Despite how right my hand felt in his and how much I wanted to sigh with all the feels.

His footsteps finally dwindled in volume, making me believe he'd crossed the room to his desk. I picked up my phone and rehearsed my spiel in my head before dialing the number to the Paris location.

The secretary greeted me in a bored tone.

"Good morning. I'm Iris Blakely, owner of Aṣọ in Ọlọrọ Ilé, Africa. I'm calling to sign up for the fashion show."

"Which one?"

"The one this December." *Please have a spot open, please, please, please.*

The woman snorted. "*Madame*, there is a wait list for that show, and the odds of a cancellation are nonexistent."

"Does that mean I can't add my company to the list?"

"If you want to torture yourself thinking you stand a chance, give me your information."

My jaw jutted forward. "Actually, could you just pass me through to Steph? I'm not sure you'll truly add me."

"Stephyne Jordan?"

"Yes, ma'am. She's still CEO, isn't she?" It was good to have connections in various levels of the fashion industry. Steph had been my mentor when I first started out, and we still chatted once a week.

"Madame, I cannot patch you through simply because you say you know her. Do you know how many people make that claim on a daily basis?"

"That's fine. I'll call her direct line. Thank you so much for your help."

"Wait—"

I hung up and smiled in satisfaction. Steph would be made aware of her secretary's terrible attitude. I knew signing up for a December show in September had slim-to-nil odds, but that didn't give the woman the right to be rude.

"That was well done."

I jolted. For a brief moment, I'd forgotten I no longer had the office to myself. Heat flushed my cheeks as I gazed in Ekon's direction. "Sorry. I hope I didn't disturb you."

"No. That was highly entertaining."

My back stiffened, and my teeth clenched. "Now that I've provided you with your daily dose of amusement, why don't you get back to work?" I motioned to the stack of papers in front of him.

He smirked but turned to give them his attention.

I sighed quietly and leaned back in my chair. This was going to be a long three hundred and twenty—no, nineteen—hours. Not that I was counting.

THREE

Ekon

The words in front of me wavered. I had lost count of how many times I had reread the same page. Not because the English language was difficult, but because of the *ododo* informing her friend of the curt reception the secretary had given her.

Iris. A perfect name for the woman who reminded me of a flower, beautiful to admire, elegant in nature, and easily crushed. Her emotions seemed as vibrant as her namesake. The impression of her hand in mine and the heat that had flowed between us with that one touch still remained present. I rubbed the palm in question down the buttons of my shirt and refocused on the brief in front of me.

The council had put a hefty expectation upon Ms. Blakely. It was no surprise she felt like there was still too much to do. If I were going to be of any use, I would need a memo pad to jot down notes and suggestions on how to tackle the mountain of regulations. I had not been part of the startup process of Diallo Enterprises and had no idea there were rules on how much power we could use. Though that made sense, considering the outages we experienced from time to time.

My ears tuned in to Ms. Blakely's conversation, noting her call coming to a close. I stood and walked over to her desk as she made her good-byes and hung up the phone.

She arched an eyebrow. "Can I help you? And please tell me you didn't finish reading that fast."

Her theatrics made me want to smile, but I refrained. "I did not. I merely wanted to borrow a pen and paper."

She crossed her arms and raised her brows. "Just *one* sheet of paper?"

Okay, I smiled. She was feisty. "A memo pad would be best." I slid my hands into my pockets.

"Did the dancing taxi driver steal your briefcase with all your supplies?"

My body stiffened at her censure. Clearly the queen's best friend did not hold me in high esteem. If I wanted to return to living my previous life, I would have to get in Ms. Blakely's good graces. Perhaps I could humble myself a tad.

"I did not want to assume what I would or would not need." Plus, she was the employer. She should ensure her employees were outfitted with the supplies they required. However, I would save that idea for the list I would create on that paper—if she ever handed me some.

"Hmm." She swiveled in her rolling chair and grabbed a pad behind her, then swiveled back around, extending it to me along with a pen. "Anything else?"

"No."

"Have at it, then." She shooed me away like a pesky fly.

I pushed down the frustration building in my chest. Was this what I had been reduced to? A *commoner* who took orders from an American barely cognizant of what living in Ọlọrọ entailed? No longer did I work as a COO directing people as *I* saw fit. I was now some American's lackey. The change seemed to have altered my self-assured state. Losing my title, servants, and possessions had upset a delicate balance within me.

One little slipup, and suddenly I was a pariah not worthy to represent the Diallo empire or show my face to mere servants. Now this ododo thought she was better than me? I stalked back to my seat, rage coiling in my middle, ready to strike like a mamba.

Who did Iris Blakely think she was? Certainly she had not lived a life of importance before coming here. If it were not for the queen, where would she be? A piece of me wanted to blame Brielle Adebayo for my troubles. Dayo had convinced me she would only bring our beloved country to ruin. After all, the queen was American born and only half Ọlọran. She knew nothing of our ways or our people. She had not been raised to rule a country but to teach secondary education.

As soon as the queen arrived in Ọlọrọ, she had caused havoc at the palace. At least, those were the words from Dayo. Until then, my older sister had never sought my help. Father could barely spare me two glances, too eager to make the next deal and spread his empire far and wide. It had been nice to be needed. All I had to do was charm the queen—then a princess—into marrying me. My half-sister had assured me I would be doing a service to the council once my efforts were successful.

Since I had always believed an arranged marriage would be my future, marrying the future queen had seemed advantageous. With Father informing me daily of the expectations of a Diallo wanting to inherit his sizeable fortune, I had mistakenly believed he would be proud.

Then I met the queen, took her on a date, and saw how much she tried to adhere to the customs and desires of the people. A few questions of my sister later, and I came to the realization that Dayo had not been truthful.

She expected me to turn over the crown for her personal reign. *Not* to let me be the first Diallo on the throne of Ọlọrọ.

Not only that, but there were those who believed the queen would usher in progress for so many who felt disenfranchised. The chaos at the palace was created by Dayo. A gross misjudgment of my half-sister's character on my part had nearly landed me in prison. If not for the queen's mercy, my punishment surely would have been harsher than the community service hours I had been sentenced to.

I ran a hand down my face and reread the last paragraph once more. Perhaps I would be able to turn the page and make it through this monstrosity of orders soon. If not, I would spend the entire eight hours in mind-numbing reading. If I could focus and ignore the ododo humming happily at her desk, my task would be easier. Perhaps I should call Ms. Blakely a bird instead of a flower. Not that I needed to focus any more attention on her.

I trained my gaze on the documents in front of me. I could do this. I *would* do this. The desire to prove myself worthy would fuel me and keep me on schedule. I opened the memo pad and uncapped the pen.

The council might have stripped me of my title, and Father might have taken all my earthly conveniences, but I would not let them take my invisible crown. The one that allowed me to walk into a room and command it. I would show Ms. Blakely, Father, and the royal council that I was still a prince through and through.

Suddenly Ms. Blakely stood before me. "Did you hear me, Mr. Diallo?"

I blinked, rubbing my face, then glancing at my wristwatch. Three hours had passed? "Apparently I was engrossed in my research. Could you repeat that?"

"I asked if you wanted lunch. My secretary, Oka, offered to get some."

"Where is she going?" I did not eat just anything. Who knew what Ms. Blakely took for fine dining?

She named a food stand near the building. I resisted the urge to curl my lip. When was the last time I had eaten from a roadside booth? If only I had brought lunch with me. *Because breakfast was exceptional?*

Roadside food it was.

"Yes. If you could order me something." Tomorrow I would have to bring . . . who knew what? If I could successfully make my own breakfast, then I could figure out lunch.

"Great. How many *paiis* and what kind?"

She said paiis a little enthusiastically. Were they her favorite? "Two beef ones will be fine."

"No shrimp or crab? They're divine." She beamed with excitement.

My lip curled. I could not help it. I *detested* seafood. Who wanted to eat cockroaches of the sea? "I am not a seafood aficionado, Ms. Blakely."

"Oh, then I'll let Oka know you prefer beef."

I reached for my wallet.

"No need. Consider it a welcome aboard."

I nodded and returned to my work. Now that I had found my focus, I did not want to lose it pondering what Ms. Blakely thought of my dislike for crustaceans. Yet her desk was so close to my own, and I could still detect the lingering feminine scent of . . .

Perfume? No, her fragrance did not have that type of odor. Shampoo? Or perhaps she used a scented lotion?

Why are you thinking about how the ododo smells? Focus, Diallo.

I blew out a breath and began reading from the top of the page, slowly adding more notes to the pad of paper I had begun filling. Time flew until Ms. Blakely cleared her throat and thrust two paiis under my nose. The smell awoke my stomach with a surprisingly tantalizing aroma.

When I was growing up, Father had never stopped at the

food stands in Etikun. He had informed me that Diallos could afford the finest chefs and choicest meats. Stepping up to a roadside stand was something only tourists and the poor did. Ms. Blakely definitely fit the tourist persona. She had not been in Ọlọrọ long. It was my understanding that she had arrived this summer along with the queen.

I bit into the paii and held back a moan. *Incredible.* A vague recollection of eating something similar when I hung out with friends during secondary entered my mind. Other than during my days at university in the UK, I had not eaten such pedestrian food. Though England had roadside stands, I remembered those being mostly Middle Eastern in nature. That was how I had my first kebab. Today almost felt like the first time I had ever tried a paii.

The sound of someone clearing their throat made me look up to meet the stare of Ms. Blakely. I swallowed my bite. "Yes?"

"Is there anything in particular you want to say?"

"No. I still have more reading to do."

"I meant about the food."

"It is surprisingly good." I stared at the contents, wondering how the cook had fashioned the fried meat pie.

"How about a *thank you*, Mr. Diallo?"

I blinked. The queen was fond of thanking people. Was that an American thing or something the lower class did? "Thank you."

"You're welcome." Ms. Blakely stomped over to her desk.

I watched as she laid down a napkin, tucked one into her neckline, then dug into her meal. She ate with gusto, as if sincerely enjoying every bite. Fascination filled me. How could someone take such enjoyment over a simple meal? And one not prepared by a chef, at that?

Father had always stressed that food fueled our bodies and nothing more. Granted, Father did not take pleasure in much—myself included. I pushed the thought away, taking another bite of the paii. The spices inside awoke my palate, but as much as I tried to eat and clear my mind, thoughts of my father pushed through.

I had lived my entire life adhering to his rules except for a few minor rebellions in my younger days. Perhaps it was time to embark on my own journey, discover my own way of living. If he could cut me from his life without thought or pause because the council found me guilty of betraying the crown, what did I care for his rules?

As long as I never trusted another person again, I would not find myself in the same predicament Dayo had placed me in.

I turned away from Ms. Blakely and set aside the second paii. Perhaps I would save it for dinner, since I had no idea what to cook.

Maybe you can hire your own servants.

But that was a problem for later.

One thing at a time, and work was number one on my list.

FOUR

Iris

The guard opened the back door of the sedan.

"*E seun*," I murmured, thanking him. I was still unused to the pomp and circumstance that accompanied me when visiting my best friend.

Bri had invited me over for our weekly Thursday girls' night and sent her driver to pick me up. Her Friday nights were reserved for her new husband, while her weekends usually had volunteer work packed in, which meant Thursdays were the best time to visit each other. I didn't mind what day I saw her, as long as we could continue to meet up. Still, knowing I couldn't see her whenever I wanted was strange. She was no longer simply my best friend.

Now she had obligations to both her new husband and her new country as queen of Ọlọrọ Ilé. Fortunately, we lived in the same country. When I first came to the island—located off the west coast of Africa—Bri had found out she held the title of crown princess and that her grandfather, the king, was dying. If that hadn't been enough of a shock, when she chose to become his successor, the royal council dictated she marry before the king died, or they would deny her ascension to the throne. It had been a harrowing journey for Bri, but she'd managed to come through it all with the grace of a true royal.

Which was how I now found myself in a Mercedes sedan being escorted to the palace to hang with my BFF. I couldn't wait, since we hadn't seen each other in a couple of weeks. She'd had some engagements with foreign dignitaries that made her cancel the last two Thursdays. Though we did text on a daily basis. She was the one who'd informed me that Ekon would be my business consultant as part of his sentencing.

My stomach had dropped to my toes at her pronouncement. Distinguishing if that dip was the result of nervous butterflies or excited ones had been impossible. I'd never confessed to Bri my feelings—very mixed-up ones—regarding Ekon. How could I, when he'd been a potential husband for her? After he'd entangled himself with the treason business, that didn't seem like a good time either.

What was wrong with me that I could still feel a flutter of attraction after everything he'd done? Interacting with him this week had been one wave of torture after another. It was like I'd been on some confidence course where the obstacles were smiling enough to show attention but not attraction, delegating work to remind him he was under my authority, and ignoring every hammer of my pulse when he got too close.

My cool façade had failed a few times. I'd smiled too brightly when he came into work with a bow tie. A *bow tie*. He'd looked too good for my own comfort. Not to mention the relief I'd felt when he found a way to bring in more capital without incurring a high-interest loan. The urge to fling my arms around him in gratitude had almost succeeded until I recalled we didn't have that type of relationship. At the end of today, I'd shooed him out of my office in order to lock up and ended up dragging an extra-long inhale to collect the notes of his cologne.

I still couldn't figure out what ingredient gave his scent its intoxicating smell. I had half a mind to go to a perfumer and sniff all the men's colognes until I discovered Ekon's. Was there a hint of vanilla? No, maybe it was sandalwood I detected. Whatever the mixture, the cologne was enough to send my senses spinning.

Stop thinking about him!

Instead of focusing on Ekon Diallo and the reasons he was a *very* bad idea, I stared out of the window. I loved the lush tropics of Ọlọrọ, and being chauffeured to the palace allowed me to decompress and enjoy the scenery. Although my mind wanted to focus on the needs at Aṣọ.

My to-do list included hiring a production team, pattern makers and others for the design team, not to mention the everyday roles like communications and human resources. I couldn't do everything myself, and the board was there to ensure I checked every box. The one thing I hadn't considered in my endeavor was how removed from the creative aspect of fashion design I'd be when running the enterprise.

Not having my hands in all the design aspects carved out a little piece of me and left a hole I wasn't sure how to fill. Hopefully Ekon would have more suggestions on how we could meet the council's requirements soon. Yesterday, he'd finished reading the council's missive. I'd found myself noting how his lips pursed when deep in thought. Not that I stared at them the entire time. That would be creepy, borderline stalkerish. Not to mention workplace harassment.

I just couldn't look away from his face sometimes. It was so . . . beautiful. Sure, the lines formed a masculine picture, what with that impressive jawline. But I couldn't get over how put together he always looked. Was that what living a life of luxury brought you?

"We're here, Ms. Blakely."

The guard broke into my thoughts as he stepped out of the car to open my door. I quickly reached for the handle. I wasn't royalty and didn't need to fall into the trap of thinking so. I appreciated the palace security's concerns and why picking me up was better than me driving myself, but I didn't need doors opened for me.

I thanked the guard and walked through the royal entrance into the palace. Looking up at the beautiful ceilings made me remember the first time I'd come here. How the beautiful marble floors with gold etchings had captivated my attention. Or the breathtaking tapestries that hung at focal points, telling the history of Ọlọrọ.

My heels clicked across the tile as I hurried toward the elevator that would take me to the royal guest suite. Tonight's movie session with Bri would hopefully bring some much-needed relaxation for the both of us. First, we always discussed how she was adjusting to being queen, and I shared my struggles with getting my company off the ground. Then we'd watch a movie while eating junk food.

I punched the up button, waiting for the chime and the opening of the doors. Once inside, I tapped out the code that granted me access to the royal floor. Even though Bri had her own lounge room attached to her suite, we always went to the guest suite that had been ours when we first came to Ọlọrọ. We'd meet in "my" old room and veg out.

Which was why I'd brought a change of clothes with me. Every girl needed something to laze around in, and I was desperate to rid myself of work attire. Bri usually showed up ten to fifteen minutes after I arrived, which left me enough time to change into my sweatshirt and yoga pants. As much as I loved my stilettos, my fuzzy socks held my heart even more.

When I came out of the bathroom, Bri sat in the lounge area, feet curled up underneath her. She jumped to her feet when she saw me.

"Iris!"

We hugged, and I held her petite frame. Although I only had

a couple of inches of height on her, she always seemed so tiny to me. Well, until I saw her in her coronation gown and crown. She'd looked fierce, and I couldn't have been prouder.

"How are you?" she asked.

I pulled back and took the opposite cushion on the sofa. "Exhausted!" I leaned my head back, staring up at the ceiling. The brown crown molding caught my eyes, the royal crest protruding from each corner.

"Is Ekon behaving?"

My cheeks heated, and I kept my gaze glued above. With my head tilted this way, surely she wouldn't notice the blush. Right? *Should have kept your hair down instead of putting it up.*

"He is," I murmured.

A sigh escaped Bri.

I sat up and looked at my best friend. "Were you worried he wouldn't?"

Did she think he was dangerous? He hadn't laid a hand on anyone in the plot to overthrow Bri, but was I being naïve, thinking that meant he was harmless? Well, relatively so, considering the whole conspiracy charge. Still, my heart pounded as my mind spun scenarios that had me wishing for a paper bag.

"I honestly wasn't sure if he felt any sense of remorse. It's so hard to get a read on his character." Bri's eyebrows wrinkled. "Sometimes he says all the right things, but there's a lack of warmth and sincerity behind his words." She shrugged. "But I try not to judge. I just pray he really did have a change of heart."

Pray. Something I hadn't done once. I gulped. "You're such a good person."

Bri laughed. "Please. Like you're America's Most Wanted."

"No, but I haven't once thought to pray for him." And shouldn't I have? If I really wanted him to be the man of my dreams, wouldn't I have begged God to make it so?

Or did my lack of prayer show how much I knew deep down

that a relationship with Ekon was a fantasy and never a possible reality?

"That's okay. You don't have to pray for every single person you come across."

"But shouldn't I at least pray for the people who work for me?" Shame filled me. I was failing Ekon in the most basic of ways, not to mention the rest of my employees.

Lord, please forgive me. Please help me keep my faith at the forefront. And please, please speak to Ekon's heart and demolish that fake persona he's holding on to like a shield. Because I'd seen glimpses of another person. The one who had pulled a genuine smile from me a couple of times. Then a shutter of indifference would take its place, and back was the egotistical man who made me want to scream in frustration.

"I can't tell you if your prayer life is lacking, Iris. But I can tell you to be gracious to yourself. We're always harder on ourselves than God would ever be."

"You're so right." Still, I would make a commitment to do better. I wrapped my arms around my legs. "So, tell me what's been up with you."

Bri groaned. "We've been trying to find a new alàgbà to fill Mr. Oladele's old spot."

The position of head elder, who led the royal council, had belonged to Jomi Oladele before he'd conspired with Bri's secretary and been sent to prison. Who would want to fill that spot after all the drama? "Is it rough going?"

"You could say that. Some of the elders and princes in the Etikun tribe don't appreciate how we—*I*—handled the situation." She looked off into the distance. "Mr. Ladipo suggested we get an official statement from D-Dayo." Her tongue seemed to trip over the name.

If I had to guess the reason, Bri was still wrestling with forgiveness. She'd believed Dayo was a friend.

"Confirming that Mr. Oladele and Ekon were the only accomplices," Bri continued. "Mr. Ladipo believes it best if I don't ask for the confession. He hopes it will satisfy the tribal elders. They also want to make sure no one else fell prey to Dayo's schemes. Until further notice, the Etikun council spot remains vacant on the royal council. And as long as it's empty, the hearing of petitions will be postponed."

My heart twisted at the heartache on Bri's face. I reached over and squeezed her hand, trying to keep my tears at bay. Being an empath meant that seeing distress in others triggered my own waterworks. It was why I had a special stall in the bathroom for when I needed to cry and avoid the stares of others.

I could only imagine the citizens' stress at having their petitions delayed until further notice. I'd once gone before the council, seeking approval to open Aṣọ. The wait for their decision had had me on my knees and squeezing my favorite stress ball to calm myself.

Bri sighed. "I'm trying not to worry."

"Is Tomori helping?" Her husband was so good to her. You could see the love he had for her whenever he gazed at Bri. "Are there any duties he can take on to ease your burden?"

"He is helping." A huge grin curved her lips. "He's been wonderful. He went to talk to some of the elders in Etikun this morning. I feel like we're closer to a resolution because of it."

"That's wonderful."

She nodded, a dreamy look in her brown eyes. "There's more."

"What?" I breathed. Did he rub her feet at night? Draw her a bubble bath? Not that I thought my list of romantic things could compare to real life.

"I'm pregnant."

My mouth dropped as I gasped—then squealed. "Oh my goodness!" I leaned forward and wrapped her in a hug. "I can't believe this. This is great. Oh my *goodness*."

I stifled another shriek, heart pounding from the excitement.

We broke our hug, and I sank into my cushion. My cheeks bunched so high they started hurting, but I couldn't have wiped the smile from my face if I'd wanted to.

Bri dabbed at her eyes. "Mori was so happy when I told him."

"I bet."

She bit her lip. "He's also a little nervous, so we've been keeping it quiet. The royal physician, you, and my mom are the only people who know."

"What about his mom?"

"Mori said she wouldn't be able to keep a secret that big to herself." Amusement danced in her eyes.

I didn't feel like keeping the news quiet either but certainly would. "When will you tell everyone?"

"We're going to wait until the first trimester is over. After that, we'll tell his family. We'll tell the world when they begin speculating on my baby bump."

I laughed. "Didn't they do that last week? After you wore Keke?"

Bri was a big deal in women's fashion all over the world. Every fashion designer wanted to claim the queen wore something they made specifically for her. The royal family mostly used Kikelomo Musa, known affectionately as Keke. I hoped that once my company was up and running, I would be able to be added to their list of approved designers. Since I didn't want to be accused of favoritism, I hadn't asked.

Still, I'd made Bri's Independence Day dress when she was introduced to the country as the new princess and heir to the throne, as well as her wedding dress. Shouldn't that garner me a spot? *Patience, Iris!*

"Yes." Bri shook her head. "When they spied one of the guards at the paii stand, they retracted their headline and blamed the weight gain on enjoying my new cuisine."

I chuckled. "I let out the waist in a couple of my favorite dresses. Maybe I should lay off the paiis and find a salad for lunch instead." I shuddered inwardly. I'd never been a fan of lettuce unless it was a garnish. Something to make a burger look pretty.

"Nah, just go to the gym."

I made a face, mimicking a GIF going *blech*.

Bri laughed. "The gym isn't that bad."

"There's no earthly reason to put myself in a state that would require me to sweat."

"You do realize we live in Africa now, right?"

"Eh, it's the tropics."

We laughed, leaning over each other. It wasn't actually that funny, but working five days a week in a stressful environment would make anyone a little punch-drunk. Suddenly dad jokes were the best thing ever.

We laughed, ate ice cream, watched an old favorite, and talked until Bri struggled to keep her eyes open.

I peeked out of the door leading to the hallway. Merrick, the queen's personal bodyguard, nodded at me.

"Hey, Merrick, she's asleep. You may need to get the king to carry her away."

Which I was perfectly sure Tomori would do. He loved Bri with a fierceness despite their marriage being one born of convenience. Their mutual respect had quickly developed into a love that would be told of for generations to come.

Five minutes later, Tomori arrived, apologizing for his intrusion.

"No, please. I'm sure Bri would rather sleep in her own room." Next to her husband of a couple of months.

He smiled down at her. "She told you, yes?"

I nodded. "That's why I had them call you." No way a pregnant woman wanted to sleep on the sofa all night.

"You will stay the night? She will probably want to have breakfast with you."

I glanced at my watch. It was midnight. "Yes, thank you. What time is breakfast?"

"Seven. She has an early meeting tomorrow."

"That's fine. I need an early start as well." My time at the ball was over, and the clock had already reminded me of the responsibilities waiting for me.

"Good night, Iris. Thank you for putting a smile on my Brielle's face tonight."

I wanted to clutch my heart and swoon at the two of them. Instead, I said my good-nights and went to the guest bedroom.

One day, Lord, I want a love like that.

FIVE

Ekon

I adjusted my tie, then gave myself a once-over in the mirror. Father would expect me to arrive looking immaculate. Even though I no longer held the title of prince, I still had to adhere to Diallo expectations.

The black tie went well with the maroon button-down shirt and black slacks I wore. An afternoon shave made my face smooth. I was all set to attend the commanded dinner.

I flicked off the bathroom light, then grabbed my mobile and wallet. I had wised up and called a transportation company that offered rides that were not as common as taxis. Instead, a sedate sedan would drive me to my father's house and prevent the shame of arriving in public transportation. I walked out of the lobby and into the night air. Fortunately, the paparazzi had been ordered to vacate the premises by the building owner's request. The driver acknowledged me with a dip of his head. It reminded me a little of my previous chauffeur.

Was I the only one bothered by my mode of transportation? Mother would not mind what I arrived in. She would merely be happy to see me. This morning she had texted me, overjoyed by the news of my dinner attendance. I did not have the heart to inform her that Father had woken me up with a message that I *would* show up tonight, *or else.*

I never asked what the *or else* was. Years of experience had taught me I did not want to know.

The driver was a lot quieter than the cabbie who had been taking me to Aṣọ on a daily basis. It did not matter if I called five minutes later or earlier to arrange a pickup, the same enthusiastic dancing man came to chauffeur me. Once I had informed him of my strict time schedule, he became less energetic when singing on the way to Ms. Blakely's company. At the end of the day, he would take the long way back to my penthouse and jam to his music the whole ride home. Apparently taking me home did not demand a rush.

I honestly could not decide if I should use a different taxi company or continue my silent watch of his erratic dance moves. Conversely, my current driver had barely spoken two words. Only enough to confirm my destination.

In the past, this would have been enough to ensure a pleasant drive. My old chauffeur never said much—though I never engaged him in conversation—and when I drove one of my own cars, I never listened to music. Now I found the silence stifling, giving me too much opportunity to think.

When would I ever be able to escape my thoughts? The ones that wondered if Iris Blakely was as genuine as she presented. The ones that wondered why I had not turned down Dayo in the first place. If I had alerted the council to her schemes, I would have avoided my current predicament. But then I might have also risked fracturing a relationship with my half-sister that had been tenuous at best.

I also could not escape wondering if following every expectation of Father's was really worth the cost. Because what did I have to show for my blind obedience? Yes, I had known that dating the queen was part of Dayo's plan, but Father had backed the relationship as well. He had simply had no knowledge of my half-sister's input. He had viewed the endeavor through the lens of having a queen for a daughter-in-law. Sometimes I think he was not so much angry that the council had reprimanded me but that the queen did not pick me to marry. After all, she chose a commoner and passed over all the Diallo name had to offer.

At the time, I had been insulted. Now I believed she had dodged calamity and not the other way around. An image of her kind eyes at the council meeting filled my mind. Took over the thoughts pulsating in my brain. She saw something in me I did not believe existed. Would I fail her a second time?

I cleared my throat, adjusting my tie as the driver turned down the road leading to our home. It was more a mansion than a house. The expansive home certainly did not resemble the little shacks that littered most of Etikun. The clay-colored sandstone structure sat on a hill, gleaming against the cedar-shingled roof. A balcony wrapped around the house, as part of the front sat on stilts, protruding from the hills.

I started to get out of the car, but the memory of the look on Iris's secretary's face when Iris had thanked her for a job well done stopped me. Did people really want to be acknowledged for their work? I cleared my throat, glancing at the driver. "Thank you."

He dipped his head.

My Adam's apple bobbed as each step drew me nearer to my childhood home. Once I crossed the threshold, I would have to be the Ekon Father desired me to be. Unfortunately, I had played the game for so long, I no longer knew who *I* wanted to be separate from Father's expectations.

Was there a chance I could break free, or would I be tethered forever to the Diallo name and all it represented?

It does not represent a man stripped of a title.

Before I could knock, the door opened, and the butler bowed before me.

The show is on. I strolled through the foyer—with an air of confidence as my shield—then made a right into the sunken living room. Cedar floors gleamed throughout the home, and the white living room furniture preened for show. The sitting room was not a place to relax in, and for that reason my bedroom had always been my sanctuary. The only place I could breathe. That was, until I moved out when I went to university.

However, Father kept his hold on me by gifting me the keys to the penthouse. Thankfully he had never visited me there, merely ordered me home to submit to his mandates.

Mother rose, her hair perfectly coifed in a curled bob. I kissed her cheeks, and when I finished, she held on to mine.

"How are you, my son?"

"I am fine, Mother."

Her black eyes studied mine. "Are you?" she whispered.

I nodded. Not because it was the truth but because to be anything but okay was not the Diallo way.

"I am praying for you."

I barely bit back a scoff. Why did she insist on the pretense of prayers? The god she prayed to was one of judgment and punishment. I had had enough of that in my life and did not need an eternity of it. I stepped back, and she dropped her hands.

"Your father is finishing up a phone call." She sat, tucking her dress under her.

Far be it from him to break himself away from business after demanding a meet and greet.

Instead of showing my irritation, I flashed a smile, slipping a mint into my mouth. The burst of coolness broke up my frustration and gave my mind something else to think about. "How have you been, Mother?"

"I am okay. I went shopping with your aunt yesterday. Wait until you see the new dining table."

Mother had an obsession with shopping that fueled her decorating bug. Yet she always gravitated to the same color scheme.

I smiled. "I am sure it is wonderful."

"How is . . . work?" She cleared her throat.

"It has been intensive. It is . . . interesting seeing a business from the ground up." Ms. Blakely had guts, I conceded.

"I admit I thought Iris Blakely much too intrusive to dare set up shop in Etikun." Mother patted her hair. "However, I can already see a difference in the women. They seem more . . . hopeful. I heard she will be hosting a hiring event soon."

"Yes. In three weeks." One of my suggestions she had found helpful.

Granted, she had only read one page from my recommendation list. I was not sure she would find the rest of my ideas as helpful. I had tried not to be harsh in any faults I had found. If Ms. Blakely wanted her business to succeed, she had a long way to go. Streamlining her hiring process was a must, and having all the insurance matters taken care of beforehand a necessity. I believed one of the board members was assisting in that area.

"Hmm. Seems a bit pedestrian."

I shifted against the couch cushion. Over the years, I had perfected little nuances to redirect my annoyance and appear easygoing, such as shifting in my seat. Mother might think she was better than Father, but she had no fewer opinions.

"Would you like a drink, Ekon?"

"No. I am fine, Mother."

She waved a hand, and a servant appeared. Mother whispered in Oninan, asking for a glass of wine. Had she really not had a glass or two already? Perhaps she had gotten rid of the evidence before I or Father could join her.

Footsteps sounded in the corridor. I straightened in my seat while Mother patted her curled hair, shifting her heeled feet to the side. We were well trained in how to appear before the dictator entered the living room. As he did, I rose to my feet after his eyes fell on me for a brief moment. They shifted to Mother, who rose as well.

"Father," I greeted. Not much of a salutation, but he did not expect me to spout sonnets.

"Were you late?"

No, you are the one who just walked into the room. "No, sir." I popped in another mint discreetly.

"Good." He turned to Mother. "Is dinner ready?"

"Of course, Ise."

"Then let us adjourn to the dining room."

Mother flashed me a grin. Apparently she was really proud of her purchase. I could only hope it would not be a shade that bordered on loud. She really went crazy with color in that room.

I winced upon seeing the space. Red walls screamed to be noticed, but they competed with the red table centered in the room. The square shape made seating a little too close for comfort. I would easily be able to hear my mother and father. Who knew I would miss the rectangular table that had kept us distanced for so long?

"Tife, what is this?" Father demanded, gesturing to the table.

"I went shopping with your sister yesterday."

Father muttered under his breath. I waited to see if he would explode and order the table removed immediately or choose deadly silence. When he smoothed his tie and sat down, I followed suit. It looked like we would have a wonderful evening of meeting his death glares and utter disappointment whenever he viewed the table.

Fantastic.

The servants immediately began plating our meal. Silence reigned as we began eating. Mother grabbed her wine glass before her fork, only to halt mid-air as Father shot his dark gaze her way. I wished I could eat another mint. Instead, I would have to force each bite down my esophagus at this farce of a family dinner.

"How is consulting going?" Father asked after a few minutes.

Did he actually care? "Well," I replied.

"Will Ms. Blakely say as much? You know she has the ear of the king and queen."

My back stiffened at his insinuation. Father had yet to mention the queen by herself, even though she was the reigning monarch and *not* the king. But I needed to answer his question before he found my silence impertinent. "I believe she would."

"I suppose that is something."

No, Father, stop with all the accolades. I cannot stand it. I cut my steak and took a bite, but the choice cut might as well have been ash for how my taste buds recognized the meat.

"I am sure you have wondered why I called a family dinner," Father proclaimed.

Mother's head jolted, and she glanced at me. "You did not ask to come, Ekon?"

I ignored the look of hurt on her face, choosing to meet Father's steady gaze instead.

Just in time to see him curl his lip. He had no trouble letting a snort fly free. "Please. Your son is hiding in shame. Not a Diallo way of handling adversity."

Yes, because you know what it is like to be punished by the royal council and have a princely title stripped from your name. I ate another bite.

Mother reached for her wine glass, ignoring Father's obvious disdain.

"I have been thinking, Ekon."

"Yes, Father?" Here it came. Perhaps I would discover the reason he had stripped me of my servants and cars.

"I fear I have been too lenient on you."

Excuse me?

"I do not think I was strict enough after the hearing."

Because public humiliation and airing our family secrets on national television was too tame? What more could he possibly take from me? The clothes off my back?

"I have decided to rescind the gift of the penthouse."

My fork clattered.

A predatory gleam seeped into Father's eyes. *Oh no.* I had reacted. Loudly, at that. I removed my hands from the tabletop, fisting them in my lap. Mother's hand reached underneath to squeeze my wrist. I did not know whether it was in warning or empathy.

I swallowed. "If you take the penthouse, where will I live?" My question was calm, collected.

"You are twenty-eight, Ekon. Well past the age to figure that out." Father held out his hand. "Give me the keys."

"Ise," Mother hissed. "You cannot demand the keys right this moment. What about his clothes? His things for work?"

I kept my face impassive, but my heart was trying to beat a path out of my chest. Why was Mother so shocked? Father was more than capable of keeping me from all of my belongings, including my clothes.

He pulled back his hand and picked up his fork instead. "You have twenty-four hours from the moment you arrived here for dinner. That gives you time to pack your clothes and remove any belongings you purchased with your own money."

My breath caught in my throat.

"His trust fund money?" Mother asked.

"*No.* Paychecks with his name on them, issued by Diallo Enterprises. His trust fund has been closed."

My stomach heaved upward, then hurtled toward my feet.

This past week, I had walked around as if life could not get any worse. But finding out I would leave the penthouse with nothing was something else entirely. Had I actually bought anything with the checks I earned as COO? I lived solely on my trust fund money.

"I expect to see receipts proving the items you remove were bought with salaried monies. If you cannot prove it, you will have to purchase the items from me without using your trust fund."

I licked my lips. "The value of most items has depreciated. Am I able to purchase them at a lesser value?"

"Whatever the average rate they are going for currently."

I nodded, knowing no good would come from arguing. Instead, I placed my napkin on the table. "May I be excused? It appears I have some packing to do."

Father flicked his wrist and resumed his meal, the business of my existence already replaced in his mind. Yet I found I could not ignore him so easily as I left the house and pondered my next steps.

SIX

Iris

Something was wrong with Ekon. He'd been oddly subdued this morning, and every now and again, I'd catch him glancing at his watch. Did he have somewhere important to be? Was working for me so tedious that he had to count down the minutes?

My pen clicked against my notepad as I tried to focus on the task at hand, but once again, Ekon stared at his wristwatch.

I cleared my throat. "Do you have someplace more important to be?"

I resisted the urge to raise my eyebrows in speculation. I wanted him to think I was the perfect picture of professionalism despite the way I fidgeted in my seat. Only he didn't even turn and acknowledge me.

"Mr. Diallo?"

I angled my head, trying to see if he had earbuds in. *Nope.* My voice wasn't quiet, which meant he'd *chosen* to ignore me.

The clacking of my pen upticked in pace while he glowered at his watch. What was going on with him?

"Mr. Diallo!"

He jumped in his seat, whirling around, mouth dropping in shock. "We occupy the same room. Must you yell?"

"You didn't answer me the first few times."

His eyes widened, and he ran a hand over his close-shaved head. "I apologize. I did not hear you."

I wanted to believe him, but . . . "I asked if you had somewhere more important to be."

"No, Ms. Blakely. Not for another six hours and fifty-four minutes."

I wanted to laugh but schooled my expression. "How precise of you."

A sheepish expression stole over his face, adding a vulnerability that made my nurturing instincts kick into gear.

He licked his lips. "It is only because I am very aware of an impending deadline after work."

I so badly wanted to know what was going on, but what right did I have to invade his privacy? I hesitated, questions on the tip of my tongue. Just because the council had put me in charge of his mandated consulting hours didn't mean I had the right to poke and prod through the rest of his life. But he looked so . . . so . . . *sad*.

"Is everything okay?" I asked.

A deep sigh fell from his lips. "It has to be."

Wow, talk about cryptic. Fortunately, getting to the heart of a matter was my specialty. Being empathetic made me a good listener, and I was so ready to see his gloom fade into lightness.

"Do you want to talk about it?"

Ekon's dark gaze met mine. Then he sprang to his feet, striding to my desk before I even knew what hit me.

He sank into one of the chairs opposite me. "This needs to remain confidential." His gaze pierced me.

I barely held back a gasp at the severity in his dark eyes. They beckoned to me, making me wish I could drown in his gaze and declare the feelings bubbling within me. Only this was no romantic conversation. Something was wreaking havoc with his thoughts. I needed to stay focused. And, of course, remind myself that we could never be. *Keep your head in reality!*

I nodded.

"I mean it. I do not want the council—or the *queen*—learning of this."

My mind tried to come up with different scenarios before I agreed to his condition. Only they didn't matter. He needed to bare his soul, and I was a willing listener. "I promise this will remain strictly between the two of us."

Why did my brain do a little squeal at the thought of an *us*? I was pathetic.

He gave a relieved sigh and sagged back against the chair. "I am going to be homeless by the end of the day."

"What?" I straightened, then tempered my voice. "What do you mean?"

"My father has taken all my material possessions as punishment for my conviction. Last night he summoned me to dinner and informed me he would also be taking the keys to my penthouse. He is permitting me to leave with only the items I paid for from my salary." He slid his hands along his pants, a grimace twisting his beautiful lips. "I do not believe I have ever bothered to spend those funds."

"Does it go into a separate account from your"—I paused—"trust fund?" What other monies did a man like him have, if not a trust fund?

He nodded. "Father insisted I keep two accounts."

"Okay, so how much is in your salaried account?" If he'd never touched it in all the years he'd worked for Diallo Enterprises, he shouldn't be destitute.

Ekon shrugged.

I sighed. "How do you not know?"

"I have never needed to access those funds. They were secondary to my trust fund, and that is in no danger of running out any time soon."

59

He probably had a black card. Wait, did Africa have unlimited credit cards like they did in the States? I had no idea, and obviously, I was following a rabbit trail. "Do you have your account info?"

"Uh, no?"

At my look of frustration, something flashed across his face.

"Look, I can admit I have led a pampered life, but please keep your judgments to yourself."

I gaped. "I wasn't judging." Was I? "It's just hard to understand how you don't know if you do or don't have that information."

"Fair enough." He pulled his wallet from his back pocket, then passed it to me. "That has credit cards and anything else I might have found useful. However, I am not certain if anything in there will answer your question. Perhaps that is something I filed away and promptly forgot about."

I reached for the leather wallet, face heating. This felt so . . . *intimate.* Was he really going to let me look through his things?

"Are you sure?" I asked.

"Yes, please." He gulped. "I need the help."

That admission must have cost him. I opened the black billfold, stopping to look at his driver's license. It was the one thing missing from my wallet. My New York identification card had sufficed up until now, since I'd never taken the driver's exam. Unfortunately public transportation was a lot more difficult in Ọlọrọ. Did I really want to continue to get to work using taxis and the regional bus?

I shook off the thoughts and began to rifle through Ekon's credit cards, masking the shock at seeing a couple of black cards. So Ọlọrọ *did* have unlimited credit cards. Just how rich were the Diallos that Ekon had not one but—I counted—three black cards?

Stick to the task at hand, Iris. I finally found a debit card from a local bank. I pulled out the green card and waved it at

Ekon. "This is probably the one your paycheck is going to." I turned the card over. "There's a number on the back. Call them, tell them your name and that you want to check your balance."

"Is that it?"

I shrugged a shoulder. "They may ask to verify your identity, which you can probably do with your social security number." I shook my head. "Uh, the national social fund number." I kept forgetting that not every word easily translated down here. Ọlọrọ had no Social Security Administration but a national social fund instead.

Focus, Iris. "It might be easier to visit in person if you want account information and the ability to log in online to track your info that way."

Ekon nodded slowly. "I will call them first and find out how much I have." He swallowed.

Since when did an Adam's apple look sexy? *For the love, Iris!*

"What will you do next?"

"Find out how much it costs to rent a place." His eyes drifted to the side, gazing blankly. "Perhaps I could find a hotel, if they do not cost too much."

"My complex is leasing." My heart raced at the thought of having him for a neighbor.

"I will keep that in mind." He rose, pointing a thumb over his shoulder. "Do you mind if I step out to make the call?"

"Go ahead. You might want to go in the stairwell. Although, Oka won't listen if you do talk in the reception area." At least, I prayed my secretary wouldn't eavesdrop on his conversation.

The same thought must have crossed his mind, because he stared at the door, thought lines furrowing his brow.

"Listen, you can stay in here and make the call." I grabbed some earbuds. "I'll pop these in and turn up the volume on my playlist so you can have some privacy."

"Thank you."

I nodded, slipping the buds into my ears. I hadn't listened

to my millennial pop list in a while. Or maybe my boy band list would keep me from daydreaming, Ekon front and center. Before long, lip-synching took me to another world, memories of my brother telling me I was silly for having posters of boy bands from all eras hanging on my walls. He didn't understand that once you became a fan of boy bands, you had no choice but to listen to them all.

Of course, my favorites were from the 2000s and on. There was nothing like that pop sound that *NSYNC and the Backstreet Boys and countless others had perfected. I grinned, trying not to dance in my chair as I responded to correspondence Oka had forwarded to me.

A hand appeared in my face, and I screamed, scooting my rollaway chair backward. I crashed into the wall behind me, wincing at the sound. I popped the earbuds out of my ears.

"I did *not* mean to scare you." Ekon looked appropriately contrite, yet the telltale twitch of his lips gave away his true thoughts. Whether they were about my reaction to his sudden presence or my chair dancing was an entirely different matter.

My office door flew open, and Oka stopped just inside, a ruler in her hand brandished like a weapon. Laughter bubbled up inside me, and I let loose. I heard vague murmurings of Ekon explaining the situation as I reined in my laughter and reached for my professional veneer.

"Sorry," I gasped as the last of my amusement faded. "I was a bit distracted."

Ekon's lips tilted to the side in a half smirk that sent my pulse racing. "I noticed."

"Did you need something?" I stood, rolling my chair back in place in front of my desk. Anything to keep the focus off my flaming face. Why did I have to blush so much around him?

"Yes. A bit of guidance, if you please." He took the chair in front of me.

"All right." I followed suit, folding my hands in front of me. "What do you need?"

"I know my balance now. The employee informed me that no funds have been spent since its opening."

Holy moly. Did he have an account that collected interest? "That's good, right? You've worked for your father for how long?"

"Since I turned seventeen."

"So, eleven years?"

His brow furrowed. "You know how old I am?"

My face took on the hue of the ruby-red lipstick I'd passed over this morning, or at least it felt that way. "I saw it on your driver's license." His birthday was New Year's Eve. What kind of parties had he had growing up?

"I see."

Did he feel like I'd breached his privacy? "I'm sorry. I didn't mean to pry."

"No apology is necessary."

Phew. "Then how can I assist you?"

He was obviously overwhelmed. Hopefully the question would help him focus instead of being lost in thought. Me as well.

"I need a place to live. My father gave me a deadline—today, actually—and I need somewhere to stay. I'm not even sure if I can rent a place that fast. I called a few friends last night, and . . ." He licked his lips.

A despondency I didn't understand stole across his face. Had his friends abandoned him? Did he have no one to turn to? The need to offer support rose within me, feeling like a very real nudge from God.

"Anyway," he continued, "I need somewhere to live."

"All right. Have you ever made a budget? Do you know how much you want to spend a month on rent?" These questions sounded ridiculous to my ears, but if he hadn't known how to check his own personal account, I was assuming nothing.

"We use budgets at Diallo all the time. However, I have never lived on such a low fraction." He gulped. "Have you? I mean, how much?" He rubbed his face. "I do not want to make assumptions, Ms. Blakely, but I *am* assuming you do not spend as much as I have in the past. Perhaps creating a budget with so little funds is easier for you than for me. I am hoping you can tell me what is realistic for a man of my means."

I wanted to laugh as he sat there and judged me but tried not to. The irony of it tickled something inside of me. Yet seeing the discomfort on his face stopped my mirth from escaping.

I shuffled papers around as I gathered my composure. "I am used to budgets of all ranges. The biggest question is, will your father continue to pay your salary while you fulfill the council's sentencing? If not, then what you have in your account has to last until you're back on payroll with him." Assuming his father would welcome him back when this was all over. He sounded a little on the harsh side.

Understatement.

Ekon's lips flattened. "He has cut me off. What I have in that account is it." He rubbed his face. "I am not sure he will employ me afterward. I have tainted the Diallo name, you know."

My heart ached for him, and a crazy idea formed in my head. But no. One step at a time. I quietly blew out a breath. "If you don't mind telling me the amount, I'll help you from there."

His eyes darted back and forth, roaming my face. I wasn't sure if he was studying me for sincerity or happy I'd offered.

He reached for a sticky note on my desk, took a pen from his pocket, and wrote on it. Then he handed the neon-pink note to me. I entered the conversion from Oloran francs to dollars in the calculator app on my cell to see what he was working with.

I gaped at the number on my screen.

Ekon Diallo was a millionaire *just* from his salaried position with Diallo. He had 1.25 million dollars sitting in the local bank.

SEVEN

Ekon

I could barely focus on the images on Ms. Blakely's computer screen. She had made room for me to sit behind her desk so we could explore my housing options, which meant our close proximity tempted me to notice her as a woman instead of strictly my employer.

It helped that she kept up an almost continuous dialogue of renting versus owning. If monthly payments did not bother me, renting would be a navigable route, she assured me.

"Or you could purchase a small place outright. Then you only have to worry about taxes and maintenance."

Honestly, both options were a little unnerving. Everything I had ever owned had been purchased by my father. Or by the trust fund he had allotted for me. I had never really purchased anything with my own funds. What if I made the wrong decision?

But that was not the worst question my brain had conjured. I could not help but worry if Father would ever forgive me. Would he require me to give up my birthright and find another job outside Diallo Enterprises next? A daunting thought, especially since my crimes would most likely follow me. What were the odds someone with no relational ties would hire me?

My mind immediately jumped to the rental process. Would landlords prefer not to rent to a person found guilty of crimes against the crown? Perhaps buying a home would be best.

"If I wanted to purchase a home, what would I do for tonight?" It pained me to ask, but I needed to know. In the past, I would have simply handed over a credit card, knowing my trust fund would pay the balance. "Do I have enough to check into a hotel? I honestly have never looked at the expense." My neck felt warm. She must think me an idiot.

"They can be expensive. It depends on their nightly rate. If you're leaning toward purchasing a home, I could let you stay in my guest room until you find a place."

I froze. Gratitude filled me but was quickly burst by a bolt of shame. I was now a charity case. "I do not think that is a good idea, Ms. Blakely. I work for you." Well, not officially, but all the same. "You are like my . . . parole officer. Would not that be a conflict of interest if I reside in your home?" Now my shame knew no bounds. I shifted my chair away a bit to cool my face.

"You're not going to stay with me forever." Her voice trailed off, and a look I could not describe settled across her features. Those wide ebony eyes took on a dreamlike quality, but that made no sense. Had she been sucked into thoughts about another person?

"Ms. Blakely?"

Her black eyes blinked at me, and she smiled. "How about I call my realtor? He's great at knowing what's available in the area. Oh!" she gasped. "Do you want to stay in Etikun?"

"It would make commuting here easier."

"Yes, but what about after? Oh, wait. Diallo Enterprises is located in Etikun, right?"

"It is. About twenty kilometers away."

"Then I can tell him to keep his search local. Tell me the price range you wish him to stick to. That way you'll still have money to live on. Do you know the interest rate your account accrues?"

"I do not." How many questions would she ask that I would not have the answer to? How carelessly had I lived? I cleared my throat. "The bank official I talked to helped me set up a username and password. I am sure that information is available online." At least, I hoped it would be.

"That can help you know how to budget for the future. If the interest is good enough to live off, then you can spend a little more."

"I will look. Meanwhile, if you could call your realtor friend?" Did she hear the note of desperation as well?

This was not me. Then again, finding out that not a single one of your friends would return your call would do that to a man. My mind went back to last night, when I had scrolled through every single contact in my mobile, asking them if I could stay at their place for a night or two.

Out of the thirty-something people I had called, only five had responded. All had said no. One had bluntly told me he could no longer be associated with me and to lose his number. I was pretty sure some of the unanswered calls meant I had been blocked.

I scooted away from Ms. Blakely. I needed to think. Renting a place would drain my pocket every month for the unforeseeable future, whereas a home would be a quick purchase and one I could negotiate. Then, *if* Father ever forgave me, I could use it as a rental property and return to life high in the sky.

"A home, please." I named a figure I thought was respectable.

The whites of Iris's eyes grew bigger. "That's too much. What will you have left to spend on daily expenses like groceries and taxis?"

I did not want to live in a hovel, though. "Can I afford to buy a car?" Perhaps not one of the same caliber as my previous ones, but a respectable one, at least.

"Not if you want a house that costs that much."

My hands clenched at my sides. How could Father do this to me? He acted like I had murdered the queen instead of trying to marry her. Granted, conspiring with Dayo was wrong, but did he really think this level of punishment necessary?

Stupid question. He obviously did.

I looked at Ms. Blakely. "I trust your judgment. Perhaps you could recommend an amount that is respectable and will allow me to pay for daily expenses."

"All right. I'll set up a meeting with the realtor so we can start looking right away. That way we'll get you a home as soon as possible." She paused. "And the offer to use my guest room stands."

I nodded. If I checked into a hotel, the paparazzi would fill the headlines with my plight. "Very well. Will we do this after work? I need my hours to meet the council's requirement."

"Oh, I'll cover this under the work umbrella."

"How so?"

A mischievous grin curved her lips. "Because then you can set up a finance class for the women we'll hire. They'll need to know how to manage their funds and what they can realistically afford in Etikun. Purchasing a home and anything else we may buy today will help you help them. Make sure you bring that notebook to take notes for the curriculum."

I stared at Iris, then smiled. I could not help myself.

She was such a breath of fresh air and seemed *genuinely* nice and caring. I had never met a woman who possessed these characteristics. Most of the women in Father's circles were looking to marry up or stay in a lifestyle they were accustomed to. One that provided drivers, maids, chefs, the works.

"Thank you." I hoped she could hear the depth of gratitude I felt.

"Anytime," she murmured.

I drew in a ragged breath, then stood. "I will work until the realtor is ready to show us a house."

She nodded, holding up her mobile. "I'm on it."

And she was. I could barely concentrate on the work in front of me as I listened to her plead for the man to fit us into his schedule right away instead of later on. Finally, she said the magic words of *cash offer* and then hung up.

I pretended that the paperwork in front of me held the secrets of life instead of resembling a puzzle I had no clue how to construct. I was much too distracted to focus.

"Okay, Ekon."

I jolted. She had never said my first name before. "We are using first names now?"

Her face turned a pretty pink. "Sorry, Mr. Diallo. Um, Dumeme, my realtor, will be by in ten minutes. He has a spacious car, so we don't have to worry about transportation. He has a few homes in Etikun he thinks you'll like."

"Great." I studied her. "You *can* call me Ekon, if you want." A small part of me wanted her to. Just to hear how my name sounded on her lips again.

I had already studied how they looked. Tried to memorize the shade of maroon that matched her dress. The gold medallions on the fabric provided a pop of color that she wore confidently. Everything about Iris Blakely screamed *notice me*, but in a way that did not point to arrogance. The more time I spent with her, the more I wondered if she really was this innocent.

I had no time to think further on the subject, as her secretary came in, asking if we wanted lunch. Iris informed her we had other business, and Oka studied me out of the corner of her eye.

For the first time since I had stepped foot in Aṣọ, I wondered if my father had spies here. Obviously, he was not concerned about competition. The jewelry business did not need to compete with the fashion industry. In fact, they were quite complementary to each other. Still, perhaps he simply wanted to keep tabs on me.

I wanted to pull Oka to the side and question her, but in the same breath, I did not want the veil of ignorance ripped away.

Iris and I took the elevator to the ground floor in silence. I wanted to say something, but words failed me. What did you tell a person who was helping you but had changed the scenario to one where you were assisting her? She had managed to figure out a way for me to get my eight hours in but also keep me from living on the streets.

"Dumeme is a great realtor. If you don't like something in the first place we see, let him know why. And if you don't know why you don't like a place, then say what you're partial to, and he'll use that to help you find something better."

"Understood."

She smiled, her straight white teeth gleaming in the sunlight. I wondered if she had worn braces as a kid. Somehow the idea made me want to smile with pleasure. She was turning me sappy.

I looked away and scanned the parking lot. A few seconds later, a black car turned into the lot.

"That's him. I'll sit in the back so you two can talk."

I balked. "No, I can sit in the back."

"There's more leg room in the front. You don't want to squash that frame." She pointed a finger up and down, spanning my height.

"It is not like you are a short woman." She had to be about 175 centimeters. A quick calculation turned that to five feet nine inches.

"But I am still shorter than you. Stop arguing and get in the car, Ekon."

I shook my head but opened the back door for her.

"Thank you, sir."

"*Kò tópé.*"

Her mouth parted, and for a brief moment, a look of attraction flashed across her face. At least, it *seemed* like attraction.

Perhaps my good manners just impressed her. I slammed the door by accident as want pulsed through me at the idea.

What was I thinking? She was all wrong for me. She did not even understand how I grew up. She was not an Ọlọran. I scoffed as I opened the front door. If Father was angry with me now, linking myself with an American would be the perfect clincher.

His one request when I went off to university had been that I not fall in love with a foreigner. He did not want any grandchild of his not being full-blooded Ọlọran. I could not think of any in our circles who had an interracial relationship or one that spanned different countries.

Iris stuck her head between our seats and introduced me to her realtor.

"Dumeme, this is Ekon. Ekon, this is Dumeme."

We shook hands, exchanging greetings in Oninan. "Ms. Blakely says you want a house, two bedrooms at the least and located in Etikun."

"Yes, ògbéni."

"Very well. The first place you will love. It is about three kilometers from Aṣọ. You could walk if you were inclined."

I was not. Summers in Etikun were hot, and I did not want to have to deal with the elements. Yet a three-kilometer cab ride should be less expensive than the jaunt I had made from the penthouse.

Dumeme went on to espouse the benefits of the home, and a minute later, we pulled up to a house with a thatched roof. *A thatched roof!* Only poor people lived in a building that did not have real shingles. I kept my mouth shut, though my jaw took the brunt of my effort.

Iris spared me a glance or two as we walked up the stone path. Weeds were everywhere, and the stairs were crumbling. I halted before them, then turned to Iris.

"Perhaps I should lift you over the threshold." I pointed toward her heels. "You do not want to fall."

"I'll be fine." Yet she looked wary, as if she knew the odds of twisting an ankle.

"It is not a problem."

"Of course not." A strained smile covered her face. "Because I'll be walking on the two feet God gave me."

"God did not give you those skinny sticks to balance on." Why did she always wear stilettos?

To better show off her legs, Ekon. Which I refused to let my gaze wander upon.

I must have been staring at her feet longer than was comfortable, because Iris cleared her throat. I looked into her ebony eyes, and she shifted, taking off one heel, then the other.

"Problem solved. Now you don't have to carry me."

"Good, then let us enter," Dumeme interjected.

So what if I followed dejectedly into the house? I had not actually wanted to carry her anyway. Had I not just gone over the uproar dating a woman like her would cause? I would never get back into Father's good graces if I aligned myself with Iris. No, I needed to stay on the path that would lead to my redemption. I would show Father that I could be self-sufficient and not squander the money I had earned working for Diallo Enterprises all these years.

A decade of dedication to the Diallo legacy had to be worth something. But as I looked at the home Dumeme was showing me, I knew it would not be this place that would earn back Father's respect.

EIGHT

Iris

To say Ekon hated Dumeme's first option would be a disservice to the word. Granted, Ekon did his best to hide his distaste, but I could tell how much he loathed the humble home. He was afraid to touch anything, as if the poverty would taint him by mere association.

As Dumeme led us from the master bedroom, I pulled Ekon aside. "Listen." I lowered my voice so it wouldn't carry to the realtor. "The women we'll hire will most likely live in a home like this."

His eyes widened. "How could anyone live in such a place?"

"Careful, your snobbery is showing."

He pulled back, an affronted look dropping his jaw.

Oops. Apparently, we didn't have the type of relationship where I could censure him. But seriously, he needed a heart check. There was nothing in the house that a little TLC couldn't fix.

I tried to appeal to him in a different manner. "What I mean is, you have to remember that people do buy homes like this and live happily. More than that, they're *proud* of their accomplishments. Don't look down on them. See this house's potential."

"If I want my father to—" He broke off. "*Trust* me. This place will not work. Not for me."

"Fine." At least I'd stood on my soapbox for a bit. "Dumeme can cut the tour short and take us to the next place."

"Thank you," he murmured.

Did it pain him to show gratitude? Bri once told me that he'd told her she said *thank you* too much. Did he feel like this was all completely beneath him? The great Ekon Diallo shopping for a home with the bare necessities—though I'd take his $1.25 million and trade it for my more modest savings—when he'd been living the penthouse life with cars, servants, and anything he could ever want.

My parents had a little money, but they'd never spoiled my brother and me. We were taught that hard work was an honor to oneself and what made one dependable. Our parents never wanted anyone to believe we hadn't earned the possessions and accolades we'd—at least they hoped—accumulate.

I'd been able to purchase the building Aṣọ sat in because of a monetary graduation gift from my parents and the smarts I'd used to invest it over the years. Some of the board members were also investors, as they believed in the company's vision. My other capital would be provided by good ol' bank loans.

Ekon assumed appropriately that I knew how to live on a budget, but he was wrong in thinking I didn't understand a life of luxury. After all, my best friend was now the queen of Olọrọ Ilé.

I hastened past the infuriating man to let Dumeme know we needed to see the next house. The realtor's face fell. He glanced over my shoulder, and I turned to see Ekon coming down the hall.

Ekon cleared his throat. "Excuse me, ògbéni. I know you rearranged your schedule to accommodate me. I appreciate your time and dedication. Unfortunately, this home will not be a fit for me. This house appears to need more work than I am capable of."

"Bééni, ògbéni. Yes, it needs much love. Surely you can afford the upkeep."

I hid a wince. Maybe I hadn't been clear enough in stressing Ekon's budget to Dumeme. I had been discreet, not naming Ekon—the Diallo name would be a red flag—but Dumeme would have to be blind not to know who he was. Ekon's face had been plastered all over the news.

Ekon shook his head. "I do not have the skills nor the funds."

Dumeme stared at Ekon, and Ekon met his gaze head on. I resisted the urge to fidget or wave a hand and ask if all was okay.

"Very well." Dumeme pulled out his phone, studying the screen. Suddenly a huge grin lit up his face, and his eyes twinkled with merriment. "I have just the place. This next home is owned by a family who desires something bigger. They must sell quickly. Any repairs needed in the home are superficial at best."

"Sounds like something to see," Ekon stated.

Dumeme led us out, locking up behind us. I wanted to applaud Ekon for his diplomacy, but his initial snobbery still rubbed me the wrong way. This house didn't need that much work.

A step crumbled beneath me, and the thought flew out of my mind as my body sailed forward.

"Ack!" I screeched, squeezing my eyes shut as I waited for the stone steps to pulverize my face.

Strong arms encircled my waist and halted my flight toward humiliation. Still, embarrassment clung to my cheeks, heating them more quickly than an egg on hot asphalt. Ekon turned me in his arms, examining me. I took in his concerned expression as his gaze roamed my figure, stopping at my heels.

Don't say it.

"Are you okay?" he asked.

How could I tell him that my pulse had skyrocketed at my potential plummet and soared even higher at his touch? That his nearness made my insides melt like a molten lava cake? And worse, that the worry in his mocha gaze made my heart trip right at his feet?

"Iris?"

Swoon! My knees buckled at the husky way he said my name. *Lord, save me from myself!*

"Ms. Blakely, do you need a doctor?" Dumeme asked.

I blinked. Right, I was fine. Nothing had been broken but the last vestiges of my pride.

"I'm fine." I stepped back, the clouds clearing from my mind as Ekon's touch fell away. I dragged in a breath and aimed a smile at Dumeme, purposely avoiding Ekon. "Shall we go to the next one?"

Shall we? I don't talk like that. Admittedly, my mind was still addled from being held by Ekon. It was everything I'd imagined—with a side of embarrassment at my clumsiness. Too bad losing my balance was the way it had come about.

But he caught you like the heroes in the movies you love so much.

A soft sigh escaped my lips.

"Béèni, béèni, let us go."

I blinked and headed for the car. Ekon held the door open for me once more. I slid onto the seat, ignoring his probing gaze. He couldn't know how much I was attracted to him. It was detrimental to our business arrangement and my friendship with Bri. How would it look if I showed up to a dinner at the palace with the island's biggest persona non grata hanging on my arm? Ekon probably wouldn't make it past the gates. As soon as the guards saw who was in the car with me, they'd make us turn around, regardless of my relationship with Bri.

We sat in silence as Dumeme pulled away from the home and drove a few miles—er, kilometers—to the next one. My breath caught as I saw the brown sandstone structure complete with a cedar-shingled roof and orange shutters around the front windows. The house was elevated in the front like a few of the other residences down the street, and an attached front porch seemed to be perched precariously on cinderblocks. It was cute. I prayed Ekon would like it or at least let Dumeme show us the whole home this time.

I kept my hands in my dress pockets, thankful I'd had the good sense to add the inside compartments when I'd made the apparel a couple of weeks ago. The dress was an idea I'd been contemplating for one of the women's lines of Aṣọ.

As we exited the car and walked up the sidewalk, I eyed the front steps. *Phew.* They looked completely stable. No mishaps here. Still, I clung to the rail as I walked up the four-stepped flight, stopping on the porch landing when it groaned a little. Okay, maybe the porch would take me out this time. I'd fall right into Ekon's arms, wrap my arms around his neck, and then our eyes would meet, establishing a connection unlike any other. Overcome with the intensity of the moment, he'd dip his head, and I—

"Ms. Blakely?"

I blinked at Dumeme and Ekon, who were beckoning me inside.

"Sorry about that." I swallowed, trying to push away my daydream.

My breath caught at the openness of the home. The living room opened to the back of the house with a view of the hills and all the wonderful greenery of Etikun. I walked straight to the wall-length windows, peering out.

"This is a gorgeous view." I sighed, imagining what it must look like during sunrise or sunset. Footsteps sounded behind me, and I glanced over my shoulder.

"It is," Ekon said softly.

A note of longing lingered in his voice. I peered up at him and froze as his gaze connected with mine.

"Have you ever wanted something that was bad for you?" he asked.

I'll say. I flushed and reverted my gaze back outdoors. "Yes."

"Me too," he whispered.

We faced forward, not another word spoken, but something like electricity hummed between us. Or was it all in my mind? Maybe I was projecting my daydreams on him and wishing he felt the undercurrent of attraction like I did.

"Ah, this home has wonderful views." Dumeme came to stand between us. "Wait until you see them from the master bedroom."

Ekon turned to explore, and I trailed behind the two men. Why couldn't I shake off my thoughts? I needed to ground myself in reality. Curse my vivid imagination. Now that I knew what it was like to have Ekon's arms around me, it was all I could think about. And touring homes with him certainly wasn't doing me any favors.

I opened a door in the hallway. *A closet.* I wasn't sure what it would be used for, but at least Ekon would have some kind of storage. I continued down the hall and into the master bedroom. The room was a half-moon shape with four floor-to-ceiling windows overlooking a small pond.

"This actually falls on your property," Dumeme said. "It does not belong to the neighbor."

"Is there wildlife in it?" Ekon asked.

I held back a snort. My idea of wildlife was snakes, lions, tigers, and bears. *Oh my!* But fish—and possibly frogs—didn't count.

"There is fish, ògbéni, nothing else."

"All right."

The bedroom also had a small ensuite bathroom. From my understanding, most of the homes in this area only had one communal bathroom. No bedrooms had their own ensuite. Would Ekon appreciate that concession? As much as his arrogance had bothered me during the first tour, I'd had a chance to think about his point of view. How vastly different these homes were to the penthouse he used to live in.

We exited and crossed the living room to enter a smaller guest room. Then Dumeme took us behind the guest room to the kitchen.

"No dining room?" Ekon asked.

"No, ògbéni. But you have room to build on." At Ekon's look of dismay, Dumeme hurried on. "Of course, it is just yourself. Perhaps you could get chairs and a table and put them outside. Enjoy nature."

"That is an idea," Ekon agreed grudgingly.

Boy, this prince—*ex-prince*—was having a rough time of it. It made me wonder what his penthouse looked like. Was it covered in all-white marble? Or did he go for the dark look of black with chrome finishes?

Regardless, Ekon would have to alter his view of what he needed in a home in order to find something. This was a lot nicer than the streets. Not that I would take back my offer of letting him camp out in my guest room. A shiver went down my spine, imagining sharing the same four walls.

Get out of your head, Iris. Don't go down this path. Remember, you're not his girlfriend, and you'll never be his girlfriend, so stick to what's real.

The thought bruised my heart and made me want to curl under a blanket and tell Ben and Jerry my woes. Until then, I had to keep up my guise of joy and happiness. I sighed and trailed the men. Dumeme spouted numbers and facts to Ekon, and I tuned them out.

I dug my cell out of the bottom recesses of my handbag. After inputting my pin, I opened the app to chat with my mom back in the States. Right then, I wanted to hear her voice so very much, only that would break out the waterworks, so texting would have to do. My family used to tease me whenever we played Monopoly growing up and insisted that the utility property should always be owned by me. Of course, my brother led the teasing. I even missed his ugly mug at the moment.

Iris:

Hey, Mom. Whatcha doing?

Mom:

Wondering what's wrong with my daughter. Are you okay?

Iris:

What makes you think something's wrong?

Ekon drew my attention, motioning that we were leaving. I headed toward the car. "I'll remain in the back." I held up my cell. "Need to answer some messages."

"Are you sure?" Ekon eyed me skeptically.

"Yes." I smiled, forcing my cheeks higher to make it believable.

"Okay, then."

I buckled in, then read Mom's response.

Mom:

Whenever something's bothering you, you ask me what I'm doing. And to answer that, I'm in the garden.

Iris:

How are the flowers?

Mom:

Basking in the sunshine. How's my little bug?

I stared at the front seat, thankful the headrest blocked Ekon from my view. My mom never called me *flower*, saying I was named after one for a reason. Instead, she called me *little bug* or *ladybug*.

Iris:

A little weary.

Mom:

Are you taking in too much negative emotion?

Iris:

No

Mom:

Empathizing with people?

Iris:

No

Mom:

Ah, in your own head, then.

Iris:

How do I get out?

Mom:

Sing to the Lord. Praise His name, and I bet you'll transform your thoughts.

I hugged my cell to my chest. Mom was the best. Even a thousand miles away, she knew what to say.

Iris:

I love you.

Mom:

I love you too. When are you coming back?

Iris:

Mom . . .

Mom:

Fine. When can I visit?

Iris:

When you're ready.

I put my cell in my handbag. Mom wouldn't visit. She had a fear of flying and went nowhere a car couldn't take her. She'd taken my news of moving permanently to Ọlọrọ the hardest. Dad would visit, and even my brother might. But Mom would only visit through FaceTime and the pictures I sent her daily.

I miss them so much, Lord.

I closed my eyes and sang a hymn as I waited for the day to end and Ekon to find his perfect place—for now.

NINE

Ekon

This was the longest day I had experienced in a while . . .
and it still was not finished.

I unlocked my front door—well, not mine any-
more—to the penthouse and ushered Iris inside. I cleared my
throat. "I packed last night. I simply need to grab everything."

"Sure." Her voice sounded a little high-pitched, which
matched the state of her eyebrows as she turned in a circle to
admire the place.

The flash of pride that usually came with showing off the
top-floor flat remained absent. Even if Father forgave me and
returned the keys, would I ever feel the same sense of satisfaction living here?

How could I after seeing all the properties in Etikun that
were not half as nice as this one? I had started the tour with
irritation that my address would be like a commoner's. By the
time I viewed the last property, I came to the realization of how
fortunate I had been all of these years.

The house with the pond was the best of the offerings. Dumeme had shown me a few places that made it appear like

the royal palace. Coming to a decision was simple after seeing those. As he drove us back to the penthouse, my thoughts had turned away from my misfortune to those born less fortunate.

How had the elders of the Etikun tribe failed our people so? Why were we not giving the citizens better accommodations and making houses more affordable? Or, like Iris, employing more people to elevate their situation in life?

My thoughts continued to tumble one after the other as I entered my bedroom and grabbed my packed luggage. The only things inside were the clothing my mom had gifted me on birthdays and holidays. Surely Father would not consider those trust-fund items, since I had not purchased them for myself. Earlier at lunch, I had sent him a text asking how much he would charge for my cologne, watch, and shoes. We had worked out an agreement, and my bank had drafted a check in order for me to leave with the items I found necessary.

I refused to touch anything else, including my jewelry, sports equipment, and the paintings that hung on the wall. Those were now items of my past. I would have to decorate the pond house with niceties more aligned to my new budget. Once that was done, perhaps I could invite my family over for dinner.

As soon as I learned how to cook.

When I entered the living room, Iris's gaze dropped to the one piece of luggage I carried.

"Is that it?" she asked quietly.

"All I am allowed."

"Oh." Her voice sounded small, and her eyes began to water.

I halted in horror as not one but *two* tears spilled down her cheeks. "Are you . . . are you *crying*?" I did not know what to do with a weeping woman.

"Why is your dad being so mean?" she wailed. "He's leaving you with nothing. What if you hadn't bought a house today? What if you were truly penniless and destitute like so many in Etikun?" She started to hiccup as she spoke through her tears.

My breath came in spurts as I hurried to the water closet to grab something to mop up the mess on her face. I did *not* deal with blubbering women on a regular basis. I was not even aware tears could come so rapidly nor be accompanied by countless questions.

I thrust the paper handkerchief toward her. She dabbed under her eyes, then peered up at me. Her ebony irises were glossed with a storm of hurt.

For me.

When was the last time someone had genuinely cared about my well-being? Mother asked after me occasionally, but only when I visited for family dinners. Gin and wine were what my mother worried about. How little she had left in her glass. How much she had already consumed. And whether or not Father was aware of the growing number of empty bottles in the trash.

Iris Blakely had known me for two weeks and was already shedding tears. Without thinking, my arms wrapped around her and brought her close.

"Shh, I will be fine." I held her, hoping my quiet tone would soothe the ache in her heart. Watching her at work had shown me just how deeply she cared. Or perhaps her emotions simply got the better of her.

My thoughts fled as she buried her face in my chest and squeezed my waist. My chest pounded at her touch and the care she exhibited. The longer we held on to one another, the more tension seeped from my being, and a peace I had never experienced took over.

Quiet descended, and I realized Iris had stopped weeping. How long had she been quiet? Had she wished to remove herself from my embrace and could not for fear of an uneasiness? I jolted backward, dropping my hands.

"I apologize." I stopped. What else should I say?

"For what? I was crying, you gave me a hug, and I stopped crying. I should be thanking you."

I arched an eyebrow. "But you will not?"

"Uh. No. I, uh, thanks." Her face turned bright red.

I nodded, sliding my hands into my pockets. Why had I directed us toward this awkward path? Now the only way out was a change in subject. "We can leave, if you wish."

"Right. Yes. Come on."

Iris had hired a taxi, since Dumeme had other business. The driver sat waiting at the entrance to take us to her place.

Us. Talk about upping the discomfort level. Even though I was buying a home, I could not occupy it straightaway. There was paperwork to be processed and the transfer of ownership to be handled, which was why I had accepted Iris's invitation. That and the desire not to be stalked at a local hotel.

When we exited the elevator doors, I walked over to the concierge.

"Omoba—I mean, ògbéni—how can I help you?" The concierge winced as he misspoke, using my old title.

I ignored the feeling of shame and passed him the keys. "Can you deliver these to my father?"

"Of course, Ògbéni Diallo."

I thanked him in Oninan.

His eyes widened. "Kò tópé."

The taxi driver popped the boot for me to deposit my luggage. By the time I was ready to get in the car, Iris already sat in the back. I buckled in, ignoring the loud silence as she gave the driver her address.

"Should we grab dinner first?" I asked.

"I was planning to cook."

My mouth salivated at the thought. "Really? You do not order out?" I had always assumed most New Yorkers ordered takeout for everything. I guessed that was the difference between reality and TV.

"No." She laughed. "I can cook. My mom taught me."

"Oh." Further proof she had not lived a pampered life. They had no chef.

Only, I was beginning to believe that was not such a bad thing. Look at where my upbringing had landed me. If it were not for Iris's generosity, I did not know where I would be right now. The sting of my so-called friends' rejections still smarted.

I had originally believed my desire to lie low was why I had not heard from any of them. Calls had been few after my house arrest became public knowledge. Once my friends had confirmed the charges against me were true, the calls had stopped. I could not truly blame any of them. Who wanted an ex-prince—a convicted one, at that—for a friend?

"What are you cooking?" I asked. What did one make one-self? I still had not figured out how to crack an egg.

"Chinese food. I miss it, so I thought I'd try my hand at making it. I found a recipe on Pinterest and managed to locate some ingredients at the store."

"How often do you cook for yourself?"

"Most nights." Her lips curved. "Ordering out is not where I choose to spend my money."

"What do you mean?"

A bemused expression crossed her face before it quickly switched to neutrality. "I adore all things fashion, which means buying clothes, shoes, accessories, and sometimes the fabric itself so I can make my own outfits. In order to indulge my passion, I make concessions elsewhere. Which is why I cook more than I eat out."

That made sense. Was that something I could incorporate into the classes for Aṣọ?

"What about you?" Iris asked. "Do you have a hobby or something you spend more money on?"

I took a moment to give her question some thought. I had always purchased whatever I wanted with no regard to the ex-pense. "I suppose I am not the collecting kind."

"Really? You don't own two of something?"

"I had multiple cars, but I doubt that is what you mean."

She laughed. "Maybe that's a rich man's collectible."

There was no malice in her words, but the way they hit my gut had me examining myself once more. I was no longer a rich man, so who was I? I had seen Iris's face when I told her how much rested in my bank account. She obviously thought the amount high, yet she had cautioned me to not spend it all. In my estimation, that meant it was *not* that much. Sometimes the contradictions of my new circumstances made my head spin.

I had gone from a life of guaranteed money for anything I wanted to not knowing what would come my way tomorrow. It was enough to depress a man. As it was, a headache had been pulsing in my forehead since last night's dinner.

At least I had a home. Now I simply had to figure out how to furnish it and if I could afford a vehicle as well. If I asked for Iris's help, she would probably take me bargain hunting. Which might not be a bad idea.

"Iris?"

"Yes, Ekon?"

Chill bumps popped across the back of my neck. I swallowed and concentrated on my request. "Would you be willing to help me furnish my new home and find an affordable vehicle?"

"Sure. Did Dumeme say when you would get the keys to your place?"

"He will know more tomorrow once the offices are open and he can begin filing paperwork."

"Oh, good. I know of some great places for furniture. I've found so many pretty things and had to make myself not go crazy furnishing my place. You'll see."

As she spoke, the taxi driver turned into a building complex. "Here we are, Ms. Blakely."

"Thank you, Abeo. See you tomorrow."

"I'll be here, miss."

I grabbed my luggage, then closed the boot of the car. "You know the taxi driver?" We walked down the sidewalk to one of the buildings of flats.

"It made sense to use the same person instead of getting a different one every morning."

"Why have you not purchased a car? Are you not spending a lot on transportation?"

Her face flushed. "I don't know how to drive."

"You do not have a license?"

She shook her head.

My mouth dropped. "Never had a license?"

Another shake of the head.

Interesting. I peered down at the top of her curly mane. "I could teach you."

"Really? Why would you help me?"

Was she jesting? After all she had done for me? "You are helping me. Can I not do the same?"

"That's common decency." She waved her hand. "Anyone else in my position would help you."

I snorted. "I know many who would not agree." Like the contacts in my mobile.

"There's got to be something you don't know how to do that I could teach you."

The answer popped into my head immediately. "I cannot cook." I still dreamed of omelets.

"Can't or won't?"

"Definitely cannot. I tried to make an omelet after watching a YouTube video. I could not even manage to get the egg into the bowl."

Iris giggled, her rosy cheeks blooming.

"You laugh, but I went hungry that morning."

"*Pobrecito.*"

I laughed, feeling joy that I had not felt in a long time. Even at being called *poor baby* in Spanish. "Do we have a deal?"

"Fine. You teach me how to drive, and I'll teach you how to cook."

"Perfect." I could practically envision tomorrow's breakfast.

We exited the elevator and came to a stop. A woman stood in the hallway, waiting. Her eyes widened as they flitted from my face to Iris's.

"Ẹ kúròlé," Iris greeted.

"Ẹ kúròlé." The woman swallowed, her gaze flicking to mine. "I'm Ada Ekezie. I live down that way," she said in Oninan, pointing to her left.

"Nice to meet you," Iris said, switching to English. "Um, I caught your name but not the other part."

"She lives that way," I interjected.

The woman looked at me nervously. Perhaps I should wander down the hall and leave them to talk. I moved away, nodding at Iris.

"Does he live here?" Ada whispered in English, albeit poorly. I could hear her clearly as I walked to the other end of the building.

A few minutes passed, and then Iris caught up to me. "Sorry about that."

"I think I made her nervous."

Iris gave a strained smile. "How about you drag your luggage into the guest room, and we can have your first lesson." She opened her front door, then pointed toward a room. She looked down at her dress. "I'll change. Who knows what food you'll fling my way if you can't even crack an egg?"

"Ha."

I wanted to ask what Ms. Ezekie had had to say but did as instructed. No need to focus on a person who saw me as a criminal when I could converse with a woman who treated me with respect.

Maybe living temporarily with Iris would not be demeaning after all.

TEN

Iris

I needed coffee and a chance to ignore the presence of my new roommate.

I hadn't slept a wink, too busy replaying every exchange, every momentous event that had happened between Ekon and me, starting with that hug.

I'd cried in front of him. How could I do that? Not that I was ashamed of my tears, but generally, losing my composure in front of a man only came after a certain amount of time in a relationship. Ekon and I were really only acquaintances. But when he'd walked out of his luxurious penthouse bedroom with that one suitcase and the clothes on his back, I'd lost it.

Even if that bag had been stuffed to the gills, it wasn't enough to outfit a week—unless he was a phenomenal packer. After gazing at all the gorgeous artwork on the walls and the figurines situated here and there, I'd had a better idea of what Ekon was losing. Living a life paycheck to paycheck like the majority of Americans wasn't even in his vocabulary. It had quickly become apparent that he didn't even understand how most of his own tribal members lived. To toss him into the unknown without a life float—though some could argue the million dollars in his bank account made a pretty cushy float—seemed cruel of his father. If I ever met the man, I'd give him my two cents on how a parent was supposed to come alongside their child and show them the right path, not dig the knife in and twist so there was no hope of recovery.

Despite all the emotions that had been going through my mind and obviously leaking down my face, I hadn't expected Ekon to throw tissues at me or offer a hug when it became clear I couldn't stop crying.

The waterworks had ceased almost immediately when his arms closed around me, enveloping me with his warmth. Hearing the steady beat of his heart had soothed the ache in my own heart at the treatment he'd received from his father.

I'd always thought being held in Ekon's arms would come with a rush of hormones that would reduce me to a human puddle. But the gentle way he'd held me encouraged me to snuggle closer. It was only after a few minutes that I'd realized my tears had dried. Even so, I'd clung to him like I'd found my penguin.

As if hugging him hadn't been momentous enough, we'd shared a meal. The laughter had remained steady throughout the night. *Literally!* I'd gone to bed around midnight simply because I knew I had to work today, not because we'd run out of things to say. Now my eyes were swollen, and my heart double-timed, knowing Ekon resided on the other side of my apartment.

I rolled onto my stomach and groaned into my pillow. Life wasn't fair. I couldn't call Bri and ask for advice. I'd had to tell her a work-related issue came up yesterday when I canceled girls' night. I didn't want to hurt her by falling for the guy who'd been part of a coup and once been rejected by her—obviously, in good sense. There was more to her not picking Ekon than his arrogance, but my mind couldn't seem to recall what Bri's issues had been in the face of the memories I'd made with him over sesame chicken.

Oh, sesame chicken, I'll never think of you the same way.

Because now my heart beat to see that rare but gorgeous half smile Ekon was so great at. Staring into his mocha gaze against the backdrop of his dreamy dark-chocolate skin, I was a goner!

Still, life called. I needed to dress, ride to work, and act like we hadn't spent yesterday finding a new home for him, then enjoying his first cooking lesson. I huffed and threw back the covers. Now wasn't the time to continue my obsessive investigation of *does he or does he not like me.*

Still, as I rifled through the clothes hanging in my walk-in closet, my mind automatically asked the question—would he think I looked pretty in this?

"I don't know," I murmured, staring at a pantsuit.

I never wore pantsuits. I wasn't even sure why I'd bought this one, except the pattern was out of this world, and Bri had insisted the outfit made me look like a runway model. Who didn't want to look that beautiful at some point in their life? But if I was going to manage to act any semblance of normal, I needed something comfortable but stylish to feel my best.

Since I'd worn a dress yesterday, a skirt was a must today. But what kind? Pencil skirts were out. There was nothing worse than feeling like a mermaid on dry land. The constricted feeling didn't appeal to me, even if I could agree on how stunning a lot of women looked in them.

I grinned when I spotted a black skirt with a ruffled bottom. It flared if I twirled and had pockets—life's perfect ornament in women's clothing. Fortunately, they weren't those skinny pockets big enough only for a tube of lipstick. I could slide my hands into these babies, adding my cell phone *and* the lipstick if I really wanted to. Which most times I did.

I grabbed the skirt off the hanger and laid it on my bed before scanning my blouse section for the perfect complement. An emerald-green wrap blouse with a nice bow to tie at the waist caught my eye. I had some fantastic gold hoop earrings that would go well if I put my hair up in a French twist.

Thankfully I'd braided my hair in a few two-strand twists last night to make it more manageable this morning. I couldn't always let my curls go free, or they'd get damaged from too much manipulation or look like a bird's nest upon waking. Such was the curly-haired life.

Satisfied with my ensemble, I headed for the kitchen. I slid to a halt at the sight of Ekon wearing all black and a silver tie. He looked like perfection.

Keep strong. He's business, strictly business.

Pretty sure my brain wasn't buying the pep talk. Not after all the lines I'd crossed yesterday. I just had to figure out how to redraw them and erect more barriers to ensure no one snuck over to the other side. But each step that lessened the distance between us threatened to break my resolve. Especially when I came close enough to reach out and touch him—if I wanted.

Wouldn't it be wonderful if I had the right to wrap my arms around him and wish him good morning? As if we were newly husband and wife, our families having attended the wedding ceremony and sent us off with well wishes and blessings to last a lifetime. Of course, that was an alternate reality I'd already explored. Reality had proved there would be no wedding, no honeymoon, and no babies to come.

"Good morning, Iris." Ekon smiled and handed me a cup.

"What's this?"

"Coffee. You have a Keurig, and even I cannot mess that up."

I laughed. *See? Funny.* "Thanks. It was the first thought on my mind when I woke." More like opened my eyes and gave up the pretense of sleeping. Something had to fuel me through the day if I was giving up on my daydreams of being Mrs. Diallo.

"I enjoy a cup in the morning as well."

"Are you almost ready to go?" I glanced at my watch. "Abeo will pick us up in twenty minutes."

Ekon's mouth turned downward. "I was actually hoping for a breakfast cooking lesson."

"Well, I usually grab a smoothie." I opened the fridge and showed him one of the bottles. "Want to try one?"

"Sure." Yet his smile appeared dimmer.

My heart pricked. "I'd be happy to teach you tomorrow. Besides, cooking lessons are best on the weekend." Because obviously I wouldn't fall asleep again if he kept looking so boyishly handsome.

"Great."

His full grin lit me up like Times Square at night. We drank our smoothies in silence before I grabbed my bag and he took hold of his briefcase. It was all so perfectly domestic and yet not.

Abeo talked a lot on the car ride to work. I chimed in a few times, laughing at his jokes, but the entire time, my mind was all too aware of one thing and one thing only: Ekon. How had he so ensnared himself in my heart? And how could I remove him without doing damage? I didn't want to get hurt, and any feelings for him were bound to lead to heartache. His own father wanted nothing to do with him. What made me think we could have any semblance of a healthy relationship? I was banking on wishes and dreams and should be praying for his redemption and to be kind like God asked. Nothing more, nothing less.

Oka raised her eyebrows when we stepped off the elevator together but said nothing.

I stopped in front of her desk. "Ẹ káàárò, Oka. Any messages this morning?"

"Ẹ káàárò, Ms. Blakely. You have no messages. Your package of flyers did arrive, though." She motioned to the box resting on her desk.

"Oh, goodie. We'll get those distributed, then."

"We?" she asked, peering over my shoulder.

Probably tracking Ekon's movements. I shifted. "Yes, please. You said you would take some to your beauty shop?"

"Oh, yes." Oka offered a stiff smile.

I got the feeling she didn't like me too much, but she did her work and wasn't rude, so I couldn't complain. "Don't worry, I won't make you hand them all out. I have some places I'll take them as well." Maybe Ekon could distribute some also.

The hiring event had to turn out well. It just had to.

I dipped my head at her. "All right, let me know if anything important comes through."

"Yes, madam."

When I walked into the office, Ekon already sat in front of his desk, head bent in concentration. I tried to keep my gaze off of him. Boy, would this make for a long day. Why had I let him stay at my place?

Why, Lord?

Perhaps if I went to talk to the ladies in design, I could give myself a breather before staring at him again. I dropped the box of fliers on my desk.

"I'll be on the second floor," I called over my shoulder as I hustled out of the office.

As I headed down the stairwell, I stopped, resting my back against the wall. My mind had been filled with nothing but Ekon since he'd stepped foot into Aṣo. Now I needed to pull my head out of the clouds and remind myself what was at stake. Rules and regulations had to be met, loans had to be secured, and employees needed to be hired.

For now, I would talk to the few designers I had managed to hire. Zam Manufor was a wonder when it came to design for Qloran men. She was going to transport Aṣo to the top. First, I had to answer her many emails, the last one labeled urgent. I continued down the stairs until I exited onto the second-floor landing.

Wide tables littered the design floor, and a few women had their heads bent over notebooks. Hopefully brainstorming ideas for our fashion lines. We had one for men, one for women, and one for children. We hadn't yet discussed if we would branch out into any specialties.

"Madam, you are here." Zam pushed her black-framed glasses up her nose. "Come. I show you the problem."

Problem? I guessed I should have read my emails before escaping my office. "*Kíni àròyé rę?*" I tried to ask what the problem was in Oninan with confidence, but the words sounded so foreign to my ears, and I was afraid I'd butchered the correct pronunciation.

Bri had been helping me with the language. With her guidance and YouTube videos, I would become more fluent. I *had* to. What kind of owner would I be if I didn't try to learn the language of the country I desperately wanted to be a part of and help?

Zam smiled. "Keep practicing, madam."

"Please call me Iris."

She shook her head. "No, you are the boss."

This wasn't our first disagreement over the moniker they'd pegged me with. As much as I wanted to be one of the ladies, I really wasn't. "Okay."

A look of relief flashed in her brown eyes. "The lights keep flickering. We need better lighting in here."

I wanted to scream in frustration. Since I'd bought the building and hired someone to take care of the power, we'd battled blackouts. "What about the generator? Does it not keep them from flickering?"

"That is why they flicker. The power goes out, generator kicks on, power comes on, generator goes off. It is fortunate we do not have epilepsy."

I stifled my groan. "I'll call the company once more."

"Perhaps you can use your connections?"

My back stiffened. Did she assume I would run and tell Bri my woes? "What do you mean?"

"Mr. Diallo. I understand he is a consultant. Perhaps he can talk to the elders. Take our concerns to the royal council."

But they hadn't elected a new member to fill the Etikun seat yet. I rubbed my forehead. "I'll run upstairs and figure it out."

"Thank you, madam."

I nodded.

"Also, we wondered if we could do a fashion show. Show the country what is coming from us."

A *fashion show! In Ọlọrọ!* I squealed. "Zam, you're a genius. Let me see what the board says." I wanted to hug her, but the lines between employee and employer had been drawn. Instead, I clapped my hands and waved good-bye.

Steph had called me back and apologized for her rude secretary. Unfortunately, her company didn't have an opening in her show. She'd given me some suggestions of others to contact, granting me permission to drop her name, but their shows had been filled as well. Zam's idea would be a great way to introduce our lines of clothing and maybe even alert the others in the industry.

I dashed back into the office.

"Ekon?" I asked.

"Yes?" He looked up, turning sideways in his chair in order to see me.

"What do you think of having a fashion show?"

His head cocked, and that look came upon his face. The one that furrowed his brow and made him rub his smooth chin in consideration. "That is actually brilliant."

"You think?"

He nodded slowly. "I have an in with a jeweler who would love a chance to showcase his many necklaces and the like."

My models wearing Aṣọ clothing and Diallo jewels? That did paint a pretty picture. But . . .

"Are you sure your dad would go for that?" Because I got the impression of an entirely different man.

"Yes. He is all about business; however, I will call him and present the offer officially, if you wish."

"Please."

He nodded and picked up his cell phone.

I tried not to eavesdrop—well, as much as I could, sharing an office with a person. Even though I caught some of Ekon's conversation, I couldn't tell if it was a yes or a no. Finally, he hung up and stood, taking a seat at my desk.

"He is willing to help. I offered to be the liaison between here and Diallo. He has accepted."

Color me surprised. I wasn't sure if that was a good thing or a bad thing. It couldn't have been an easy call for Ekon to make. "Thank you so much."

"You are welcome." He got right back up and went over to his desk without another word.

I wasn't sure why he'd walked the few steps when he could have remained in his own area, but I'd be lying if I said pleasure at his presence hadn't filled me. I hummed softly to myself and pulled up my to-do list.

ELEVEN

Ekon

Did waking up extra early to ensure I would be ready for my breakfast cooking lesson reek of desperation? I did not even know if the sun was up. Yet I had already finished my grooming and dressing for the day. Although, perhaps that was not such a good idea. The last time I had attempted to crack an egg, the insides had ruined my shirt. But since Iris was going to teach me, I would be safe from yolk slime, right?

I picked up my Lure cologne and sprayed the liquid, then walked through the mist. Thank goodness I had negotiated a price with Father to bring this with me. It was a little piece of my old life that helped me not feel so lost. Since the bottle cost a fortune, I had changed my standing order to be billed to my personal account.

I headed for the kitchen, careful not to disturb the quiet. Iris probably still slept, and I did not want to disrupt her, no matter how impatient I was to eat. Oddly, the quiet calmed me, unlike the day I discovered my servants had been dismissed.

The silence would afford me a few minutes to prepare myself

before seeing Iris. Ever since that hug—had that truly only been two days ago?—I could not push the idea of an *us* far enough from my thoughts. She was so much more than I had ever expected.

Not that I actually expected much from women. The ladies of my past always enjoyed hanging on my arm like an expensive garment. All for the pleasure of saying they knew a prince or a Diallo. Their end goal had been to manipulate me into spending money on them. Outside the standard date-night dinner, or wherever I took them, I never squandered money on my dates. I made it clear they would never be my girlfriends, much to Mother's chagrin and Father's annoyance. Why would I bother when they had my life mapped out and none of those women were on the approved list?

Father wanted me to provide an heir to the Diallo fortune, and Mother simply wanted grandchildren. They both had a woman or two in mind who could bring the fruition of their dreams. When I had escorted the queen on a date, Father had flaunted the association with his business colleagues. It was no wonder he had taken all my possessions.

Even though I had never truly been serious about a woman in the past, Iris made me think *what if*. What if I had met her before the queen? What if I had not betrayed my country and monarch?

That was the thing about what-ifs—they only led to delusions and depressed a person's spirits. I had *not* met Iris before Brielle Adebayo. I indeed *had* betrayed my country and queen in assisting and feeding into Dayo's delusions.

Not to mention, Iris was an American and, if I had to guess, of mixed ancestry. It was one thing to tell Father I wanted a relationship with an American, but to also hint that she was not fully African-American would be another mark against her.

Do you care what Father wants anymore? After all, he has washed his hands of you.

Only, I could not let go of the spark of hope that I could show him I was capable of being a better man. After all, he had granted me the opportunity to be the liaison for Iris's fashion show. In two months' time, the country would be introduced to Aṣọ. That gave us time to hire all the people needed to manufacture some clothing to show the world. With Iris's connections in the fashion industry and probably a favor from the queen— though Iris did not seem the type to beg a favor—the fashion show should be the most sought-out event in Ọlọrọ.

"Good morning," Iris called out.

I whirled around and inhaled sharply. She looked beautiful, hair out in full glory. Her dress was floor-length, the color changing from light blue to dark—a picture of relaxation. Attraction buzzed through me.

"Ẹ kóojúmọ́." It was early yet. I cleared my throat. "How was your rest?"

"Good." She turned away and popped a pod into the Keurig.

I took in the spotless counters, my thoughts spinning. One would never know the granite had been covered in cornstarch yesterday. My adventure in homemade sesame chicken was an experience I would never forget. The feel of the chicken rolled in the white powder had evoked senses in my fingers I had never experienced before. Previously, chicken had always been served to me already cooked by the finest chefs. Who knew it was pink in its raw form? I was yesterday years old when I learned that bit of information.

Iris hummed softly as she poured a cup of coffee.

"Are we making breakfast this morning?" Did I appear as eager as I sounded to my own ears?

"Yes." She smiled, but her eyes did not appear as bright as usual. "You want an omelet lesson, right?"

"Yes. Please." I halted, unsure if I should ask if she was okay.

"All right." She eyed my shirt. "Do you want to use my apron? I'd hate for you to get your clothes messy."

"Am I going to make a mess?" Did not a lesson include knowledge on how to avoid messes?

"Don't you recall the cornstarch snafu yesterday?" She laid a hand on my arm.

I forced my gaze to remain on her ebony eyes instead of remembering how slim her waist was and how good she felt in my arms. I swallowed. "I was simply ensuring the chicken was thoroughly coated."

Iris snorted, mirth dancing in her eyes.

Pleasure filled me, knowing I brought that look there. Even if it was at my expense.

Since when was I willing to be so self-sacrificing to make sure another smiled? Yet the sound of her laughter was like a slap on the back with a *good going*.

"Fine. That's your story." She clapped her hands together. "Okay, grab some eggs, cheese, and . . ." She tilted her head to the side. "What else do you like in your omelet?"

"Meat or vegetables."

"Okay." She nodded. "I have some green onion and other stuff in there." She motioned to the refrigerator. "Find your ingredients, and we'll get going."

I nodded and perused the contents. She had a lot of fresh vegetables. I wondered if she went to the market. Would she let me tag along? Shopping on my own would be a new experience. I had never bought food to cook for myself. Yet I did not want to have to admit to lacking another life skill many probably mastered in childhood or their young adult years. A man could only take so many hits before he lost all the respect of a woman who interested him.

Not that this can turn into anything. Remember that, Ekon. There was no room for Iris on the narrow path to Father's good graces.

Twenty minutes later, I had managed to make us both omelets, though the shape left a lot to be desired. Mushrooms and onions poked through the exterior instead of being folded discreetly within the eggs. I would do better next time, but at least now I could say I had managed to make some breakfast.

As we sat at her table for two, I looked at Iris and took a gamble. "Iris?"

"Yes?" She looked up, fork holding her next bite.

"Could you teach me how to cook dinner?" Why did my neck have to warm so?

"We made dinner last night."

"No, not that kind." I swallowed, hands suddenly damp from the anxiety taking over. "I want to make a traditional Ọlọran dinner and invite my parents to my new home."

"Oh," she whispered. Her tongue darted out of her mouth, licking her lips.

Not that I purposely stared, but the image branded my mind. *Focus!* "You see, I want to show them I am capable of being on my own."

"You *are*." Her head bobbed in agreement.

"Thank you. I figure once my place is furnished, I could prepare a meal and have them over. Show them I am learning to be independent." Then perhaps Father would finally be proud of me. He knew I had the smarts to run a company, but did he know I could be a man on my own two feet?

"I would love to help, Ekon, but you do know I'm American, right?"

I chuckled. "Yes. The accent kind of gave it away."

"Oh, I talk funny? Is that what you're insinuating?" Her eyes danced in merriment.

"No, not at all. You have a lovely accent." If she kept saying my name in that way that made it sound brand-new and important all at once, I would continue to listen to her.

Her face turned rosy. "Thank you. So do you." She covered her mouth, a slight cough sounding behind her hands. "Um, anyway, I just mean that I don't know how to make an Ọlọran meal. Do you have a friend, a *girl* friend, who could help?"

Was she trying to find out if I was single? Satisfaction spiraled through me, then quickly fizzled out as I recalled her question. "I do not have friends who could help. They are no longer accepting my calls."

Dismay fell across her face, dousing the light in her eyes. I bit back an oath. I should not have said anything, but something about this woman made me share the words I so often held close. If I did not speak certain truths, they held no real power over me, right?

"You need to make new friends."

I almost laughed. No one would be lining up to become associated with me in the near future. "I am a criminal. That removes me from the friendship arena."

Her face blanched. "Ekon . . ."

"I am finished." I placed my fork on the plate. "I will clean up the mess in the kitchen before I leave." What could be better than leaving one humiliation for another? Because today was another day of community service.

"Wait, let's talk."

I shook my head. I had done enough conversing for the day. Now Iris Blakely knew how pathetic I was and why she should keep her distance. It was also a reminder to myself to ensure I did not taint her innocence and *joie de vivre*.

An elder picked me up in front of Iris's apartment building. This time it was Mr. Ladipo. Most likely he would assign someone else under his employ to watch me pick up trash. Ms. Keita had stayed, but rumor said otherwise of Ladipo. He did not have the time to spend watching a peon such as myself.

Half an hour later, he pulled over to the side of the road. I grabbed the traffic vest and slipped on the neon-yellow garment. With each movement, my face heated as shame fell upon me like a weighted vest for an X-ray. I grabbed the trash bag and claws to aid in picking up waste.

"I will be back to pick you up eight hours from now. Do stop for a brief lunch," Mr. Ladipo directed.

Right, because I wanted people to see me eat from a roadside stand. I said nothing and exited his luxury Mercedes sedan.

A few people slowed in their cars, watching as I used the claws to grab a plastic bottle. I kept my gaze on the ground. Orange dirt mingled with the green of the grass. Despite the undignified task, the day was nice. The sun shone brightly, and a breeze softened the heat that touched my skin.

Time passed slowly as I made my way down the street, bag filling up.

"Ògbéni, ògbéni!"

I turned at the masculine cry and found a man waving to me down the street. My heartbeat raced as I tried to ascertain if he was a threat. But the moment he got within a few meters of me, he smiled. Several of his teeth were missing, but that did not prevent the wide grin.

"You are Ekon Diallo, yes?" he asked in Oninan.

I gulped. "I am."

He held up his mobile. "Take a selfie with me."

My stomach soured. "I cannot. Council policy." It was a lie. One I willingly committed in order to avoid showing up on his social media feed.

"*Má bínu.*" He apologized, then pointed to my left. "You missed one." He sauntered away.

I stared at the can that had escaped my notice, wishing it was big enough to cover my head and make this miserable day disappear.

TWELVE

Iris

My stomach was in knots. The lemon-lime Suga—the Ọloran brand of pop—I'd drunk all afternoon had done nothing to quell the burn churning in my gut. Now that the driver had arrived at the palace, I'd come to a conclusion. My feelings for Ekon were growing, and I needed to tell Bri.

I couldn't keep hiding my feelings. They were literally making me sick. At the same time, the thought of admitting them to another person made them all-the-more real. I shouldn't like him for so many reasons.

One, obviously he didn't feel the same way. I'd gone from zero to crush based off of his *picture*. Meeting him in person, working with him, and now sharing my flat had me producing heart eyes and planning our wedding. Okay, so I managed to rein my thoughts in and dial back before I got past the wedding gown.

Two, we worked together. Hadn't he called me his parole officer? I didn't want some Stockholm-syndrome romance. I wanted a true partnership where I was respected for me and not what I owned or didn't.

Three, we lived together. It bore repeating. Though Dumeme said Ekon could move into his new home tomorrow. Being in close proximity all day—work and home—hadn't led to any flirting or even a spark of interest in his eyes. I was truly alone in my feelings, and I needed to be okay with that. Because it was very apparent that Ekon needed a friend more than he needed a girlfriend. The only question remaining was if I could be that to him.

Lord God, please help me know how to be Ekon's friend. Please help me not to desire that our relationship would turn into more. If I'm going to be his friend, could You please protect my heart and remove these feelings?

Something told me God wanted me to be a safe person in Ekon's life. One who was genuine and meant what they said when they said it. I couldn't do that if I kept dreaming about happily ever afters . . . *or* kept secrets from my best friend.

My heart pounded with every step that led me down the palace's marbled corridors and into the sleek elevator. I hadn't brought an overnight bag with me or a change of clothes this time. Why bother, when I was pretty sure Bri and I would be cutting our night short?

We'd never had huge arguments. Disagreements, yes. Little tiffs that lasted a few hours, of course. But my feelings for Ekon and my desire to listen to God could potentially put a huge dent in our friendship.

Please let me be wrong, Lord. I don't want to lose Bri or have her be mad at me. I value her friendship. I love her.

I didn't have any sisters, and Bri was very much the sister of my heart. She fit in with my family, and my brother even teased her like he teased me. I considered her part of my family and knew she felt the same way about me, especially since she was an only child.

Still, nerves had me pacing back and forth in the living area, waiting for her to show up. Maybe I shouldn't say anything.

She was pregnant. How would this news affect her pregnancy? Could I cause such turmoil that her baby would feel it?

I sat down. *You're being ridiculous, Iris.*

I shot up and resumed pacing. I would just say the first thing that came to mind when I saw her. *Yes, good plan.* I let out a breath and sank back down onto the couch.

The door opened, and I shot to my feet again. "Bri!"

She grinned and gave me a hug, and the door shut quietly behind her. Probably one of her personal bodyguards taking up sentry outside to ensure she was safe and that we had uninterrupted time.

"How are you feeling?" I asked.

"I'm so tired. All. The. Time." She rolled her eyes. "It's like I've turned into an old lady who can't make it through the day without a nap or going to bed early."

"Do you do both?"

"I did yesterday." She looked sheepish.

"On purpose or by accident?"

"Well, not by accident, per se. I scheduled a nap. It worked out perfectly. Then when Mori and I were having dinner last night, I nodded off. That was completely by accident."

I chuckled. "Is it normal to be so tired?" I'd heard pregnant woman complain of that before, but I had no personal experience. Just what I had seen on shows or movies.

"It is. At least, that's what Dr. Falade says."

"And everything is going okay? Baby is fine?"

She smiled. "Perfectly fine."

"Oh, good."

Bri squeezed my hand. "What's up with you?"

I froze. I hadn't meant to, but it was like something shorted my brain, rendering me mute.

"What's wrong?" Bri asked softly.

"I don't know how to tell you, to explain." Finally, my words were working.

"Just start at the beginning."

The beginning. Right. "So, when you came here and the council gave you the list of potential husbands, I went to Dayo." I winced at the name of the woman who had tried to take the crown away from Bri. "I asked *her* about them, and when I saw a picture of Ekon, my heart leapt as if recognizing he was—"

I stopped. What was I actually saying? That was absurd. *Focus, Iris.* I peered at my friend, who looked interested, but more importantly, caring.

"I didn't mean to develop feelings, especially knowing you could potentially marry him. Then he was involved in crimes against the crown, and . . ."

I drew in a breath, my head swimming with my emotions and trying to make Bri understand I'd never meant to hurt her. But my heart hadn't listened to any reprimand. *None.*

"Calm down, Iris. You don't have to rush and tell me the whole problem in one breath."

I choked out a laugh. "I just want you to understand."

"That you like Ekon?"

My eyes widened. "You know?"

"Girl, your face got red every time I mentioned him. At first, I just chalked it up to you being warm. Then I noticed it happened every time I said his name. When I told you I'd decided to marry Mori and not him, I could tell you were relieved. Just like I could tell you were heartbroken when I shared his involvement in Dayo's schemes."

I *had* been heartbroken. By that time, I'd built up this fantasy of how we'd meet now that he was off Bri's list. Leaving him no choice but to fall hopelessly in love with me. We would marry, have babies, and live the rest of our days in wedded bliss. Always, my dreams ended like all the great rom-coms and romance stories in the world.

"Are you mad?" I stared at my hands, heart pounding while awaiting her answer.

"Iris, you can't help who you're attracted to. I imagine working with him hasn't made things any easier either."

I bit my lip. "About that . . ." This time I met her gaze. I needed to know just how much shock she'd be in. "He's been living with me since last week."

Her head reared back. "What? Why?"

This was where it got tricky. Ekon hadn't wanted anyone—Bri, specifically—to know of his issues. "It's a long story and not really mine to tell, but it *is* temporary."

"Wow."

Right? But did she mean *wow, how could you do this* or *wow, you're such a good human*?

"He's moving soon, so . . ." That was safe, right? "I just wanted to help him." Understatement of the century. I truly wanted to make everything better for him.

"Are you?"

"Of course. He doesn't know how to do the basics, the things we take for granted. I've been helping him learn how to cook." Boy, he'd looked adorable with cornstarch everywhere. I was surprised it hadn't landed in his hair. "Um, he offered to teach me to drive in exchange. Not that I'm going to take him up on his offer." Something about getting behind the wheel freaked me out a little bit.

Bri laid a hand on my arm. "Did you come here to apologize for liking him or to ask for my permission to like him?"

I gaped. "*Apologize*, obviously. I would never ask your *permission*." I groaned. "I didn't mean that the way it sounded. I'm definitely sorry I allowed myself to have feelings for him. But also, I wanted to find out if you had a problem with me being his friend. He has no one; none of his old friends are returning his calls. He looks so lost, and I feel like God wants me to be his friend. So . . ." *Breathe, Iris!* My emotions were topsy-turvy, and I didn't want to head for Tearville.

"Okay. Let's clear some things up."

"Please." I wrung my hands, waiting for her verdict.

Bri shook her head in bemusement. "I don't hate Ekon, Iris. I never did. I thought him arrogant, and then I felt sorry for him."

"You *pitied* him?"

"Well, yeah. He doesn't believe in love, and it made me think that meant he didn't believe in God either. I wondered what had happened in his life to make him believe those things. It was the main reason I chose Mori."

What? He didn't believe in love? How had I forgotten this tidbit? Had Bri told me? If she had, most likely I'd chosen to forget it, since it didn't fit my narrative of a fairy-tale ending.

I groaned, dropping my head into my hands. Why couldn't I just live in reality and stop trying to romanticize everything or see the silver lining? I needed to ground myself in the present somehow, someway.

"I thought I told you," Bri said.

"You probably did," I mumbled against my hands. Then I straightened. "I promise I'm listening now. I'll leave my head out of the clouds."

"That's one of the things that's great about you. You see the best in people."

I raised my eyebrows. "You mean I see illusions."

"No," Bri countered. "You see possibilities."

"That doesn't really help if they don't come true."

A sad smile tinged her lips. "Probably not, but it also encourages a person to be better."

"I can't be his salvation." I didn't want to. What kind of relationship would that leave us?

Again with the hopeless romantic thoughts!

"No, you can't. But maybe you'll point the way."

I shrugged a shoulder. I didn't want to hear logic and things that made sense. I wanted to stew in the hurt and berate myself for my willful ignorance.

"Iris, if you believe he needs a friend, be that. I'm not going to cast judgment. Besides, I've been praying he changes."

"Then pray that I do too. I don't want to live in a fantasy world anymore. It does me no favors." Maybe my heart would ache less if I could remember that the stuff of novels wasn't real life.

"Oh, friend, don't harden your heart. You can create boundaries, you can eliminate things that are harmful, but don't do something out of hardness of heart. Seek God's wisdom first."

I sighed, flopping back against the couch. "You're so wise."

"I remember many a time you were wisdom for me. It's about time I return the favor. I know how you can let your emotions overwhelm you. I'm just offering you another perspective. From the outside looking in, I see a woman who cares deeply and will go to bat for anyone. That's not something I think God would want to change."

My bottom lip trembled as I battled tears. "Thanks, Bri," I whispered. I leaned my head against her shoulder. "Let's change the subject."

"To what?"

"Baby names?" I suggested. Something happy and not me-centric.

Her face lit up. "I've been looking at those online."

"Will you pick something American or Ọlọran?"

"Maybe a mixture?"

That made sense. "Any contenders?"

Bri sighed. "Not yet. I can't stop wondering what the world will think about the name. If they'll feel it's royal enough, not royal enough, too American, too Ọlọran."

I looked at Bri. "Make sure you and Mori like it. Pray God inspires the both of you. If you both come up with the same name, maybe you'll know it's royal enough and a nod to both cultures."

"That's a good idea."

It turned out I was wrong about it being a short night. We chatted over dinner, talked about the things we missed about New York and America and the things we didn't miss. We talked until Bri fell asleep at eight o'clock, when I alerted her guards and asked one to drive me back to my flat.

As I walked down the hall, my name echoed against the corridor. I whirled around and saw my neighbor, Ada. I wished her a good evening in Oninan.

She beamed, lighting up her countenance and showcasing her expertly applied makeup. It was subtle, causing her skin to glow. The shade reminded me of a beautiful brown chiffon bridesmaid dress I'd seen once before.

"How are you?" she asked in English.

"Good. You?" I wasn't yet sure if Ada was interested in me because of who I was or who I knew.

"Tired. I got home not too long ago, only to discover I did not prepare a meal ahead." She shook her head. "I had a lot on my mind."

If I didn't have a flatmate, I'd invite her in. However, she seemed wary of Ekon and he equally as guarded against her. "Are you going out to eat now?"

"Yes. Would you like to join me?"

Actually, I would. I couldn't let Bri be my only friend, especially since the women at work were keeping me in the employer box. "Yes, please." I tilted my lips up, hoping she recognized the sincerity.

"Great. Let's go. I know the perfect spot."

I followed her back out into the night. She pointed to a tan sedan in the resident parking lot. "That is me. It is quicker to drive."

I slid into the car and bit back a sigh. It felt so good, sitting up front and riding in a normal car. Not a rideshare. Not a taxi. Not even the palace vehicles. Just me in a car. Now, if only Oloro would add a subway system, maybe then I would feel more at ease.

It was silly to feel choked up over the lack of a rail system, and yet . . .

Ada asked me questions about work, steering clear of anything related to the queen or Ekon. Finally, when we pulled up to the eatery, I turned to her. "Should we talk about the two elephants?"

Her cheeks bunched. "I respect your relationship with the queen. No need to talk about it."

"Fair enough. And the other elephant?"

Her lips turned downward. "I am not sure I want to."

"Okay." I gulped. "Then I think it's only fair you talk about your job now."

Ada chuckled and opened the door. "Prepare to be bored."

Yet hearing her adventures in dental hygiene left me lighthearted and thankful God had sent someone my way. My thoughts were not completely silent on Ekon, but the pressure of thinking solely of him lifted.

Tonight, when I returned home, I would head straight to my room to pray. Knowing I'd willfully ignored the state of Ekon's salvation had taken some of the shine off my feelings. I guessed the rose-colored glasses were finally off. Even though I thought it necessary and potentially beneficial, I wasn't sure if that was enough to guard against more feelings.

I needed to put on some armor, because if I was going to be his friend, then I needed to ensure my heart would remain intact.

THIRTEEN

Ekon

I stared down at the silver key Dumeme had passed me. The last time a man gifted me keys to a place, it was to a penthouse suite. I remembered the pride that had rocked through my center when Father handed over the keys to the palace in the sky. My friends—*former acquaintances?*—had taken me drinking that night to celebrate. My chauffeur had seen me safely home afterward. I truly had believed I had reached the height of success.

The feeling unfurling in my chest right now could be labeled as pride, but it felt so very different. I had worked for this purchase. I looked up at Dumeme. "I appreciate all your help," I said in Oninan.

"My pleasure, ògbéni. You will make this a wonderful home."

That was my goal.

Dumeme left, and I unlocked the front door and stepped over the threshold. The first time I had entered this house, the views of the hills had drawn me in. The windows did not provide the same bird's-eye perspective of the penthouse. Instead, trees and other greenery surrounding the home beckoned me. With a bit of cleaning, paint, and furnishing, the house would be fit for company.

I wanted badly to remind Iris that she had agreed to help me shop, but there had been something different about her this morning. She had smiled at my jokes, listened to my suggestions at work, then given me a brief lunch lesson on the appeal of hoagies. Yet throughout the day, there seemed to be this invisible wall between us. As if, were I brave enough to reach out, I would hit glass unexpectedly. Much like birds often did with freshly cleaned windows. Not wanting to be bruised, I had maintained space and kept our conversations cordial.

Now, alone with my thoughts, seeing the vastness of the home and wondering if I could truly afford to furnish every room, my thoughts naturally turned to Iris. How her eyes had not shone as brightly as usual. How her chatter had been more subdued. She had not even hummed while working today.

Not that I would admit to missing the sound. I never knew the songs and always assumed they were American ones she listened to in her earbuds.

I slid my hands into my pants pockets. I could wonder about the conundrum that was Iris Blakely later. Right now, I had to figure out what I would sleep on and what to eat for dinner. Iris had informed me I could still sleep in her guest bedroom, but since I was no longer homeless, it was best for both of us if I removed myself from her life. I could not extract myself from the work situation, but she should not have to be forced to see me in the evening as well.

A knock sounded, and my brows shot up. Had Dumeme forgotten something? I crossed the wood floors and opened the door.

"Congrats!" Iris shouted. Her arms were full, holding a gift basket.

I reached for it and stood aside, motioning her forward.

"Thanks, that was heavy. I'll be right back." She darted back out to the taxi.

I watched, bemused, as she came back with two more bags. What had she brought with her? The driver took off, and my mouth dried. Did he know to come back for her?

"I know you have nothing," she started in that breathless way she used when about to talk a great deal, "so I grabbed some things as a housewarming gift. I intended to buy just one thing, but I kept seeing useful items. Then, of course, I had to get you something completely fun, because who wants to be boring and only have things you *need*?"

"You did not have to go through the trouble, Iris."

"Of course not, but that's what friends are for, right?"

Friends? She considered me a friend? Time slowed as my limbs felt heavy. Iris continued to jabber words that made no sense. How could they, when the ringing in my ears had taken over?

"You consider us friends?" I asked, suddenly snapped from my trance.

She stopped flitting about and met my gaze. "Obviously." Her brow creased. "Wait, you don't?"

"I did not think you would want to be my friend."

She shook her head. "Well, now you know how wrong you were." She motioned to the basket in my hand. "There's kitchen utensils that will allow you to make breakfast tomorrow and bring a sandwich to work for lunch."

Laughter filled me. Such an Iris gift. "And in the others?"

She held up one big bag in her right hand. "Air mattress. It's mine, so this is a loan. Return it once you have a bed of your own." She switched, raising her left hand instead. "And these are sheets and a pillow. Since someone wanted to be stubborn and move out before he had furniture."

"I thought you would appreciate having your space back."

"Meh." She set the bags down. "I also bought you a board game."

My lips twitched.

"I have one more surprise, but I'm not sure when it'll get here."

I raised a brow. "Something better than feeding me and providing a place for my head to rest?" I pointed to the game. "And entertainment?"

"If not better, then just as good." She grinned.

Since she stood so perfectly before me, I took the time to catalogue her grin. I compared it to the ones in my memory and noted that the light still remained absent from her eyes.

Apparently, the wall stood strong.

"What is the surprise?" I murmured, confused by how disappointed I felt. Still, I would act normal. It seemed we would not discuss our innermost thoughts.

Perhaps though, her distance was because of the surprise.

Iris peeked out the front door, then grinned. "It's here."

I set the wicker basket on the floor and moved to the doorway. An old car drove down the street. I guessed I would meet my neighbors eventually. Instead of turning into one of the other gravel driveways, however, the vehicle stopped in front of my house.

"Who is that?" I asked.

"Not who, *what*," Iris stated.

"No, pretty sure people are *who*. I know English well enough to understand that distinction."

She laughed. "The driver is of no consequence."

I begged to differ. A tall man got out, then shut the door. Did Iris have a boyfriend? If so, how had I missed that fact?

"He just came to drive your gift."

Understanding dawned. "Is the vehicle a loan?"

She nodded. "I figured it would give you an idea of what it's like driving a cheaper car. Then you can decide what you'll do about owning one yourself. Not to mention save money on taxis."

"Um, do you not see the irony?"

She giggled, then shrugged.

I lowered my voice. "Who is the guy?"

"Oh, that's Matt. He's the marketing director at Aṣọ."

The man walked onto my front porch, sending a grin Iris's way. She threaded her arm through his and patted him on the chest. My jaw ticked.

"Ekon, meet Matt Wallace. He'll be doing all of our PR and working out publicity on the international scene. He just arrived back from the States. Matt, this is Ekon Diallo."

Jealously coursed through me and had me tightening my grip as I shook the grinning Matt Wallace's hand. He brimmed with energy and seemed unfazed by my show of strength.

Instead, he returned it and winked. "Isn't Iris the best?"

Not something I could argue, and he knew it. Why was I even playing this game? Iris had put me in the friend zone. I slid my hand from his and into my pocket, discreetly wiping my palm on the inside pocket lining. "She is."

"You guys are too kind. Well, Matt has already called for a car to pick us up. I hope you enjoy your new home, Ekon."

"Thank you for all you have done." My chest tightened as I tried to ignore the scrutiny from the smarmy Matt Wallace. Was this the kind of guy Iris liked? One who oozed charm, wore expensive suits?

That was you, remember?

Unfortunately, I did. Men like him—*me*—were bad news.

"Of course, Ekon. We're friends, remember?"

"Iris is a good friend to have," Matt stated. "She collects them everywhere she goes."

Was he insinuating that there was nothing special about me?

Iris, oblivious to the undertones, laughed good-naturedly. "I'll see you tomorrow." She waved.

"Have a good night."

I closed the door and pressed my forehead against the wood.

She had taken the move out of my hands. I no longer had to worry about the possibility of us being together. I was her *friend*. She had a Matt Wallace waiting in the wings. And now that I knew that, I would make sure to keep things strictly professional. I would not cause problems or cause Matt to think I was more than what I was.

My life was a lot different at twenty-eight than I had ever imagined. Maybe it was time to reinvent myself. Turn myself into someone respectable enough to have a woman like Iris in my life.

My stomach dropped to my toes. I would never be that man. Not with the council's decree and punishment hanging over me. People in Ọlọrọ had long memories. When my community service and business hours were complete, they would still remember my act of treason.

The only thing I could hope for was to show them I was no longer the same man. I did not know how I could change, but something different had to happen. I could not live in this limbo.

My mobile chimed, and I pulled up the notification that filled my screen.

Someone had tagged me in a social media post. There I was, bent over with garbage bag in one hand and the claw in the other. The caption read, *Prince falls from grace.*

I winced. This was my present and, most likely, my future. The stares and comments would not stop, which meant I needed to find a better way to handle the attention. First step, removing the alerts on my phone. Other people's opinions would only derail me if I truly wanted to start fresh.

Still, a part of me wondered if Iris ever saw these posts or the ones that made national news. Did she feel embarrassed to have me working for her?

No, she called you friend, remember?

I knew deep down I could trust Iris would truly be my friend, despite how the media portrayed me. Perhaps I would keep that at the forefront when I felt the shame too deeply. Someone called me friend.

And I call her friend too.

FOURTEEN

Iris

"Y ou're looking beautiful this morning." Matt shot me
a grin as if he'd just paid me the highest compliment.
But I was pretty sure he was peering at the mirror
behind me and not talking to me.

"Do you have a moment to talk about the fashion show?"
he asked.

He'd yet to look me in the eyes, but since I *did* need to discuss
the logistics of the event, the point was moot. "Sure, let's talk
in the conference room."

I had a feeling it would be too uncomfortable to have him in
my office with Ekon in there. He was creating a finance class
for our future new hires, and our conversation would probably
distract him. I pivoted away from Oka's desk and strolled down
the hall to the conference room.

I loved this whole building. The concrete floors had a pol-
ished look, and all the rooms had at least one floor-to-ceiling
window letting in a flood of light. The abundant sunshine was
glorious. I had yet to experience a cloudy day in Ọlọrọ, and I
loved it. It made me feel like a plant that needed to soak up the
sun, my face instantly angling for the best vitamin D exposure.

Which was why I chose a spot in the light and gestured for Matt to take a seat across from me. He ignored that chair and chose the one next to me, tossing a friendly smile my way. Matt and I had never dated, and I'd never carried a torch for him. He had to be one of the few guys who hadn't entered my daydreams as a possibility for Mr. Right. Matt was okay-looking—if you liked that James Bond, coiffured type—but there was just no spark.

"What did you want to talk about?" I asked.

Matt tilted his lips to the side, one eyebrow joining, in full-out charm mode. How did he *do* that? "I'm glad you asked. I need people who have marketing experience. Experience implementing media to reinforce a brand. And I'll need the exact dates for the fashion show. We want this to be a success."

I opened my calendar app. "November fifteenth through the nineteenth."

Matt's eyes widened, and he sank into the leather seat. "This year?"

"Yes." I didn't want to wait forever. I needed orders for the spring line, and that would only happen if we could get our wares in front of buyers.

"We should really push it back to February. That would give us a chance to run a full PR campaign."

"Yes, but we need buyers now."

"For what product?"

My back stiffened. "For the lines Zam, Rapulu, and the others are creating." Not to mention myself. I might not be involved in the everyday design aspects, but I still had an idea or two popping in my mind and landing on sketch paper.

Matt's lips quirked into a condescending line. "Iris. The fashion world holds their shows in February or October. November is too late."

I drew in a deep breath. Matt was here to help, and I had to keep that perspective in mind instead of becoming irritated.

Though the rapid rise in my emotions told me I was close to losing composure. "The western world does host fashion week in those months. However, there are places in Africa where they do it outside of those time frames. Ergo, we will be fine hosting our show in November."

He tapped the tabletop. "Just consider pushing it back until February. It'll be better for the team and the company as well."

Before I could reiterate my stance, my phone buzzed. I glanced down. My brow wrinkled as the caller ID flashed *MOM* across my screen.

"I'm sorry, Matt. I need to take this." I swiped the phone to answer as I strolled out of the conference room and safely into the hall. "Mom? Are you okay?"

"Of course I am. Can't your dear mom call you from time to time?"

"Yes. It's just that I'm at work." And my mom was a smart woman. She could easily figure out the time zone difference. I glanced at the time. She should be asleep right now.

"Are you busy?"

"I'm in a meeting." I glanced through the windows to see Matt leaving the room. "Or I was." Now I'd have to catch up with him before the board meeting in an hour.

"Then I won't be long. I simply wanted to let you know that we've decided to come see you."

I blinked. "Excuse me?" My hand tightened around the phone. Surely she wasn't saying what I thought she was.

"We miss you. *I* miss you. So I got to talking with Dad, and then Junior was over for dinner. The next thing I know, we all decided a trip was necessary. We're coming to Ọlọrọ Ilé. Did I say that right?"

I smothered a laugh. "No, Mom. It's Oh-low-ROW ill-LAY." But that didn't explain how she was going to get here. "How are you guys traveling?"

"By plane, of course. You didn't think your father and Junior would indulge my whimsy of a boat ride, did you?"

Ha! That would have been funny to see, but no. "Hence my confusion. You don't fly."

"My only daughter has moved to another country. Obviously, I have no choice but to put on my big-girl undies and take a Xanax so I can come see my precious baby girl."

I laughed because she would expect it, but my heart turned over in my chest. Mom did *not* fly. To say she hated it would be understating the very real fear that held her prisoner and made her believe road trips were the best thing ever.

Which they weren't. Nothing could be better than hopping a plane and landing in your destination within a few hours. Sure, there were places that took longer than that to fly to—*ahem,* Ọlọrọ—but most flights weren't international ones. She'd probably need a horse tranquilizer in order to board safely and not have fellow passengers seeking the undercover marshal for the unruly passenger in seat B3.

"Are you sure that's a good idea?" I worried my bottom lip as I tilted my foot on my stiletto.

"I'll be fine, Iris. I've already called my doctor to make sure I have something that will sedate me before the plane takes off."

"Will it last the whole flight? What about layovers?" My mind spun, conjuring all the scenarios that ended with Mom in a padded room after experiencing a nervous breakdown. Did people recover from that? Why wasn't that something that was talked about?

"Breathe, sweetie. I can practically hear your thoughts scrambling from here. Your father is renting a jet so we can go straight there."

That was a relief. Still, I couldn't believe she would willingly subject herself to a flight across the Atlantic. Her parents—my grandparents—had died in a freak airplane accident. Mom had never been on one since. She'd been the only survivor.

"I love you. I can't believe you're doing this. It means a lot."

"I'd do anything for you, bug. Even defy gravity."

I stifled a laugh. Mom put on a brave face, and I wouldn't have her thinking I thought lightly of her fears. "Thanks, Mom. I can't wait to see you guys."

"Same. We'll be arriving Sunday night. I know life isn't the same as last year, but please, let Bri know we'd love to see her, if possible. Or do I have to call her Queen Brielle now?"

I grinned. "I'm sure she'll insist on remaining Bri. She has enough people calling her *queen*. I know she'd love to see you."

"Wonderful. Have a good day, bug. Oh, and let us know a good hotel near you."

I rolled my eyes. Like she really wanted to stay in a hotel instead of at my place. "You know you can stay with me."

"I thought you only had two bedrooms."

"I do. You and Dad can have my room, and Junior can sleep on the sofa."

She laughed. "I'll be sure to let your brother know. But seriously, we'll all fit?"

"Of course. I do have an air mattress I can sleep on if Junior wants the guest room." My sofa really wasn't for sleeping on. But it looked cute!

"You know he's not going to let you sleep on that. He'll take the air mattress."

"It'll be here for whomever." Oh, wait. I'd loaned it to Ekon. *But now you have an excuse to talk to him.* Not that I needed one. I was his boss, after all.

Still, a heady sense of relief filled me. I could stop being so terribly awkward and find out if he'd bought a bed yet. Then get the air mattress back and go back to keeping my distance but trying to remain friendly.

It was exhausting, going against my nature of dreaming and imagining what-ifs, but I was determined to kick the habit.

Please help me change, Lord. Keep me grounded. Keep me in reality.

I said my good-byes and glanced at my cell's clock. There was no time to speak with Matt before the board meeting. We were gathering in the conference room in fifteen minutes. That gave me enough time to run to my office, grab my notes, and return.

Perhaps I'd have Ekon sit in on the meeting as well. He'd gone through the stack of requirements Aṣo needed to fulfill and had come up with a plan of attack. The board would love an update.

"Ekon, can you attend the board meeting?" I asked as soon as my heels crossed the threshold of my office.

He glanced up from his desk. "Yes. I am yours to direct."

Don't I wish. I bit back a groan. My thoughts were running loose like a kid set free in Chuck E. Cheese. "Then grab your notes."

I reached for my legal pad just as the door burst open.

Oka's eyes were wide.

"What happened?" I asked.

"The electrician came regarding the lights on the second floor. He says the whole electrical system needs to be replaced."

"What?" My stomach dropped to my heels, and I pressed a hand to my middle, trying to keep the roiling from reversing in my digestive tract. She handed me a slip of paper with an astronomical number on it, and I dropped into my chair. "This can't be happening."

Oka clutched her hands together. "I am sorry, madam. I do not want to be the bearer of bad news."

Too late. "Ẹ seun, Oka."

She dipped her head and exited.

My throat felt raw. I rose unsteadily, clutching the piece of paper. "I'll meet you in the conference room," I murmured.

"Are you okay?" Ekon asked softly.

He came into my view, and I stared at the buttons on his

shirt, refusing to meet his gaze. If I did, the tears I was suppressing would make an unwelcome appearance.

"I will be." I gulped and rushed around the table.

I had about five seconds to make it to the restroom before the waterworks erupted and I lost all composure. As I rushed down the corridor, the first tear slipped free. I sniffed, and another appeared just as I pushed open the bathroom door.

Tears fell one after the other. I didn't know how I could afford to replace the whole electrical system on the second floor. I didn't even know if Oka meant the floor or the building, but judging by the price, it was the whole building. Heaven help me if that price was per floor.

Why had I thought I could do this? I had no experience owning a company. How could I expect people to follow me? I had no idea what I was doing, and if I didn't figure it out soon, my dream would not only crash and burn, but it would take a bunch of casualties with it.

Lord God, please help. I don't want to fail the people of Etikun, the board, or the council. They all believe in me. Please help me believe in myself.

Or was that vanity?

Never mind. Please help me keep my eyes on You. I know You'll equip me, but I just feel so ill-equipped at the moment.

I needed to present a confident front when I faced the board and told them of this setback. Maybe I could get our COO to find the funds to cover the unexpected expense. I didn't want to do another loan. Ọlọrọ had outrageous interest rates, and the rest of the countries in the region weren't much better. I could ask our investors for more, but they had already provided so much.

I blew my nose and fixed my makeup. This was what board meetings were for. We'd figure it out. There was no other choice.

FIFTEEN

Ekon

I stared at the door Iris had rushed out of. Something about her red eyes tore my insides apart. How big of a deal were the electrical issues? Did she have funding set aside to take care of the repairs?

Despite the unanswered questions, I could not help but wonder what had happened between her and Matt Wallace. Not that I necessarily cared if they were interested in each other. It was not as if *I* could be interested in her. Father would never go for it. The queen either, for that matter.

Not to mention I simply was not good enough for someone like Iris Blakely. A woman who wore her heart on her sleeve and had no problem loaning it to others in need. I would never be her equivalent. Not with my past of getting through life without a care in the world. Even the baby steps I took in the direction of selflessness weren't enough.

"Ekon?"

I looked up, surprised. When had Iris returned? Had I been so deep in thought that I missed the clack of her heels or the sweet scent that followed her?

Ugh, listen to you. She is off-limits.

I cleared my throat. "Yes?"

"The board meeting?"

"Right." I grabbed my paperwork. "I was leaving."

She nodded, gaze averted. I hoped she did not believe I would cast judgment on her tears. Not that I had visual evidence of her crying, but why else had she left only to return to her office? Had she not informed me we would meet in the conference room?

I headed for the exit, wondering if the tension in the room was all my imagination. Her heels followed me down the hall, but I kept my gaze locked forward. Soon we filled the conference room along with the members of the board. My face heated as eyes followed my person until I reached a seat in the corner. I was about to sit when my gaze fell on Iris. She gave a discreet shake of her head, and her finger covertly pointed to an empty seat at the table. I adjusted my movement and reached for the chair.

"Thank you for coming," she said in stilted Oninan.

I hid a wince, glancing around the table to note the expressions of the board. They did not seem offended by her efforts, more like amused. A puff of air escaped me.

She switched to English. "You should all have received my agenda for today's meeting."

One of the board members, Bisi Okusanya, raised her hand.

"Yes, Ms. Okusanya?" Iris asked. At least she'd pronounced her last name correctly.

"I heard the electrical wiring needs to be replaced on the entire second floor. Why is that not on the agenda?"

Iris's face blanched, and I quickly scanned the boardroom. Who had informed Ms. Okusanya of that, when Oka had relayed that information to us only moments before?

"How did you hear that?" Iris asked.

"So it is true?" Ms. Okusanya asked.

"I do not have the full details, but I will by the end of this afternoon."

"You mean you were unaware?" Dera Ibeh asked.

Iris's face flushed. "I was informed today. As we had this meeting scheduled, I did not have more time to ascertain the details." Her head tilted as her eyes landed on Ms. Okusanya. "How did you hear so swiftly?"

"Mr. Wallace informed me in the elevators."

My hand fisted around my pen. How had Wallace found out? And why would he go to the board and not to Iris? What had happened in their meeting? I could not tell by the shade of red filling Iris's cheeks if she was humiliated or furious. My bet was on the latter. Though perhaps because that was where my emotions were taking me.

"I see," she gritted through her teeth.

"He thought we would want to brainstorm ways to fund the repairs."

What conceit!

Iris stared at the tabletop before speaking. "We will need more funding for the repairs."

"How much is it?"

Iris named a figure that stole my breath. If I had access to my trust fund, I would sign a check right this second. Still, there had to be something I could do. *Right?*

Some of the board members shook their heads. "We cannot afford that. This company has already incurred two high-rate interest loans." Tola Balogun, hair braided in a crown, folded her arms with finality.

"I'm well aware, Ms. Balogun."

"Well, then you should be aware of how detrimental multiple loans can be."

"I am. Which is why we have investors."

Iris made a good point. I wanted to applaud her efforts.

"Yes, but we can't keep going to them for money," Ms. Okusanya said.

"Why not? Is that not their purpose?" I asked.

Silence descended as I hid a wince at my faux pas. I had not meant to speak aloud.

Ms. Okusanya sniffed. "Really, Mr. Diallo, I was not even aware your presence was required, as this is a *board* meeting, and you are not a member."

"He is not," Iris interjected. "But he is here at my request. He has been instrumental in ensuring we meet the royal council's requirements. Fixing the electrical wiring and guaranteeing we have the funds to pay for it is all part of that."

My face heated at her praise. Fortunately, my brown skin would prevent anyone from seeing the effect of her words.

"Very well," Ms. Balogun said. "Let's continue."

The board members were able to come to an agreement to ask for more funds from the investors. Ms. Okusanya agreed to draft an email with the request. After that, we moved on to the other topics listed in the agenda.

At the end, Iris and I strolled back to her office.

"You did just fine," I said softly.

Her gaze flicked to me. "Thank you. Sometimes I feel—" She cleared her throat, leaving her sentence hanging.

"You feel?"

She waved a hand. "Never mind. Hey, I was wondering if—" She bit her lip, worry crinkling her eyebrows. "If you'd bought a bed yet." Her cheeks flamed red as her eyes darted forward.

"No. Not yet."

"You see, my mom called before the board meeting." She held up her mobile. "Apparently she's coming to visit. Well, her, my dad, and my brother."

"Ah. You need the air mattress back."

"If you haven't found a bed yet, I can get another mattress."

"No, no." I opened the door to her office, waving her through. "I can go after work, if you can recommend a good location."

"I could go—" She stopped short, her face now red all over.

I looked down, trying to keep laughter from exploding. She

looked so embarrassed. So adorable. Still staring at the table, I shook my head. "I can handle that. If you can tell me the best place to shop in line with my budget."

"Of course," she squeaked. "I'll write the names of a few places down for you."

"Thank you, Iris." I spared her a glance. "You are truly kind."

Her eyelashes fluttered. "That's a big compliment coming from you."

"It is the truth."

She nodded slowly. My hands fisted by my sides as she met my gaze. I did not understand this weirdness between us, but I could acknowledge the intelligence of the distance she had created.

"Ekon, would you like to join me at church on Sunday?"

Surprise filtered through me. "I . . ." I did not want to burst her bubble and tell her I did not believe in her god. How could I, when nonsense followed me wherever I went? Good people died. Innocence was lost. Evil reigned. And people like me, we coasted. It was all a form of chaos I would never attribute to a god or a fallen angel.

"You don't believe, do you?"

I listened to her tone, replaying her question in my head, trying to discover the nuances. All I could hear was simple curiosity. "I do not."

"May I ask why?"

Should I regurgitate my thoughts from a moment ago or give her a better explanation? I rubbed my chin. "The world seems too chaotic to be ordered by an all-knowing god. I do not buy the theory that a fallen angel brought that chaos into play."

"Would you be interested in having that belief tested?"

I bit back a sigh. How could I answer without hurting her feelings? Because the answer was unequivocally no. I was fine with the status quo.

Are you really?

"I am fine, Iris."

"Are you, though?"

Her dark eyes searched mine, and I turned away. If she probed too deeply, she would understand what a waste I really was. "Yes." I picked up the pen from my desk. "I should get back to work. My boss is a stickler for me not wasting my time."

"Ha."

But the feigned laughter did not spark any real humor in her eyes. She looked sad, and I hated that I had put that look on her face. Still, I would not change my beliefs just to put a smile on a pretty woman's face. She deserved more than polite interest that would lead nowhere.

I needed to change the subject. "When is your family coming?"

"Sunday. They'll get in late."

"Good. Tell them to go straight to sleep to get on Ọlọran time."

"I will." Her heels clacked as she walked to her desk. "Have you finalized the onboarding process for our new hires?"

"I need a couple more days, and then we will be ready."

"You realize our hiring event is next week."

I turned to look at her fully. "I will not leave work Friday unless everything is in place."

Her shoulders dropped. "Thank you, Ekon."

I nodded. Helping out was why the council had ordered me here in the first place.

That and the community service I had been assigned. Picking up trash around Etikun last weekend had been an adventure. So many people recognized me and shuffled away when they saw what I was up to. I was supposed to go to the Òkè region this Saturday, according to Mr. Ladipo. I imagined the council would have me cleaning up the whole country before the month was over. I still had yet to clean every square kilometer of Etikun. Just enough to be seen and ignored.

I tried to continue work, but the little noises coming from

Iris's direction completely distracted me. The shuffle of papers, clicking of her pen, and the little humming she used to keep the silence from growing loud.

"Why do you not listen to music?" The words were out before I could think better of them.

"Pardon?"

I turned to face Iris. "You hum every day, sometimes all day. Would it not be simpler to listen to music?"

Her mouth parted, shut, parted once more. I wanted to laugh at the surprised look on her face, but would she understand the humor?

"I listen with earbuds sometimes. But honestly, I don't want to disturb you by playing anything louder."

Too late. She was already in every thought process I possessed at work. "It is no bother." Maybe it would mute her noises and allow me to focus on the task at hand.

"Okay," she said quietly. She reached for her mobile, and soon music filled the room.

I scanned her desk for the external speakers. Only then did the type of music penetrate my mind. "What *is* this?"

Her cheeks bloomed. "My boy-band playlist. I can change it to something else if it disturbs you."

"Boy band?"

"You know, music by bands made up of all boys? Well, men." She scratched the back of her neck. "Come on. Olorans have bands made up of more than one male singer, right?"

"Yes, but I can honestly say we have nothing that sounds like this."

She laughed. "I'd imagine not. How about we take turns? First hour I can play whatever I want, and you get the next hour."

It would probably not be a good thing to point out that I did not care for music. It was all noise to me. Instead, I simply nodded at her suggestion and turned back to my desk. At least now I would not have to hear her hum and imagine the words were something about forevers and overcoming adversity.

Not that I was projecting in any sense of the word.

Time sped by, and soon I found myself preparing to leave the office for the day. I closed my briefcase and glanced over my shoulder. "Are you heading out? I can give you a ride home."

Buying a car was on my agenda for the day. I did not want to be beholden to Matt Wallace for one more minute.

"That's kind of you, but I have a late night prepared."

I frowned. "You are going to remain here at night?" In the dark with no security?

Her brows rose. "Yes. I do stay late occasionally."

"But you do not employ a security guard."

"I do, actually. The queen's personal guard recommended a few men to me. They are already on company payroll. Whoever is on shift will walk me out to the taxi tonight."

"You are still taking a taxi?" My grip tightened on my briefcase. Did she know what kind of men drove those things?

"Is there a problem, Ekon?"

"I do not feel comfortable with you riding in a taxi alone in the dark. If you would, let me come back and get you. You can call me when you are ready."

Her eyes searched mine, and for once, her expression gave no hint as to her thoughts. Had I overstepped? Did she believe I was being overbearing?

"Okay. That's kind of you."

I scoffed. "I have never been accused of being kind." If I had, perhaps I would not be in my current predicament.

"But you are."

I had no desire to argue with her. "I will see you later."

She nodded, and I left. There was nothing else to say. She was intent on seeing good that was not there. Perhaps I should invite her to my family dinner. Spending a few minutes in the presence of my father would make her realize how many faults I had. Father never had a difficult time listing them.

I shook my head. I needed to buy a new car before Iris called me back to pick her up. I would *not* drive her around in that prima donna's vehicle. I had spent time researching what kind of automobile would be most beneficial. A part of me filled with regret and longing for my old vehicles. The other was ready to live a life of simplicity.

There were a couple of car dealers near me, but I knew nothing of their reputations. I made a phone call to the man who sold me my Porsche and asked his opinion on used-car dealerships. He had a cousin who owned one, so I drove straight there after work.

"Mr. Diallo, welcome, welcome," Bizzy greeted me.

I nodded.

"My cousin tells me you are looking for a vehicle."

"Yes. Something simple that will not require a lot of upkeep." It seemed I had always been taking my old cars to the shop for some maintenance. Granted, when you owned multiple vehicles, one always had to be serviced.

"I must admit, I am surprised you do not want to purchase another vehicle from my cousin. He has the best ones."

My gut tightened. Was he fishing for details? "I prefer simplicity these days."

Bizzy nodded sagely. "That is probably best. You do not need any more spotlight on you."

Ouch. I kept my face impassive and followed him around the lot as he suggested a few different vehicles. After test-driving two of them, I picked one that was ten years old. Mr. Odell offered to deliver it to my home, since I had Matt Wallace's car. Instead, I got him to deliver Mr. Wallace's to its rightful owner.

When my phone rang with Iris asking me to pick her up, I smiled all the way back to work. She would not be picturing Matt Wallace in that ratty ol' vehicle any longer. I had a new ride.

SIXTEEN

Iris

Jide scanned the parking lot, then pushed open the lobby door. His stocky build filled the frame before he moved aside to let me through. "Looks like your ride is here, Ms. Blakely. Have a good night."

"You too, Jide." I waved, then turned and froze.

Ekon bought a new car! I snapped my mouth shut before a fly or some other winged creature could mistake it for a hideaway.

I knew for a fact that he'd left work in Matt's car. But seeing him leaning against the passenger side of a clean vehicle, feet crossed at the ankles and arms folded across his chest, had me doubting myself. I took a cautious step forward, then another.

"Do you like it?" he asked.

"I do." It was a pretty navy-blue SUV. Although I didn't think Ọlọrans used that term. Still, it was nice and didn't appear brand-new. Part of me was afraid to ask how much it cost. The other part was still in shock.

Ekon grinned and opened the door. "A ride home as promised."

"When did you get this?" I placed a hand on the door panel, inhaling the clean scent of the SUV.

"After I left here."

I waited until Ekon got in the car and buckled in before unleashing more questions. "Where did you go? Did you get a good deal? Where's Matt's car? I thought you needed furniture?"

Ekon smirked. *Smirked!* Just when I was finally ignoring the little things that made my heart race, he had to lift those full lips to the side and look at me as if I were cute. I could practically hear the words in his mind. Although, maybe he thought it in Oninan, which—*swoon!*—would probably sound so much better than in English.

"I went to Bizzy's. He is the cousin of the man I used to get my cars from. I told him I wanted something simple but dependable. He showed me some above my price range, but after I reiterated my requirements, he began showing me vehicles within my budget."

"I didn't even know you'd created a budget for a car." Why did I feel left out?

"I am not a child, Iris. I have studied how to budget on less income. After all, you have had me working on such things for our new hires. Correct?"

Yes, but I never thought he'd go and do this.

The man is grown. He doesn't need you to shop with him.

But I love shopping.

Maybe that was the source of my shock and not hurt that he'd moved on without me. Picked up on my cues that we needed to create distance. Distance I now loathed and wanted to shoot up with Nerf darts.

"Obviously you're a man and not a child." Whew, did I need to fan myself? "I'm a little surprised, is all."

"But not in a negative way?" he asked cautiously.

"Not at all." If I could simply put my wounded feelings

aside. How hard would it be to lock them away? How many times would I try before they remained hidden? I shifted in my seat. "I'm glad you got something useful and within budget."

"I've also decided utility vehicles are cool-looking."

I shook my head. "A woman probably flirted with you at a stoplight in order to change your opinion."

He grinned.

My heart dropped to my toes. Did that mean I'd guessed correctly?

"Also, I had Bizzy arrange for Mr. Wallace's car to be delivered to him. I got his info before I left the building earlier."

"And furniture?"

"I bought a bedroom suite. The place you recommended was next to Bizzy's shop. Once I picked out this beauty and signed the paperwork, I went and browsed the furniture section while waiting for the car to be detailed."

He'd gone furniture shopping as well? Clearly, I was no longer needed. "Did you get all the furnishings you need?" My voice came out quiet and maybe a tad unsure. With any luck, Ekon wouldn't notice.

"No. I only purchased everything for my bedroom. I will look at the other places you mentioned for the living and dining areas."

I exhaled instead of asking to join him. When my tongue was under control, I spoke. "Did you invite your parents over yet?"

Ekon shook his head as he slowed at the stoplight. "No. I still need to figure out how to prepare the perfect Ọlọran meal."

"Hmm." I pulled out my cell and opened a text message to Bri.

Iris:
Do you know someone who can teach Ekon how to cook an Ọlọran meal?

Bri:

Good question. I could ask one of the staff
here.

Iris:

Is that a good idea? Will the council object?

Bri:

Perhaps. Give me a minute.

"Who are you texting?" Ekon asked.

I stared at his profile. His very *handsome* profile. I jerked
my gaze away, staring at the sea of cars before me. "Bri. I'm
hoping she knows someone who can cook."

"You just texted the queen about me?"

Something in his voice made my fingers pause over the keyboard before I responded to Bri's text. "Yes," I responded hesi-
tantly. "Is that bad?" I held my breath.

"It depends on what you said."

"She knows we're friends. I only mentioned the cooking to
her."

Ekon put on his blinker, pulled off to the side of the road,
and parked the car. He turned to me. "You told the queen we
are friends?" His dark gaze searched mine.

"Aren't we?" What was going on in his head? "I thought
we agreed we were friends." *Please don't take this away from
me too.*

"We did. We are."

I sank into the seat. "Then what's the problem?"

He ran a hand over the back of his head. "She is the *queen*,
Iris. The very one I was found guilty of committing crimes
against."

I laid a hand on his arm. "She doesn't hold a grudge, Ekon."

"How could she not?" His stark whisper filled the interior
of the vehicle and snatched my heart.

146

"Ekon . . ." *Lord, what do I say?* "Bri isn't the type to have ill will toward someone. She's the kind of woman who'll pray their heart changes and that they make better choices from then on out."

His Adam's apple bobbed as he stared unseeingly out of the windshield. "I do not deserve her kindness nor yours."

"You have it nonetheless."

He shook his head, then signaled to get back onto the road.

We drove in silence until I couldn't stand the quiet any longer. "Are you okay?"

"I am a little shocked. I am trying to figure out why you two would give me a second chance after what happened."

Because you took hold of my heart long before we met face-to-face. I widened my eyes, trying to keep tears from forming. I stared straight ahead so he wouldn't realize just how close I was to bawling and begging him to care for me.

How. Utterly. Pathetic.

Why couldn't I shake this hold he had on me? He didn't even *realize* how serious my feelings were. *I* hadn't until this moment. Everything I had learned about him made it easy for him to claim my heart. Was there a way to stop my emotions before I was too far gone?

Aren't you already?

"I do not know why you would want to call me friend, but I am thankful for you, Iris Blakely."

The tender way he said my name was another example of why my feelings continued to break free from the barriers I'd erected. "You should thank God."

"Pardon me?"

I swallowed. "God told me to be your friend." I gazed at his profile, thankful my own feelings had managed to gain some semblance of composure.

He inhaled. "Why would he do that? You know, assuming he is indeed real."

Oh, Ekon. He is very real. "Because He wants you to know He's real without a doubt."

Ekon's hands tapped the steering wheel, but he made no comment. Silence followed us all the way to my apartment building. One I didn't break for fear the waterworks would start.

When Ekon pulled into a parking spot, I unclicked my seatbelt and grabbed my purse. "Thank you for the ride."

"Anytime."

I reached for the door handle, but Ekon's hand gripped mine. "Iris."

My breath came in spurts as warmth pooled in my middle and tingles spread through my extremities. "Yes?" I squeaked, willing myself not to turn and look at him.

"If the offer still stands, I will come with you to church."

My head whirled around, meeting his delicious gaze. "Really?" *Calm down, girl. It's not a marriage proposal.*

No, this was so much more. No one who had ever met God had walked away unchanged. At least, not to my knowledge. I supposed the most stubborn could refuse to believe His truths, but I prayed that Ekon would soften his heart toward the Lord. Maybe then he would stop chasing the impossible and trying to live up to standards he was never meant to live up to. I had a feeling his dad needed a God encounter as well. Something to add to my prayer list.

I blinked. "I go to the English translation one."

"You do not attend with the queen?"

I shook my head. "I do not want to make the drive there. I've been attempting to learn Oninan, but there's no way I understand enough to sit through an entire service spoken in it."

"Understandable. What time is the English service? Do you go to the Etikun church?"

Had he really never set foot in church? The Etikun chapel was beautiful. "Ten, and yes."

"You will not be too busy readying for your family?"

"I'm pretty neat. What can't be done tonight will be finished after church."

He nodded. "Then I should pick you up at what time?"

"Nine thirty." It would give us time to drive to the chapel and for me to greet the few people I talked to.

Some of the congregants steered clear of me. I didn't think it was a language barrier, considering I attended the English service. I think it was my status as the queen's best friend that made them stand back and gift me only with a smile.

"I will be here then."

"Great." I couldn't stop a smile at the thought of him in church. *Lord God, please touch his heart, soften it toward You, and show Ekon who You are.*

"And Monday?" Ekon asked.

"What happens Monday?"

He flashed a smile. "Would you like a ride to work?"

"Oh. Yes, please." *No! Stupid, stupid girl. You should have said no.* Only the pleasure on Ekon's face kept me mute. Besides, I *would* save money on a taxi if Ekon picked me up.

"I am happy to take you anywhere you want to go."

Goose bumps broke out across my arms. For a moment, it sounded like he was *flirting* with me. *That's craziness.* I pushed the door open, needing to get out of the car before my resolve broke. Why wasn't the fact that he wasn't a believer shutting down my feelings?

Because you're not a robot. I waved good-bye and walked away, patting myself on the back.

Knowing about Ekon's past and his disbelief in God should have me running for the hills. I *knew* being unequally yoked was a no-no. The knowledge didn't shut my feelings off, however. If anything, I needed to pray that I didn't adopt some misguided belief that I could change him.

Which I was in danger of if I didn't redirect my feelings or get it through my thick skull that Ekon was off-limits.

Please, Lord, please. Take these feelings away from me. This can only end in heartache. And I was so anti-heartache. In what way was getting your heart ripped out fun for anyone? I'd seen friends over the years deal with breakups and ruined relationships. It was never pleasant. I simply wanted to experience the fun of falling and the promise of a fairy-tale ending, like my parents had.

They were that insta-love that made most people want to gag from the sweetness. Dad and Mom had been set up on a blind date by good friends. Miracle of miracles, it worked. Dad said he knew from the moment she laughed that he wanted to be with her. He didn't stop to think about it, just went for it. Mom always said Dad's humor made her fall hard and fast. She went home and told her mother she'd met the man she would marry.

Sure, they'd faced opposition when each of their families realized theirs was an interracial relationship. Thanks to me and my brother, our extended family changed their tunes, but it could have been ugly. As it was, my parents had a justice-of-the-peace wedding because they didn't want the drama from their families. Fortunately, they made up for it on their twenty-fifth wedding anniversary. Where I'd sobbed buckets at the beauty of it all.

Something told me that going into a relationship with Ekon would find me divorced and the prime example in a Bible study of what not to do.

I'm listening, Lord, I promise. He's not for me.

I dropped my keys on the hook inside my apartment just as my cell rang. Matt's number flashed across the screen, and my lips pursed in irritation. I could still recall that mortifying feeling, knowing he had divulged information he shouldn't have even been privy to. The marketing department didn't reside on the second floor.

"Hello?"

"Iris, girl. How are you holding up?"

"Is something wrong?"

"Uh, you know the wiring issue?"

I propped a hand on my hip, the other clutching my cell. "Actually, I do know. The question is, how do you?"

Stammering filled my ears until Matt cleared his throat. "Are you actually upset with me?"

"You told one of the board members. What gave you the right?"

"I am a department head."

"Yes, but last I checked, *owner* didn't follow your title." I squeezed my eyelids shut, but it was no use. Tears fell with every huffed breath my anger exacerbated.

"I was just trying to be helpful. I know how busy you are. I figured you hadn't had a chance to tell them."

And like that, the anger left with my next breath. I sank into my sofa cushions, dropping my head back. "Matt, that's not your position."

"Noted. I apologize."

Too bad his apology didn't give me the warm fuzzies. "It's fine. I handled it."

"You have the funds to cover it?" Surprise raised his voice an octave.

"Again, not your department."

"Fine. Fine. You want to go out tonight?"

Never had I been so thankful for unexpected out-of-town guests. I was in no mood to act chipper while he inserted his foot in his mouth. "Actually, my family is coming to visit. I have to get my place ready."

I stared at the air mattress I'd left at the front door. That was going to be a joy to puff up.

"Oh, well then, I'll let you get to it. Maybe once they leave?"

"Sounds like a plan."

I set my phone on the coffee table, then scanned my flat, mentally writing a to-do list. Of course, I'd have to actually get up instead of sitting here, or a mental cleaning list served no purpose.

"I'm up, I'm up." I stood and rubbed my hands together. My family would be here soon.

The thought put a smile back on my face and pushed thoughts of Matt out of my mind.

SEVENTEEN

Ekon

Why had I agreed to go to church with Iris?

Right, because she had told me god wanted her to be my friend.

I could not help but look at her skeptically when she had said that. How could she truly expect me to believe that a cosmic being told her to be my friend? Did he speak audibly? In a dream? Or had she simply imagined I needed a friend and chalked it up to her faith so she would make the charitable move?

Although I believed it to be the latter, something tugged at me within. Iris was not charitable for charity's sake. She was genuinely kind. Just the other day, I had seen her consoling a woman who could not buy food until the next payday. The company had already set a program in place for such a need. Apparently, the employee had been unaware. I had quickly added that information to the onboarding program I set up for Aṣọ. The woman had been overwhelmed with gratitude and was an example of another person who valued Iris.

The real reason I had accepted her invitation was to prove

that her god did not exist. Not because I wanted to take away any innocence Iris possessed, but because I wanted to be right. *Needed* to be. Because if *she* was right, then I had been living life wrong.

My *whole* life.

The idea did not sit well and answered why I now tried not to fidget as we sat in a middle pew. I would have preferred the very back row, but Iris wanted the front, and the middle became our compromise.

"Are you okay?" she whispered.

I nodded. Lying probably was not the best thing to do in this building, but if I was not struck dead, then either her god did not exist or he did not work in that way. Regardless, I would continue living my life as I had always done until I had a good reason not to. But then, perhaps my current situation was an example of why I should switch it up.

The annoying thoughts that kept creeping into my head were starting to get to me. My life was *fine*. Yes, I needed to make some changes. I had already checked becoming independent off my list. I was not done with my transformation, but owning my own home, car, and furnishings ensured a good start.

Plus, I had a cooking lesson this afternoon. Apparently, the queen's sister-in-law could cook and had agreed to assist me in that area. I had offered to pay her for the tutorial and was promptly refused. Nika Eesuola said she would teach me how to prepare a meal for lunch since she had a family dinner to attend later. I hoped that would be sufficient preparation for the dinner I planned for my parents or would perhaps lead to more lessons.

My thoughts turned to Iris and her family. Had she mentioned me to them? If so, in what manner had she referred to me? As a friend, like she claimed we were, or as an employee who had been ordered by the council to do community service?

I let out a sigh. Community service remained a horrendous

part of my day. A palace runner had driven me the two hours to Òkè yesterday, and then I spent the day picking up trash, to the ridicule of those around me. It was like the elders had sent out a notice to every person in Òkè and informed them where I would be cleaning. People had walked by, laughing at my misfortune. Several had taken pictures. Once again, I landed on someone's social media account with the word *loser* attached—though that was pure assumption on my part. I did not actually search for confirmation. They certainly would not label me with the title of prince.

Without that moniker, who was I?

Music filled the air, and I blinked, realizing the program had started. People stood, and I turned to Iris to find her standing, arms raised in the air as she swayed back and forth.

O-kay.

I glanced around the room and noticed no one had remained seated. With resignation, I rose to my feet, sliding my hands into my pockets. The people sang about how well they were. Were we not all well? Was this something to raise their hands about? After the slow melody ended, the band picked up the tempo, and people began clapping.

My skin felt too tight as the back of my neck heated with embarrassment. Only the thought of sitting down and incurring more looks kept me frozen. *You said you would come and listen, so do it.* No matter how much this strangeness made me want to crawl out of my own skin and disappear.

Fortunately, the music did not last an eternity. After a total of six songs, we were permitted to sit. The preacher made his way to the podium and grinned as he looked around the room. "I am so happy to see so many brothers and sisters this morning. Blessings to you all."

The people clapped, and I did my best not to roll my eyes. Still, some of his joy reminded me of Iris and how she happily greeted everyone at Aṣọ when she arrived.

"Brothers and sisters, I woke up this morning happy to greet the day, happy knowing I would see you. I took a moment to greet my God and prepare my heart for the Word today, and a new message took root." His cheeks bunched with pleasure. "You know I had no choice but to let the Holy Spirit have His way."

"Amen," someone shouted from the back.

All right, I knew a little about Christianity. I had heard of Jesus and how he was supposed to be god but man as well. But a holy spirit?

"I hope you will be gracious as I share what God laid on my heart early this morning. I was reading from the book of Isaiah, and it was in that time that these words spoke to my heart. Look at chapter thirty-two, verse eight."

Iris pulled a book from her purse and flicked through the pages. Then she shifted, holding it between us. She pointed to a small number eight in the book.

"'But he who is noble,'" read the preacher, "'plans noble things, and on noble things he stands.' Brothers and sisters, I cannot tell you what a comfort it was to read about nobility, seeing as our great queen and king are a visual example of those who are noble and how their actions reflect such standards. Did you know our great queen has taken on the endeavor to ensure that all Christian churches in Ọlọrọ have Bibles? I know there are a couple of churches still waiting, but if you do not have a Bible, we *can* provide one for you. That is watching a noble woman plan a noble endeavor."

I stared at the Bible in front of me on the back of the pew. Part of me wanted to reach for it, examine it in my own hands, knowing that the queen had helped see that the churches had Bibles. I had had no clue they were without before. Did the people all own personal ones, like Iris? No, Etikun was a poorer region. It only made sense that the citizens could not afford such luxuries.

"Brothers and sisters, I came to tell you something you may not know. Your belief in our Savior, our King, makes you noble. God has adopted you and called you an heir with Christ. Therefore, you are of nobility now. Every single one of you."

My back straightened, hands fisting. How could he be allowed to spread this falsehood? I had been born a prince and raised in a princely fashion. How could he tell these people, some who surely did not even have a roof over their heads, that they were noble?

"We know the characteristics of the nobility. The Lord tells us in Galatians when He talks of the fruit of the spirit. Brothers and sisters, do not believe the lie that you have to have a visible crown on your head in order to walk in the way of nobility. To be noble is to have outstanding character. Character so above and beyond that those around you are drawn to you. They must figure out how you are the way you are. That is when you can tell them of a God who changed you inside out and called you child. One day we will be crowned in His glory and live a life of supreme happiness."

My jaw ticked as my teeth clamped harder together.

Nobility set you apart. It was not for *everyone*. That was what Father had taught me. We were deemed better than other Ọlọrans because of our heritage and bloodlines. We were smarter, more capable, born leaders. That was *not* something that could be given to anyone who decided to believe in Jesus. That was absurd.

I pulled out my mobile and opened my notes app. Hopefully it would look like I was paying attention. Instead, I made a list of things I wanted to learn how to do on my own. If I was going to prove to Father that I was indeed as noble as my birthright, then I would show him how smart and capable I was. My work with Iris and past experience at Diallo Enterprises would prove my leadership capability.

The rest of the church service sped by as I took notes on how

I wanted my life to be and ignored the preacher and his absurd teachings. Everyone could be noble. *Ha!* Maybe I should email Father and tell him the nonsense the citizens were learning at church. Then again, the queen was a Christian. I believed almost every member on the council professed some type of faith. Perhaps remaining silent was the way.

Rustling sounds broke my thoughts, and I turned to see everyone getting up. I had missed the closing. Not that I was heartbroken over this.

Iris and I walked outside in silence.

"Iris!"

We turned, and I noted the woman from her flat complex.

"Ada! I didn't know you came here."

"I usually go to the Oninan service, but I have something else to do today." Her eyes widened. "Would you like to join me?"

"I can't. My family is flying in today, and I have to get ready. Maybe another time?"

"That would be fantastic." Ada's gaze flitted to mine then away. "I will talk to you later?"

Iris nodded, then waved good-bye. A few more people waved as we walked to my vehicle. I held the door open for her and rounded the car to get in. I still did not know what to say, so I put the car in DRIVE and headed for her home.

"You hated it, didn't you?" she asked softly.

"Hated it? No. But I am not sure church is for me." I spared her a glance in time to see the crestfallen expression on her face. My gut twisted at the thought of disappointing her.

Yet I could not lie. I had not enjoyed a single aspect. All it had done was anger me and make me wish I were anywhere else. I bet that was not the feeling Christians had when going to church.

"Most people don't become believers after one church visit." I could feel her gaze on me. "I'll continue to pray for you."

Wait, what? She *prayed* for me? "What do you pray about

when you pray for me?" I did not know whether to feel honored or offended.

"Depends. Sometimes I pray that you'll like working at Aṣọ and it'll be what you need in this time. Other times I pray the council will see you've changed and treat you accordingly. Then others I pray that you *will* change the way God desires. Basically, it varies."

Did she ever pray that there could be more between us? Because *if* I ever believed in a god who listened and cared about the people on earth, that was what I would pray for.

Instead, I replied with a simple comment. "I see."

Iris laughed. "I doubt it, but at least you know someone cares about you enough to pray."

"And praying is a big thing?"

"Very."

Hmm. "Then thank you."

"Anytime, Ekon."

My pulse double-timed at the—dared I hope—affection in her voice. "Iris?"

"Yes?"

"Why do you believe?" I glanced at her, then stopped as the car in front of me suddenly braked.

"I believe because in my darkest time, God showed me who He was and how much love He had for me."

Darkest time? When had sunny Iris ever experienced darkness? I wanted to ask, but the turn I had just made brought me to her flat. Since her family would arrive later, she probably had no time to explain further.

"Maybe you can tell me about that one day." I faced her fully, wanting her to know how sincere I was.

"Maybe." She opened the door. "Thanks for the ride. See you tomorrow."

"*O dabọ*, ododo *mi*," I murmured.

EIGHTEEN

Iris

My heart drummed loudly in my chest as I waited on the tarmac. When I'd first flown into Ọlọrọ Ilé, Bri and I had landed in the capital city of Àlàáfíà. Who knew the Etikun region had its own airport in the city of Ẹwa?

I'd ordered a van to drive me to the airport where the private plane my dad had rented now taxied. I couldn't wait to see my family. Nerves for my mother had had me praying for her all day long. I still couldn't believe she'd actually boarded the plane. Dad had texted me a picture as proof.

The airstairs dropped, and my brother flew down them. "Rissy!" he shouted. He trapped my arms by my sides in a bear hug and twirled me around.

"Stop!" I giggled. But joy filled my heart. They were really here.

"Not until I hear the magic words or you puke!" he threatened.

Brothers. Even when they grew up and celebrated milestones that proved they were adults—*ahem, thirtieth birthday*—they refused to give their younger siblings any slack. Past experience had taught me that Junior would follow through with his threat.

"You're the best brother ever!" I squealed.

He laughed and set me down.

I placed a hand against my head, trying to find my balance. "Where are Mom and Dad?"

"Dad's trying to wake Mom up." Junior rubbed his beard. "She might be out of it when you see her."

Anxiety swooped in my middle. "Was it a bad plane ride?" My hands clasped tightly before me.

"It started off well. She was asleep before boarding, and Dad carried her on and buckled her in and everything." Junior grimaced. "Unfortunately, halfway into the trip, she woke up and panicked."

"Oh no," I whispered. "She should have stayed home."

Junior snorted and rolled his eyes. An expression our dad pulled off the same way. "You can't make her change her mind. She was intent on seeing you."

I bit my lip. Staying in Ọlọrọ had felt right when I'd first made the decision. It had come after much prayer and seeking advice from Bri. But I'd known in the back of my head that I wouldn't see my family as much, which had been a bitter pill to swallow. We were so close.

"She'll be okay, Rissy," Junior murmured, hooking an arm over my shoulder.

I leaned against him. "Are you sure?"

"'Course. Dad is there to bring her around. I figure if she's mad that we let her make that flight, he'll take the brunt of it."

I laughed. "That's because you ran off the plane."

"I'm not stupid." He grinned cagily.

"Where's your luggage?"

"Right." Junior straightened and walked to one of the employees pulling the bags from the plane.

I glanced at the doorway of the plane and sighed in relief as my mom's blond head appeared. She walked slowly down the airstairs, Dad walking in front of her but backward. Did he really think that was the safest way to go down?

My heart stayed in my throat until their feet hit solid ground without incident. My mom was clumsy in all caps, and who knew what a woozy head from a sedative would do?

I ran over to my parents and wrapped my arms around their waists in a group hug. "I can't believe you're really here."

"My sweet Iris." Mom squeezed me tighter.

"How's my baby girl?" Dad asked.

I pulled back. "So ecstatic now that you guys made it."

Mom looked around. "It's dark."

"Because you flew in at night." I couldn't keep the bemused tone from my voice. What had she expected?

"True. I still was hoping for some kind of light."

"When you wake, it'll be light."

Mom scoffed. "I can't sleep."

"It's the best thing you can do to get on the right time and avoid jet lag." I remembered Ekon's advice and my own struggle to adapt to the new time zone. "The sheets and blanket have been washed. My room is now yours."

"You're such a good daughter." Mom squished my cheeks with her hand, shaking my head slightly.

"Thanks, Mom," I mumbled.

"Leave the poor girl alone," Junior piped up. "You act like you don't have another child. One that's better in every way."

I shook my head, but inside, my heart warmed. I'd missed Junior's teasing.

I motioned for everyone to follow me to the waiting van.

"When are you going to get a car, Ris?" Junior asked.

"Kind of have to learn how to drive in order to do that." I wasn't going to remind Ekon of his offer to teach me either. Not when my heart still ached that he hadn't been inspired by today's church service. Honestly, my heart had fractured at his pronouncement, and I didn't know how to sew it back together.

"I'll teach you," Junior offered.

"You have a driver's license?" Mom and I asked at the same time.

She glanced at me, a twinkle in her gray-blue eyes. We had always been in sync in our thoughts.

"I got one last year. Figured I wouldn't want to take public transportation forever."

Why not? New York's subway system made it so easy to get around. A car just clogged up the roads. But if Junior could be taught, then . . . "I should probably learn." Still, my heart was in mourning and acting like Ekon was my only possible teacher. I cleared my throat. "Dad, you want to teach me?"

He laughed, throwing his head back. "No," he stated calmly. "I dodged that bullet, and I'm not about to step in front of it now."

"Martin . . ." Mom tapped his chest in exasperation. "Someone's got to teach her."

"I'm sure they have driver's ed here," Dad said.

He continued to protest as we piled into the chartered ride. It was so nice listening to the familiar voices of my family. Dad and Junior took the third row while Mom and I sat in the middle. She threaded her fingers through mine, giving a light squeeze.

"How have you been?" she asked softly.

"Good. I really like it here." The only thing that would make it better was if my family lived here and Ekon—

Stop, Iris.

Mom's lips curved into her trademark smile, her top lip flattening with the movement.

"I'm so glad you came." I leaned my head on her shoulder. "And so sorry the plane ride was rough."

"What did Junior say?" she muttered.

"That you panicked." I lifted my head to study her, ensure she really was fine.

"Just a little bit." She held her pointer and thumb a smidgen apart. "It wasn't a big deal."

"Are you sure?"

"Positive, Iris. The sedative did its job."

"Good."

In no time, the driver arrived at my flat. Dad and Junior began removing the luggage from the back. Dad gestured for Mom and me to start walking, so we meandered slowly down the sidewalk. I didn't want to get too far ahead, or they wouldn't know which direction to go.

"I can't wait to see this in the daylight," Mom said.

"Do you want to relax tomorrow or sightsee?" My plans at work were fluid.

Oka had been advised not to schedule anything just in case my parents expected me to play tour guide. Still, I would probably go in for a few hours at least. The employees would expect me to make an appearance. The council also wouldn't count Ekon's full day if I didn't have some watchguard in place. Something I had yet to tell him or figure out a way to ensure he didn't lose any hours.

"I figured you had to work and we would be recovering from traveling," Mom said. "You know you don't have to entertain us, right?"

"But you came to see me." How could I not spend time with them?

"Yes, but your business is so new. We came here with the understanding that we might have to take a backseat to your company."

I squeezed her hand. "We'll figure it out."

"Of course we will, baby." Mom patted my cheek.

Dad and Junior caught up, and we soon stood in front of my door. I unlocked it, clicking on the light, then held the door as they all wandered in. I pointed to the left. "Junior, guest room is that way."

"Yeah, right. Just point me to the air mattress."

I laughed and pointed near the sofa, where it had been positioned after church. Outfitted with fresh sheets and a light blanket, it was ready for slumber.

"Mom, Dad, let me show you to the master." I entered my bedroom and raised an arm, Vanna White style.

"Iris, it's wonderful." Mom held her hands under her chin.

The tan color on my walls went well with the abstract paintings hanging over my ebony bed. I loved the pops of color and how the artist managed to make them cohesive-looking. Plus, I used them as an excuse to bring lots of color to my bedding and other accessories in the room.

"Thanks, Mom."

"I don't know how you expect me to sleep with all the color in this room."

"With your eyelids closed, Dad."

A bark of laughter escaped his lips. He grinned, and the slight gap between his two front teeth winked at me. His chocolate skin didn't hold a single wrinkle unless he crinkled his brow at our family's shenanigans. I often wondered if he dyed his hair, because he didn't have a single gray hair. I knew Mom did. She enjoyed her golden locks and didn't want to age. At all.

I hugged my parents and wished them a good night before heading to the guest bedroom. I'd hoped Junior would sleep on the air mattress, but I hadn't been one hundred percent sure he would go for it.

I paused in the living room. "Hey, if you need closet space, there's plenty of room in the guest closet."

"Thanks, sis. I'll worry about that tomorrow."

I nodded. "'Night, Junior."

"'Night, Big Head."

"Whatever, Big Nose."

I chuckled all the way into my room. It was so good, so *normal*, having them here. Even Junior's teasing was welcome. Life felt a little more perfect with their presence. Still, my mind wandered to Ekon as I settled in for the night.

God, please help him see how wonderful You are. And if the reason he didn't like the service was due to conviction, may You turn it up full throttle. I grimaced, imagining the turbulence that would cause within Ekon. It would feel awful, but it was so very necessary.

Make him uncomfortable, Lord. Prepare him to examine his ways and how Yours are so much better.

I paused. *And, Lord, please take these feelings from me. If You don't, for whatever reason, help me to know how to remain his friend. He needs one. Maybe You could even bring him some more friends.*

Though, how he would meet them was beyond me. From what I understood, Ekon worked, did community service, and went home.

And if . . .

No, I couldn't ask that. Even if I wanted to.

Please just help me be patient in the process. I believe Ekon will find his way to You.

He had to, right?

Not really, but imagining Ekon not finding God, not finding salvation, was something even my imagination didn't want to contemplate. I didn't want to picture the eternity he'd spin if he hardened his heart and forged ahead on his own path. Knowing how demanding his father was made me wonder if Ekon could truly understand the goodness of the Heavenly Father.

Please let him figure it out, Lord. Because the peace that would come with that knowledge was worth the heartache of wrestling with his own beliefs and measuring them against God's word. I wanted nothing but goodness for Ekon and would continue to pray for it until it came to pass.

Even if that meant I had to push my desires aside for His. It was about as difficult as *not* crying when I became overly emotional. Still, I was determined to mature in this aspect. To learn patience and the peace of walking in God's will. For there had to be peace in knowing I wasn't out of alignment, not just the uncomfortable stretching feeling of growing in the Spirit.

I sighed. Was I even making sense now? I should just close my eyes and pray for morning to come and for God to do His perfect work.

Yes and amen.

NINETEEN

Ekon

The urge to rub my eyes and verify the scene in front of me was real made my fingers itch. Only losing composure in front of Yemi Ladipo, the temporary leader of the Ọlọrọ Ilé Royal Council, would not be a smart move. Neither would adjusting my tie to keep it from choking me.

I switched my briefcase to my left hand and extended my right to greet Mr. Ladipo. "Ẹ káàárò, Alàgbà Ladipo."

"Ẹ káàárò, Ògbéni Diallo."

Ògbéni. That burned. I forced a look of interest onto my face. "What brings you to Aṣọ?" Where was Iris? Why was he sitting behind her desk?

"I called Ms. Blakely in early this morning to discuss your progress. During the course of the conversation, she let me know her family had arrived last night for a visit."

I nodded. "She is very excited."

"Were you aware that she intended to come into the office every day so that you would still have your time accounted for?"

I blinked. "Come again?"

"If Ms. Blakely is not here, your hours do not count."

My jaw ticked. Why would Iris keep this from me? Perhaps Mr. Ladipo and the other council members had prevented her from saying as much. Then again, she was like a parole officer. "Alàgbà, her family flew thousands of miles to see her, not watch her go to work every day."

Mr. Ladipo shrugged. "Not my problem."

"Where is she?" Had he said something to bring her to tears? I could imagine her hiding in a bathroom to regain composure.

"I sent her home."

"Oh." Did that mean he would send me home too? My presence apparently meant nothing without Iris to count my hours of servitude.

Mr. Ladipo curled his lip in his signature sneer. I swore he drank tears for breakfast and chewed on hurt feelings for lunch.

I cleared my throat. "What should I do, then, Alàgbà?"

"I am glad you asked, *Mr. Diallo.*" Ladipo steepled his fingers. "I will give you an opportunity to decrease your community service hours."

My mouth dried. More trash pickup? "How can I help?" I wanted to applaud myself for my steady tone and for not showing any weakness in the face of the council. Granted, Ladipo was only *one* member, but it was quite obvious he was here as *the* council. Father would be pleased to know his lessons in showing no emotion were useful.

"The queen wants the Etikun tribe to select an elder to take Jomi's seat. She offered to speak to them personally since they still have not named a replacement. I made the suggestion for you to assist."

Me? I was not a prince any longer. What could I do? "I do not understand. Why would they listen to me?"

"It seems they do not believe that you, Dayo, and Jomi were the only co-conspirators. They fear nominating another elder only for him to make threats against the queen."

Again, what could I do? The Etikun elders would not listen to me, a mere *commoner*.

Unless your father gets you a seat in the tribal meeting. I swallowed. We had not spoken since I asked him for his assistance in the fashion show. Our relationship remained estranged, as I had not seen him since the night he ordered me to hand over the keys to the penthouse.

I stared at Mr. Ladipo, knowing what tradition required of me. "What would you like me to do, Alàgbà?"

Ladipo's lips pulled up like he had successfully stolen Christmas gifts from the less fortunate. "You will go visit Dayo Layeni and get her to sign a statement listing those she manipulated to assist in her endeavors. You will then show that list to the Etikun elders and impress upon them the need to nominate the next elder to sit on the royal council and appease our queen."

And I thought my throat had been parched before. "You cannot be serious."

"I am, Mr. Diallo. Do you not want justice for *your* queen?"

"Bèèni, Alàgbà." My heart pounded. She had been more than gracious in my sentencing and deserved my loyalty. Yet I had not spoken two words to my half-sister since she had been arrested for trying to steal the throne from Brielle Adebayo. "Doing this will count for community service?"

"Yes." Ladipo glanced at his watch. "If you leave right now, I will start the clock for your community service hours. When you have the written letter in front of the Etikun elders, that will be considered the end of your day. I have seen fit to assign a palace runner to accompany you and make sure you do not make any unnecessary detours."

I glanced at my hands, making sure handcuffs were not actually shackled to my wrists. My gaze rose to see Ladipo arch an eyebrow, as if awaiting my decision.

Clearly, I did not actually have a choice. If I could not decrease my business consulting hours, then I could at least lower my community service ones. "I would be honored to assist the queen."

"That is what I thought." Ladipo rose, glancing at his wrist-watch. "The clock starts now. Your palace runner is outside. I assume you will be driving."

"Yes. I bought a used vehicle."

"Interesting. What else do you own, Mr. Diallo?"

What? Had my father said something to him? "A house."

Both of Ladipo's eyebrows rose, and his mouth parted. He cleared his throat. "I see."

"May I leave?"

"Yes, yes." He waved a hand, shooing me out of Iris's office.

I would have to text her and make sure she was enjoying the time with her family. Honestly, I simply wanted to know if she would be at work tomorrow. Not seeing her today had thrown me off. I wanted to tell her about the cooking lesson Nika had given me yesterday.

Despite having a king for a brother and the reigning queen as a sister-in-law, Nika had put me at ease. She had also proven to be an excellent cook, then proclaimed me a disaster after I burned some rice and meat. My back doors had been left wide open last night to rid the house of the acrid odor. Nika had offered to give me another lesson tonight, but who knew how long this council business would take.

> Ekon:
>
> *Omidan* Nika, could I please reschedule our cooking lesson? I am on council business today and unsure of how long it will take.

I slid my mobile into my pocket and headed outside. The palace runner followed me. When we got to my car, I said, "You can sit up front."

Surprise flashed on the young man's face. "Omoba—I mean, Ògbéni Diallo, it is best if I ride in the back."

172

"Oh, I am your chauffeur?"

He flushed. "Never mind. I will sit up front."

I got in and waited until he buckled before leaving the lot. Ọlọrọ only had one prison, and it was in the capital city, a good hour and a half away. Was I supposed to talk to the palace runner the entire way or do what I would have in the past—ignore him? Perhaps I had changed, or maybe some of Iris's mannerisms had rubbed off on me, because I could not ignore the very real person sitting in my passenger seat.

I cleared my throat and attempted small talk. "What is your name?"

"Ody Umeh."

"Nice to meet you."

"And you, òisgbéni."

I did not even wince at the *mister* this time. Instead, I gripped the wheel as my brain sought another question. "How long have you been a palace runner?" Palace runners lived to run errands for royalty and council members.

"Two years, òisgbéni. My mom needed the extra money."

I eyed him, then turned my gaze to the road. He looked like he belonged to the Opolopo tribe. He had that look that all the people from the lake region had. "Are you Opolopoan?"

"Yes."

"Are you an only child?"

"No, òisgbéni."

I sighed. "Please call me Ekon."

He thanked me.

"You are the oldest of your siblings?"

"Yes. My mom has six other children, all younger and too young to work."

"How old are you, Ody?"

"Eighteen."

He had been sixteen when he'd taken on the financial burden for his family? "What happened to your father?"

"He is a fisherman."

The fishing industry had taken a hit over the last few years. *Pity.* I asked more questions, trying to get to know this young man. Not because I was one hundred percent interested in his answers, but because it seemed like something Iris would do.

Why was she filling my thoughts so incessantly today? Was it simply because I had not seen her this morning? Some aberration of the mind that had me focused on the one thing I could not see?

I managed to rein my thoughts in as Ody began to open up. We were soon having a genuine discussion as I made my way to Àlàáfíà, then toward the prison gates. Ladipo had mentioned he would inform the guards that I would be arriving to visit my half-sister. I had to admit, my stomach heaved the closer we came to the prison.

The gray building stood sentry over its prisoners. My gaze remained transfixed despite the need to move forward. I did *not* want to step foot inside. Not that I had wanted to when Ladipo first made the suggestion. But if my country needed my assistance and the council believed I could help, I would do what was necessary. I also could not ignore that part of me that hoped this would put me in the good graces of my father and other Etikun elders. Apparently, I was still selfish in nature.

I blew out a breath and began walking to my doom. We went through the process of turning in our mobiles and being patted down before they allowed us entry. However, they would not permit Ody past the front room. I concealed my flinch as the heavy steel-bar door shut behind me.

My pulse ticked in my throat. What would Dayo say? Was she sorry she had pulled me into her drama? Did she have regrets about what she had done to the queen?

More importantly, would she sign a statement like Mr. Ladipo wanted?

My thoughts had no choice but to tumble one after the other

as I sat in an empty visitors' room. Finally, a buzzer sounded, a door opened, and Dayo shuffled in wearing all gray. I slid my hands against my slacks, thankful the table hid the telltale movement.

Dayo looked me up and down. Her mouth drew downward. "What are you doing here?"

"Please, sit." I motioned to the empty bench across from me. "No."

I stifled a sigh. "It will make things more comfortable for you." Because I could not leave until I got what I came for.

She scoffed. "I am in prison. Comfort has ceased to exist."

Probably, but surely she did not want to stand the whole time. "Sister . . ."

"No! Do not try that tone on me."

I waved a guard away as he stepped forward at her outburst. I leaned forward. "So it was okay for you to yank on family ties and make me do your bidding, but heaven forbid if I want you to sit while we talk." I shook my head. "Listen, I have a lot to say. *A lot.* I will not leave until I get the answers I came for."

Her mouth twisted, but she sat down, her shackled hands coming to rest on the tabletop. "Who sent you?"

"Ladipo."

She snorted. "That man."

A twinge of guilt flared at my mental agreement with her. "*That man* holds your life in his hands."

"His spot as leader of the council is temporary. Once Etikun nominates a new member, they will request a vote for a new council leader." Bitterness coated her every word.

"Do you think the other council members will let another elder from Etikun run the council? After what Jomi did?" She was delusional.

"What do you want, little brother?"

I drew in a breath. "Why did you lie to me?" That was not

what I had intended to say, but now that the question hovered between us, I realized I needed the answer.

"I did not lie. I told you the American would attempt to disrupt our way of life, and she has." Dayo hissed on the tail end of her sentence. I had a feeling that being imprisoned had not changed any belief she held.

"I have not seen any instance of disruption." If anything, our country seemed to be improved.

"That is because your life is cozy. It always has been."

"Father cut me off."

She cocked her head. "Aw, poor baby." Her shoulder slipped up into a shrug. "Now you will know what it is like to be poor."

"Why are you so bitter?" My brow furrowed at the venom in her voice.

Her gaze narrowed, her petite head looking even smaller with the close shave and the large prison garb. "Maybe learning that the man who I thought was my father actually is not has hardened me."

Dayo had believed the late king to be her father. It was the main reason she had tried to take the throne. Only, her father turned out to be the illegitimate brother of the king, with whom our mother apparently had a relationship. Something told me Dayo had been bitter long before that knowledge came to light.

"Dayo," I said slowly, "your only recourse is to assist the council willingly. Maybe it will be accounted to you for leniency."

"No, brother. They will never let me out. Not as long as *she* sits on the throne."

She could be right, but that did not change my task. I could not leave this prison without a statement. Judging from the clenched jaw and the steel in my half-sister's eyes, she would not make this easy.

TWENTY

Iris

Lake life was wonderful.

I tipped my head up to the sky, relishing the feel of the sun on my face. Although it was October, the temperatures stayed in the eighties—Fahrenheit; I was still learning Celsius—year-round. The heat warmed my skin as I continued to drift in the inner tube that we'd rented in Opolopo.

The family had wanted to get out and sightsee, but nothing too taxing, which had led to Bri's husband suggesting fun at the lake. Each of us had our own tube and the quiet sounds of nature to accompany us. My head dropped to scan the lush greenery surrounding the lake. This country was truly breathtaking. I loved everything about it.

"Are you saying the weather is like this every day?" Junior's question broke the silence.

"Yep." I smiled.

"That can't be accurate. Has it rained here?"

Had it? I couldn't remember a cloudy sky, but . . . "Oh yeah, but it didn't last long."

"Huh."

"Junior, don't get any ideas," Dad joked.

Well, at least I thought he was teasing. I opened an eye and glanced toward my father. He looked the perfect picture of relaxation, holding a coconut drink in one hand. His head nestled against the tube as he soaked in the sun's rays. The barest wisp of a smile showed under his black mustache.

Disappointment filled me. I actually wouldn't mind if my whole family moved here. It would be wonderful to have them close by, see them more than FaceTime and impromptu trips allowed. Though, I didn't want to impose my desires on them. They would have to make the choice on their own. Even if I could point out that Junior could work anywhere. Of course, Dad might have a little more difficulty, but he was always talking about early retirement. I was pretty sure he had enough in investments and whatnot to make it a reality.

Still, I kept silent and floated.

"Did you put on sunscreen, Iris?" Mom asked.

She'd slathered herself earlier with the highest SPF possible. She probably had a timer on her phone for when she'd need to reapply. Mom burned easily, but thanks to dad's DNA, I didn't. Not that I couldn't, it just didn't happen to me as often as it did to Mom. She could step outside, greet the sun with a smile, and be left with a sunburn on her nose.

"I did."

"Do you need more?"

Back in New York, I would have rolled my eyes. Now I was glad she was close enough to mother me. "I put some on an hour ago, Mom. Pretty sure it said good for four hours." I tempered the words with amusement, knowing she would understand my dry tone was all in good fun.

"You never know, bug."

"Leave her alone, Deb. She doesn't burn like you do."

"But skin cancer," she grumbled.

"Which is why she has sunscreen on and won't stay out here all day."

Boo. Staying out here all day sounded marvelous.

"What about you, Junior? Did you put some on?"

Junior huffed. "Yes, Mom. You do know I'm darker than you and Rissy."

"Doesn't matter," Mom and I parroted.

I laughed. I'd missed that. Somehow, we were always in sync. I didn't have troubles with my mom like some women I knew. I loved her and thanked God for two parents I could go to if I ever needed anything. Even if it was something as simple as a hug.

"When will we see Bri?" Mom asked.

"Thursday. It's our standard girls' night, and we figured it would be easier to bring you guys to her than for her security to scramble for her to come to my place."

"We certainly don't want to inconvenience her," Dad said. "I can't imagine what running a country's like."

"Her husband is a great support," I said.

"Good. He should be." Mom pulled the brim of her straw hat closer to her sunglasses. The shades were huge, covering a majority of her face.

I was surprised she actually had on a bathing suit instead of something that covered her arms and legs. Granted, her one-piece was modest, and she did have a wrap around her legs. Probably feared the kiss of UV light.

"How's business going, bug?" Dad asked.

"Good. We have a hiring event tomorrow. I'm sorry I couldn't change it." But we were ready. Everything was in place.

"No, don't be sorry," Mom said.

"She's right, bug. We're just happy we get to see your face. Maybe we'll venture out on our own and see the sights."

Bri had already offered to get my family tickets to any place they wanted to visit. Maybe I could get someone to play tour guide for them while I was at work tomorrow. "I'll hook you up, Dad. Bri will know the perfect places to go."

I almost invited them to Aṣọ but stopped. My parents would love to see my work, but the thought of them meeting Ekon made me want to reach for a barf bag.

What was Ekon doing now? Had he fared well in the meeting with Mr. Ladipo? Mr. Ladipo hadn't disclosed to me the task he had for Ekon. He'd simply asked me for a report on Ekon's consulting skills and whether or not he was fulfilling the council's sentencing in a satisfactory manner. Ever since, my curiosity had been imagining all sorts of assignments.

I'd thought of everything from the humiliating—Mr. Ladipo seemed the type—to the *get back in our good graces* mission. Not once had I reached for my cell and typed a simple question asking what Ekon was doing. It seemed too intimate, and I'd probably blush and end up on the receiving end of questions from my family.

How would I even tell them about Ekon? Dad would freak and assume he was the worst sort of criminal. Probably even tell me how I deserved so much more. The crazy thing was, my feelings for Ekon weren't based on some worthiness scale. I knew who I was. I knew that God loved me. This wasn't me gravitating toward bad boys or rebelling against my parents. I was just a hopeless romantic who saw love everywhere.

Including in Ekon.

Knowing that he wasn't a believer kept me up at night. Nothing could happen between us, that much was clear, and there were mounting reasons why. I tired of listing them—because obviously that took the shine off my imagined dreams—but I could no longer ignore the long list. Ekon would remain a friend and only a friend.

If only I could engrave that memo on my heart and survive the close proximity of office space.

God, why won't You take these feelings from me? He's off-limits. He has a past that's less than savory.

Yet I could remember the grace with which Bri talked about

him. If she could forgive him, and God *would* if Ekon ever asked, then who was I to hold that against him?

No, you're listing why your feelings are ridiculous and can't be trusted, not why Ekon is acceptable.

"Hmm," I murmured.

My feelings couldn't be trusted because my imagination had free rein. It often got the best of me, when I chose to create a better ending rather than face the reality life dealt. How many crushes had I entertained growing up? A simple smile from a cute guy had me full-out planning our wedding. A bit much, I knew, but I couldn't say the adult Iris was any better than teenage Iris.

My feelings for Ekon had begun in a similar fashion. A handsome picture that made my heart beat hard and my soul shout: *him!* A glance across a ballroom that made me wish I'd seen him before Bri. My what-ifs had immediately begun imagining situations where he *didn't* marry Bri.

Then life had come crashing down around me with the accusations from the council.

No way had I conjured up a life of subterfuge and plotting against the throne. I'd also never thought we'd be working closely together simply because the council sentenced him to help.

Getting to know him had provided more opportunity to add to the "cons" side of my argument. His upbringing, penchant for arrogance, and lack of faith weren't helping. On the other hand, we *were* friends, he could make me laugh, and peeks of vulnerability made me realize how much of his behavior was a defense mechanism.

But none of that matters, Lord. We're just friends. You asked no more of me, and I need to focus on that. Reality states Ekon doesn't believe in You. I squeezed my eyes, fighting against tears. *And I'm sorry that isn't deterrent enough for me. Please forgive me. Please forgive him. Please soften his heart.*

My phone rang, and I groaned, pulling the waterproof case it was in from my side. Matt's name blinked on the screen, a picture of him smirking at the camera floating above his name. "Hello?"

"Iris, I've been looking for you everywhere, and then your secretary informed me that you took a personal day." He tutted. "You do know we have the hiring event tomorrow."

"I'm well aware, Matt. Everything is set up and ready to go."

He sighed. "Why did you take a personal day?"

As if it were his business! "My family arrived last night. I didn't think one day off would hurt." Plus, I was still peeved about his conversation with the board member, despite us clearing the air.

"How about I take you and your family out for dinner? There's a fantastic restaurant I discovered."

While the thought of Ekon meeting my parents sent me on a path that ended with prayer for his salvation, the thought of Matt meeting my parents seemed weird. He'd never met them before because we weren't that type of friends. "I appreciate the offer, but we already have plans."

"How long will they be visiting? We can schedule for another day."

"Matt." I reached for a gentle tone, hoping he could hear through the lens of our past friendship. "I've been looking forward to spending time with them. I hadn't planned to introduce them to any of my coworkers."

"Coworkers? Really?"

I winced at the frost in his voice. "You're the head of marketing. Plus, we worked together in New York. Or would you have preferred I use the term *employee*?" *Darn it.* There went the kindness I was going for.

"What about friend or . . . ?"

My eyebrows rose. Was he hinting that he wanted more? Was that why he was always trying to have a meal together?

My brain scrambled for the right words. "Friendly coworkers?" I suggested.

Matt cleared his throat. "I guess I'll see you tomorrow, then."

"Yes." At work, where I could straighten out any miscommunication.

"Very well, then."

I grimaced and ended the call.

"Rissy's got an admirer."

My mouth dropped. "What makes you think that?" I eyed Junior.

"It was obvious from the *get me out of this situation* expression on your face. I've seen it a few times." He smirked and rubbed his beard.

Man-child. "More like all the time," I quipped.

He flung water at me, and I squealed.

"You're going to get my hair wet!"

"Good, tame those curls."

I did *not* want to have to do my hair. Which was ridiculous, because I had to deal with my curls every day of my life unless I decided to straighten them.

"Mom!" I shouted.

"Children," Dad and Mom scolded.

I stuck out my tongue at Junior and he flicked water again, but just enough for a few droplets to get me. I laughed and spun myself around in the tube. Family was the best.

TWENTY-ONE

Ekon

My task from the council had not been resolved in one day as I had hoped. Though I managed to secure the letter from Dayo, I simply could not show up at an elder's home unsolicited. To make matters worse, Father refused to procure me a seat at the Etikun elder meeting unless I showed him my current living situation. I had called in an emergency lesson from Nika so I would be able to serve dinner to my parents.

Thankfully, some good had come from the prison visit. Ladipo had agreed to write off a full eight hours from my community service total, though it had only been a six-hour day. Once a meeting with the elders was arranged, he would send a palace runner to attend with me. The elder meeting would count toward my community service as well.

I peeked through the clear pot lid at the rice medley before checking on the chicken. Everything *appeared* ready. Nika had left ten minutes ago with instructions to leave the rice on low until my parents arrived. The time on my mobile showed about five minutes before they would knock on my door. Father was never late.

Which meant I needed to change my shirt now. The T-shirt I had worn to cook in looked like the spice cabinet had attacked it. I headed for my closet and reached for a dark-green button-down shirt. My shorts were traded for starched slacks, and a spritz of cologne finished my cleanup.

Just as I turned off the stove, the doorbell rang. I gulped. What would Father say? I eyed the living room, which now sported a brown sofa set. The couch held two pillows in a tan-black pattern that had come with the furniture. A pottery plate collection hung on the wall above the couch, adding a nice touch of decor.

I was no interior designer, but I had watched my mother redecorate enough times to know if pieces went well or if they clashed. I could only hope she would be pleased with my efforts.

I rushed to the door and unlocked it. "*Ẹ kúròlé, Bàbá, Màmá.*" I held the door wide for them to enter.

Mother's gaze roamed my home, and her ebony cheeks bunched with joy. "Ekon! How lovely."

I let out a sigh. One parent's approval, check. "Thank you. Would you like a tour?"

"She can have a tour later," Father interjected. "I assume you have something prepared to feed us."

My jaw ticked. "Yes, Father. Please follow me." I guided them out back, where I had set up an outdoor eating area. "If you will have a seat, I will bring dinner to you."

"You expect me to eat outside?"

"Ise," Mother hissed.

I held my breath, waiting for his pronouncement.

"Very well." He unbuttoned his dinner jacket and took a seat.

"I will be right back."

"We are in no rush, Ekon." Mother patted my hand.

I dashed into the kitchen, plating the food like Nika had recommended. I steadied a plate on my forearm, then put the second in my left hand, leaving the third plate for my empty right hand. Walking back outside was slow going, as I did not want to make a mess. Making another trip was *not* an option. Father would find fault with that.

"It smells good." Mother clapped as I lowered the plate before her. "Do you have something to drink?"

"Yes. I picked up Pupa FunFun."

"That is not the best red wine." Father sniffed, affronted by my choice.

Perhaps not, but it was within my budget. Besides, did Mother really need to imbibe tonight? "It was a good price."

Father arched an eyebrow. "For who? A commoner?"

No, for the son you cut off. Instead, I offered a slight smile. "For my budget, Father."

"Very well. A glass will do."

I went back into the kitchen and filled three wine glasses. I actually did not want any but poured myself a glass in case Father granted me the honor of blessing my home. I would need a cup to toast with if so.

I set the stems down gently, then took a seat across from Father. "Would you do me the honor of saying grace, Father?"

"Of course."

As we bowed our heads, a jolt of hypocrisy shot through me. How many times had I bowed my head, listened to a prayer, and said *amen* afterward? We had never been the church-attending type, but we always had a blessing at mealtime. Why was that?

The question reverberated in my head as Father closed the prayer and began eating. I waited for someone to compliment my cooking, but no one said a word. They simply ate. I supposed I could count it a win that I had not burned the meal or made it inedible. I took a bite of the rice.

Not bad. Nika had saved the day. Had I remembered to thank her?

"Who cooked this?" Father asked.

I tensed. His tone gave nothing away. "I did."

Lines furrowed his brow. "How?"

Did he want a tour of my kitchen? Was he asking in the very literal sense?

"In his kitchen, Ise. Be serious." Mother tapped Father on the arm and took a gulp of her wine.

Good thing I had only bought the one bottle.

"I understand the mechanics of cooking, Tife. What I do not understand is how a man who has never stepped foot in a kitchen can suddenly construct a meal fit for his parents."

Was he angry at me? I straightened in my seat. "I had someone teach me."

"Let me get this straight." Father pointed a finger at me. "The council removes your title, and you decide it is time to act like a commoner and learn how to cook?"

"I thought you wanted me to become self-sufficient," I stated cautiously, though indignation burned. What had been the purpose of stripping me of all my possessions if not to make me self-reliant?

"You mean to tell me you could not *hire* a chef? Etikun is crawling with people who need jobs. One of them surely knows how to prepare a satisfactory meal and accept a low wage in return."

My jaw tightened. "How do you expect me to pay them, Father? You told me I could only use my payroll account. You removed my access to the trust fund and took away the keys to the penthouse and all the cars I thought were gifts or that I had bought personally."

"*Personally* with the money *I* set aside for you. My money gave you all of that."

"Well, my money bought this house, the car in the yard, and

the food you are eating." I curled my fingers into my palms, fighting the urge to pound the table. Why was nothing ever good enough for him?

"I wanted you to realize how good you had it," Father shouted. "I wanted you to keep yourself out of trouble. I did not imagine—*could not* imagine you would learn the ways of the poor."

"Ise," Mother muttered, laying a hand on his arm.

He knocked it aside, standing abruptly. "I will *not* recommend the elders give you a seat at the meeting."

Heat burned my throat like an aged whiskey. I nodded slowly, picked up my napkin, folded it, and placed it beside my plate. "Fine, Father. I will tell Mr. Ladipo."

Father's eyes flashed. "What does that mean?"

"Alàgbà Ladipo came to my work this morning and gave me a task. I have already informed him that I could not complete it in one day as he wished, as I need access to the elders' meeting. Now I will have to find another way to acquire a seat with the elders."

They had already imposed their own sanctions on me, ashamed at the black mark against all Etikun tribu members because of my aid to Dayo. My mind filtered to some of the taunts and insults she had thrown my way earlier today.

"You are worth nothing. It is no wonder you are no use to all who know you."

The words had stung and loosened something inside of me. I did not know if that was a part I needed or not.

"Yemi Ladipo wants you to see the elders?" Father asked skeptically.

"Yes."

"Why?"

"I am not at liberty to say." And would never share with my father even if I could. He would find some way to take the glory for himself.

I needed this. I needed to show people I was not useless. I could be counted on. Somehow.

"Very well, then." He straightened. "I will get you into the meeting. However, after that, consider yourself no longer associated with Diallo or Diallo Enterprises in any capacity."

Mother gasped. "You cannot mean that. He is our son."

Father stared at me, his dark eyes assessing. "He is no son of mine." He stalked out of the room.

A painful lump formed in my throat as I stared at his vacant seat. I had done the opposite of what I had intended, of what tonight should have been. I wanted to gain favor from Father and had gone down the wrong path . . . *still*. Somehow, I had managed to make myself too common.

"Ekon?"

I turned to Mother, who had tears streaming down her face. "Yes?"

"I must go." She stood, looking at the house. "I am proud of you," she whispered, then left me alone.

"Brothers and sisters, do not believe the lie that you have to have a visible crown on your head in order to walk in the way of nobility."

I blinked. Where had that thought come from? Why remember parts of that sermon at a time like this? My emotions had shut down, ushering in a deep abyss. I stared at the table, at the food they had left unfinished. All that work for a man who continuously refused to give me his approval.

I went through the motions, standing to clear the plates. My mind held no thoughts as I entered the kitchen. Operating on autopilot, I put away the food that had not been eaten, then washed the dirty dishes. When all was done, I went to my bedroom, passing the mirror on the back of the door. The one I had stood before to ensure I looked ready to greet my parents.

My reflection filled the glass. From the moment I had been

sentenced by the council until now, my appearance had remained unaltered. The face peering back at me still the same. Groomed arched eyebrows, mine. Dark brown skin, the same that had covered me since birth.

Only my possessions and location had changed. Oh, and the lack of a title. My lips twisted. Apparently, now I could add no Diallo legacy to adhere to as well.

All my efforts had been for naught.

I sank onto my bed, elbows coming to rest on my knees as my back hunched over. *All for naught.* What had seeking my father's approval ever gotten me?

My mobile chimed, and I pulled it out of my pocket.

Iris:
How was your day?

I stared at the question. Did she want my real answer? Wait a minute, this was Iris. Of course she wanted my real answer.

Ekon:
Terrible

Iris:
Want to talk about it?

Ekon:
No. How was your day?

Iris:
Good. Spent it at the lake. Now I look like a lobster. Just in time for this great hiring event. What color doesn't clash with sunburn?

I winced.

Ekon:
You did not wear sunblock?

Iris:

Of course I did. My mom even harped reminder
after reminder. But I must have enjoyed the
sun a little too much because even my mom
managed to escape the sun's wrath.

Ekon:

I am sorry.

Iris:

Don't be.

Ekon:

Are you ready for tomorrow?

Iris:

Not at all. I feel like I'm going to throw up.

Ekon:

Do it, then you will feel better.

Iris:

I don't think that's how that works.

Ekon:

Sure it does. That is its purpose.

I laughed at the *ew* GIF she sent back. Trust Iris to keep the
darkness from swallowing me whole.

Ekon:

Fine, have chocolate.

Iris:

That I can do.

She sent a picture of a chocolate bar half eaten.

Iris:

It's delicious.

> Ekon:
> I could use some chocolate as well.

She sent a GIF of a person stuffing chocolate in their face. I laughed once more, the pain in my chest waning.

> Ekon:
> Looks good.

> Iris:
> LOL. I'll bring you real chocolate tomorrow.

> Ekon:
> It is not necessary.

> Iris:
> Then what cheers you up?

You.

But I could not say that. It would tear me to pieces if she rejected me just after my father's abandonment.

> Ekon:
> I am not sure. Chocolate will be fine.

> Iris:
> Chocolate it is. Oh hey, my family is ready to eat. See you tomorrow.

I sent a good-bye and set my phone to the side.

What did I do with myself now? I could only hope that the meeting with the elders would not be such a colossal failure as dinner with my parents had been.

TWENTY-TWO

Iris

There were so many women here. I wanted to cry with relief and joy. We were having such a good turnout for the hiring event. Many of the women had brought some of their sewing pieces as proof of their skill. Ekon had created a process for the hiring team to ensure the women weren't exaggerating their experience or showing someone else's work. They also made sure the ladies understood we were willing to hire unskilled workers and teach them what they didn't know.

Ekon also had a hand in creating the training class. Well, the concept anyway. He had no idea how to use a sewing machine or the countless other tools related to fashion. He always got a blank look on his face and gestured as if waiting for me to fill in the missing term. It was cute. *He* was cute.

Stop, Iris.

But already I was glancing over my shoulder, searching for him. I spied him talking to a group of men, some I had spoken to earlier. Some were here for the sake of fashion. But the others were hoping we had more jobs available other than making clothes.

Ekon nodded at them but didn't look wholly interested in what they were saying. Something was off with him today. It was killing me that I hadn't had a chance to ask the thousands of questions swirling around in my brain. Why did he have a *terrible* day yesterday? Was he ready to talk about it? Did the chocolate bar I'd given him earlier cheer him up any? Most importantly, had he considered praying to God for help?

Instead, I kept busy ensuring the hiring event went smoothly. Eventually, I would have to take a step back from overseeing every tiny detail and let the employees do their jobs. I couldn't have my hands in every piece of the pie, but for now, I couldn't help myself. This was my baby. Still, I didn't want the women to feel like I was micromanaging them. My goal was for Aṣọ to have a family-like atmosphere.

"Iris?"

I turned. Matt walked toward me with a man I didn't recognize. The gentleman was shorter than me and probably in his fifties. I reached for my most professional smile and walked over to greet them.

"Iris Blakely, please meet Mr. Jaya Kalu. Mr. Kalu, this is Iris Blakely, Aṣọ's owner."

I greeted him in Oninan, trying to hide my wince. I was always sure I butchered the pronunciation, but Ọlọrans were always gracious, smiling at my attempts.

"It is nice to meet you, Ms. Blakely. We in Etikun are thankful for your dedication to our people and for the opportunity to employ them."

"It's my pleasure. I fell in love with the area, and fashion has always been my passion." Ọlọrọ held a wealth of beauty in fabrics and skill. If I could use fashion to rid the area of poverty, I would.

"You are doing good work." Suddenly, Jaya stiffened. "I see the rumors are true."

"Rumors?" I looked over my shoulder, trying to locate the

source of his disapproval. Not finding anything, I turned back. "What do you mean?"

"We heard that Ekon Diallo was working for your company and overseeing several areas for the hiring event."

O-kay. I needed to tread lightly. "Mr. Kalu, Mr. Diallo was ordered by the royal council to consult for free as part of his penance. Fortunately for Aṣọ, he has the education, experience, and background needed to ensure we adhere to the council's business requirements. He has been instrumental in seeing that new hires will go through a financial class to ensure they are making the most of their wages and improving their quality of life."

Mr. Kalu's head jerked back. "You sound like you approve of him."

Ekon wasn't some child. He was a grown man who didn't need my approval. But I kept those feelings behind my clenched teeth and sucked in a breath. *Lord, please give me the words. Please soften this man's heart.* "Mr. Kalu, do you not believe in second chances?"

He blinked at me, eyes large behind his round spectacles. He ran a hand down his black tunic, stopping at his rotund middle. "I do."

"Then wouldn't Mr. Diallo be the kind of person you'd want to make the most of his second chance?"

"He brought shame to the Etikun tribe," he countered.

"I cannot imagine the hurt you must feel over his actions." Although I could relate because of Bri and my own feelings on the matter. "However, if your queen can find the grace to give Mr. Diallo a second chance and not count him lost, shouldn't you?" I wasn't sure if he was a believer, or I would have asked *what would Jesus do?* In a non-cliché manner, if that was possible.

Mr. Kalu stared at me.

I met his gaze, resisting the urge to fidget or blurt a bunch of my thoughts begging for release.

"I suppose you are right. Please, take me to him."

I glanced at Matt, then at Mr. Kalu. "I can do that."

We started to cross the great room. I loved the warehouse and how much space was on every level, but right then, it seemed like an ocean stood between Ekon and me. He must have sensed our presence, because he turned away from the men he was talking to and stared straight at us. Ekon straightened quickly when he took in who stood next to me. I gulped. How big of a name was Jaya Kalu that Ekon would react so?

Please be in the midst of this conversation, Lord.

"Mr. Diallo," I said, recalling my professionalism and Ọlọran customs. "This is Mr. Kalu. He wanted the opportunity to talk to you. Jaya Kalu, please meet Ekon Diallo." My hands were clammy as I gestured between the two men, my brain trying to say a prayer at the same time.

Ekon bowed and began speaking in Oninan.

My stomach tensed. I couldn't follow their conversation. How was I supposed to know how well it was going? *Hello! Don't you know it's rude to speak in another language?*

Was it considered eavesdropping if I couldn't understand a single word they uttered? I needed to stop ignoring the daily prompts to use my language app and spend more time practicing.

As it was, I stood there for a few minutes, trying to guess what their facial expressions and body language conveyed. Ekon maintained respectful eye contact, his gaze never wavering from Jaya Kalu. Whatever they talked about had Ekon tense until Mr. Kalu dipped his head in dismissal. He nodded at me before walking away without a good-bye.

"What was *that* about?" I asked.

"Tribal issues."

"Is he mad at you? I told him he should forgive and give you a second chance."

Ekon's mouth parted, and then his jaw snapped shut.

Wait, was he mad at me?

"What did you say to Mr. Kalu?" he asked cautiously.

"That if Bri could give you a second chance, he should take her example and do the same. Does no one practice forgiveness anymore?"

Ekon gaped at me, then grabbed my hand. He pulled me away from the crowd, out of the room, and down the hall. I scrambled to keep up as his long legs ate up the distance. He pushed open a door and flicked on a light, shutting the door behind me as soon as I crossed the threshold.

"What in the—" But my words were stopped by his lips.

Oh my. I sighed as the feather-light touch stroked my mouth once, as if asking permission. "Yes," I whispered, pressing my lips firmly against his in case there was a roar filling his ears like mine and preventing him from hearing my answer.

Ekon took charge, exploring my lips as if he were starved for affection. My body heated like molten lava, and I gripped the hands that held my face lightly but firmly. I wasn't sure how long we stayed there kissing, but I had no plan to move until he pulled away.

"What am I going to do with you, ododo mi?" he murmured.

I wanted to mention that we should continue kissing, but I couldn't think. Couldn't speak. Could only feel the buzz in my swollen lips, the fast beating of my heart, and the tingles in my middle.

Ekon kissed me. *Kissed me!* A bona fide, swoony, for-the-movies type of kiss. I was probably wearing a bemused expression, because my brain just couldn't connect the dots and get me talking.

"Why do you believe in me so much?" he asked.

Why did I? I stared into his warm brown eyes. "Because every time I look into your eyes, I see endless possibilities." I wouldn't mention that half of them were about our future. No reason to show him just how much I lived in a fantasy world, especially when I'd been trying to ground myself.

Crap!

I'd kissed Ekon. We'd kissed. How had I let that happen?

He started it, and you eagerly continued. I pressed a hand to my middle.

"I have never met anyone who believed in me as much as you do, Iris Blakely." His eyes darted back and forth, studying me with wonder.

"No one? Not even your family?"

He drew back, dropping his hands from my face and sliding them into his pockets. "My father wants nothing else to do with me."

I blinked. "What do you mean?"

"He came over for dinner last night, and one thing led to another. He told me to never contact him again."

An ache spread into my chest. "How could he do that?"

A bitter smile filled the lips that had just kissed me with a gentleness that still had me reeling. "Easily. My mother will probably avoid talking to me out of respect for his wishes."

Tears filled my eyes. "I'm so sorry."

He nodded jerkily. "Then you tell me what you said to Jaya Kalu. I . . ." He ran a hand down the back of his neck. "I lost my head."

My stomach dropped to my toes. Was he about to—? Was he going to—?

"I should not have kissed you, Iris."

He was. I drew in a jagged breath, hoping to keep my tears from spilling. "You're sorry?"

"I . . ." He clamped his mouth shut, rubbing his chin. The jawline I had been dreaming of kissing since his first day in my office.

"Ekon?"

"No, okay." He threw his hand in the air. "I am *not* sorry. I have been wanting to kiss you for a while. But you *are* my boss. I *am* a convict. This has made matters much more complicated."

He squeezed his eyes shut. "You have always been careful to treat me as a friend and nothing more. I have messed everything up once again."

"I kissed you back." I didn't want him to make himself a martyr on my account. Besides, I had my own regrets that I would have to examine. *Later. Right now, figure out what's next.*

That crooked grin appeared, and it was all I could do to stay in one spot and not fling myself into his arms. "You did."

I smiled. I couldn't help it. Until seeing the happiness on my face triggered Ekon to erase all delight from his.

"Iris, I am not good enough for you."

Funny, hearing the words directly from him that I had been trying to tell myself for weeks now didn't bring me any joy.

"You have everything ahead of you. I cannot—will not—drag you down."

"What are you saying?"

He stepped forward, trailing a fingertip along my arm. "That as much as I want to be more than your friend, I cannot."

My mouth dried out. "Can't or won't?"

"Does it matter? It is semantics at this point. You deserve so much more than me."

Tears threatened to breach as I dragged in a shaky breath. "What about what I want? What I think of the situation?" Because I would wholeheartedly choose him.

"Iris, if I asked you what you thought, you would present the glass half full. I am here to tell you there was never a glass to begin with. I am not right for you."

No, no, no. "What if you are?" I rasped.

He scoffed. "Then I somehow found a way to go back in time and change some major life decisions."

"Then that's it? You kiss me"—my lips were still quivering from the sensation—"tell me you're no good for me, and what, we go back to being friends?"

"We go back to me being sent here by the council to fulfill

my community service. When that is complete, I will leave and never bother you again."

I gasped, back slamming against the wall.

Ekon turned his head away from me. My breath came in spurts as the reality of his words sank in.

Reality.

Something I'd constantly tried to alter to my liking, and now I couldn't outrun its truth. I whirled around, opened the door, and ran from the present.

TWENTY-THREE

Ekon

There were moments in life when rock bottom appeared as innocuous as the average day. The evening sun shone against the hills of Etikun, casting a warm glow across my backyard. If I were to take a picture of this moment and post it on social media, someone would applaud my view and tell me how fortunate I was to be able to experience it.

What they could not know was how horribly I had destroyed my world. How the view was shared by me and me alone. No friends to come over and tell me how lucky I was. No woman to keep me company and dream of being a part of my world.

Granted, that last one was on me. Well, no, it all was. I had made choice after choice that ended with me standing outside in a T-shirt from a local store and joggers that would most likely fray before the end of the year. Devoid of any designer label that made the simple fabric worth more than it should be. The shirt made cheaply because it had to adhere to my budget now that Father had cut me off from his finances and out of his life. I still could not believe he expected me to live like before.

That was neither here nor there. I had no one else to blame for how my life had turned out. It was all my fault.

The one woman who would have gladly listened and kept me from feeling isolated . . . well, I had offered her hope, then shattered it to pieces. Her beautifully expressive face could not have hidden the hurt I had inflicted if she had tried. Even attempting to explain I was no good did not lessen the pain.

My stomach rolled from the day's events. I wanted to justify to myself how very necessary breaking all ties was. Iris needed to rid herself of the positive outlook that somehow we could live a life like in the movies. Only I was no prince charming. I snorted. I was not even a prince anymore. That had been my first stop on my downfall.

How could she think I could ever be worthy of her? I was a nobody now. No one of consequence. I had no purpose on this earth but to keep inhaling air and expelling toxins. Though I was not even sure that was a significant mark on the world, considering plants could purify the air, nullifying my worthless contribution.

Toxic. That was what I had become.

"Do not believe the lie that you have to have a visible crown on your head in order to walk in the way of nobility. To be noble is to have outstanding character. Character so above and beyond that those around you are drawn to you."

Why did those words keep reverberating in my mind? How could I be noble of character if I was not noble in name? Was character dealt at birth like royalty? Was it too late for me?

I stared at the rolling green scenery. *"Because every time I look into your eyes, I see endless possibilities."* Could I really become a man I would not be ashamed of? Did I still have something to offer?

I peered up into the sky, thinking of how Iris believed in a god who would send me a friend. "Are you real? Do you really care enough about me to send me a friend?" I winced. *Look what you did to your friend.*

I had to. Distancing myself was the only way I knew how to watch out for her. Someone had to, because she certainly would not. She would befriend a mass murderer if she thought they could be redeemed.

I rubbed my forehead. "I do not see how you can be real. Nevertheless, I am desperate enough to ask. To actually look for some very real answers." I looked back into the sky, the sun dipping a little since I had first made my way out to my yard. "Show me who you are. Please," I whispered.

I turned and walked inside. I could not go back in time, but I could be proactive about my future. If I wanted to stop making bad choices, then a change was necessary. Not just outwardly, but inwardly as well. Perhaps I could actually make the queen's hope come true. There was nothing to stop me from seeking a different viewpoint. Not anymore. Father had washed his hands of me, effectively removing himself from all my decision-making.

I winced. What would be my measuring stick if it was not Ise Diallo? How would I figure out how to be a better person? Other than trying to figure out if Iris's beliefs were true or not, I had no direction. What was I supposed to do now?

The couch beckoned me, and I sank into the cushions, not even sure why I kept moving from one space to another. Perhaps to ward off the loneliness. I had no one to call. No one to ask for help.

Ask Iris.

No. I could not go back on my declarations and treat her as a friend. It would be spiteful to call and ask her to help me figure out my life. She had already done so much for me.

I pulled up my mobile, opening my contacts. There had to be someone in here who could help. Someone I had yet to delete after being blocked first.

Someone. Anyone.

My fingers paused when I reached Nika Eesuola's name. She

had been kind when giving me a cooking lesson. Could that somehow translate to life lessons as well?

I tapped the side of my mobile, trying to figure out what to do. It was not as if I could fall further from here, was it? Reaching out should be a step in the right direction. I hoped.

> Ekon:
>
> Hello, are you busy?

> Nika:
>
> I'm not. Do you need to schedule another cooking lesson?

> Ekon:
>
> May I call?

> Nika:
>
> Sure

I gulped and pressed the phone icon.

"Hello?"

"Hi." I swallowed, unsure of what else to say.

"This is a surprise."

"Yes." I ran a hand down my chin.

"Is something the matter?"

"Yes."

A soft chuckle reached my ears. "Do you want to tell me about it?"

I did. I spilled everything that had gone wrong today, yesterday, and all the way back to helping Dayo. "I know I probably should not be saying this, since you are related to the queen, but I have no one else to talk to."

I muffled a groan. That was offensive, right?

"And what do you want to do now?"

Not be alone. Not feel like a waste of space. I cleared my throat. "Be better."

"Then be better."

"But how?" I sighed. "Iris . . . um, she believes in god. I went to church with her once, and something the pastor said has been echoing in my mind. He talked about character and how we could all act nobly."

"Sounds like a good message. Did you understand it?"

"Not really." Then again, how much of that had been my anger blinding me to it?

"Did you believe it?"

"At the time, no. A big no. Now I would like to." *Needed* to.

"Okay, Ekon. I can't believe I'm suggesting this but write down this address."

I reached for the pen and paper on my coffee table. I did not even remember leaving it there, but fortunately, the pen worked. I jotted down the address Nika gave me, which was somewhere near the capital.

"What is this for?"

"I go here every week for Bible study. My friends and I meet up to discuss the hard questions life throws at us. If you truly want to know how to be better, then a foundation in God is a must."

I jolted back. "Are you saying I cannot be a better man unless I believe in god?"

"Yes."

She did not speak rudely, but she also did not try to make the words sweeter. I blinked, startled by her quiet admission. "And if I try on my own?"

"You will fail."

Had that not been how I had operated my entire life? On my own merits? Now failure all but swallowed me whole. "When do you meet?"

"Wednesdays at six. So, tomorrow. We each bring some food to share, and we talk afterward."

"I can only make rice and chicken."

Nika laughed. "Bring rice. That will be sufficient. We can schedule another cooking lesson later."

"Thank you."

"Sure. Do not forget. Six o'clock."

"I will be there."

I hung up. Nika was no Iris, but that was a good thing. I needed someone I could truly count as a friend who did not make me wonder if there could be more. I did not need distractions while righting my wrongs. But I would still have to figure out a way to work in the office with Iris.

I thumped my leg. Why had I kissed her?

There was no way I could walk into the office, smell her floral scent, see her beautiful happy face—though I was sure she would throw daggers my way—and work as if nothing momentous occurred in the janitor's closet.

I could still recall the feel of her plump lips, the warmth of her hands wrapped around my wrists. I dropped my head back against the couch. Now would be a good time to work out or listen to some music. Anything to stop the onslaught of memories and the wishes of what could have been.

Perhaps a bicycle would help. It would get me out of the house, keep me fit, and exercise the memories. I grabbed my wallet, mobile, and keys, then headed out the door. Surely there was a store in my neighborhood that sold bikes.

If not, I would have to find another outlet, and fast.

TWENTY-FOUR

Iris

There wasn't enough ice cream in the world to coax away the pain that gripped my heart in its talons. Coffee wasn't helping either. I set down my mug and stood to make my way to the balcony. The apartment was quiet, as my family still grappled with the time zone change. Then again, it could be because I'd woken at four this morning and no one else was up. The sting of yesterday's rejection still pricked at the back of my eyelids. My face was puffy from crying myself to sleep.

Maybe it had been a mistake not to confide in my mother when I came home yesterday. But she'd been so happy and overjoyed at all the sights she'd seen with Dad and Junior that I'd put on a brave face and kept quiet instead.

I hadn't even texted Bri about what should have been a momentous occasion—Ekon kissing the socks off me—but instead ended in a heart shattered. Of course, I could still walk around and breathe, so obviously the organ still pumped my blood. But the part that made me *me*—optimistic, often to a fault—

was MIA. I felt like I'd been drop-kicked into a hole with no chance of rescue.

I touched my lips, remembering the fullness of Ekon's pressed against mine and the pure, unadulterated joy that had beamed from my heart as if I were Leeloo in *The Fifth Element* discovering love really existed in a dark world.

Ekon had stomped on that belief, switching his emotions with a pace I couldn't even comprehend. *How?* How could he have kissed me, offered my dreams the sweetness of his touch, then crushed me in the next breath with his words?

Saying he wasn't right for me.

He's not!

I squeezed my eyes tight. Not in avoidance, but in hopeless acceptance. Ekon *wasn't* right for me. He didn't believe in God, he was an Ọlọran convict, and apparently he had decided to accept the consequences of both.

Lord, forgive me. Because as much as I professed I wouldn't change Ekon, I *wanted* to be the one to change him. To make him see the light and truth of how glorious God was and would always be. I wanted him to see that having the council punish him for his crimes—which he deserved—wasn't the end-all and that he could still become a better man.

I wanted to make him a better man.

I'm so sorry, Lord. It's not my job to be someone's Holy Spirit. It's not my wheelhouse and obviously such a foolish, foolish desire. Somehow, I had dived into believing I had some kind of power over Ekon.

Judging by the ache in my heart, he had all the power.

A tear spilled down my cheek, and I wiped it away.

"There you are." Junior pushed the sliding door farther open and stepped out onto the balcony.

"Hey." My lips trembled with the effort to smile.

"Uh-oh." Junior plopped down in the seat next to me. "What's going on?"

"What makes you think something is wrong?" I sat up, trying to appear my normal self.

"Please. It's easy to tell. You usually exude happiness, and now you reek of"—he took an exaggerated sniff—"heartache." He arched an eyebrow. "Do I need to beat someone up?"

The thought of Ekon's handsome face bruised and battered cracked the pieces that were left of my heart, and tears poured forth.

"Rissy, Rissy." Junior wrapped an arm around me.

I leaned in, pressing my face against his shoulder. I didn't know if it was because Junior was once the one I'd depended on to slay the monsters under my bed or if it was being able to unburden myself, but I pulled back, and words poured forth.

"There's this guy I've had a crush on since I first saw him, and it was ridiculous, and I *knew* it was a bad idea, but that didn't stop my heart from imagining all kinds of futures with him. Then I got to know him and developed a friendship with him, which only intensified my feelings. And yesterday, he kissed me." I stopped there, memories warming my heart before bitterness followed. "*Then* he decided that we were a bad idea, *after* he kissed me. Said we should just revert back to a—"

I stopped. I couldn't tell my brother that Ekon was my employee or at Aṣọ under orders of the royal council.

"He friend-zoned you?" Junior's voice rose.

I nodded instead of erupting more truth that Junior wouldn't want to hear. Because right now he was calm and playing the role of comforter. If he knew the whole truth, he'd probably Hulk out and step into the role of protector.

"Do you see this guy every day?" Junior asked cautiously.

Was that his way of trying to find out if we were coworkers? "Most days," I hedged.

"Hmm. What do you want to happen now?"

"It doesn't matter what I want," I replied bitterly. Ekon had made that quite obvious. "I need to be able to see him again and act like nothing ever happened."

"Ouch." Junior exaggerated rubbing the space over his heart. "That'll twist the knife in the dude."

"What? You're supposed to be on my side, Junior." I nudged him with my elbow.

"Iris." Junior squeezed my shoulder. "I don't know everything that went down, but judging from some gaps in your story, there's obviously more to tell. I'm also betting he had a moment of panic and spoke before thinking."

I couldn't hope for that. Even if Ekon felt he'd made a mistake in relegating me to employer-only, he wasn't wrong about not being right for me. We were unequally yoked. Falling in love with him would only lead to heartache. *Are you sure you haven't already?*

That was neither here nor there. Still, what more could I tell Junior in order to get a balanced answer? Not simply one I wanted to hear.

"Come on. Tell your big brother the *whole* story."

I looked at Junior. "I can't."

"Can't or won't?"

My mind traveled back to that janitorial closet. My heart in my hands, hoping Ekon would accept my love. "His name is Ekon Diallo, and he works for me." I sighed. "Well, not really, because the royal council ordered him to community service in two parts: actually helping in the community and offering me business consulting."

"What did he do to deserve that?" Junior asked quietly.

"Worked with Dayo Layeni to see that Bri didn't become queen."

"Wait, he's *that* dude?"

I nodded, staring at the sweater wrapped tightly around me. I figured Junior had kept up to date on the news. After all, his knowing Bri and my living in Ọlọrọ pretty much guaranteed he cared about the news that came out of this country. Add to that the fact that Ekon had made international headlines, and it was hard not to know who he was.

Silver lining: tourism had seen an uptick despite the craziness of the situation.

"Is he as evil as the news and social media portray him?"

"Not at all." I met Junior's gaze. "He *is* a little arrogant, but seeing as he was spoiled, entitled, and a trust-fund kid, that makes sense. However, he has changed in that arena." I couldn't divulge that his father cutting him off had been a catalyst for the transformation. My heart wrenched, remembering his despair.

I swallowed. "He's not the same man who stood before the council and received his sentencing."

Did you forget how he crushed all your dreams yesterday?

I hadn't, but I couldn't discount the life blows Ekon had been dealing with either.

Yes, you can. Ekon Diallo is not your problem. He cannot be fixed.

I gulped. "None of that matters. He's not a believer."

"Ah." Junior looked out into the courtyard that my apartment overlooked. "No chance of him becoming one?"

I shook my head. "He didn't like church."

"He went?"

"I asked. He said no, then changed his mind and went."

"Maybe he'll change his mind about God, then."

Not likely. "I can't sit around waiting for that. I can't live on hope and expectation." Look where it had gotten me so far. Single, Rocky face from tears, and anxiety over our work situation. No wonder people cautioned against workplace romances.

"But, Rissy, that's one of the things we do when we believe in God. Live on hope and expectation of His promises."

I snorted. "Ekon's not God."

"No. I'm not trying to say he is. Just saying that you've been living that way for so long."

I wrapped my arms around myself. "I can't do that anymore. It hurts too much." I didn't *want* to live that way anymore. Living in a dreamworld was a boon for fashion and a handicap for relationships.

"Rissy, you can't close yourself off."

Watch me. Except I kept my thoughts to myself. No need to freak Junior out. "I can put up guardrails and warning signs, though." *With enough armor to withstand love's calling.*

Junior's mouth turned downward. "I suppose you can."

I would. Somehow. Someway. I would prevent myself from being hurt again. *God, please show me how to guard my heart. To guard against false hope like I had with Ekon.* I paused, trying to figure out what else I wanted to say.

But my mind was numb with pain and my heart too wounded to give me any talking points.

Please, God.

Hopefully the Spirit would intercede on my behalf and make sense of my incoherent prayer. I stood. "I have to get ready for work now."

"I'll be praying for you, little sister."

"I appreciate that, big brother."

A black-and-white color-block dress that hugged my curves in a professional-looking way became the first garment in my armor. The black pearls dangling from my earrings matched my mood and served to remind me not to open up. I opted for a nude shade of lipstick and pulled my curls into an updo. Yet my stomach tossed and turned like a sailboat in hurricane-churned waters. Knowing Ekon would be at the office kept me from feeling any spark of happiness. Already, I wanted this day to be over.

I headed for the lobby of my building, thankful for the taxi I had called to take me to work. Yet the sight outside stopped me in my tracks. Ekon's car sat in the circular driveway, right behind my ride. My stomach lurched toward my chest, and I swallowed the saliva pooling in my mouth.

My mind flashed to yesterday, how he'd driven me to the hiring event. After what'd happened there, I'd assumed his offer to chauffeur me to work was null and void.

Ekon must have sensed my confusion, because he got out of the car. His long strides had him standing in front of me before I could mentally prepare. At the smell of his intoxicating cologne, my insides whimpered like an injured dog.

Buck up! Don't let him see how much his presence bothers you.

I straightened my shoulders, lifted my chin, and met his gaze head on. "What are you doing here?"

"I told you I would take you to work."

"No." I spoke slowly, steadily, and pointed at the taxi. "That's my ride."

"I am perfectly capable of driving you."

"I'm sorry. You weren't employed to chauffeur me around."

He stepped back, mouth flattening. I would *not* read into the supposed hurt in his eyes. For all I knew, his eyes always looked like that. Saying you could read a person's emotions in two colored irises was stupid and only something found in a romance book. I was *so* not feeling romantic.

"I'll see you at work, Mr. Diallo."

His Adam's apple bobbed as if he wanted to say something, but I didn't wait around to hear it. I rushed toward the taxi, praying my composure would hold up. The flood of longing that hit me at his presence took me by surprise. Images of being held in his arms, his hands cradling my face, had almost taken me out at the knees. Why hadn't the memory of his rejection kept me from feeling?

I needed to find a better place for Ekon to work today. No way I wanted to endure him sitting in *my* office, smelling like he did. *Looking* like he did. I wouldn't survive the onslaught to my emotions and past dreams.

I opened my messages and pulled up Oka's number.

Iris:
Please find a different place for Ekon to sit. I have a lot of work to do.

My finger hovered over the SEND icon. If I sent this, Oka would know something was wrong. Every employee at Aṣọ would know something was wrong. Would the council find out somehow? They were the ones who had told me to keep a close eye on Ekon. They wanted to make sure he actually worked and didn't just pretend to.

I groaned, flopping my head back on the headrest. Was there no way out? I was stuck with him. *Stuck!*

God, please help me.

TWENTY-FIVE

Ekon

This was the longest workday I had ever experienced in all my years of employment.

Sitting at my table in Iris's office had been torturous. Every noise she made pulled at my attention, but no more so than the smell of her floral scent every time she passed by my desk. Not to mention every feigned indifference while she snubbed my presence. Then there was the added surprise and pain of her choosing to ride in a taxi instead of my vehicle this morning.

She had not uttered two words to me the entire day. However, she seemed to have no problem drafting an email, detailing all the work she wished me to accomplish. Shame had heated my face each time I saw her name in my inbox. Had I really been reduced to email contact only?

"We go back to me being sent here by the council to fulfill my community service. When that is complete, I will leave and never bother you again."

I grimaced at the echo of my words. All right, so it made sense why she had reduced our communication to email.

However, that did not erase the ache in my chest whenever a message arrived. She was only ten feet away and more than capable of saying my name.

Enough wallowing. Leave.

With a nod, I shut off my laptop and straightened my area. *You can do this. Just say good-bye and offer to pick her up tomorrow.* I would hate myself if I did not try to bridge the gap my senseless words had created. There had to be some way to erase the pain I had inflicted.

"Um, Iris, I am done for the day. Do you need anything before I go?"

She made a shooing motion, her head positioned downward to stare at the fabric samples littering her desk.

It was now or never. "Would you like a ride tomorrow?"

She shook her head.

My hand fisted. "I promise you, it is not a problem for me."

She shook her head once more.

This was not working. I clearly needed to respect the boundary she had erected . . . for now. "Have a good night."

I walked out of the office, despite my good sense trying to turn me around to beg her for forgiveness. *Remember, the distance is necessary.* Plus, I *had* set all this in motion. Iris had been willing to see beyond my past, and I had stubbornly ignored her attempts to do so.

As much as I hated seeing her hurt and obviously angry, I needed to remember that I was *not* good enough for her. She needed a man like Matt Wallace. Someone who had his future mapped out in gold. What could I ever offer her?

Your heart.

I scoffed. That was probably the most damaged portion of my entire being. What did I know about relationships? Watching Father ignore Mother and her drink away her feelings had not given me a front seat to normalcy. All I knew was how to spend money to fix a problem, and that was now in shorter supply.

None of that mattered, though. I would not offer Iris damaged goods. She was worth so much more than I could ever give.

I started my car, then peeked at the address Nika had sent me. Tonight was Bible study night. Should I feel wary or nervous? Had Nika told everyone I was attending? Would they object and tell me to find someplace else to discover if god was real or not?

I did not know what to think, but I pointed my car in the right direction. Perhaps it would all work out. My thoughts turned to Iris again as I joined the other cars making their way around Ọlọrọ.

Would she ever smile again? Seeing her with a closed-off expression had been shocking. Then again, what had I expected? That moment in the janitor's closet had felt so right. Holding her in my arms had shifted something in my heart. While I had had some physical reactions to that moment—*wow, could she kiss*—it was like my whole being had been engaged in that instant. My mind had catalogued her features, my body had memorized the feel of her, and my soul . . . my soul had shouted the rightness of it all.

My hands gripped the steering wheel. There was no point in revisiting those seconds. Though part of me wanted to tuck the memory away in a box for later, I had a feeling burying it deep would be best. I feared the temptation of sliding into my old habits and expecting her to accept me how I was now, warts and all, would beckon if I kept returning to that room on the main floor.

That is not the plan. Stick to the plan.

I wanted to be a better man. I needed to be my *own* man. Not one guided by Father's dictates. Entering a relationship now would be disastrous for me *and* Iris. The truth was, she was the only woman I wanted to be with. Yet I was a man without a compass, now that Father had disinherited me. I had lived my life adhering to his standards—or trying to. Now that he wanted no part of my life and I had severed any chance with Iris, I needed to figure out what would guide me going forward.

If god was real, perhaps he could be my moral compass. Though committing my life to something unseen seemed irresponsible. Hence, I would reserve judgment and see how this Bible study went. Who knew whether it would be any better than the sermon I had sat through?

Next to Iris.

I sighed. How had she invaded so many parts of my life? How would I be able to move forward with thoughts of her tugging me backward? What would she think if she knew where I was headed?

Oh no. Tonight was supposed to be a potluck. I pulled over, stopping at a roadside stand. How had I managed to leave the rice I had cooked by my own hands on the kitchen countertop? Hopefully an order of paiis would not be unwelcome.

Fifteen minutes later, I pulled up at the address Nika had sent me. The neighborhood resembled some of the ones I had searched for a home to purchase in. The street was lined with humble homes topped with thatched roofs. There were a couple of other cars in front of the house. A red dirt path led to a wraparound porch that circled the abode. My mouth dried as I ran my palms against my slacks. I should have asked Nika how many people would be in attendance, but now it was too late. I climbed the two steps to the porch, then knocked on the wooden door.

The door opened, and Nika beamed. "Ekon. Come in, come in."

I stepped through, glancing around quickly to see how many people were here, but no one else was visible. "Am I the first to arrive?" Nausea tossed my stomach to and fro.

"*Rárá.* We are all in the kitchen."

I held out the food. "Thanks for inviting me."

"Of course." She took the paiis, studying me. "Are you okay?"

I shrugged. "Nothing I did not bring on myself."

"Oftentimes that is when we feel the worst. We believe there is no outlet for our emotions."

Was there? If I was the source of heartache and pain, did I deserve to feel any negative emotions in response? Should I not direct my sentiments to catalogue my own stupidity? I remained silent.

"Come on. You are the last to arrive."

"I apologize." My nerves made my words come out stiffly. This was all unnerving.

"Do not. I did not mean that in a negative way. We are glad you made it." She smiled. Her spiraled curls bounced with her movement.

I could not help but think of Iris's gorgeous curls. Nika's resembled black corkscrews, while Iris's had more volume, making her appear regal and graceful.

Ha. Iris was more noble than I for certain. Perhaps all the time I considered myself noble, I was the most common of all.

We entered the small kitchen, and all conversation came to a halt. The two men and two women looked at Nika then me like a gem under a loupe.

"Everyone, this is Ekon Diallo. He is joining us to learn more about God. Ekon, meet Tito, Kitan, Kamso, and Fola." She pointed to everyone around the table.

"Nice to meet you."

Fola arched an eyebrow and flipped her long braids behind her shoulder. Apparently she recognized me, knew what I had done, and—judging from the pursed lips—was not too happy I was here.

"Everyone will make Ekon feel welcome, right?" Nika asked, hand on her hip, eyes landing on Fola.

"Why would we?" she responded, gaze on Nika and not me. "It is not like he has anything to be concerned about, is it?"

Nika straightened to her full height, which was an inch or two shorter than Iris. "No one comes to Bible study ready to have their past thrown in their face, Fola. We are God's ambassadors, and we will act as such. Remember what we talked about."

Fola blinked, then studied me before speaking. "Welcome, Ekon."

"Thank you." I swallowed, trying to ignore the heat in my neck. I dipped my head, acknowledging everyone before my gaze stopped on Nika. "What exactly does 'God's ambassadors' mean?"

"You've come to the right place," Tito said in Oninan. "We will teach you everything you need to know."

"Not everything," added the man called Kamso. He rubbed his bald head. "We could never truly know everything."

"Agreed." Kitan smiled at me. She was pretty, but all I could think of was Iris.

"Have a seat, Ekon," Fola said. "We eat, then talk."

I grabbed a chair at the table and filled my plate as they passed me the dishes. Tito said grace before we all dug in. The silence felt awkward, but perhaps that was only me. Yet the memory of the introduction pressed on me, making the food turn dry in my mouth. I should not have come.

But you have to be better. This is the first step. Do not cower now.

I looked around the table. "Do you already have a topic in mind to discuss, or do you make suggestions?" I was not sure how this worked.

"Usually what is most heavy on our hearts. Nika told us you were coming," Kamso said. He glanced at Fola. "We debated whether it was a good idea or not."

Fola threw her hands up in the air. "I lost the vote, but I am sure God will fix my attitude."

I wanted to laugh at her candor, but seeing as her issue was with me, amusement seemed self-deprecating. Besides, I was too curious how Fola thought a god could fix her attitude.

"We decided that we would let this be an introduction for you," Nika said. "We want you to ask the questions that are on your heart. We figured at one point or other, most of us have probably had an experience with whatever you throw our way."

"I doubt that. Unless you are a prince or princess who got their crown stripped away, was forced to do community service, has eaten one too many humble pies in the process, or has been disinherited." My face warmed. I had not meant to announce that last part.

Tito raised his hand, his caramel skin in contrast with his black afro. "I have been disinherited."

"I have been forced to do community service," Kamso said.

"I am all about eating humble pie," Fola said with a grin.

I turned to Kitan, her honey-brown eyes taking me in. "Are you a princess?"

She laughed. "Illegitimate daughter of a prince. No crown or title, since I was deemed unworthy before I was born."

Perhaps I really was in the right place. I turned to Nika. "Sorry, I did not leave any issues for you."

She patted my back. "I am the sister-in-law to the queen. That has come with its own scrutiny."

I was sure it had. The king's family had been thrust into the spotlight with his marriage to the queen. A commoner, he had been crowned a prince when they got engaged and elevated to king after the queen's coronation.

I looked around the room and smiled. "It looks like I am in the right place."

Perhaps I could truly find the answers to the questions I sought. If not, hopefully I would at least make some true friends.

TWENTY-SIX

Iris

I couldn't wait to talk to Bri, but unfortunately, my family felt the same way. They jabbered excitedly as the guard drove us to the palace. My mom oohed and ahhed at the wrought-iron gate barring entrance to the palace.

"The guards look so impressive in their uniforms," she murmured.

The black uniforms with purple, white, and blue tribal stitching were impressive. Especially with their gold buttons and military-style hats. They reminded me a little of the United States Air Force's headwear.

"You're just checking them out," Dad joked. "After thirty years, I'm hip to your game, woman."

"Hush, Martin." Mom giggled.

Junior and I turned toward one another with twin gagging motions, but inside, the ache I'd carried around all day only intensified.

Was it so wrong to want what my parents had? To have inside jokes and be assured that, regardless if Mom actually was ogling the guards at the gate, she would never forsake my dad?

Junior must have had an idea of the direction my thoughts turned, because he reached over and squeezed my hand. I wasn't sure what to do with a kind brother. I much preferred the one who teased and told me I was hideously ugly. This version only made the tears rise to the surface that much quicker.

"Do we need to bow or curtsy, Iris?" Mom asked from the middle row.

"No. It's Bri. You'll probably embarrass her if you do."

"I'm bowing," Dad and Junior stated simultaneously.

I shoved Junior, glad he was sitting in the very back with me. "You would."

"Hey, you shouldn't have said it'll embarrass her."

"Where will we eat? Somewhere formal, or do they have a private kitchen area?" Mom continued, suddenly acting nervous. She pulled out her compact, checking her makeup.

"Most likely the family dining room." I wondered if I could pull Bri aside and spill my woes before Mom managed to hog all the time with her.

Maybe I should have texted Bri the moment Ekon broke my heart after soaring it to the sky with his kisses.

"I can't believe she's the queen. We know a *queen*, Martin." Mom squeezed Dad's arm with barely suppressed glee.

"Yes, dear."

The car came to a stop, and we exited. Still Mom continued her barrage of questions.

"What if she has kids? Then we'll know a prince or princess."

Junior chuckled. "When you meet her husband, you'll know a king, Mom."

She squealed, clapping her hands. "This is so exciting."

I shook my head in amusement. At least Mom was enjoying her vacation. I took the lead, Junior walking by my side. The guards opened the door leading to the side entrance, and I thanked them in Oninan.

"They just let you waltz in, huh?" Junior asked.

I rolled my eyes. "Bri and I have a standing date. Every Thursday the palace sends a car to pick me up. I come here, we have a girls' night, and then they drive me home. Besides, we wouldn't have been allowed through the gate without clearance."

"Ah, so we're encroaching upon girls' night." Junior turned around, walking backward. "Hear that, Dad? It's supposed to be girls' night."

Brothers. But my melancholy lightened with each teasing comment.

"Junior, hush," Mom scolded. "You're missing the beautiful decor." She gestured around, eyes wide with wonder.

"Seen one carpet hanging on the wall, you've seen them all." I repressed the urge to laugh. "It's a tapestry, big brother."

He scoffed. "Carpet."

"Tapestry." I pressed the elevator button to go up.

"What's the difference?"

"You walk on carpet, and you hang a tapestry as part of the design scheme." I pointed at the nearest artesian woven rug. "Tapestries tell a story."

"So does carpet."

This I had to hear. "How so?" I crossed my arms.

"Every fleck of dirt trapped in its fibers tells you how many people walked by, each with their own story." His mouth turned solemn as if he had just spouted some wisdom to be quoted on social media.

I laughed and pushed him into the opening elevator. "You're ridiculous."

"But you laughed," Dad stated.

"How could I not? He's ridiculous, like I said."

Mom shook her head. I could practically hear her say, *Children,* as if we had never grown up. When Junior and I were around each other, we reverted to childhood. But I supposed that was true of a lot of siblings, no matter their age.

Our conversation slowed as the elevator lifted, and then the doors opened.

Mom squealed.

Bri stood on the other side, wearing a maxi dress and looking regal. Her hair fell in soft waves, and her diamond earrings glinted in the hall's light.

"Mrs. Blakely," Bri cried.

Mom flew into her arms and swayed back and forth. "I can't believe you're a queen." Mom stepped back, taking Bri in. "You look gorgeous. Royal life suits you."

Bri smiled and placed a hand over her stomach. "I think the glow is related to something else."

Mom gasped and grabbed Dad's arm as if in shock. "She's pregnant." Her stark whisper echoed in the hall.

"We're keeping it hush for the moment, but I figured you'd love to know," Bri said.

"Uh, yeah. I was just saying how if you had a child, we'd know a prince or princess."

Bri grinned. "Counting your connections?"

"You know it."

Bri motioned for us to follow her. "Tomori is already in the dining room. I wanted the time to greet you by myself."

"You didn't have to wait for us at the elevator, Your Highness," Junior said, then bowed when Bri looked back at him.

Her face flushed as she shook her head. "Still the same ol' Junior."

He laughed. "I can't grow up just yet."

"Maybe when he hits forty," Mom quipped.

Dad laughed. "Good luck with that."

We reached the dining room, and I smiled at the skillfully carved blue doors. All the doors in the palace had a scene depicted in the wood. It was wonderful to just stop and gaze at them. The men in my family pushed forward without a thought, but Mom noticed the intricate carvings.

"Are all the doors like this?" she asked.

"Yes. Beautiful, aren't they?" I brushed my hand against the grain.

"Amazing. Can you imagine the talent required to do something like this?"

Tomori stepped forward, resting a hand on Bri's waist.

"Mr. and Mrs. Blakely, please meet my husband, Tomori. Mori, this is Deb and Martin Blakely."

"Please don't call us Mister and Missus," Mom said. "We keep telling Bri to call us Deb and Martin, but she refuses."

Mori smiled down at Bri. "I am afraid I will follow suit, then."

"Bri told us the good news. Congratulations, young man." Dad shook Mori's hand.

"Thank you, sir."

We took a seat around the rectangular blackwood table. I stared at the head of the table, remembering the first time I met the previous king, Bri's grandfather. He had passed away a few months ago after losing a battle with lung cancer. I met Bri's gaze, her own eyes sparking with tears.

She came around the table and gave me a hug. "Something's wrong with you. Do you need to talk?" she whispered.

"I do, but later."

She pulled back. "No. Let's do this now." She turned to Mori. "Hey, I want to talk to Iris for a moment. About that thing."

He nodded and gave her a smile.

Bri pulled me toward the back of the room to an exit that led to a hallway.

I studied her. "What do you want to talk about?" Surely she hadn't made up something just to get me away from everyone else.

"Well, I do want to ask you a question, but I want to know what's wrong first."

Good, because I couldn't hold back any longer. "Ekon kissed me, and it was perfection and bliss that gave me all the feels.

I would have swooned if he hadn't wrapped me in his manly arms." I shivered at the memory.

Bri's mouth dropped open. "Shouldn't you be over-the-moon happy, then?"

My lips pursed. "*Afterward*, he said it was a mistake."

"Oh, Iris. I can't believe that." She squeezed my hand, then let go.

"Neither can I." I wrapped my arms around my waist, wishing I'd worn a sweater.

"Did you talk about it? Try to find out why he felt that way?"

I nodded. "He says he's not good enough for me. Nothing I said changed his mind or seemed to matter. He didn't want to discuss it any further. Said we were just employee and employer." I hiccupped, remembering the punch of those words. "Then he had the nerve to show up at my apartment yesterday morning to offer me a ride to work." I threw my hands in the air and then swiped them against the tears that had begun falling.

The last two days had dragged, as it took every part of my being to ignore Ekon and his presence in my office.

"He hasn't said anything else?" Bri asked.

"We're not talking unless it's business-related."

"What are you going to do?"

I blew out a breath. "I need prayer, Bri. Now that I've kissed him, it's like my nerves are alerted to every movement he makes. I can't kick him out of my office without raising suspicion."

"Can you two work things out?"

I was shaking my head before she finished. "I don't *want* to. I thought my heart was safe in his hands, that he wanted the same things I did. That somehow we could overcome the obstacles stacked up against us. But I have to be smarter than that. He's *not* a believer. He doesn't have a real job. He doesn't want me . . ." My voice trailed off. At least, he didn't want me enough to find some way to overcome the odds.

Didn't you already come to this conclusion before the kiss?

Of course I had, but I had wanted to be wrong. I'd hoped that he was different than everyone assumed.

"So that's it? You don't want to take the time to breathe and work through all of your emotions?"

I nodded. "I'm done. I'm just waiting for my emotions to catch up with my head."

"It's not like you to rule with your head first."

Good! Maybe I was already learning my lesson. "I had to mature eventually."

"Iris." Bri sighed. "Leading with your heart isn't a sign of immaturity."

"How about we agree to disagree right now?"

Bri studied me, then nodded. "Okay. I'm so sorry, girl."

"Me too." I stared down at my shoes. "He's a really, really, *really* good kisser. Now I just have to pray Mr. Right can out-kiss him."

Bri laughed. "Trust you to think like that."

"What can I say? My mind is like a Jackson Pollock painting. Messy but art all the same." I waved a hand as Bri shook her head at me. "Enough about my drama. What did you want to ask me?"

"Mori and I were talking, and we want to ask if you'd be our baby's godmother."

I gasped, covering my mouth. "For real?" My voice was muffled behind my fingers.

She nodded.

"I would be so honored." I wrapped her in a hug, swaying her back and forth like my mom had done earlier.

"Thank you so much." We broke out of the hug. "And, Iris?"

"Yes?"

"If something were to happen to me and Mori, would you raise the baby?"

Chills went down my arms. Was that what being a godparent entailed? "Are there threats against you?"

"No." She shook her head. "No. Nothing to worry about. I

simply meant generally speaking. You know, *what if*. What if we were in some accident? I want to know that our child will be looked after and loved."

"You don't want your mom or one of Tomori's relatives to care for the baby?" Not that I wasn't honored, but was she really putting me above everyone else? I clasped my hands together.

"We've discussed it, and we've come to an agreement. We believe you would be the best person."

"Then yes. Of course I would."

She sighed. "Thank you so much. I'm not sure if the council has to be consulted or anything, but knowing you said yes helps. I'm sure if there are any legal hoops, we'll navigate them."

I linked my arm through Bri's as we walked back to the dining room. I wasn't sure if the royal council would let an American with no ties to Ọlọrọ—other than my business—raise the heir to the throne if something happened. However, I knew my acceptance would give Bri peace of mind, and that was good enough for me. Knowing I could be there for her if something were to happen—*Lord, please keep them safe*—made me happy. Bri was the sister of my heart, and I would do anything for her.

I wished I could find a man with similar dedication to a romantic relationship.

Patience.

Goose bumps broke across my arms at the quiet voice. A voice that didn't sound like my neurotic musings. Was God speaking to me?

Lord, You know patience isn't my strong suit.

Patience.

I heard it again, more clearly, and definitely with that Holy Spirit nudge that God was telling me something important. I gulped. I wasn't sure how to be patient, but I would learn.

Okay, Lord. I'll be patient if You'll just show me how.

TWENTY-SEVEN

Ekon

As much as I loved the hills of Etikun, it was refreshing to see the Fadaka *odò*. The river snaked all the way through Ọlọrọ to the Gulf of Guinea. Tito and Kamso had invited me on a kayaking-camping trip. It had been a couple of months since I had explored the water. After the tense situation at work and the tedious hours of community service, I was ready for a different outlet. Fortunately, the men had not minded waiting until after my service hours were finished for the day.

I tightened my life jacket strap, then pushed the kayak into the water. The hatches had already been filled with a sleeping bag, first aid kits, my clothing, and other items. We had to split the camping equipment between us, each storing the items in our own kayaks. Now all I had to do was step in and start our journey.

"You ready, Ekon?" Tito asked with a grin on his face.

"Ready."

"You ready, Kamso?" Tito asked.

233

"Yes, yes," Kamso replied. He placed some shades over his eyes. "Let us go before you float away from us with your excitement."

Tito laughed and clapped his hands together. "Then we will." He stepped into his kayak, reaching for his paddle.

I followed suit, as did Kamso.

"Remember, we stick together."

"This is not our first time, Tito," Kamso stated dryly. Then his gaze turned to me. "Right?"

"Right." I had been kayaking plenty of times with my old "friends."

Of course, I no longer owned any water-sports equipment, but Tito had an extra kayak he had happily lent me. I found these men to be different from my old crowd in ways I would never have noticed if I had not been actively searching.

They did not look down on others, always smiling and greeting people we passed. They also did not try to outdo one another to obtain accolades, something I had not even realized bothered me.

After I established the rhythm of my kayak, I looked around at the countryside. Green trees swayed with the wind, cocooning the riverbanks. The river stretched wide before us and reflected the blue sky above. Peace filled my being as I exhaled, paddling on my left, then my right.

We maintained our silence as we continued downriver. Birds chirped, and some type of animal answered in return. I breathed out, thankful for this time of relaxation. Perhaps I should have worked out a deal to buy my water-sports equipment from Father. I could at least ask for my kayak back.

"How is working for an American?" Tito's voice broke the silence.

I turned toward him. "All the employees love her."

"Do you?"

I startled, the kayak swaying with my jerky movement. I concentrated on righting myself and keeping upright. Once the ọkọ stopped rocking, I answered Tito. "Of course not. I am her ward, nothing more."

Because you made it so. I refused to have an argument with myself. What was done was done.

"You protest, but you give us no viable information. What do you think, Kamso? Is he in love with the American?"

I scoffed.

Kamso shook his head. "Please grow up, Tito. You will have him running for the hills if you keep this up."

"Ekon is not afraid. Look at how he has handled the paparazzi. They were forced to find another subject because he refused to engage with them."

"I wish the people would follow suit instead of taking pictures and posting them on social media," I said.

"I hope you do not have an alert to be notified when you get tagged on social media." Kamso's brows rose.

"I turned it off."

"Wise."

We paddled in silence until Tito pointed ahead. "That is our campsite."

I directed the kayak toward the right and soon found myself pulling the ọkọ onto shore. Tito chattered about the site and how great the outdoors was. His constant prattle reminded me of Iris.

I blew out a breath. I had almost made it a half hour without thinking of her. Not counting Tito's inquisition. Hopefully he would forget his questions while we set up the campsite.

Kamso worked silently, and before long, we had one-man tents up and a fire going. It was not for warmth but to provide us a way to cook our meal. I had already informed them of my distaste for seafood. Tito called me ridiculous, and Kamso simply shrugged. I had brought beef, keeping it separate from their fish and other cockroaches of the sea.

We settled around the fire, using nearby logs. The area had the markings of being used often for a campsite, yet it was tidy.

I wondered if another parolee had lent their hours to beautifying the grounds, or if the campers cleaned up after themselves. Fortunately, Ọlọrọ did not have any bears to worry about, but the small monkeys would peek from within the canopy to see if they could get away with thieving.

"So, Ekon." Tito paused, his fork hovering above his tin plate. "Why did you do it?" He arched an eyebrow.

I gulped, then glanced at Kamso before meeting Tito's gaze. "At the time, I believed that having an American as our next monarch would be detrimental to our values." Why? Had I really cared about Ọlọrọ, or was I simply saying what I thought people wanted to hear? "Dayo spun a good yarn, and I believed aiding her would be helping our country."

Kamso cocked his head. "Is it true that you kidnapped the queen?"

I shook my head. "No. I went on one date with her. I am not sure why it was only one. We had an amicable meal. She did not run screaming."

"Ah, but she did not smile and laugh throughout the meal either, did she?" Tito asked.

My mind flicked to Iris. How she used to laugh at my attempts to joke. How she had always greeted me with a smile. Now she presented me with her profile or the top of her head at every turn. Though, she was not the current topic.

"She did not. Little did I know that she found me lacking. Dayo believed I could try harder, and if I was not successful, then she would step in."

"That is when you broke your silence?" Kamso asked.

"Not exactly. I did not believe she would harm the queen or go further once I was out of the running to be the queen's husband. I happened to go to the palace for another matter when I overheard someone mention the trouble the queen was receiving. It was then that I put two and two together."

"Then you informed them?" Tito asked.

"Then I waited. I tried to set up a meeting with Dayo to see if she had concrete plans to get what she wanted." I shook my head. How had I ever believed she would let the matter go once Tomori Eesuola was named prince? I peered at my two new friends. "That is when I informed them of her desire to take the crown for herself."

"And they put you on house arrest? Some thank-you," Tito groused.

I froze. "You do not believe I should have been punished?"

"Oh, sure. You were going to try to overthrow an Adebayo. But I do not believe you should be doing countless hours of community service."

"It builds character," Kamso said wryly. His lips twisted, and humor filled his eyes.

"Or breaks character," I said. "I admit I thought myself above picking up trash. It has left me with some humiliating feelings." I swallowed, thinking of the first time I was photographed as well as the most recent time. "But I have learned to ignore the insults, the taunts. Instead, I have seen the anger that drives the people. I hurt my countrymen. I insulted our way of life by trying to circumvent the heir to the throne. Even if all I did was date her in the hope that she would pick me and I could become a ruler."

"Yes, about that." Kamso held up a finger. "Did Dayo expect you to kill the queen once you married?"

I shifted on the log. "She thought that I would be able to persuade her to turn over the reins to me. Then I was supposed to sign the crown over to Dayo."

Tito snorted. "Did she not know you? I cannot see you being crowned ruler, then handing over the power to that woman. Why did you even listen to her? Were you in a relationship, like your father suggested?"

My food curdled in my stomach. I took a breath. "She is my half-sister."

"What?" They echoed one another.

Tito's mouth had dropped, and Kamso wore a similar expression. Though he was the more stoic of the two, his *what* had been as animated as Tito's.

"It is not something my father speaks of. My mother is not my biological mom. She could not have children, and when my mother—Dayo's mother, as well—discovered she was pregnant, Father made a deal to raise me as his legitimate son. Despite my illegitimacy and his shame for having an affair. He figured if no one knew, then . . ."

Kamso rubbed his jaw. "The elders would go berserk if they knew the truth."

I nodded.

"So now you need us to keep quiet," Tito stated.

My innards tensed. Would they betray me? Tell the world the truth and cause problems for Father and Mother? *What do you care? They have not spoken to you in days.*

True, but they were my parents. I could not out them.

"I would appreciate your silence."

Quiet descended as I waited for someone to speak.

Finally, a grin broke across Tito's face. "Of course we will keep your confidence, my friend."

I leaned back in relief, only to fall on my backside. Apparently, logs did not come with a chairback. Kamso and Tito laughed, and soon I felt amusement bubble up and fill the forest with mirth.

We kept up a steady dialogue throughout the night, and in the morning, we kayaked back to the start of the river before parting ways. I felt restored and ready to start the week, now that I had been able to do something normal.

Still, my thoughts turned to Iris and what she was up to. I could only hope her weekend was as carefree as mine.

TWENTY-EIGHT

Iris

I wrapped my arms around Mom. "I don't want you to go," I whispered.

Spending time with my family on a daily basis, even if I'd had to go to work for a few hours, had been a complete joy. It had been a while since I had laughed so much and felt so joyful. Even Junior's teasing and Dad's terrible jokes didn't bring me down. Instead, they buoyed me until I floated past everyone at Aṣọ.

Even my neighbor, Ada, saw the benefit of my family's visit. We invited her over one night, and my parents had thought her delightful—Mom's word, not Dad's. She even kept up a witty banter with Junior. I found it strange that she had not been shy like when Ekon was present.

I guessed that went to show she wasn't his number-one fan.

Now I stood on the tarmac, saying good-bye to my people. The ones who got me and loved me just the same. My heart panged at the thought. Part of me even regretted not introducing them to Ekon. On the other hand, it would be disastrous for them to meet the man responsible for my use of extra coverage for the bags under my eyes.

Mom squeezed me extra tight. "I'm going to miss you terribly, bug. Don't worry, we'll be back."

I sighed, then pulled away. "Do you think you'll get over your fear of flying?"

"Not overnight." She brushed back one of my curls. "But I'd conquer every fear if it meant seeing you in person."

My lips wobbled into a grin. "You're the best."

"No, I am." Junior stepped toward us and wrapped his arms around us.

Then Dad joined, and we stood there, huddled like we were waiting for the quarterback to tell us the play. The only thing spoken was . . .

"I love you," I choked out.

"We love you too, bug." Dad squeezed my shoulders.

Then we all stepped back. Dad kissed my forehead before ascending the airstairs. Junior stuck out his tongue with a laugh and ran up behind Dad. Mom gulped.

"Do you need me to walk you up there?" I asked.

"No. But call me whenever you can. I don't care about the time difference."

"Love you, Mom."

She sniffed, trying to say it again. Before I could give her a hug, Dad appeared and guided her to the private jet.

I stood there, watching as the airstairs lifted. As the plane taxied. As it soared into the air and left me in Ẹwa, missing my family even though they had literally just left.

I ambled up to my ride. I couldn't go back to my apartment. Though the silence always felt welcome after a busy day at Aṣọ, the empty space would seem isolating after my family's departure.

Since it was the weekend, I had no reason to darken Aṣọ's doors and work to chase away the blues. That also meant I couldn't see Bri. I was pretty sure she and Tomori were on the mainland, meeting with other dignitaries. Yesterday, a post on social media had flagged Bri's name with a pregnancy rumor. I couldn't wait for the reporters to find out that for once they were right.

Which meant I had no one to talk to, no one to hang out with. Ada had to work, and I didn't know anyone else in my apartment building. I hopped into the car and requested the driver take me home. Maybe by the time I neared, I could figure out a better place to pass my time.

Halfway home, my cell rang. Matt's number flashed across the screen.

"Hello?"

"We have a problem."

"What's wrong?" My stomach twisted. Was it Aṣọ? Something else?

"One of the marketing assistants spotted a typo in the fashion show announcement."

I gasped. "The one going out in the mail Monday?"

"The very one."

"What was misspelled? How did the copy editor miss it?"

"I'm not sure, but you'll be happy to know I fired her."

"What?" I screeched. The driver swerved, eyes widening as he met my gaze in the rearview mirror. I mouthed *sorry*, then focused on Matt. "Why on earth would you do that?"

"She made a mistake. We can't have mess-ups of this magnitude happening close to launch."

"You're not part of HR, Matt. You have no authority to do that." Not to mention he opened us up to a lawsuit for wrongful termination.

"I was trying to be helpful. You need to ensure you're hiring the right kind of people."

My nose flared. *The nerve!* I had hired the perfect people to operate the human resources department. To insinuate that I didn't know what I was doing pricked at my desire to do right by my employees and my insecurity that I had bitten off more than I could chew.

"Matt, please call my secretary Monday morning and make an appointment with me." I used my most professional voice despite the rising heat in my face.

"Are you . . . are you *mad* at me?"

"You fired a person when you had no authority." I stopped. "Like I said, make an appointment with Oka, and we will discuss this further."

"I can't believe this. But if that's what you wish."

I rolled my eyes.

"What are you going to do about the typo?"

"Fix it, obviously. We'll get a reprint."

"That's going to cost money if it's a rush job."

I did *not* need him to mansplain everything. "I got this."

"Fine." He hung up.

Not a moment too soon. "Ugh." I stretched out the word, since I couldn't very well scream in the cab's interior. I didn't want to cause my driver to crash because the people I worked with were being less than smart.

Lord God, help me. I'm furious! How could Matt even think he had the power to terminate my employees? The gall of that man. It burned me up and made me want to stomp my feet in fury. Instead, I had to try to be prim and proper in the back of this cab.

I stared out the window, hoping the scenery would calm me down. Even though the island landscape created a relaxed atmosphere, the greenery, colorful homes, and roadside stands did not calm me down.

I peered at the driver. "Could you take me to the Etikun chapel?" I asked in stilted Oninan.

Amusement glinted in his eyes. "I would be happy to, Ms. Blakely."

"Ẹ seun."

Soon the white building appeared. Twin white steeples flanked the red-tiled roof. White crosses affixed to each steeple gleamed in the sun's light. Stained glass filled the arched windows. When the sun shone through the glass, colors danced within the sanctuary. It always made the artsy side of me smile with delight. Plus, I was always reminded how the Bible described God as many gemstones, and seeing those colors across the floor, on the backs of pews, made His presence feel very alive. Something I needed desperately to feel right now.

I thanked the driver once he came to a stop and exited the vehicle. Sometimes the church was locked up, and other times they had meetings in it. I prayed that someone was inside so I could sit, soak in God's presence, and let Him renew my mind.

There seemed to be so many things pricking at my dreams. Matt acting out of his purview and trying to sabotage my work.

No, that was being dramatic, even for me.

I pulled on the door and sighed when it opened.

Matt wasn't malicious, but apparently he was slow to understand I had hired him to make marketing decisions and marketing only. Firing a copy editor didn't fall under his list of duties. Telling the board that I needed new electrical wiring on the second floor hadn't been his business either. Thankfully, a new investor had been willing to cover the expense. I was going to be forced to talk to Matt on Monday, and that turned my insides out.

Working with Ekon still ranked number one for awkward and torturous all at the same time, though. His cologne, his presence, called to me. Since I'd stopped talking to him verbally and only communicated via email, it was like his work efforts had increased. As if he wanted my attention. But that was ridiculous. Thinking that kind of hope-filled direction was what had landed me in the rejected/unwanted pile.

I sank onto a pew and stared at the podium. "Lord, please bring peace to my storm."

My company had officially entered a pandemonium level of drama as each department worked on a checklist to get our own fashion show off the ground. If there was a typo in the flyers, that could set us back. How was I supposed to find someone who could provide a quick turnaround on a Saturday? The island came alive as people left their work worries alone and celebrated leisure on the weekend.

I couldn't let the flyers be delayed. And I had to figure out a way to get my copy editor back without alarming the board regarding Matt's behavior. I dropped my head into my hands, resting my elbows on my thighs.

Lord, please help.

"Are you okay, madam?"

I peeked through my fingers and sat up. "Àlùfáà!" The pastor! Had I disturbed him? "I'm sorry. Is it okay if I'm here?"

"Yes, madam. Yes. Please sit."

I sat back down, smoothing my skirt under my legs.

"You are troubled, yes?"

I nodded, staring at my hands. "I have a lot I'm dealing with." I winced. I hadn't meant to switch to English, but I guessed that was my default setting.

"Ah, a weary mind," he stated in my native tongue. "Have you come to seek rest from our Father?"

"I have."

"I find that being still is a skill we must train for. It is not one we are born with."

"Really?" I thought of women like Bri, who seemed to have it all together. Who had a peace, a stillness about them that steadied me. "Are you sure?"

He threw his head back. "I am. For some it may be easy to learn. For others it is much, much more difficult."

"I belong in the latter camp."

"Ah, Ms. Blakely. You are a mover and a shaker."

I didn't think so. I just did what I felt led to. I said as much, transitioning between English and Oninan.

"Ms. Blakely, you can converse in English if it is best for you. I understand."

I sighed in relief. "Thank you so much."

"And thank you for all you are doing in Etikun. Many of the people are happy to be employed. To have health benefits. To know money is going into the national retirement savings. You have allowed them to feed and clothe their families. That is no small thing."

"I feel like I could fail at any moment."

"Good," he boomed.

I gaped. "What do you mean? How is that good?"

"What did that feeling prompt you to do?"

My brow furrowed, and he motioned around the room. "You mean come here?" I asked.

"That is it exactly. You did not stay away but sought to be closer to the Lord. You feel your frailty. Your weakness. But you know the source of your strength. That takes great character and shows me you do know how to be still. To seek rest. To lean on the Lord."

Tears filled my eyes. His words were like a balm to my weary soul. I had not realized that coming here would be considered a step in the right direction. My only thought had been to gain peace.

"I'm weak," I murmured.

"We all are, Ms. Blakely."

I nodded slowly. "I really appreciate you stopping to talk to me."

"Anytime. Perhaps next time you come on a Sunday, you will stay for the feast afterward."

"There's a feast?" I thought everyone left.

He stood. "Yes, madam. It is the next road over. That is where we all go. I apologize that you did not know."

"It's okay." And it was. Knowing that I had been invited into the church family lifted my spirits.

I pulled up the app for a rideshare and waited patiently in the stillness of the chapel.

TWENTY-NINE

Ekon

It had been two weeks since I kissed Iris. Two weeks of trying to forget the feel of her lips on mine. Two weeks of being on the receiving end of her cold shoulder. And two weeks since my first Bible study with Nika and the others.

I wished I could say that I had been magically transformed—*wait, magic is a no, right?*—but I did not feel any different. I still did not know if god existed, and I still did not think I was good enough for Iris.

Except now was not the time to dwell on the torture seeing her at work inflicted on me. My eyes could not help but note the elegant way she dressed, the smile she graced on others, or the joy she put into each endeavor.

Whenever she interacted with others, her face beamed in full wattage. Yet as soon as we were alone, her lips dropped their curve, and not a word passed between us. Our email communications had become the custom.

I both hated and loved going to Aṣọ. Hated because Iris continued to ignore me but loved because I saw her five days a week. Plus, I was aiding her in the endeavor to turn Aṣọ from an idea to a reality. The seamstresses from the hiring event were in full collaboration mode as they worked to bring Ọlọrọ its first fashion show. Every employee had been tasked with a specific undertaking as time dwindled.

In fact, my appointment with one of the loan specialists at Diallo Enterprises to discuss the jewelry we required for the event was coming soon. I had thought for sure that Father would instruct someone to cancel the meeting, but it remained scheduled.

Today, however, I had a more significant appointment. The Etikun elders had finally granted me a meeting—thanks to Father—to finish the task Yemi Ladipo had assigned to me. Iris was aware I would miss a few hours in order to get this accomplished, since I had informed her via email and verbally confirmed it before leaving. She made the same maddening shooing motion she did every time I wished her a good evening.

I smoothed my hand down my navy-blue tunic. My slacks and button-down shirt had been traded for a traditional Ọlọran outfit. Hopefully my nod to our heritage would soften the elders toward me. I walked up the sidewalk to Mr. Kalu's house. He retained the rank of chief elder and was the shoo-in for the Etikun seat at the royal council, in my opinion. A letter from the tribal leader had been sent to my home, instructing me to arrive here, where all the other Etikun elders, which included some princes, would gather.

My stomach knotted as I knocked on the door. Better to get the appointment over with before I could make myself ill with the unknown.

The door opened, and I bowed before the lowest-ranking elder who greeted me.

"Come in," he said.

I stepped over the threshold, my eyes adjusting to the dimmer light. This was my first time attending an elder meeting, despite my previous title of prince. Father had always sat in the Diallo seat. Even then, I had been unnecessary. My eyes made their way around the room, but I did not see him. Was that because I was here?

Every eye fixated on me, and nothing but air dared make a sound. I dropped to my knees and lowered my head to the floor in honor. Then I rose and greeted the elders and princes one by one in Oninan and thanked them for allowing me to attend.

"You have the floor."

Jaya Kalu pointed to the empty space within the circle the elders had created. My mouth dried as I moved forward. The paper Dayo had written and signed rested in my pants pocket, but now I wished it rested in my hands. Perhaps then my fingers would have something to grip instead of curling into my palms. I would probably have half-moons indented in my skin once this meeting finished.

"*Eni baba*, Alàgbà Yemi Ladipo tasked me with an errand on behalf of the royal council and our *olorì* Brielle Eesuola Adebayo."

"Go on."

I swallowed. "It has come to their attention that there are those in Etikun who fear more tribal members conspired with Dayo Layeni. The council believes this to be the reason the Etikun seat on the royal council remains empty. Therefore, they tasked me to find out the truth from Ms. Layeni herself. She detailed the actions of those involved in this letter"—I pulled the envelope from my pocket—"which she signed, as well."

"How did you come by this letter?" Elder Kalu asked.

"I went to the prison to petition her to write it. She signed the paper as proof she was not under duress and as verification she wrote the contents." I could recall the smells of the prison as if I were standing there right now. It would be a while before that visit struck itself from my memory banks.

"Was she offered leniency for her cooperation?" another elder asked.

"She was not."

He snorted. "I cannot believe you would dare show your face, considering your own crimes."

Neither could I. My original intent had been to find myself back in favor with those who had power over my current situation. Now I simply wanted to help the queen, who had seen something in me that eluded my vision. Perhaps I wanted to be worthy of her grace. To show Queen Adebayo my heart was not as damaged as all believed.

And for Iris.

I cleared my throat. "Eni baba, I would not have dared come before you if not on the behest of Alàgbà Ladipo. I am not fit to stand before you, considering the aid I gave Ms. Layeni."

"Let Ekon Diallo read the letter," Jaya Kalu instructed. He eyed me. "Some people deserve second chances."

My heart thumped in my chest. If Iris had not told him that, would he be vouching for me today? Another plus for her goodness.

"Very well, then. Read the letter," an elder pronounced. The others nodded in agreement.

I pulled the sheet out of the envelope, unfolding the trifold. I took a deep breath. *If you are real, please help them understand.*

"'To the elders of the Etikun tribe,'" I read in Oninan. "'When I was a little girl, my mother wove tales of how I was a princess and deserved to rule a kingdom that could benefit from my leadership. She told me so often that I began to believe it was true. But we only lived in the palace because she worked as a housekeeper and not because she was married to the prince. When I became a teen, I questioned her about the story she used to tell and if there was any truth in it.

"'She assured me my father indeed was royalty. She died months later from cancer. By that time, I had become acquainted with her duties as head housekeeper. I assumed some of her responsibilities despite the palace assigning someone else to her role. I then worked myself up to a secretarial position for the princess we now know as Queen Brielle Adebayo.'"

I cleared my throat and continued. "'When I learned about the princess, I was already in a relationship with Jomi Oladele. He informed me they would let her become crown princess. It was then that I hatched my plan to take the throne. I blackmailed Jomi into helping, threatening to inform his wife of our relationship. He then added Ekon Diallo to the list of potential suitors for the princess to consider for her future husband at my request.'"

My heart pounded, and I dared not look up as I continued reading Dayo's letter. "'I urged Ekon to make himself desirable to the princess, as I was well aware of the trouble she had experienced on her first two dates with other contenders. I wanted him to succeed. I stressed that she was detrimental to our Ọlọran values so he would be motivated to do his best.'"

"And were you motivated?" Jaya interjected.

I looked up from the paper. "I was for many reasons."

"What reasons?" a prince asked.

This was where it got tricky. Did I divulge everything or a piece of the whole?

I licked my lips. "My parents both wanted me to marry. My father had been dropping hints but had kept quiet as to who he thought I should wed. When I told him I was going to go on a date with the future queen, he was overjoyed. He gave me tips and told me not to mess it up."

Yet I had anyway. She had found something lacking in me, as everyone eventually did.

"Is that all? Parental expectation?" Mr. Kalu asked.

I swallowed. "Ms. Layeni is my half-sister."

"What is this?" one of the princes cried in outrage.

"My father had an affair with Ms. Layeni's mother. The product of that affair was me. He was ashamed of his actions and what that meant for his seat with the elders. I was told not to divulge our private business. It was a desire for kinship that led me to listen to Ms. Layeni."

"Did you believe your *sister* would harm our queen?" Mr. Kalu curled his lips in disgust.

"Never. When I agreed to be added to the queen's list, Ms. Layeni did not seem unstable. I believed all the lies she told me. It was only later that I began to worry. That was when I informed the palace of her intentions."

Glances were exchanged, but mouths remained shut.

I sighed. "Should I continue reading?"

"No," Mr. Kalu barked. "Pass us the letter."

I handed it to the man who had opened the door. One by one, the elders and Etikun princes read Dayo's words as I stood there, waiting for their next steps. When they had all scanned the document, stares and rumblings began to fill the room. I resisted the urge to fidget. Instead, my hands rested behind my back as I opened and closed my fingers. I had to get the nervous tension out somehow.

After minutes of whisperings, Jaya Kalu met my gaze. "Ekon Diallo, we will inform the council of our vote. Please take your leave so we may continue our deliberations."

"Thank you for your time, eni baba." I bowed.

"Before you go, may I impart some wisdom?"

He wanted to share something with *me*? "Please."

"Do *not* follow the path of your father. Aspire to be your own man and the one God created you to be. Understood?"

I nodded, too stunned to do anything else.

He waved a hand, effectively dismissing me. I turned and exited the house, exhaling loudly when the door closed behind me. I breathed in the fresh air, thankful I had survived a meeting in front of them.

I pondered his words admonishing me not to follow Father. Had the elders felt that way before I informed them of my parentage, or did they not hold my father in high regard now that they realized he had raised an illegitimate son to be a prince?

I shook my head. How had I never considered how others saw my father? I had operated under the assumption that he was well-respected wherever he went. That Diallo Enterprises was one of the best businesses in the country.

Yet with one piece of advice, my wheels were turning and my views upended. As for god, even the elders believed he existed. Was I the only one who did not?

"Is there something wrong with me?" I whispered.

The questions I had raised at Bible study had been answered, but the answers they gave had not resonated with me. Sure, there was a logic to sin entering the world and explaining why we had murderers and the like. But believing that god sent his son to pardon the sins of all who believed in him was a little hard to swallow.

How did he know if any of us were worthy?

I make you worthy.

Chill bumps broke out along my arms. The words were as clear as day in my mind. Questions rose one after another, but I pushed them aside, pulling that voice and statement to the forefront.

Could I really be worthy of redemption? And if so, what did I have to do?

THIRTY

Iris

Going to the Àláàfíà market was one of my favorite
things to do on a Saturday. The drive down to the
southern coastal capital town rejuvenated me. The
beauty of Ọlọrọ could be perfectly explained using a postcard
or a viral Instagram photo.

The booths at the market made my heart go pitter-patter as
I imagined the goods I would buy and fill my home with. The
colorful canopies beckoned me to explore all they had to offer.

"Anything specific you want?" Ada asked me. She shielded
her eyes with her hand as we walked through the market entrance. Her presence had been a godsend. It was nice to have
a friend to shop with, since my BFF had queen duties and still
dealt with morning sickness. I also appreciated getting to know
Ada because it eased the ache of missing my family.

Keeping busy and staying away from my quiet flat helped me
ignore the intense quiet. Unfortunately, with the whole Ekon
fiasco, I couldn't shake the blues. Joy was very absent in my
day-to-day life. It didn't help that my heart refused to forget
how kissing him felt like coming home.

Working with him day in and day out was the worst. I'd been texting Bri for strength. Ada and I avoided all talk of Ekon. Since he wasn't my boyfriend, I didn't feel the need to address the elephant in the room.

"Whatever catches my eye. You?" I asked her.

"I have a few items on my list, and that is it. Should we split up?"

I saw a booth selling yams. *Yum.* I could make a good lunch or dinner with them. "Sure. I'm going to buy a couple of yams."

She waved and sauntered away as I turned to the vendor. I bought two and thanked the merchant before meandering down the aisle and checking out the other produce. I pulled up short as Ekon and another man walked toward me from the opposite direction.

Eek! My fight-or-flight response kicked in, ratcheting my pulse to tachycardia ranges. Only pure panic froze me to the spot. What was I supposed to do? Could I truly ignore him outside of work? Would he try to speak to me? I hitched my bag over my shoulder to turn, but he spotted me.

Drat! I froze, waiting to see what he would do.

He slid his hands into his pockets. The man talking next to him noticed Ekon's distracted focus. He followed his gaze to me and grinned. They began walking once more, right in my direction.

Great. I was going to have to talk to the man who had been plaguing my days and nights.

Ekon's Adam's apple bobbed as he neared, and he stopped a couple of feet away. "Iris," he rasped.

I nodded.

His tongue darted out, and it took all of my willpower not to stare at those full lips. Though his warm brown eyes weren't much better at keeping me from wilting at his feet.

"Iris," he started again. "This is Tito. Tito, this is Iris Blakely. She's the owner of Așo."

"Very nice to meet you," I said, grade-school manners kicking in.

"Nice to meet you too." Tito had a small afro, his skin the same shade as mine, but his accent was definitely Ọlọran.

"How do you know Ekon?" I asked, keeping my eyes on Tito.

"Oh, he goes to my—" His eyes bulged as Ekon elbowed him in the ribs. Oninan was angrily whispered, and then Tito straightened. "We're friends."

"Oh." Hadn't all of Ekon's friends abandoned him? Had this one reached out to bridge the gap, or was he a new pal?

None of it mattered, but something had to break the silence. "What are you two up to today?"

"Ekon offered to cook dinner tonight, so we decided to get some fresh food."

My gaze flicked to Ekon's. He knew how to cook now? I looked at Tito. "Are you teaching Ekon how to cook?"

He laughed. "I am not that skilled. Nika is his teacher."

Nika? Tomori's sister, Nika? The words caught in my throat as my heart beat a hundred miles a minute, imagining the two of them cozied up in the kitchen. I thought they had only met for one lesson so he could invite his parents over. How many lessons had she given him?

I whirled and stomped away, too hurt to say good-bye or anything else.

"Iris."

I halted at the pain in Ekon's voice. A rush of air caressed my bare arms, and then Ekon stood before me.

"Please do not go. I know you want nothing to do with me but listen to me. Please."

I wrapped my arms around my waist and started tapping my foot. I couldn't look at him. If I did, I would lose all composure.

"Nika is a friend. She has been helping me with cooking and other things."

Other things? My head almost rose to ask the question, but I clenched my teeth and made myself remain still.

"Everything I have done since that day has been to better myself."

That day? Was that what he was calling it? "So being with me would have been detrimental to you?" Tears sprang to my eyes as I realized I'd voiced the question out loud.

"No," he rasped. "No," he stated stronger. "Being with me would have been detrimental to *you*. I will not do that to you."

My head snapped up. "You can't make other people's decisions for them, Ekon. That's not how relationships work."

"We are not in a relationship."

I reared back.

He muttered an oath and dug his chin into his palm. "I did not mean that like it sounded."

"Yeah, color me surprised if I believe that."

"How can I make you understand?" He stepped forward.

I held out a hand. "Don't bother. Like you said, we're not in a relationship. You don't owe me any explanations. You're almost done with your service hours. Then you'll be rid of me."

"I do not—" He clamped his mouth shut. "I will not bother you anymore."

I almost asked what he'd been going to say originally. *Almost.* I'd like to think myself wiser, which was why I studied Ekon's face one last time, then turned and walked away.

Tears streamed down my cheeks, but I refused to wipe them away in case he watched me go. He couldn't know how much he'd hurt me. Was *still* hurting me.

And why was that? We hadn't dated. Why was my stupid heart so invested in this man?

Because you're a dreamer. You've always been a dreamer.

When I was far enough away, I wiped my face and texted Ada. I hated to cut our trip short, but I needed to leave.

And Lord, if You're taking any requests, can I get another personality trait? Maybe being a cheerful giver. I had been called stingy by Junior a time or two. *Or maybe give me that teaching quality.* I shuddered. No, I would leave that to Bri. *I don't know, Lord. Something other than this head-in-the-clouds persona. It's trite, and I'm getting on my own nerves.*

"Iris."

I groaned, spinning on my heel. Ekon bent over as if he had exerted all his energy chasing after me. I doubted it. "What?" I snapped.

"Do you need a ride home?" He squinted up at me.

"No." I waved my cell in his face. "I came with a friend."

He straightened. "You did?"

"Ada. My neighbor."

His shoulders dropped, and my phone chimed. I peered down at her text, dismay filling me. Apparently, Ada had run into her old boyfriend. She wanted to grab lunch with him. She wondered if I could possibly find a ride.

Ugh. She'd already informed me of his *one-who-got-away* status. I couldn't be the cause of her losing another chance.

Iris:
Sure. Have fun.

Ada:
I hope to.

"Is there a problem?" Ekon asked.

"Nothing a taxi won't fix.

"That is so expensive. Let me help you."

"I have the funds."

A pensive look changed his countenance. "How about I give you a driving lesson today?"

My heart leapt, but I swatted it down like Serena Williams facing a tennis ball. "What part of not bothering is this?"

The color drained from Ekon's face. He looked like someone had socked him in the stomach. *My* words had done that. Remorse filled me. "Ekon . . ."

He gulped. "You are right. It is just that you taught me how to make an omelet. I owe you a lesson in exchange."

I wanted to ask what foods Nika had taught him to make. I couldn't believe how insanely my heart pounded with jealousy.

"That was all. I simply wanted to be a man of my word."

Ugh! Kill me with the *woe-is-me* attitude. But my heart-strings fell in line as if commanded by a master puppeteer. Still, I couldn't cave. "That's okay. You're with your friend."

"Tito does not mind." He pointed over his shoulder. "He saw another friend and wanted to talk to her for a bit. I know a place where we can go close to here for a lesson."

What were the odds Tito was with Ada? I bit my lip. I couldn't be in a car with Ekon, but I was so very tired of paying for taxis. It would be wonderful to save money and just purchase a car. Then again, a guard at the palace had offered to teach me as well. Though I thought his request was more of a flirtation than a genuine offer of help.

"One lesson. That is all you need. You will not be sorry," Ekon added.

I eyed him skeptically. "One lesson?"

"One."

"What if you're wrong?" It always took me a while to learn a new task.

"Then you can tell the council I did not complete my community service hours in a satisfactory manner."

Oh, that *was* tempting. Though I would never lie just to make someone else miserable. Even if a part of me wanted to see Ekon miserable.

What do you call his expressions at work?

"Fine."

260

His half grin appeared, and disappeared just as quickly. "Follow me."

Ekon led us out of the market and to the grassy parking area. He unlocked his door, then opened the passenger side. I held my breath so I wouldn't smell his cologne as I passed him to get in the car.

I wasn't sure what I would do once he was sitting in the driver's seat.

When he got in, I lowered the window. If I took shallow breaths, maybe I would smell nothing. Unfortunately, that wouldn't keep me from remembering the warmth of his embrace. I even missed the awful jokes he used to tell at the end of the day.

I simply missed talking to him, really.

"This will be easy. You will see."

"It better be," I muttered.

He chuckled. "I never thought I would see you fear something."

I swung around. "I'm not afraid of driving."

"Sure."

The word held the right tone, but I didn't believe his sincerity. "I'm not."

"Mm-hmm."

A few minutes later, he stopped in the middle of an empty lot. He got out of the car, then opened my door.

"What are we doing?"

"Switching spots. Go sit in the driver's seat."

"Now?" I squeaked.

"Yes, ododo mi. How else will you learn?"

I fought a shiver at the low tone of his words and the tenderness in his eyes. I didn't understand what game he was playing. I skirted around his body and the front of the car and slid into the front seat.

He pointed to the pedals below. "Brake. Gas."

261

"Simple enough."

"Pull your seat up so you can easily navigate the pedals with only your right foot."

I did as Ekon instructed and continued to listen as he pointed out parts of the car that I needed to use. I knew most of it. I had watched movies, after all. Still, felt foreign sitting behind the wheel, knowing I'd be expected to put the car in DRIVE and navigate like I knew what I was doing. *One lesson?*

After a few minutes, that was exactly what Ekon told me to do.

I swallowed and maneuvered the gear into DRIVE, then slowly took my foot off the brake. The car inched forward, and my stomach swooped for my toes. "Oh my goodness!"

Ekon chuckled. "Go ahead and ease your foot on the gas."

"Are you sure?"

"I am sure."

"What if I crash?"

"Into what?"

I laughed. I mean really laughed for the first time in weeks, because there was literally nothing out here to hit. I pressed the gas, and the car jolted forward. I yelped, slamming my foot against the brake.

Silence filled the interior as I stared out of the windshield, refusing to see what Ekon thought of my horrid driving.

"It is all right," he murmured. "You do not have to press the pedal that hard. Try again."

Every instruction Ekon gave me, I followed. Soon I was making circles in the parking lot as I laughed with delight. I could drive! I wouldn't have to call a taxi.

"This is so much fun."

"Good. Now you are going to take us out of this parking lot and turn right onto the road."

I gripped the wheel. "There are cars out there."

"Yes. In order to see how you behave with other vehicles, you will need to drive with them. Do not worry, I am here."

Suddenly every nerve ending prepped to do the opposite. Because the moment I got out of this car, he would drive away again. Convinced we were better apart.

Maybe you are? Operation Ignore Him needed to continue.

"You can drive yourself home." Ekon's voice broke through my musings. "Tomorrow I will bring you a test booklet so you can learn the rules in order to pass the Ọlọran test."

"Okay."

We didn't talk much once I turned out of the parking lot, but Ekon was right. I could drive, and when I turned into an empty spot in front of my apartment building, I squealed with happiness.

I placed the gear in PARK and turned to Ekon, wrapping my arms around him. "Thank you so much. I can't believe I just drove for an hour."

"It was my pleasure." Warm air caressed my ear as he spoke quietly.

I jolted back, quickly escaping his arms. It was time to leave before I forgot my plan. I made my good-byes and headed inside.

Once in my apartment, I leaned my head against the door and closed my eyes.

Lord God, it's me again, coming to You with the same prayer I've been asking since the Incident. Please take these feelings from me. Please change me. I don't want to be a dreamer anymore. I can't take the pain.

Because when some other guy—*would I really get over Ekon?*—failed to live up to my expectations, I would only experience more hurt.

THIRTY-ONE

Ekon

If I thought a little driving lesson would thaw the atmosphere in the office, I was mistaken. We were back to email communication and frosty air.

> Dear Mr. Diallo,
>
> We have a financial workshop scheduled today for our new hires at ten this morning. When I went to add it to your calendar, it was denied. Do you know the reason for this discrepancy?
>
> Respectfully,
> Iris Blakely,
> Owner and CEO of Aṣọ

I frowned—because of the scheduling error or the frigid tone of her email, I could not decide. With a click, I opened my work calendar and shifted to today's schedule. Written in bold letters at ten o'clock were the words **Diallo Enterprises.**

Oh no. I exhaled, rubbing the bridge of my nose.

When I called to verify the meeting with my father's company,

I had been informed that they would come to Aṣ̣ọ, not the other way around. Apparently, Father wanted *no* chance of running into me.

I turned my head to stare at Iris. Should I walk over to her desk and tell her the reason for the conflict? Would she speak to me civilly or maintain the silence she had started by ignoring my greeting this morning? She had even chosen to send me an email to thank me for the driver's manual I had placed on her desk.

Email it is. I clicked REPLY and typed up a response.

Dear Ms. Blakely,

I do apologize for the conflict in scheduling. It was not my intention to disrupt the schedule, but the jewelers from Diallo Enterprises will be arriving to discuss our needs for Aṣ̣ọ's fashion show. Will you be able to attend the meeting? Do I need to reschedule?

With regrets,
Ekon Diallo

I paused, wondering if I should add a title below my name. I never had in the past, but I was feeling a little unsure. I wrote *Consultant by Order of the Ọlọrọ Ilé Royal Council,* pressed SEND, then went back to my work.

Iris gasped.

Had she just read my email? I stared at my inbox, waiting for a new one to show up. Instead, the sound of her clicking heels reached my ears. My body tensed, and I slowly turned in my seat.

"Is your father coming?" Iris's ebony eyes showed concern as she stopped at my desk.

"I doubt it."

She bit her lip. "He hasn't called you?"

"No."

"Your mother?"

I shook my head, half amazed she was talking and half amazed she seemed to still care.

"If I attend the meeting, who will oversee the financial workshop?" she asked.

"The COO or someone in his department?"

Her nose scrunched up. "How long do you think the meeting with Diallo will last?"

"At least an hour."

She blew out a breath. "What if we push the financial workshop back an hour? Those attending could continue with their work and then go to the conference room at eleven instead of ten."

"If that is what you wish to do."

"Yes. I want us both in that meeting."

"All right." I tapped my pen against the desk. "Do you want to show me the drawings of the pieces you plan to showcase at the fashion show?"

Her eyebrows shot up. "Why?"

"That way I can guide the men to offer the right jewels if they do not do so themselves."

"Oh." Her mouth parted.

I blinked, then dragged my gaze away from her pink lips. For the past two weeks, she had been wearing ruby-red lipstick, but today her lips were a soft shade of pink that made her mouth seem all the more kissable. I tugged at my collar.

"I'll get those sketches right now."

I forced myself to stare at my desk and not watch her walk away. *You are not good enough for her. Not worthy.*

Yet I could not help but remember that voice that had claimed to make me worthy. Was it merely referring to redemption? To salvation in Christ? Or could I one day be worthy of a woman like Iris? I snorted. Not *like* Iris, but *Iris*?

She came back with the sketches, and I studied the designs. I was not a fashion connoisseur and had no idea if the elite would find these designs worthy. However, they evoked a sense of Ọlọran pride in me as I looked at each sketch.

"These are stunning," I said.

"You think so?" she asked quietly.

"I do."

"Will looking at them help you know what jewels to ask for?"

My mind was already thinking of ideas. "Yes."

"Good."

I turned to the next picture. A pregnant model graced the page. Rumor said the queen was pregnant. An idea sparked. "Are you going to showcase a wedding gown?"

"What?"

Hearing the shock in her voice, I looked up. "You designed the queen's, right?"

"As well as her Independence Day gown."

"Maybe you should do another wedding gown for the show. The fashion world loves matrimonial garb, correct?"

Iris tapped her chin, mumbling under her breath. Her eyes widened, and she whirled around, heels clacking as she scurried to her desk. She grabbed her sketchbook, pencil flying over the page.

I stared, mesmerized by her focus. When I first started working for Diallo, I had dabbled in jewelry design. Father quickly prevented me from continuing in that vein. Diallo men did not design jewelry; we ran the industry and hired people to do that menial task.

That thought took me back to the time when I had watched countless videos of jewelry design. Learned what paired together. What tools were imperative. What would take Diallo Enterprises to the next level.

I had actually enjoyed the process. Could I afford any of the tools on my current budget, or would that be considered a frivolous purchase? Could I sell the things I made? I shoved the questions aside and continued my current work.

There were only a few more weeks of consulting before I would be left solely with my community service hours. No longer would I be able to see Iris on a day-to-day basis. We would no longer be forced to endure the awkward silences.

And you will be unemployed.

I tried to hide my wince. My unknown future was beginning to keep me up at night. I had asked the Bible study group what they thought I should do. Kitan told me to polish up my résumé and hope for the best. Fola simply said good luck. Nika had offered to share the résumé around. Tito and Kamso both gave me sympathetic glances and pats on the back. Although they did not voice their thoughts, it was apparent they believed a royal council pariah would not be hired.

Perhaps selling jewelry on my own would be a viable option. I could work under a different name—completely legal and necessary—and earn an income that way. Definitely something to ponder.

A tiny part—well, more significant than I was willing to admit—wanted to continue working for Iris. I thought we made a good team, and I was good with financials on a scale like Aṣọ's. Unfortunately, I had already made myself her nemesis. I supposed that wish was just that.

Soon the clock struck ten o'clock. Iris picked up her notepad, and I straightened my tie, nerves gripping me. We strolled silently down the hall toward the conference room to greet the representatives from Diallo Enterprises. Before she could reach for the door handle, I opened the glass door and held it for her. She took position at the head of the table as I settled in the spot to her right.

"Security will escort them up here, right?" I asked.

"Correct."

I exhaled. Who would Father send? Would he treat Iris like a top-notch client or as if she were barely worth Diallo Enterprises's time?

My questions were answered when security showed up with two guests. Jide nodded at Iris as he let in my father and Zoro Njoku, his right-hand man.

I shot to my feet, my stomach twisting itself into a pretzel. "Ms. Blakely, may I introduce Ise Diallo and Zoro Njoku from Diallo Enterprises."

Iris stiffened at the mention of my father's name.

"Gentlemen, this is Iris Blakely, owner and CEO of Aṣọ."

She bowed before them, and they dipped their heads in acknowledgment. "Have a seat, please," she said in Oninan, pointing to the chairs across the table from me.

I waited until she took her seat before taking mine. My gaze stayed riveted on the blackwood table, although part of me wanted to look Father in the eye and ask why he had come. Since when did he attend meetings like this?

"I thank you so much for coming," Iris said warmly in English. "We're really excited about putting Ọlọrọ Ilé on the map in the fashion industry."

Father cleared his throat. "While that is admirable, Ms. Blakely, I am afraid Diallo Enterprises cannot be associated with Aṣọ as long as Ekon Diallo is employed with your company."

I froze, but my eyes rose to stare at Father of their own accord. Then he had not come to help. He only wanted to strip me further of my dignity.

"I'm sorry to hear that. If that is your wish, you could have canceled this meeting with my secretary instead of wasting my time."

My head jerked toward Iris, surprised at the venom in her voice. Since when did ododo mi talk to another person in such a manner? Yes, she could be passionate, but I had not realized she could be fierce as well.

My father spluttered. "You dare—"

"No, *you* dared." Iris pointed a finger in his face. "Your

personal relationships should never interfere with business, but since you decided to merge the two, let me be clear. I will never, *never* use Diallo Enterprises in any of my dealings as long as you are head of the company. I will make sure to let all of my contacts in the fashion industry and those beyond know of your disrespectful handlings in business. I hope they'll think twice before dealing with a man of such ill repute."

I bit down on my tongue at the odd phrase. It made me want to laugh, though there was no humor in the situation. I could not believe Iris was going toe-to-toe with Father. It made me love her all the more.

Cold washed over me.

Love?

I could *not* love her. There was no way I could walk this life with such knowledge and know she was out of reach. It was one thing to like her or be attracted to her, but *love?*

Please, God, make it not so. I have nothing to offer her.

I blinked rapidly as my brain jumped from one shock to the other. First a claim of love, and now I was talking to a God I had never been sure existed. Clearly this meeting had messed with all of my senses.

Father rose, and his henchman glared at me before following in Father's wake.

I turned to Iris, but she picked up her sketches and ignored my stare. I *knew* she could feel the heat of it, but she walked out of the conference room without a backward glance.

Just as well. The way I felt, who knew what I would say or do if she said one word to me. I sank back in my seat. I would ignore my revelation regarding Iris and focus on the one about God. Did that prayer mean I believed? Had my subconscious believed before my head or heart?

And if so, what would I do next?

"When you believe that Jesus is your Savior, confess your sins before Him, and He will forgive."

Nika's words washed over me. Somehow my soul had come to a conclusion about God before my head had caught up. I instinctively knew that if I were to make any headway in life, I would need Him for my guide. Had that not been my purpose in seeking Him?

I bowed my head. *God, I have made so many mistakes. Lived a life that would satisfy me without care for the consequences of my actions. These past few months, I have been all too aware of how unworthy I am. I am not a good person, but I want to be.* I swallowed, my heart thudding. *I have sinned in countless ways. Some in ignorance, some intentionally. Please forgive me for them all. Please show me the way, Your way. Please forgive me and make me worthy to walk the path You set before me. Please pave a way for me. Amen.*

I breathed out and blinked in surprise at the moisture that had filled my eyes.

THIRTY-TWO

Iris

How could someone's parent be so cold? More than that—*heartless*. My heart broke for Ekon and how his father had tried to shame him at work. At *work*, for heaven's sake!

I hadn't had the nerve to meet Ekon's eyes in the conference room. I was too afraid I'd burst into tears and wrap him in a hug while asking him a million times if he was okay. I would be *crushed* if my father treated me so coldly.

As it was, I was crying softly in the bathroom. Thankfully, I'd had the foresight to stash extra makeup in here so I didn't have to leave this room looking like my face had gotten into a fight with a cheese grater. Splotchy red circles always developed on my face when I cried, and considering that I kept wiping at them with the rough tissue in here, who knew what damage my skin was going through.

I sniffed, remembering the way Ekon's father had ignored him. *Ignored him!* After cutting Ekon off a month ago and refusing to speak to him, you'd think Mr. Diallo would have something to say. Anything, really. Instead, he'd acted as if Ekon didn't exist.

Haven't you been giving him the cold shoulder yourself?

Oh no! I hiccupped as the sobs built. I was no better than Ise Diallo. Refusing to talk to Ekon just because he thought he was no good for me and that I deserved better. I mean, in a way, wasn't that sweet? Wasn't that kind of . . . noble? I sniffed, trying to keep my snot internal and my tears from exploding in my heartache.

A soft knock rapped on the bathroom door. "Iris? Are you okay?" Ekon's voice filtered through the wood.

I peered at the watch on my wrist. How long had I been in here? "I'm okay," I croaked. I rolled my eyes. Yeah, that was believable.

"You do not sound okay."

I sighed. "I'll be fine. I'll be out soon."

"Open the door, Iris."

And let him in this enclosed space? *I don't think so.* "Sorry, can't do that."

"You are decent, right?"

"Of course I am. Who gets naked at work?" I slapped a hand over my mouth. When would I learn to shut up?

Soft chuckles reached my ears, and a smile filled my face. I loved the way he sounded when he laughed. It so rarely happened. Probably because his father was a jerk.

"I did not think you were unclothed. But maybe you do not feel presentable."

"I'm not. Go away, Ekon."

A heavy sigh reached my ears. "I cannot when I know you are upset. Are you crying?" he asked cautiously.

I didn't want to lie. . . . "Yes."

"Why?"

This was stupid. I opened the door a smidge and peeked out. "Your father's a jerk." Points for Ekon for not gasping at the ugliness of my face. I could feel the redness.

"He can be difficult."

I pulled the door open all the way and gaped at Ekon. "Difficult? He threatened me, tried to shame you. Add what you've already told me about him, and me calling him a jerk is being nice."

"Iris," he whispered. "There is no need to be upset on my behalf."

"How can you say that? If I'm not, who will be?" Why was he so willing to take such harsh treatment?

"God."

I reared back. "What did you say?"

He stepped back. "God understands what I have been through. He understands what I *will* go through."

Was I having some kind of out-of-body experience? I hoped not, because I probably looked like an enormous guppy gasping for air. "You said God." I pointed at him.

"I did."

"You believe in God?"

"Yes."

I wanted to scrub my ears or pinch myself, something to prove this was all real and not something my mind had spun in the midst of my emotional turmoil. "When did this happen?"

"In the conference room." He rubbed the back of his neck. "I have been searching for more and had a moment in the conference room where everything kind of cemented itself." He shrugged as if shocked himself. "My heart believed before my mind could catch up."

Searching for more? I wanted to lean back on the sink but gripped the door instead. "When did you start searching for Him? *How* did you search for Him? Did you ask questions? Read the Bible? What made you want to try? Are you sure you—"

Ekon laid a warm finger on my lips. Heat flooded my body, and my breath suspended. I couldn't have moved or spoken even if I'd wanted to prattle out the rest of my questions.

"Do you really need to know all the answers now?" he asked. I shook my head, then stopped as tingles erupted over my mouth.

"Good. Make yourself presentable and come. I have an idea for the show."

I blinked, hoping Ekon would realize my lips were being held hostage by his finger. I didn't want any more warmth spreading through my body. I'd had enough feelings for the moment and needed to gather them back in and stuff them in the trunk of my mind. Not that I was always successful in shutting the top and locking them away.

Ekon pulled his hand away, gave me one final look, then closed the door.

My forehead dropped to the door as I breathed in and out, clearing my mind. I moved in front of the sink to cleanse my face, then added a layer of foundation before redoing my makeup. Ten minutes later, I walked out of the restroom and headed to Ekon's desk.

His head popped up from whatever he was studying.

"What's your idea?"

He looked at me. "If you are willing, I will create your jewelry."

I frowned. "What do you mean?"

"When I first went to work for my father, I dabbled in design. I showed him my ideas, but he did not wish for his son to be a jewelry designer."

My mouth dropped. There were so many things wrong with that. However, considering the source, I shouldn't be acting the shocked maiden. "Do you have some ideas already?"

Ekon nodded and lifted the notepad before him. I inhaled sharply at the stunning necklace design. Even though he'd penciled it in black-and-white, I could tell it would be amazing with real gems. I'd had no idea he could draw like this.

"What gems would you use?"

"For this one, I imagined the V-neck dress you have in navy and red."

I nodded, recalling the exact pattern he was referring to. The high-low number was fabulous, if I did say so myself.

"I'd pair it with rubies and diamonds. The rubies will go here." He pointed to different points in the necklace. "Diamonds everywhere else."

"That would be stunning." Could I get that for myself as well? Rubies always seemed like an understated jewel.

A hesitant look crossed his face. "You like the idea?"

"I love the idea." I clapped my hands, repressing a squeal. "What do you need from me? Do I need to purchase the stones?" How much would that hurt the company's pocketbook?

"Actually, let it be my gift to you."

"What? No." No way I'd let him earn nothing. "The company will commission the pieces."

"No, please." He reached for my hands, squeezing them gently. "Listen."

"Fine." I pulled my hands away, trying not to whimper at the loss of his touch.

"I am a pariah in Ọlọrọ. If you are willing to let me design these and showcase them at the fashion show, then if people love them and ask where they were designed, you could refer them to me. I will operate under a business name, not my own. That way I can actually cultivate clients."

I hated that he was right. I saw how the people of Ọlọrọ treated him. "Are you sure you don't want Aṣọ to be your first client?"

"You will be. I have simply refused to charge you. The exposure is worth more to me."

I bit my lip, thinking of possible ramifications. Except my mind kept focusing on his horrible father and how he'd tried to humiliate Ekon. "How about we consider it a loan? We'll return the jewels to you after the fashion show."

Ekon nodded slowly. "All right."

"Where will you get the stones?" Though the louder question in my mind was how he could afford them.

"I have some already. Plus, I know where to get some others."

"But your budget . . ." I didn't want him going into debt because of me.

"I will be fine. I promise." He gave me that half smirk, and my mind flashed back to the first day he came to Aṣọ.

So much had changed since then. Ekon had grown leaps and bounds. I could only pray he would one day see the man I saw. *It doesn't matter who you see. He's off-limits, remember?*

I swallowed and spun on my heel to go sit down. Far away from Ekon and the dreams he made me want to resurrect.

We worked in silence, but this time it wasn't forced because of some punishment I thought he deserved. When we exited the office to leave for the day, I made eye contact and said good-bye.

"Iris?"

"Yes?"

"Would you allow me to make you dinner?"

My mouth dried. As much as I tried to act like a grown-up—aka the opposite of Mr. Ise Diallo—I didn't want to put myself in a position where I would sink further into a dream world with Ekon. "I don't think that's a good idea."

"I need to practice my skills before my friends come over."

My back stiffened. "The guy from the market?" And Nika? He let Nika come over to his house?

Ekon slid his hands into his pockets. "It is my turn to host them this week."

"Host what?" Would I have been invited if I hadn't given him the cold shoulder for the last two weeks?

"Bible study."

Shock turned the edges of my vision black, and I swayed.

THIRTY-THREE

Ekon

I reached for Iris as her eyelids shut. Was she faint? My mind immediately catalogued how right it felt to hold her. I whispered her name.

Her eyelids fluttered, and relief flooded through me.

"I'm fine," she murmured.

My brow furrowed in skepticism. She had wobbled, and her eyes had closed. Was this a reaction to the news of me going to Bible study or simply an accumulation of the day's events?

"You certainly don't look fine."

A wry chuckle escaped her lips and she stepped back. I slid my hands into my pockets, squeezing them tight at the loss of contact.

She put a hand against her head. "My mind is having trouble keeping up with all these miraculous changes." She chuckled. "It almost sounded like you were hosting a Bible study."

I stifled a smirk. "Imagine that."

"You wouldn't believe what I've imagined," she mumbled. Or at least that was what my ears heard. "Ekon?"

"Yes?"

"Did you really say you believe in God now?"

I nodded.

"And you're going to Bible studies?" Her eyebrows rose.

I nodded again.

She stared blankly at me.

"So . . . dinner?"

A shutter came over her face, and for the first time since I'd met her, I couldn't read her expression.

"It's not a good idea."

I opened my mouth, then shut it. Why did she not want me to cook for her?

You did say your relationship with her was strictly employee-employer. I could not keep dangling the friendship gambit then yanking it away, could I? "I hope you have a good night, then."

She nodded, but a flicker of sadness crossed her features.

I bit back an oath. Iris had no one but the queen to talk to. Wait, she was talking to her neighbor now. Still, I did not know how deep that relationship had become. As she was the CEO of a new company, had she been able to connect with other CEOs in the country? I had not seen her talk to Matt Wallace lately. Had something gone wrong in their friendship?

"Come on, Iris," I pleaded before I could stop myself. "I do not want you to be alone."

Her mouth dropped, and her back stiffened. "Are you kidding me right now?"

Great. How do I always manage to anger her? "I meant no insult."

"First you say we're friends, then you kiss me like you're starving, only to tell me we're simply employer and employee." She pointed at herself, then me.

My mind halted at the *kiss me like you're starving* bit. Was that a bad thing or a good quality? If I kissed her now, would she slap me or welcome my affections?

"Now you pity me and only invite me to dinner so you can practice for your *real* friends."

"I do not pity you." Far from it. I wanted to care for her. Watch over her.

"Then what do you call it?"

"Concern?"

"Are you asking or telling?"

I cleared my throat and stepped forward. "As much as I do not want to care, I do."

"If that's not some Mr. Darcy–type bull, I don't know what is."

"Who?"

Iris dropped her head in her hands, muttering to herself. I could barely make out the words, only catching a few such as "figures," "why me," and the last one sounded a lot like "why, Lord." If she was going to bring God into this, then so would I.

I am not sure what is going on, but I messed up. I am always messing up. But You said You are the One who makes me worthy. I do not know how, and I still do not know if I fully believe I can be, but I want to be worthy of this woman before me. Please help me. Please.

I continued praying, and finally Iris looked up and met my gaze. My heart prompted me to speak.

"Will you come to my home as my friend, Iris?"

She studied me for so long that I almost startled when she spoke. "Okay."

I held my breath, waiting for the joke.

She waved a hand in the air. "Or we could stand here and starve."

"No. I can feed you."

She sniffed, tilting her chin in the air. "Thank you. I *am* hungry."

Now I just had to figure out what food I had in my refrigerator that would be worthy of her taste buds. I gave myself an inward punch to the face. Iris had softened me in a way I was not sure was good, but I could not deny its effects either.

I held my car door open for her, shutting it as she slid into her seat. As I rounded the corner of the car, I shot off a *thank you* prayer to God. He was showing me in little ways how He really was there and cared about me. I did not know *why,* when no one else did, but I was grateful.

The conversation between Iris and me remained horribly stilted on the way to my place. What could I do to make it better? Would my words annoy her? The growing silence made me want to crawl out of my skin.

Just speak. "Did your family enjoy their visit?" That was a ridiculous conversation starter. They had departed a few weeks ago.

"They did. They're already talking about visiting again."

My shoulders relaxed. "That is good." It was nice to know there were functional families in the world.

"Are you going to talk to your dad about today?"

My hands tightened on the steering wheel. "I do not think I should push against a door he so firmly closed."

"How does that make you feel?"

"Why do you want to know?" I glanced at her before reverting my gaze back to the road.

"I'm not asking to be nosy or anything. I guess I want you to know I'm here to listen if you want to talk about it."

I sighed. Did I? "I am not sure how to feel, honestly. Perhaps relief that I do not have to meet his high expectations anymore? Maybe hurt, that he could so easily ignore my existence." I swallowed around the lump in my throat. "Either way, I am over the initial shock of it. I feel okay. And all the emotions I expected to have are missing." I shrugged. "I do not even know what that means."

"Maybe you're numb?"

Was I? "No, I do not believe that is it. How can I feel anything toward a man who constantly prevented me from developing proper feelings? Always, he said Diallo men did not let emotions cloud their actions. That they were for the weak. Perhaps that is why I cannot decide how I truly feel."

I searched for further explanation. My tongue felt tied up as I tried to express the countless memories I had of myself as a child seeking affection from a father who prevented me from receiving hugs. Or the times he had refused to allow my mother to soothe me if I had hurt myself. There was no praise if I did well in school, no accolades for graduating with honors. These things were expected of a Diallo and not something to celebrate.

"My father had definitive expectations of what we did or did not do. Anything that could be listed under a positive emotion was ignored, and negative emotions were corrected out of me."

"Do you have an example?"

"I did not receive hugs."

She gasped. "You weren't hugged? At all? Not even as a child?"

"No. Mother was forbidden to hug me."

She turned in her seat. "Your mom. That reminds me. I may have heard a rumor that you are related to Dayo? Is that true? Is she your half-sister?"

I wiped my left palm on my slacks, then the right. The queen would not have shared this, which meant someone in Etikun had. "Where did you hear that?"

"The break room," she whispered. "I'm sorry."

"It is not your fault. But yes, she is my half-sister."

"How?"

"We have the same mom."

"I thought Dayo's mom was a housekeeper. Didn't she pass away? Yet you make it sound like your mom is still alive."

If people in Etikun were spreading rumors, it did no good for me to keep the truth from Iris. "When I reference my mother,

I am referring to my adoptive mother. She is the woman who raised me. I never knew my birth mom."

"What do you mean?"

I rubbed my jaw, hating that I had to share this part of my past. But I did not want to hide this from Iris. Perhaps now she would understand what I meant about not being good enough.

"One night, my father got drunk and slept with my birth mother, whom he met while at the palace on business. When she came and told him she was pregnant, he agreed to pay her medical expenses if I was indeed his child. If not, she would owe him. When I was born, they did a DNA test. He made her sign over her rights, and he brought me home for his wife to raise."

"He was already married?"

I nodded.

"So your mom raised her husband's product of a one-night stand?"

My jaw tightened as I nodded.

"Does anyone know?"

"The elders of Etikun do, as well as the royal council and queen. When I was fifteen years old, Dayo approached my father, asking permission to get to know me. I do not know what he told her, but I did not see her again until I was in my early twenties. Father stressed that I would not be deserving of my princely title or any future role as an elder if my illegitimacy came to light."

"Does your adoptive mother treat you well?"

"She does . . . well, did. I have not seen her since Father announced I was no longer his son." Then my heart had felt something. Did that mean I was over it now? "I believe she pitied me at first. Perhaps even pitied my birth mother. She has always cared for me as much as my father allowed."

"He can't dictate emotions."

I snorted. "Did you forget what he tried to do in our meeting?"

She huffed. "No."

"All right, then imagine that but a much harsher, starker reality. *That* was my childhood. That is my mother's life. He can and *will* dictate emotions. My mother will not call me unless he allows it, and I do not see that happening."

"He's not a good man."

"Good and bad are relative." I would have once characterized myself as good, believing I had never done any real harm. Now I could not escape the very real truth that I had done bad things.

My hands gripped the wheel. I needed to formally apologize to the queen.

"How can you say that?"

Iris's question brought me back to the present. "When you grow up like I did, seeing all the so-called good things of life that come to the wealthy, what you see as good may be someone else's bad. Wealth is not always a good thing. Not when it is detrimental to your family." *Ugh*. I had not meant to say that last part aloud.

"And now? Now that you are doing Bible studies and talking to God, do you see good and bad differently?"

"Now I am more confused than ever."

She laughed. "I can understand that. The Bible can be so backward to society's ways. And when you consider how you were raised . . ." Her voice trailed off.

"Yes." I cleared my throat. "Have you ever heard this thing about God making us worthy?" My face heated as the question left my mouth. Maybe I should have kept it closed and not shared the question that had plagued me some days. Frankly, some of my nights as well.

"I have."

"What does it mean?" I turned into my driveway and parked the car, turning to take in Iris's expression.

Her ebony eyes gleamed. "This will be a wonderful conversation to have over dinner."

"Will it?" My heart lightened.

"Yes. Come on, let's go. You can show me how your skills have advanced, and I can tell you why God makes us worthy."

I followed her, trailing behind as she walked up the few steps of my porch. I had bought a couple of chairs so I could sit on the veranda and enjoy the scenery. Though they were no match for how I had set up the backyard. I could not wait for her to see.

My nerves ramped up as I unlocked the door and let her in.

"Ekon, this looks fantastic." Her voice held wonder.

"You like it?"

She turned slowly, her gaze roaming every piece of furniture, artwork, and decor stamping the inside of my home. "I adore it."

I smiled, placing my keys on the hook by the entrance. "I am glad."

"I didn't know you had it in you."

I laughed. "I have seen my mother decorate enough to learn a thing or two."

"You picked up more than one skill."

"Do you want a tour?"

She nodded.

I showed her the different changes I had made, ending with us in the kitchen. I leaned against the entryway, my hands itching to wrap her in my arms and kiss her. There was something about seeing her in my house that did me in.

I was not sure if I would ever feel good enough for Iris Blakely, but right then, in that moment, I committed myself to the effort. *Show me the way, Lord. Please.*

THIRTY-FOUR

Iris

The night had been absolute perfection. The food was amazing, and if my pencil skirt—the one I'd finally put into use—hadn't objected, I would have continued eating the delicious meal Ekon prepared. As it was, now I had nothing preventing me from looking into Ekon's warm brown eyes. I could feel my desire to dream possible endings for our future pushing against my concentration to stay in the present. *Practice patience. Stay in the moment. Don't jump ahead in life and miss this now.*

All true. Tonight had been wonderful. Never in my imaginings had I thought we'd have such stimulating conversation about the worth of a person, the gift of salvation, and the effects loving Jesus had on people. Ekon wanted to understand everything on a heart level and not just head knowledge. Yet the depth of God's love continued to trip him up.

If I could, I would sit Ise Diallo down and tell him what a horrible man he was and how much his child-rearing method had wounded Ekon. Mr. Diallo was supposed to be an earthly example of God's care as the Father. Only, I had a feeling that somewhere in Mr. Diallo's past was another bad example of a dad. I wasn't sure if that person had been his father or someone just as close. Maybe his mom?

The thought made me wince. *Lord, please help Ekon's father. Please rid him of the chains keeping him from showing appropriate emotion. Help him find love. Help him find You.*

I sighed as the sun kissed the earth in its downward descent. The colors displayed on the horizon were better than any painting or picture I could find on Instagram. The scene before me had me thinking of the song about how much God loved us. I peeked at Ekon from the corner of my eye.

He had served dessert in his backyard, proud of the oasis he'd designed. As he should be. The fire pit created a cozy vibe as much as the cushions on the outdoor sofa. Although I'd behaved and stayed in the present of tonight by enjoying the food he'd cooked, the discussion of my beliefs and the emergence of Ekon's had my mind trying to pull me to the future.

I wanted a relationship with Ekon so badly that I could visualize every detail. Instead of focusing on thoughts of us sitting out here after a long day at work—both of us at Aṣọ, with a son or daughter playing at our knees—I catalogued his features now.

He, too, stared at the setting sun, an arm resting on the back of the sofa. I wanted to ask why he'd pushed me away. If he would change his mind. Because my mind brought up the kiss incident at least once a day. It often battled for prime real estate in my frontal lobes against anything and everything to do with our fashion show.

But Ekon would be leaving sometime before the fashion show. His consulting hours would be complete. Not only that, but the Lord had never given me a green light on a relationship with Ekon.

The last thought shot shame through me. I'd been so hung up on my wants that I'd never once run my hopes and dreams by God. *How did I end up here, Lord? How did I get so enthralled with the idea of a forever that I never asked You if this fell into the plans You have for me?*

I squeezed the sofa cushion, hoping the move would keep tears from forming. Still, I could feel the waterworks coming on. I sniffed.

"Iris?"

I inhaled, reaching for a light tone. "Yes?"

"What is the matter?"

I turned to look at Ekon, who was already staring at me. "How did you know something was bothering me?"

"You have this telltale sniffle that means you are about to cry but trying not to."

How had he realized that? Did he watch me? Why didn't that thought creep me out? "I realized I'd forgotten to ask God something. It made me sad."

"Asking God something is important to you?"

I nodded. "Yes. Believing in Jesus is the first step in entering a relationship with Him, but it's not the one and only. We do things to grow the relationship. I thought I'd gotten to the point where I didn't mess up, but . . ." *You're still human, Iris.* I wasn't perfect, and I needed to grant myself grace for when I messed up.

"But you are human."

I laughed. "Exactly."

"What did you forget to ask Him?"

My cheeks burned. "Just something personal."

"You will ask now that you remembered."

"I will. Probably when I'm alone and can talk everything out with Him."

Ekon chuckled softly. "Do you give God a chance to answer, or do you talk the whole time?"

A great question. "Depends. Sometimes I have to rein myself in." A sheepish grin covered my face. Anyone who knew me wouldn't be surprised. "But I have grown in the listening department."

He smiled at me. "You have always listened to me."

"I'm happy to. Everyone needs a person to talk to."

Ekon turned to me. "Is the queen that person for you?"

"Definitely. I can tell her anything and know she won't judge me and will have the best advice. Even if she doesn't know what to say, she'll be there for me." I paused. "What about you? Your new friends in your Bible study, are they your listening ear?"

He shrugged. "I am still navigating my way in that group. They have an older friendship, and I am the new guy. They do answer all my questions about God, though."

"That's good."

He gazed at me. "You are the one I talk to about stuff I did not even know I needed to say."

I swallowed. I wanted to fall into his arms. I wanted to know that if I kissed him, my heart would be safe with him. Only the past rejection and my mistake in not conferring with the Lord stopped me. "I'm honored," I said instead of regurgitating the thoughts in my mind.

A soft smile curled his full lips.

I blinked, looking down at the sofa cushion. It was time to pull myself out of this situation. I couldn't stay here without succumbing to every vision my heart wanted to create for this moment.

"Hey, I think I'm going to go before it gets too dark." Now that the sun had made its full descent, it was only a matter of time before complete darkness enveloped Ọlọrọ.

"I will drive you home."

"No." I stood, shaking my head. "I can call a cab."

He snorted. "I do not think so. I have a car and can safely see you home."

But would I survive the car ride? My willpower felt nonexistent at the moment. Still, it was better than getting a lift from a stranger at night. "Thank you, Ekon."

"Anytime, ododo mi."

I wanted to ask him what that meant, but something cautioned me against it. Maybe next time I could just have Google translate up and ready when he said it.

"Iris?" Ekon asked as we neared my building.

"Yes?"

"Could you help me gain an audience with the queen?" He paused. "I would like to apologize to her."

"For what?"

"My crimes. My part in Dayo's schemes."

My heart turned over. "I will see what she says."

"I appreciate that."

He stopped in front of my building. I thanked him for the ride, even though my heart pounded and the urge to kiss him made my palms clammy.

"Thanks again for dinner."

"Anytime," he said quietly. "I mean it."

"Sure." I reached for the door handle.

"Iris?"

"Yes?" I didn't turn back. *Wouldn't.*

"Do you want to come to our Bible study?"

My head swiveled of its own accord. Get a glimpse into the world that had changed the man before me? *Lord, is this okay?* I swallowed, waited. "Sure."

He beamed. "Great. I will see you at six on Wednesday?"

I nodded, then left, tossing a good-bye over my shoulder. As soon as I made it to my apartment, I opened my cell and texted Bri.

Iris:
I'm weakening!

Bri:
They make OJ with vitamin D now.

Iris:
😒 I need you to be serious.

Bri sent a serious-face GIF.

Bri:

I'm listening.

Iris:

Ekon is exploring Christianity.

Bri:

He's exploring it, or he believes?

Iris:

He believes but still has questions about a lot of it.

Bri:

Give him space. Let him work that out.

Not the answer I wanted to hear.

Iris:

But he's sooo hot!

He invited me to Bible study.

Bri:

Gird yourself. Put on the full armor of God.

Iris:

I can do that.

I let out a breath I hadn't realized I'd been holding.

Bri:

Have you talked to God about all this?

Iris:

About Bible study? Yes. Everything else? Going to have that conversation tonight.

> I also need to ask Him if He thinks I should offer Ekon a job . . .

Because what if no one else in Ọlọrọ offered him a job? He couldn't live on the money from his former job forever, could he?

> Bri:
> Oh wow. Do you think Ekon wants to work for you?

> Iris:
> I don't know. He's already mentioned how most Ọlọrans don't like him. He does have a business idea, but I'm not sure if it'll be successful. Though he did mention he'd use a different name in hopes that he could get clients that way.

> Bri:
> I'll pray for him. And for you.

> Iris:
> Please do! I need lots of prayer!

> Bri:
> Iris, is this only physical attraction for you?

A valid question. It was definitely one I'd asked myself already.

> Iris:
> No. There's so much more to my feelings besides how his handsome face makes my heart go pitter-patter.

Because I saw the strength in his heart, the man he could be when he finally let God do His good work. It was how he made me feel safe. How he brought laughter to my world. How I just *knew* a future with him would be bright.

Iris:

I just hate that his self-worth is so low.

Maybe that was the reason the word *patience* rang in my head so often these days. Ekon had a lot to work through. A romance probably wouldn't help in that area.

Bri:

That's sad but understandable, considering what he's been through.

Only Bri could have such compassion.

Iris:

He wants to meet with you. To apologize.

Will the council allow that? Will Tomori?!

Bri:

I'm not sure, but I'll find out.

I thought of Ise Diallo and what he'd put Ekon through.

Iris:

Oh! Pray for Ekon's father and that my ill feelings toward that man dissolve.

Bri:

There's a story there.

Iris:

Wait until Thursday! I can't wait to see your preggo belly.

Bri:

It's a small bump, but big enough that I had to wear an empire waist dress today instead of the skirt and blouse I wanted to.

> **Iris:**
> Ohhh, does that mean I can make you some maternity clothes?!

Good thing we were doing a maternity line at Aṣọ.

> **Bri:**
> Yes! They would be gorgeous!

> **Iris:**
> Sweet. Gotta go! Need to talk to God and sketch!

> **Bri:**
> Have a good evening. Praying for you!

I raced into my room and looked for my sketchbook. Sketching and talking to God always helped me think and verbalize what I wanted to say, and I had *lots* to say today.

THIRTY-FIVE

Ekon

My pulse drummed through my ears as my feet brought me closer to the safe-deposit box. The bank employee opened the vault, then motioned for me to enter. I walked over to box number 358. The silver-etched numbers beckoned me. The key on my fob would unlock the contents Father would not wish me to have.

Contents that had been given to me by right of birth.

Fortunately, he had not removed the safe-deposit box from my keeping, and when I informed the teller I wanted to empty the contents, no protest was made. Now all I had to do was unlock it and remove the gemstones that rested inside.

Taking a deep breath, I slid the key into the lock and twisted. The drawer popped open. I pulled it all the way out and lifted the box from within before lifting the lid.

Instead of gemstones, a note lay on the bottom. I closed my eyes, shock coursing through me. *Why, Lord?* I picked up the letter.

Ekon,

We both know I could not let you walk away with thou-sands', if not millions', worth of Diallo gemstones. These gems were intended for the son I could be proud of. Not the son who would bring me shame.

Do not bother returning the key. I have no use for it.

Why had I assumed he would not remove the gems from my possession? He had taken everything else.

What was I going to do now? I could not ask Iris to pay for the fashion pieces when I had already informed her I would cover it. Perhaps there was a way to buy untreated gemstones. I ran a hand down my face, blew out a breath, and shoved the box closed. There was nothing here that could help me. I would have to find another way to start my business.

Before leaving the bank, I stopped momentarily to inquire if I had any daily withdrawal limits. As tempting as it was to remove a bunch of money from my account, it would not be the smart thing to do. Not when I did not have a new source of income.

I left the bank in the haze, driving aimlessly with no destination in mind. The missing gemstones had thrown my plans out the window. Well, they were not truly lost. Father had them. Part of me wanted to drive to his house and ask him why. Why did he treat me this way?

My jaw tightened, and I turned at the next light. Why was I scared of Ise Diallo? He had already stripped me of everything. Driving by his home would not cost me any more. My brain emptied of all thought as I made the journey to the mansion in the hills.

Soon the cream-colored structure stood out amidst the dark green trees. I parked on the redbrick driveway and hurried up the steps. The butler showed no surprise when he opened the door, simply awaited my request.

"I want to speak to my father."

"He does not wish to see you, sir."

I stiffened my spine against the injustice. "I will not leave until he does."

He blinked at me. "Very well. I will inform him." The door shut in my face.

I glanced at my watch to mark the time. Father would make me wait. The question was how long.

Five minutes passed with not a word from anyone inside. I played a game on my mobile, unscrambling colors in beakers. Fifteen rounds later, I checked the time again. Twenty minutes had passed. I switched to the message app.

> Ekon:
> How is your evening going?

> Iris:
> Wonderful. Some chocolate from the States arrived.

> Ekon:
> Ọlọrọ has the best chocolate.

I smirked, waiting for Iris's reaction.

> Iris:
> Idk. There's something nostalgic about a Kit Kat bar.

> Ekon:
> I will bring you my favorite tomorrow and prove it to you.

> Iris:
> What are you up to?

I glanced at the closed door. The one that prevented me from entering the place of all my childhood memories.

Ekon:

Waiting.

Iris:

On?

Ekon:

Whether my father will see me or not. We have some things to discuss.

Iris:

PRAYING!

Ekon:

I appreciate that.

Iris:

You've got this!

It was a good thing she had sent that, because the door behind me opened. I whirled around.

The butler dipped his head. "Mr. Diallo will see you now."

I glanced discreetly at my watch: thirty minutes. Not as bad as I had thought.

The butler led the way to Father's home office. Once the door closed behind me, silence filled the air. Suddenly I wished I had gone over my talking points while waiting on the front porch.

Lord, please guide me.

"You wanted to see me?" Father continued viewing the papers before him, refusing to meet my gaze.

"The safe-deposit box is empty."

A sly grin erupted on his face. "You did not think I would forget to remove them, did you?"

Clearly, I had. My silence and heated embarrassment were answer enough.

"I told you only the things you bought with your salary were yours." He smirked.

Frustration filled me. "I do not understand how you can take back a gift."

He shrugged. "I bought it. Therefore it is mine to do with as I see fit."

"But why? Why strip me of everything? Did you not think the punishment of the council good enough?" Because every time I picked up a piece of trash or appeared in someone's derisive social media post, I was reminded of how far I had fallen. Why did my own father have to contribute to such shame?

"Community service?" he spat. "That was weak! The *queen* was weak. I cannot believe she would recommend such leniency. You are a disgrace and should be in a cell next to that *woman*."

"The queen did not think my crimes on par with Dayo's." *Thank You, God.* That was beginning to become a repeated prayer.

"Do not speak *her* name in *my* house."

I swallowed. "I simply want to understand how my own father could turn his back on me. How you could strip me of basic necessities. Take away the roof over my head. The clothes in my closet. The food in my refrigerator. Leave me with nothing."

"I left you with millions! Are you homeless?"

I gulped. "No."

"Are you naked?"

My neck warmed. "No, sir."

"Are you hungry?"

"I am not." I wanted to crawl away, a proverbial tail tucked between my legs.

"Then what is your complaint?"

What was my—? "You are my father! You should have loved me. Guided me when you thought I had lost my way, not dug the hole deeper and shoved me in!" My breath came in spurts as the words tore from my chest. All I had ever wanted was to know he loved me for me, not for what I could do for him.

"I am *not* your father."

My mouth dried. White noise filled my ears. Father's lips moved, but no sound penetrated the high pitch in my ears. "What?" I rasped. I blinked him into focus, trying desperately to ensure I would not miss a single word. "But you said . . ." Had he not told me that my biological mother and he had an affair?

"I lied," he spat. "I am not your father. I never slept with that woman's mother."

"Then . . ." Why could I not form a coherent sentence?

"Tife could not have children. Every month she mourned the loss of the possibility of becoming a mother. Life with her was becoming unbearable, so I did what I thought prudent."

"Which was what?" My hands became clammy as his story slowly penetrated the shock in my mind.

"I found a woman who could not afford to have another child. Your biological mother could barely feed that *woman* who calls herself your sister, let alone care for you. I offered to claim you as my own. Her one stipulation was that you know she was your mother."

I sank into the nearest chair. "Then who *is* my father?"

Father—no, *Ise Diallo*—pursed his lips.

"Who is he?" My heart thudded in my chest. I felt dread at the answer, but also anticipation that perhaps the answer would be better than who I had thought my father had been all these years.

"She did not say."

Being illegitimate, I had always known a princely title did not truly belong to me. But I could not believe this. All the times I had felt smug about being titled despite Father's affair. His lies had earned me prestige when others were denied because of their illegitimacy. Yet it turned out my real father was not a prince. How could he be, if my mother could not afford to raise me?

I had been born a commoner.

I turned away from the man in front of me.

"Where are you going, Ekon?"

"What do you care?" I could not spare him one more glance. He had destroyed all I knew. Now I could only think of him as Ise Diallo. Even the last name made me want to wince. Was I even legally adopted?

"You are still my son."

How? "In name only," I scoffed.

"In all the ways it counts," he thundered.

I spun toward him. "Yet you took the house, the clothes, the keys, the gems. You took everything. You withheld love. Even made sure Mother—" I stopped, cleared my throat. "Even made sure Mrs. Diallo withheld her love. So no, you did not make sure that I was your son in all the ways it counted. Otherwise, I would still be here for weekly dinners. You would have supported me despite my downfall. No. Like you said, we are done. We will no longer associate. We will no longer be family."

"Then you will give me my last name back."

I froze. He truly did want to take away my identity and all I had thought made me who I was. I stared into his eyes. "What made you like this? *Who* made you like this?"

He did not answer.

I walked out of the room, out of the house, and out of the Diallos' life.

Who knew what would happen? Would Father—*Ise*—really make me take another last name? Would I have to go by Layeni, after my biological mother? Or would the courts let me pick my own last name?

I did not know, but I had had enough drama, enough thinking, enough hits for the day. I wanted to be somewhere that did not deplete me or drain me. And only one person came to mind. Yet how could I arrive on her doorstep broken once more?

Could I ever be more to her than a wounded project?

Lord, what do I do?

303

THIRTY-SIX

Iris

Waking up to a summons to the royal council wasn't how I wanted to start my morning, but I guessed that came with living in a monarch-ruled country. I scrunched my curls as my diffuser worked to dry my hair but not ruin the volume or shape pattern.

I'd already started the long hair-washing process before the call to attend the palace at nine. The council members wanted a statement on Ekon's consultant hours. Thankfully, I'd been keeping notes the entire time he'd worked for me. I hadn't been sure they would want evidence of his work and time, but I wasn't completely ignorant either.

Half an hour later, I walked through the palace halls on the second floor, where the council chambers were located. I'd chosen a dress with a lovely print in Oloran colors of purple, blue, and white. The plaid pattern gave a nod to the country and a hint of nostalgia to the States, in my opinion.

A guard stood outside the chambers and eyed me as I came to a stop before the gorgeous maroon doors.

"I will announce you, Ms. Blakely."

"E seun."

He knocked on the door once, then opened it wide enough to disappear into the darkness. I drew in a breath, clutching the portfolio of notes tighter to my front. Who knew having an at-home printer would come in handy when I needed to show why Ekon Diallo had done all the council had demanded, all I had required, and more? I prayed they would see he was truly a changed man and not the person who committed crimes against the crown.

The double doors opened, and I walked in, taking a stand in the center of the room directly in front of the half-moon table. There sat the royal council members, Yemi Ladipo of the Òkè tribe and temporary head of the council, Lola Keita of the Opolopo tribe and the only female member, and Jamal Ibrahim of the Musulumi tribe. Only the Etikun tribe lacked representation. I was a little surprised they hadn't at least wanted a temporary member at the table, but who was I to speak of such things?

I wonder why Bri is not here? She usually sat on the council in case there was a tied vote or the council wanted her opinion.

I bowed before the council, greeting them in Oninan and trying not to wince at my deplorable pronunciation.

"Iris Blakely," Mr. Ladipo began in English, "you have been called before the Ọlọrọ Ilé Royal Council to discuss the terms of Ekon Diallo's business consultant service hours as a result of his punishment for crimes against queen and country. Do you understand why you're here?"

Wow, way to introduce the severity of my presence. I licked my lips. "I do."

"Do you agree to answer all of our questions in truth?"

Good grief, they sounded gloomy. Was I in trouble? "I do."

"Then we will proceed." Mr. Ladipo looked at the other council members. "Who wishes to proceed first?"

Ms. Keita raised her hand.

"Proceed, Lola."

"Thank you, Yemi." Ms. Keita folded her hands and placed them on the tabletop. "Ms. Blakely, as of today, has Mr. Diallo fulfilled all the consultant hours?"

"Almost. He only has today and tomorrow to finish." I wanted to press a hand to my stomach to still the angry hornets buzzing at the thought. My office would be so empty without him.

"Has he ever arrived late?"

Get your head in the game. "Only the first day. His taxi driver delayed him, but he stayed later to make up the difference. From then on, he arrived on time or early."

"Has he ever tried to get out of work?"

"No, ma'am."

"Has he ever missed a day?"

I looked at Mr. Ladipo, and he nodded. "One day he did an errand for the council."

Ms. Keita looked at Mr. Ladipo, and he leaned over to whisper in her ear. She straightened. "Yes. We are aware and have counted those hours. In fact, Yemi has now informed me the errand has fulfilled his hours for the business consultant as well. If Mr. Diallo chooses to work today and tomorrow, then the hours he works will go to his community service time."

What had Ekon done, and why had I never asked him? I needed to rectify that.

"Do you have any more questions, Ms. Keita?" Mr. Ladipo asked.

"Have you lied about his hours?"

I tried to keep my face stoic, but shock at the question caused my jaw to drop. "No!"

She smiled. "Very well. I have no more questions."

"Mr. Ibrahim?" Mr. Ladipo directed.

"Yes." Mr. Ibrahim cleared his throat. "What kind of work did Mr. Diallo do on a daily basis, Ms. Blakely?"

307

I held up the portfolio. "I kept detailed notes in case you wanted a record. The notes show the type of tasks he performed on a daily basis, what initiatives he suggested to make Aṣọ better, and the flaws he saw in our operations that were against Ọlọran regulations, the African Kings Alliance, or other conventions Ọlọrọ Ilé has entered into."

A palace runner took the portfolio from me and handed it to Mr. Ibrahim. He perused the documents slowly. I waited to see if he would ask further questions or if they would want copies or something.

"Jamal, do you have any other questions?" Mr. Ladipo asked.

He held up a finger, flipping through a few more pages. I wasn't sure how much he was speed-reading and how much he merely skipped. I'd tried to make a heading for everything to give an overview, and hopefully that was helpful right now.

Finally, he looked up. "Yes, I have one final question. If you thought there would be no objections, would you offer him a permanent position with your company?"

"No objections from the council or the countrymen?" I asked.

"With anyone, Ms. Blakely."

"Then yes, I would." I folded my hands in front of me, trying to hide how badly they were shaking.

I didn't know why his question put me on edge, but my nerves were now shot. I no longer felt like I was on the stand as a character witness for Ekon but on trial myself.

"Ms. Blakely," Mr. Ladipo started.

I tensed. Bri had told me how awful Mr. Ladipo had been to her in all the council meetings she'd attended leading up to her being officially declared princess and then queen. I also remembered the objections he had spouted when I came before the council to request permission to start a business in the Etikun district.

"Do you believe the punishment the council directed against Mr. Diallo was appropriate?"

Not what I thought he would ask. "I can't begin to imagine how someone with no judicial background can determine that. However, I believed it to be fair."

"Do you believe he should have any of his sentencing reversed?"

I bit back a gasp. Were they seriously thinking of doing that? I thought back to the original sentencing. They'd ordered community service and business consulting service and had stripped him of his title of prince. The only thing they could reverse was the latter.

My mouth dried. "I think the community service did him good. I believe it served as a reminder to the people of Ọlọrọ that even the rich and famous can be punished for their crimes. That the council would not let favoritism rule the country. It also shows that those in power can serve them on the streets and not just in meeting rooms."

I held my breath as the elders exchanged glances. I wasn't trying to insinuate anything, but seriously, helping people wasn't just passing laws from a palace chamber.

I continued. "As for his title, what you did makes a statement."

"What do you mean?" Ms. Keita asked.

"If you do not reinstate it, then other princes and princesses know their actions have grave consequences. That they cannot commit crimes and go unpunished."

"And if we reinstate it?" asked Mr. Ibrahim.

Oh boy. "Then perhaps you send the message that grace can be found after a fall. That you examine the character of a person to see if they are truly sorry and repentant and have changed for the better."

"And your personal opinion?" Mr. Ladipo asked.

"My personal opinion?" My breath quickened. What did I

believe? God taught grace, but He also taught that our actions had consequences.

As much as I loved Ekon, I couldn't discount what he'd done.

Wait a minute! Had I truly used the L-word? I swallowed, heart thumping with the realization. All the emotions I had fought so hard to suppress and asked the Lord to take away hadn't disappeared, because I *loved* him. *I love Ekon Diallo.*

"Ms. Blakely?"

I blinked. "I apologize, I am deciding. Talking it out in my head."

Mr. Ladipo sneered.

Get it together, Iris. Legally speaking, Ekon had been prepared to marry Bri for the purpose of turning the throne over to Dayo. That equaled a coup. Though I believed he was now a different person, I wasn't sure if he should necessarily get his title back.

But don't you want the best for him?

I did, so much. But what if this all had to happen so he could be in a place to meet God? My brain hurt with the thoughts swirling inside. No wonder God said we shouldn't judge. Because if I were in Ekon's position, had suffered the council's punishment, I'd want grace and my title back. I just wasn't sure if that was my flesh speaking or my soul.

I blew out a breath. "I honestly don't know."

"Thank you, Ms. Blakely."

I nodded, but my insides still churned. How many of my answers had been based on Ekon's newfound faith or because of the way he made my heart swoon? After all that time I had spent talking with God about Ekon, I still felt so unsure about what He was telling me. How could I move myself out of the equation? Or maybe I didn't even have to. The council had just said Ekon had no reason to work today, since his business hours were complete.

I could dismiss him and never have to see him again. Only the thought made me want to cry and go find some ice cream.

I loved him. I wanted a happily ever after, not a good-bye and *thanks for all the work you did.*

Finally, the royal council dismissed me, thanking me for overseeing Ekon's business consulting time. They offered me the use of a car to take me to work. I thanked them, since I had yet to get my own vehicle.

This Saturday I had a driver's test. No one knew but my brother. I wanted someone praying but also wanted to surprise people if I was successful. I'd already been looking at possible cars to purchase once I received my license.

My phone buzzed. My heart warmed as Ekon's name appeared in my notifications. *I loved him!*

Breathe, girl. God didn't give you a green light.

My heart fell to my stomach, and I tapped the messaging icon.

> **Ekon:**
> Where are you?

> **Iris:**
> Council called me in to go over your sentencing.

> **Ekon:**
> How did that go?

> **Iris:**
> Just fine.

I bit my lip. Did I tell him over text that he didn't have to go to work?

> **Iris:**
> Are you at Aṣọ already?

> **Ekon:**
> Yes. Oka is giving me a suspicious glance.

I laughed and pressed the call button.

"Hello?"

"Hey. The council said since you fulfilled an errand for them, you don't have to finish the week with me."

"Oh."

There was such a long beat of silence that I glanced at the phone to ensure the call hadn't dropped. "Ekon?"

"I still have a couple of items I need to finish."

"Well, if you choose to stay, the council is happy to shave the time off your community service."

A sigh filled my ears. "I will let them do that, then."

Light filled my heart. "I'll see you in a bit."

"Good, because I have a lot to tell you."

"I'll be there."

As I hung up the phone, I realized how much I wanted that to be true. I wanted to be there for him whenever he needed me and because he wanted me to be.

Did he still think that kiss was a mistake?

Lord, please help me stay in Your will. Please.

THIRTY-SEVEN

Ekon

I had so much to tell Iris, but I could not quite figure out *what*, exactly, to say. Last night I had taken the time to pray and seek advice from God about all the problems I had been through—even the ones of my own doing. At the end, an odd sense of calm and something like . . . *peace* had filled me.

However, was *peace* the right word to describe what I had experienced? I did not really have knowledge of that particular emotion. I only knew that the anxiety that had filled me when I left Ise Diallo's home did not grip me now.

Learning I was not truly a Diallo had opened a host of questions about my identity. Yet sitting in my backyard and laying bare my thoughts before God had quieted a few. God knew who I was. Knew everything about me and still found me worthy of saving.

I shook my head at the magnitude of that. Worthy on His say-so.

Toward the end of my conversation with God, I thought of the gems situation and possible ways to purchase my own stones. The decision to sell my car had taken a matter of minutes and a visit to Bizzy to resolve the issue. With the extra funds, I had located a gemstone dealer this morning. The stones would arrive tonight.

Except, since I would host Bible study tonight, I could not delve into the world of jewelry design. That would have to wait.

Fortunately, I felt more confident in my cooking skills since Iris's visit. She was quite a woman. If only I knew how to get out of this odd limbo we were in. When we shared that life-altering kiss last month, I had felt completely unworthy of her affections. The loss of my title, the punishment Ise had inflicted, and the looks from other Ọlọrans weighed heavily upon me. My self-worth took blow after blow, lowering my self-esteem as well. The only reasonable thought I therefore had was that Iris Blakely deserved much more than me and the baggage I carried. At that time, I never imagined life could go any lower.

Then Ise happened, and life hit rock bottom. But God lifted me up.

Though I had no car and most of my funds were tied up in untreated gemstones and tools to turn them into jewelry, I still wanted to be able to offer Iris *something*. Or was love truly enough?

Love was the reason I wanted to spend the rest of my life with her. Love was the reason she was the first person I wanted to talk to and share everything with. But was it love or fear that had kept me from telling her the depth of my feelings after that first kiss?

She deserved more than to live in my modest home, eat my simple meals, and spend time with a man who did not know what his future held. I could not even drive her anywhere anymore. She also owned her own company, while I merely had the dream of one.

I snorted. I did not even have the guarantee of a last name to offer her, for I expected a lawyer to reach out at any moment and inform me that my name had been legally revoked.

How did a person go about getting a new surname? I had thought about looking up names and their meanings online or asking my new friends for suggestions, but none of that felt right. Perhaps I needed to wait and see what Ise would do first.

Now I sat waiting for Iris to arrive at work. Oka kept giving me glances like I was the unwanted gum on the bottom of her heels, even though the waiting area in front of Iris's office had been outfitted with sofas and a coffee table. While previously the negative looks would have chipped at me, now I occupied myself with something else.

I flipped to a new page of the sketchpad. Since I had ended my call with Iris, I took the time to dream up designs that would pair well with the pieces in the fashion show. Soon the sketches would become reality. My lips tilted in a half smile, pleased at the thought.

The seamstresses were busy creating the spring line—which Iris hoped to sell this fall—including outfits for men, women, children, and a special maternity section. Aṣọ would open for export at the beginning of the new year to deliver all the spring catalog orders. At least, that was the plan.

The click of heels drew my attention from my sketchpad. My gaze continued upward until it landed on Iris's beautiful face. Her curls hung down to her shoulders, and her pink lips matched the light blush in her cheeks.

I rose. "Good morning."

"Morning." She grinned.

I stood and waited for her to unlock the office door, then followed her inside.

"You sounded like you had something on your mind." Iris set her purse on her desk. "What's up?"

"Long story short . . ." I drew in a breath. "I am adopted. Ise Diallo is not my father."

"What?" she shrieked.

I nodded and sat in the chair opposite her. "Crazy, right?"

"How are you feeling?" She shook her head. "How are you *adopted?*"

"Ise did not have an affair with Dayo's mother—*my* mother. She *is* my biological parent, but he is not. Apparently, he and Tife could not have children. He paid my biological mother to give me up and keep quiet about the whole situation."

"Oh my word. I can't even." She pressed the palms of her hands against her cheeks. "You're serious?"

"Very."

"I'm . . . I . . . wow, Ekon."

I must have held a smidgen of tension left, because it eased at the mention of my name and all the sympathy she put into those two syllables. "I am all right, Iris."

"Are you really?"

It was hard to explain all my emotions, but I would try. "We exchanged words, *heated* ones that led to the truth coming out. I admit to feeling relieved. It explains so much. Before I left, Ise threatened to make sure I cannot even use the Diallo name." Though, did I really want to?

"Because why not take the one thing you have left." She threw her hands in the air. "That man infuriates me." She made a choking motion, then yelled, "Ugh!"

I wanted to laugh, but considering I had gone through similar emotions yesterday, I completely understood. Ise Diallo could test the patience of the kindest person on earth. Hence the example before me.

"Why is he like that?"

I shrugged a shoulder. "I asked him. He did not answer."

"You what?"

"I wanted to know." Did I not deserve to, considering the toil he had put me through? "There has to be a reason, yes?"

"Definitely."

"Either he did not want to say, or he does not know the answer himself."

"That's kind of sad." Now her puppy-dog eyes were in full effect.

Was it crazy that I wanted to comfort her? "It did give me some perspective." I had spent some time in prayer, asking what to do and how to look at the whole situation. I had woken up and not felt intense dislike for Ise anymore. No good could be found in harboring anger toward him.

What was done was done.

"Then you're not angry with him?"

"Not anymore."

Iris bit her lip. "What *do* you feel?"

"Peace. He is not my father, and that explains everything I have ever been through in that house. I can now reconcile some of his actions with that bit of knowledge. It freed me to let go of the anger I have held for so long."

"Silver lining, then. Where was your mom in all this?"

"Probably drinking." I winced. "That sounds unkind. I do not mean it to be, but most likely that was what she was doing. She chooses to bury her problems in the bottom of a bottle."

"I can't imagine what the secrets were doing to her."

Valid point, and one I had not considered. The alcoholism and possible reasons for it gave me a brief glimpse into her heart. Tife Diallo had tried to love me as best as Ise allowed. "You are right. She has had a rough life."

For all our riches, we had lacked the essential thing all humans needed: love. It was not something most men talked about, but my new relationship with Christ and my friends showed me how much this was true. Without it, we were merely existing. I was testament to how that was no way to do life.

But back to business. I did not want sympathy points from Iris.

"What can I help you with today?" I asked. I only had two days left. Two days of seeing her beautiful face every day.

She jumped into a spiel on a problem with one of the sewing

machines and the delay it would cause. She wanted to do another hiring event but feared that the constant delays would prevent women from attending if they knew.

We needed to get her quality equipment. "Have you asked the investors to buy better machines?"

"I did in the beginning but kind of stopped. The board has to approve all requests for more funds." She sighed. "I'm not sure when I can have another meeting with them. I need to make sure we're up to speed for the fashion show."

"Is there something on your list that I can take over? Should I talk to the board for you?" Though they would probably have a fit.

Iris shook her head. "Perhaps you could make sure Matt has scheduled all our marketing needs." She reached for a paper on her desk. "These are all the places he plans to promote the show. Could you please find out what has been done?"

I nodded, though my insides tensed. He was not my favorite person, but I would face him if it would help Iris.

"Thank you."

She passed me the paper. I tucked it into my suit jacket and headed for the third floor, where the marketing department resided. They did not have the whole floor to themselves, as finance and human resources also had offices there.

The elevator dinged, and I stepped out onto the concrete floor. My feet carried me directly to Matt Wallace's office. He did not have a secretary like Iris did, though I had heard him request one more than once. As the company was in the early stages, an assistant was not the number-one concern. I knocked directly on Mr. Wallace's door and sauntered in upon his permission.

"Ah, Ekon. How can I help you?" He ran a hand across his slicked-back hair.

"Ms. Blakely would like an update on promotion for the fashion show."

He frowned. "Tell her I will email her that later."

I sat in the chair across from his desk. "Or you could simply give me the information. She is busy with other tasks and needs to know this is covered."

Matt pursed his lips. "Fine. What does she want to know?"

I removed the paper from my pocket and read the first item off the list. "Did you place a permanent ad in the national and regional newspaper?"

Matt's fingers raced across the keyboard. I hoped that meant he was looking for the answer versus emailing Iris. After a moment, he sighed. "Yes."

"Great. Did you submit an ad to the local news?" I did not own a TV currently, so I had not even known she was doing this.

I looked up at the long pause. Matt's face had blanched. He tugged at his tie.

"Mr. Wallace?"

"I might have forgotten to do so."

Great. Now what should I do? I grabbed a pen out of my lapel and noted the issue. Then I went through the rest of the list. Matt had missed four items. "Is it possible someone else in the marketing department picked these up?"

"No. I haven't had a chance to explain how they should do it."

"Are they not all versed in marketing matters?" Did we not do training for this?

"Well, their résumés and references hinted at the fact. . . ."

I held up a hand. "Then I suggest you delegate these matters to your team and get them completed ASAP."

Matt glared at me.

I arched an eyebrow and stood. "I will inform Ms. Blakely of the promotional status."

"Please ask Oka to schedule me a time to explain to Iris why they haven't been completed."

"You will have to accomplish that yourself. I have other tasks to complete." At least I hoped Iris would have more for me to do. I did not want to be Matt Wallace's errand boy.

I arrived back at Iris's office and repeated the highlights of the marketing conversation. She dropped her head into her hand.

"How can I help?" I asked.

"Find me a new marketer."

My back stiffened. Would she really fire Matt Wallace? I should not feel such pleasure at the thought, but knowing he would not walk the halls anymore made me inordinately happy.

"I will see what I can do."

THIRTY-EIGHT

Iris

Everything was falling apart.

The sewing machines were on the fritz. Matt was not performing well as head of the marketing department. And worse, I'd received a letter accusing Aṣọ of not meeting the Ọlọran business regulation that stated we had to receive royal council approval for the fashion show event.

While Ekon had talked to Matt, I had drafted a letter to the board requesting better equipment. We were nothing without working machines. A reply had come swiftly, letting me know they would discuss it further and inform me of their decision. I'd heard nothing by the time I logged off my laptop at the end of the day.

Before leaving the building, I had stopped by Matt's office and had a candid conversation about his work efforts. He hadn't taken the firing well, and Jide had to escort him off the premises. Fortunately for me, one of the marketing employees was still working and happily accepted the task of cleaning up after Matt. I would have to check in further tomorrow, but I had walked away thankful that had been cleared up.

As for the missed regulation, I had called the regulation office to find out where the miscommunication lay. I knew I had filed the request to do the fashion show, because Ekon had informed me of the need. So where had it gone, if not to their office?

But that was neither here nor there. Right now I was running late to Ekon's Bible study.

My phone rang as I jammed an earring in my ear, then placed the call on speaker. "Hello?"

"Hey, Rissy."

"Hey, Junior. What's up?" I said impatiently.

"Oh, *excuse me*. Did I call you at a bad time? Are you so important now that you don't have time for your brother anymore?"

I shook my head, rolling my eyes. "I'm on my way out, but you know I always have time for you."

"Mm-hmm, sure. We'll see if I believe that after I tell you my news."

"What news?" I picked up my cell, taking it off speaker and pressing it to my ear. I didn't want to miss a word.

"I'm thinking of moving to Ọlọrọ Ilé."

"What?" My mouth dropped. "Why?" I winced. *That came out wrong.* "Not that I don't want you here."

"Exactly. Your life would be miserable without me around. But honestly, Ọlọrọ is beautiful. I feel like my life would have no choice but to slow down if I moved there."

Was business that hectic? Why hadn't I done a better job of calling Junior to check on him? "Have you prayed about this?"

"Every day. The only thing I'm sure of right now is that God wants me to take a break."

"Okay." I could understand that. We were meant to take rests.

"I got the idea to visit you again. I don't want to pack up and move on a whim, so I was hoping I could crash in your spare bedroom for a while. No parents, just me. I could explore the island at my leisure. See if the move would be a good idea or not."

"What about your clients?"

"You know I can work remotely."

True. I'd done that when I first moved here. "Of course you can stay with me. *Mi casa es su casa.*"

"You're the best. I'll let you know when I have plane tickets."

"Great." I grinned. Junior was coming back. I'd have family with me again.

"Oh, and text me your fashion show date. Maybe I can arrive around then or stay until then."

"That makes sense. I'll text the info once I'm in a taxi."

Right after I ended the call with Junior, a text from Bri came in.

Bri:

Hey, just wanted you to know I had to go to the doctor this morning, and yes, everything is okay.

I sank down on the couch.

Iris:

Next time lead with that. What happened?

Bri:

I passed out.

What?!

Iris:

Where were you? Did you hit your head or anything? Is Tomori freaking out?

Bri had said he was nervous about her pregnancy but never said why. I figured it was personal reasons and none of my business.

Bri:

He's hovering over me, but thankfully not reading over my shoulder right now.

And I didn't hit my head because Merrick caught me.

My eyes squeezed shut at the image. Thank goodness for Bri's security guards.

Iris:

What did the doctor say?

Bri:

Potassium is low, courtesy of morning sickness, so he suggested an anti-nausea med that's safe for the baby and me.

Iris:

Oh good. I'll be praying for you.

Bri:

Please. And for Tomori. He looks a little shook.

Iris:

I will.

With that, I finally called for a taxi. At first, I thought it strange Ekon hadn't offered to pick me up, but then I remembered he was hosting the Bible study. I couldn't expect him to be my chauffeur when he had to cook dinner for everyone.

I shook my hands, trying to expel the nerves. Meeting Ekon's friends was a big deal. I wanted them to like me. They were the ones to impress, since Ekon's family situation was a mess. *Don't. Don't go backward and think this is some step to a happily ever after.*

Hanging out with Ada, going to church, and spending time

in my Bible had helped me get over the heartache of Ekon's reaction to our kiss. Examining my propensity to rush into a situation with emotions fully engaged and ready to believe the best had taught me that I really needed to take the time to breathe and talk to God. If I didn't make Him my first step, I would always have the problem of being let down by humans. Because people were fallible, including myself.

Lord God, please guide me. Please help me enjoy Bible study for what it is. Please help me see Ekon as a friend, employee, and nothing more.

I glanced at my watch. I needed to let Ekon know I'd be late.

> **Iris:**
> I'm sorry but something came up, and I'll be late. In a taxi now.

> **Ekon:**
> Do not worry. Just get here when you can.

> **Iris:**
> I will.

Maybe if this went well, I could invite Ada to come with me next time. We had finally talked about the elephant in the room and discovered that she was nervous around men. The fact that the guy had been Ekon wasn't even a factor. She'd been raised by women, then sent to an all-girls school. It was a reason her ex-boyfriend had broken up with her. He didn't want to be loved just because he was the first man she fell in love with. He wanted to be loved for himself. Apparently, they were taking things slowly and establishing a friendship right now.

I admired Ada and the patience she exhibited. Yes, God wanted me to learn how to exercise that fruit, but it had never been my favorite. I was more of a *love, joy, kindness,* and even *self-control* kind of girl. Patience was a bitter pill to swallow. Yet God was nudging me to be just so.

It was why I hadn't bounced off the walls waiting for the board to reply regarding the sewing machines. I'd prayed over the email, prayed for provision, and shelved the thoughts that wanted me to track every what-if option and consider damage control. I didn't want to worry about that, especially as I wholeheartedly believed that God wanted my company to succeed.

Should I offer Ekon a job? Would being able to see him every day make the love I felt worse or soften it to bearable levels? Maybe I'd meet someone else.

I snorted inwardly. Yeah, even I didn't believe that. Not that I didn't think there were other good men out there. I simply knew myself. My heart was Ekon's.

Oddly enough, I'd be okay being single if he never sought to change our relationship status. Maybe that was Victorian of me, to live a life of solitude after losing the love of a man. It sounded like a Jane Austen novel. Well, hers had happy endings, so maybe one of the Brontë sisters. Regardless, God had been working on me to be okay with whatever came my way.

Does that include what happens at Aṣọ?

I hoped so. I'd never be one to ignore my heartache. After all, self-soothing with some Ọlọran ice cream or enjoying my favorite chocolate shipped from the States was my MO. I could even shed a few tears at girls' night with Bri.

Oh goodness, I couldn't wait until her little one was born. I still couldn't believe the council had approved me to be the baby's godmother. If something did happen to the queen and king, then I'd agreed to raise the baby in Ọlọrọ Ilé. It had been an easy choice to make, and I would now be listed in their records as godmother. I had a feeling everything would be fine—making my title as godmother merely a formality—and Bri would rule this country until she was old and gray.

The taxi pulled up to Ekon's home. A few cars filled the

driveway, but not Ekon's. Had he gone out for a grocery run? Surely not. I walked up the path, then the front steps, and knocked on the door.

Nika opened the door, a big smile on her face. "Iris. Hi! Come on in. We have been waiting."

"I'm so sorry." I tripped over my words as my heart pummeled in my chest. Why was she answering the door? Had she been the closest person? Had she volunteered? Was she acting as co-host?

"Ekon just placed all the food outside, so everyone else is already in the backyard. He said you would be here soon, so I stayed by the door."

"I appreciate that." And couldn't help but sigh in relief that she'd volunteered to answer the door, not that he'd asked her specifically.

"How do you like living in Ọlọrọ?" she asked as we walked toward the back.

"I love it."

A curious expression covered her face. "Do you miss the States?"

"Sometimes, but mostly the people."

She nodded. "I would miss the people here as well." She glanced at one of the men sitting at the table.

My knees buckled, and I wanted to praise God her interest lay elsewhere.

"Iris is here," she called out.

The group turned. A few waved, and others gave greetings.

Ekon stood and walked over to me. "Ẹ kúròlé, Iris."

"Ẹ kúròlé, Ekon. Thanks for inviting me."

"Of course." He gestured toward the round table. "Please sit. We will pray and eat."

I nodded, looking at the open spots. "Should I sit anywhere?"

"There is space next to me."

I wanted to clap my hands with glee, but instead I followed

Ekon and calmly took the spot next to him. My insides were doing one of those twisty moves gymnasts did in the air, landing with jubilation. Though mine would probably do a dab to express my happy feelings.

Girl, what happened to treating him like a friend?

You try being in love, I countered.

"Iris," Ekon said, "this is Tito, Kitan, Fola, Kamso, and of course you know Nika. Everyone, this is Iris."

"Nice to meet you all." I smiled, and everyone greeted me back.

The man named Tito bowed his head and led us in prayer. Ekon leaned close to me, translating in English. I tried to stay focused on the words and ignore his close proximity, but it was difficult to do. Fortunately, the heartfelt words came through in translation, and I was swept away.

We passed the food around to fill our plates.

"So tell us, Iris," Kamso began, "what made you want to open a business in Etikun?"

I tensed. Was he curious, or did he find fault with Aṣọ like some others? "I wanted to help the women. I thought there was a better way for them to sell their designs than in the markets for mere pennies."

"But you will receive all the credit, no?"

"Actually, no," Ekon spoke up. "She has everything set up so that if one of the women has a unique design, she is listed as the fashion designer and gets a portion of the royalties. Aṣọ is listed as distributor and retains a portion of the income, since we are the ones distributing the clothing to the world."

I smiled. "But as of tomorrow, you no longer work at Aṣọ."

"Well, he does need a job," Fola stated. "Give him one."

"Fola," Ekon scolded.

"It is true," Nika agreed. "Give him a permanent job."

Ekon sighed.

I turned to look at him. "Do you want to work for Aṣọ?"

"Let us talk about it later."

"All right."

His shoulders sagged, but worry seemed to tinge his eyes. Did he not want to work with me? Or was he more concerned that I wouldn't want to work with him?

Don't worry about it right now. Just stay in the moment. I gave myself an inward pat on the back and kept eating.

We laughed and talked about our faith. Spending time with the group made me remember my friends from the city and fanned my hopes for my friendship with Ada. I truly enjoyed meeting people and connecting with as many as possible. The more time passed, the more relaxed I became. How I'd missed hanging out with a group of friends.

Moving to a new country had taken a toll on me. One I didn't often talk about. Sure, I could share my thoughts with Bri, but I always felt selfish. She had to run a whole country, and I had chosen to run a company. I didn't regret moving here, but I wished there were more opportunities to make friends. The women at work saw me as an employer only. Other than Ada and Bri and Ekon, my list was limited.

At least Junior's coming for a visit. Another person you know.

Later that evening, after we'd discussed certain passages in the Bible, Nika and I carried some of the dishes to the kitchen.

"Do you want some help cleaning?" Nika asked.

"No. I have it," Ekon stated.

"Okay, then see you." She waved and hooked her arm through Kitan's, and they left.

Fola and Kamso paused in the doorway. "Are you sure you don't want help cleaning?"

"I got it."

"Good night, Ekon," Tito shouted.

"Drive safe, brother."

The door closed, and we were alone. I looked at Ekon. "Um, could I get a ride home?"

An indecipherable look crossed his face. "I must apologize, but you will have to call for a taxi, or I can run out and ask Kamso or Tito to take you."

"Why?"

"I sold my car."

I leaned against the counter. "I need to hear this story."

He laughed. "I am starting my jewelry design business and needed some startup money."

What about his money in the bank? How much of it had he spent? "But don't you need to get around?"

"After tomorrow I will not have to go to Aṣọ, and that is the only place I really go. I can walk to the local market. Tito has offered to take me anywhere else I may need to visit."

"I offered to pay for the designs, Ekon."

He stepped forward. "I know. But I want to do this on my own. I *need* to. Please, trust me."

I searched his eyes. "I do trust you."

His lips quirked to the side. "You do not know what that means to me."

No, but I had an idea.

THIRTY-NINE

Ekon

One week had passed since my last day working for Iris. Since then, I had tried my utmost to ignore the loneliness. I missed seeing her smiling face every day. Instead of calling or texting her, I used those emotions to fuel my designs.

The transition from running a jewelry business to consulting for a fashion business to designing my own jewelry was difficult. However, I did not let that keep me from working. I had finished some bracelets and a few earrings that made a matching set. Necklaces required more work and equipment I did not yet own. Any day, more equipment would arrive.

I had managed to sell some bracelets online. Tito knew how to set up a website and had helped me get a presence. I had used the sales and a withdrawal from the bank to finance my latest machinery purchase.

Not working at Aṣọ freed me to dedicate longer hours toward the rest of my community service time. I now had a week and a half left before meeting the royal council, who would mark my sentence as served.

A knock sounded at my door, and I looked up from the Ọlọran agate I was working with. I glanced at my watch. Too early for the mail carrier. Perhaps my shipment had arrived earlier than expected.

I took off the loupe I wore and stood, leaving my home office to head for the front door. I opened the door and froze.

"Ekon."

I stared.

Ise Diallo shifted from one foot to the other. "May I come in?"

I wanted to say no. Too often this man had hurt me, but I could not do the same to him. As much as I wanted to treat him harshly, my heart—or was it God?—told me otherwise. I shifted to the side and motioned him forward.

Lord, I do not know why he is here, but please help me. Please be here with me. Please help me know what to say. Please help me forgive.

I gulped at the last thought. Forgiveness had been the subject of our previous Bible study and one that had stuck with me long after.

I gestured for Ise to follow. We walked to the living area, and I sat in my recliner. "Please have a seat." I paused. "I never expected to see you here."

He cleared his throat. "Understandable. I did not act my best the last time we met."

What was I supposed to say to that? He had not. *But neither did you. Nor were your thoughts on the charitable side.* I shifted in my seat. "You do not act your best quite often."

Father—no, Ise—winced. "You are right. I have always had such high expectations for you. The highest standards."

"That you seemed to ignore for yourself." I bit my tongue. I had not meant to interrupt, but really, did he think I would argue regarding his deplorable behavior? When I had asked him for an explanation, he had refused to give one. Now he thought he could walk in here and . . . what?

Peace.

I blew out a breath. This visit brought me anything but peace.

"I did not intend to tear you down throughout your life, Ekon, but to keep others from finding out the truth of your parentage. If the elders had known from the beginning that you were not my biological son . . ." He shook his head. "It would have cost us everything. I knew they would look at Tife and see no resemblance. With men, it is a little easier to agree there is something there."

People had never said I looked like him, but as soon as I talked, they told me my mannerisms were uncannily similar. Was that what he was trying to say? He had stifled my own personality out of me. "I understand." Oddly enough, I truly did.

"Do you?" He looked shocked.

"I do not agree with how you raised me, how you treated me after the council's sentencing. I am simply saying I understand where you are coming from."

"I imagine you are very angry."

I was and could admit some of that resentment stirred upon seeing him now. But I had also had time to think about what life had been like for my adoptive parents. To wonder what I would have done in their shoes.

"Not anymore." I stared at the man who had raised me. Who had called me son. My heart warred within me for the next step, the one God prodded me toward. I swallowed, trying to say it in my head to practice for the real deal. But I remained mute.

"What changed?" he asked.

"I am not willing to discuss that with you." It seemed too personal for our relationship. We had never had heart-to-hearts. This whole experience was surreal. The feeling in my chest welled as my pulse raced. *Say it, Ekon.*

He nodded. "I deserve that."

And so much more! I closed my eyes. *God, I cannot do what You ask.*

Peace. That word again. It was not speaking of my current situation but of my future.

I spoke. "I forgive you."

He looked down at his hands, his shoulders shaking. "I do not deserve your forgiveness," he choked out.

My chest tightened. I knew that feeling very well. One that had prevented me from accepting God's grace sooner.

We were not demonstrative, but right then, he needed to know I truly did forgive him. I stood before him and held out a hand. "I forgive you . . . Father."

His Adam's apple bobbed, and he gripped my hand. "Your mother—" He cleared his throat. "Tife learned of our discussion. She was quite upset. We had a fight."

I blinked in surprise. "She argued with you?"

A sheepish expression crossed his face. "She did." He paused. "I am sorry, Ekon. For all of it. You were right about my past." He slipped a clammy hand from mine. "I cannot share, but you were right." He pulled an envelope from his suit jacket. "Here. This is yours. I have never opened it, though I have wanted to many times."

"What is it?" I took it.

"The name of your father."

I stared down at the nondescript envelope. "You never looked?"

"No. Your biological mother assured me he would not contact you. That when you were ready, he would be ready too."

The words made me curious. I wanted to shoo Ise Diallo out the door and open the envelope, but I kept an outward façade of calm. "I appreciate this."

"It is the least I can do." He cleared his throat. "Oh, about your last name. If you wish to keep it, I will say nothing. If you want to expose me, then I will accept the consequences."

My eyes met his. "The Etikun elders know Tife is not my mother." I had not intended to tell them, but in explaining why

Dayo held power over me, it had come out. Most likely they would strip him of his seat and he would be outed.

None of that would make me feel better. It would not change my past.

"Yes. That I know. I meant the royal council."

"They already know."

"Oh." Ise looked crestfallen but left without another word. As soon as the door closed behind him, I ripped open the envelope and stared at the name.

Chima Nnadi.

The name repeated in my mind. There was an address listed below, right here in Etikun. I needed to go there. Would this man truly know who I was? Was he truly waiting for me? What did it all mean? How had he met my biological mother? Why did they not marry?

The questions flew through my mind as I requested a taxi and made sure I had some Ọlọran francs to pay for the ride.

I tapped my fingers against my pant leg as the driver drove to my biological father's address. We left town and headed for the hills, the edge of the Etikun region. As the taxi drove higher, my nerves grew. Finally, the road gave way to gravel, and the driver stopped.

"My friend, it says the house is down this road." He pointed to the GPS on his mobile. "If you keep walking, you will get there, but I do not want to tear up my car."

I stared through the windshield at the rock-filled road before us. "Will you be the one to pick me up when I am ready?"

"If you ask for me by name, I would be happy to."

"Thank you." I paid the fare along with a generous tip for his troubles, then got out of the taxi.

As I continued on foot, I realized that I had entered some of the farm area of Etikun. It appeared to be a yam field. I noticed the vines as I strolled along the road.

Suddenly the lane curved, and I could see a house at the top of the hill. The humble home had a thatched roof. People milled about out in the yard, and they all seemed to spot me at once. I could not make out their faces and doubted they could see mine, but one figure broke away from the group. The person's first few steps were slow but then picked up speed until they ran down the hill straight toward me.

My heart leapt into my throat as I realized it was a man. An older man who looked very much like me, only with gray at the temples and sprinkled throughout his short-cropped hair. He *had* to be my biological father.

Without even realizing it, I increased my pace, and I was within arm's distance of my father.

"My son," he greeted, then pulled me tightly into his arms, squeezing me as if he would never let go.

Surprise gripped me at the welcome, at the pure acceptance I felt in his embrace. And even more, at the tears that watered my eyes at the outpouring of love that flowed from him. "*Bàbá?*"

"Yes, it is I, Chima Nnadi." He did not let me go to introduce himself. We just stayed there in a hug that seemed to say, *I see you. I know you. I have been waiting for you. I love you.*

"Bàbá," I repeated, tension draining from my shoulders.

"You are so big," he stated.

I choked on a laugh.

"Let me see you."

We stepped back, and he looked me over. I half wondered if he would count my fingers and toes. "You are a strapping lad. You have that Nnadi build."

"You need it out in these hills, right?" The right side of my mouth rose in amusement.

"Yes, we do." He grinned. "I knew this day would come. I have prayed for it every day, standing on my front porch, knowing that one day I would see you come up this road, searching for me."

Chill bumps broke out across my arms. "How? I do not understand."

"Come. We will eat. I will tell you everything."

Over akara balls, Bàbá told me how he met my mother and their resulting love story. How they had lost control one night, which led to my conception.

"The shame overwhelmed me, but I wanted to do right by her."

"Did she not want to marry you?" I asked. My mind ached for them. Yet the bands around my chest loosened. They had been in love.

"She did, but then my family threatened to cut me off financially. Zita came from a poor family. She did not make a lot of money as a housekeeper in those days. Not to mention she became gravely ill with morning sickness. A few days later, after I told her my family's position, Ise Diallo approached her with the offer. She wanted to accept."

Bàbá shook his head. "I did not want to agree, but I had nothing to offer her. If we wed, poverty was our future. If I let her go, then she would find her way, and you would be taken care of."

"So you let her go," I murmured. I understood the logic, and a look at his face gave a glimpse of the heartache behind the decision.

"It was the only path I could see."

I held up the letter. "And this?"

He nodded solemnly. "I gave it to her. This home was my parents'. I vowed never to leave. If I could not have Zita, then I would never marry. That was my vow. I would work this farm and wait for your return. Maybe even hers."

Such sorrow. "You never married?"

He shook his head. "When the news about Dayo broke out, I was heartbroken to learn Zita had passed away."

"You knew my half-sister?"

"Ah, yes. We had hoped to be a family together. I was willing to be her father. But . . ." He sighed. "I was young, foolish, and did not live as God intended. It cost me everything."

"I know how that is."

He cocked his head to the side. "I have a feeling you have found your way. Yes?"

"I have. I really have." I swallowed around the lump in my throat.

"Good. God will show you your next steps. You need only be vigilant, my son."

I looked around the room. "I cannot believe you have been here all this time."

"I wanted you to be able to find me. I have kept up with you via social media over the years. I even have a binder with some clippings from magazines and newspapers." He smiled. "Do not fear my time wasted. Our greeting was all the sweeter for it."

Bàbá was right. Had I not lived the life I had, had I not fallen so short, then coming here probably would have been bitter and full of disappointment. At this time, right now, my heart was full. I could only be grateful for a father who had loved me from the beginning. Who had not treated me like a business transaction but had wanted what was best for me.

"Thank you for being here."

"I would not be anywhere else."

And I found I did not want to be either.

FORTY

Iris

Aṣọ was a madhouse, and I loved every minute of it. I
called out orders as people moved here and there to
get designs into the truck that would be driven to the
fashion show. Ekon would meet us on-site with the jewels, ready
to drape the models before they went on the runway.

A who's who of the fashion world had been flying in over
the past week, touring Ọlọrọ Ilé and bringing the world's media
with them. Fortunately, the board had bought us new sewing
machines in time, and the regulation office had found our notice
requesting to host the event. Now everyone was counting the
hours until the show started.

We—myself and the design team—had chosen to go with
four different designers' creations. We'd also asked the board
their opinion on which one represented the country the best.
I'd even taken Ekon's suggestion and designed a wedding dress,
making me the fourth designer. I worked on the design at night
to keep my heart from mooning over Ekon and wondering how
he fared. I'd been able to task some talented seamstresses at
Aṣọ to sew the dress.

Now we just needed to get the models outfitted to tell Aṣọ's story on the runway. The designers got in the SUV I'd hired to drive us. We would be seated in the front row so the media could take pictures. Of course, I'd made sure they all had time to design an outfit to wear as well. I didn't have the time, so I'd chosen to wear one of the creations that would be sold at Aṣọ in our spring line. Thankfully, the tropical air ensured my sleeveless arms wouldn't be cold.

My brother had flown in at the beginning of the week, taking up residence in my guest bedroom. I'd been overjoyed to see him, and we fell right back into the patterns of teasing. It was nice to talk to him and not hear the echo of my own voice in the flat.

Mom and Dad were heartbroken to miss the fashion show, but Junior had promised to be there as support on their behalf. Mom had made him promise to take plenty of pictures and video. I was thankful for Junior's presence and support.

Plus, Bri would attend, but under guard. She'd requested to wear something from our maternity line, as the media would snap pictures of her. She'd also had me arrange for her to meet Ekon after the show, per his request. Tomori was okay with it, and the guards would be in the room as well. Ekon had thanked me but hadn't said much else.

Was he nervous about his jewels? The show, on my behalf? Or . . .

My thoughts scattered as we turned into the parking lot of the Olọrọ Ilé Arena. My pulse skyrocketed as if I'd just downed an energy drink. The skylights were so pretty, just as I remembered from my previous visit. Ekon had recommended the arena as a venue for the fashion show. This was such a good choice.

His sentence to consult at Aṣọ and help us navigate the labor pains of a new business had been such a blessing to me. Without his input, I'm sure the business would look different—most likely, for the worse.

I sighed as I stepped out of the SUV. I needed to get out of my head and focus on business.

"Iris, Ekon is late!" Oka screeched.

That'll get your attention. I raised my brows as I walked backstage toward a panicking Oka. "Relax. He doesn't have to arrive until half an hour before showtime. I made sure there would be a car to pick him up."

I had gotten my driver's license but had been too busy to buy a car. Otherwise I would have picked him up just to see the look on his face.

"That's not what my timetable says."

I looked at the paper Oka thrust at me. "Oka, it's not four o'clock yet. It's three."

She stared at the time on her cell, then the schedule. "Oh. Sorry."

"Breathe, Oka. We're going to rock this."

She nodded. "I just really want everything to be perfect."

Truth. But God had the details. That had been my prayer upon waking this morning. "It will be just as it's meant to be. Do you have the run of show?" I'd left Oka in charge of the binder holding the sequence of events for the show.

"Yes, madam."

"Then we'll be good."

I headed straight for the makeshift dressing room. We'd hired some dressers to help the models with wardrobe changes, but I wanted to take a peek and make sure no one needed anything.

The time passed quickly as I made sure everything was progressing smoothly. Oka shooed me and the other designers to the front to mingle once guests started arriving. I still hadn't seen Ekon, but we hadn't planned to meet up at the show or anything. Just that we'd talk afterward. I wanted to see his jewelry up close and personal. Plus, I wanted to see how he was.

It had been a few weeks since we'd talked in person. He'd gotten busy with his new jewelry business and I with the fashion show. The intense ache to be with him or dream of the future had lessened. Patience had done its good work, apparently. Not that my feelings had waned, but the urgency to have my way had faded with time and been replaced with peace. God was in the details. Sometimes I repeated that phrase to chase away doubt, and sometimes I said it with the confidence of experience.

Mr. Jalu walked toward me, and I smiled. No, that wasn't his name. His first name started with a J, but his last name was . . .

Kalu! Rumor said he was the new royal council member for Etikun.

"Hello, Ms. Blakely."

"Welcome to the first Ọlọrọ Ilé fashion show, Mr. Kalu."

"It is a pleasure to be here." He looked around, observing the throngs of people. "I am impressed with what you have done."

So was I, but that seemed a little unprofessional to admit. "We wanted to make Ọlọrans proud."

"I believe you will have accomplished that by the end of the show."

I nudged one of the designers beside me. "Mr. Kalu, have you met Sofu Obinna? She designed a few of our pieces in the show and is responsible for our children's line."

"It is a pleasure to meet you." He beamed.

They bowed and began to converse in Oninan. Someone said my name, and I turned, feeling safe to let them converse without me. Bisi Okusanya, one of our board members, introduced me to a prince from the Òkè region. We talked about some of the designers and the process of how the employees were lifted from poverty. He was interested in doing something similar in his region.

I spent most of the preshow time rubbing elbows with the elite of Ọlọrọ. I talked to princes and princesses, elders, and members of the council. In the midst of all the talking, someone alluded to Ekon having had a hand in Etikun finally picking Mr. Kalu to sit on the council. I needed to hear that whole story. I would have to remember to ask him about it after the fashion show.

Oka caught my eye, giving the signal that it was time to start. I motioned to the other designers so we could take our seats. The master of ceremonies welcomed everyone as people began to settle into the chairs before the runway. My stomach felt like I had swallowed a bunch of Pop Rocks whole.

I scanned the crowd, noting the Ọlọrọ Ilé press broadcasting live and reporters from fashion magazines who'd been granted entrance. Their photographers lined the runway, sitting on the ground and waiting for the moment the first model would take the stage.

Traditional Ọlọran music started—drumbeats pulsing in the air—and a beautiful woman gracing six feet turned the corner and entered the room. Her square neckline left ample room for the beautiful sapphire necklace that followed the same shape. Her bell sleeves drew attention as she sauntered down the runway in her red-and-blue patterned dress.

However, it was the next model who left me gasping. Her green Ọlọran agate earrings dangled, catching the chandelier's rays as the model sashayed in green tones. The pine-colored top of her dress covered her ample bosom, while the seafoam skirt sported a sepia pattern. All of it showcased wonderfully with the earrings.

Outfit after outfit, accompanied by Ekon's jewels, held the crowd enthralled. Even the child models brought Aṣọ's ideas to life. I wanted to cry and squeal, then pat the ladies on the back. They had done it. We had done it. There was no doubt in my mind that suppliers would be calling us come Monday to order our spring line and ensure they had our fashions on the book.

When the show ended, the emcee announced my name as the owner and designer of the wedding gown. I stood and waved at the crowd. My cheeks hurt from grinning so hard, but I was so happy with how the show had turned out.

One by one, the designers stood with me as the emcee called their names. They bowed, and I applauded along with the rest of the crowd.

Lord God, You did it. Somehow You orchestrated all the details for this moment.

Tears filled my eyes. I couldn't sing enough of His praises or thank Him enough in my head to show how grateful I was. The designers radiated joy as various media talked to them, taking notes for what I hoped would make awesome quotes in future articles.

Tonight had been a success.

I breathed out, pressing a hand to my stomach.

"Ms. Blakely, could I get a quote for *Arẹwà*?" a writer asked.

Arẹwà was a magnificent magazine focused on beauty, from skincare to the clothes we wore. "Absolutely."

I answered question after question and gave countless statements to other magazine journalists before the crowds slowly thinned. I slipped backstage. Clothes racks were gone, and the space was tidied and put to rights. There was no evidence a show had taken place a couple of hours ago.

"There you are."

I shivered at the sound of Ekon's voice, pasted a friendly smile on my face, and turned. "Hey."

My heart tripped at his feet. He looked wonderful. My gaze roamed his face, cataloguing every feature, searching for any changes since I'd last seen him.

"Congratulations."

"You know it was a team effort."

"It was, but congratulations are still warranted."

I grinned, feeling so happy. "And congratulations to you." I looked at his empty hands. "Where are the jewels? I wanted to see them up close."

He smirked. "They are in a safe place. I cannot walk around with them unguarded."

344

"Good point." They had to cost a fortune. Or they would, once people started clamoring for them.

"Are you all done? No business to take care of?" he asked.

I nodded. "I am."

"Good. Would you come somewhere with me? I mean, after I talk to the queen?"

I'd go anywhere with him. *Slow your roll, girl.*

Besides, I had so many things to talk to him about. And I missed him. *Already you've forgotten you were aiming for friendly.* I took a breath. "Sure. How are we going to get there?" In all my planning, I had forgotten to plan for a way home.

"Kamso let me borrow a car today. He knew I had to transport everything, and I did not want to rely on a taxi service."

I frowned. "But I ordered a car for you."

"Which I canceled when they called to confirm."

I rolled my eyes but smiled when his laughter filled the air. "Meet me outside?"

"Where are we going?" I asked.

He paused, gazing into my eyes. "Does it matter?"

"No." My heart skipped.

His lips curved. "Good."

FORTY-ONE

Ekon

The queen's guard looked me up and down. My mouth dried, heart pounding at what I was about to do and say.

"May I enter?" I asked.

"She is ready for you." The guard knocked on the door and, after the queen called out, twisted the knob.

She sat with a hand over her rounded stomach.

I dropped to my knees before her. "My queen."

"Please stand."

I did so, resisting the urge to slide my hands into my pockets. Instead, I interlaced them before me.

"You asked to meet with me?" she said.

Her expression gave nothing away. I could not tell if she was annoyed by the request or curious. "I did."

She gestured for me to continue.

"Your Majesty, the council gave me an opportunity to repent of my crimes. I do not know if you recall, but I chose to remain silent."

"Yes, I remember."

I swallowed, wishing I had taken a drink of water before coming in here. "I would like to rectify that now, if you will give me the privilege of listening."

"Go ahead."

God, please give me the words. "When I was put under house arrest, I was arrogant, spoiled, and only cared for myself. I did not see how my actions were so heinous that I deserved any punishment, let alone stripping me of my title and commanding me to serve the community."

"And now?"

I shook my head. "Now I see how arrogant, spoiled, and selfish I truly was. If not for your grace, for *God's* grace, I would not be able to say that it all worked for my betterment. I am not the same man who stood before the council, keeping silent so I would not demean myself. Now I come before you to beg for your forgiveness and wish that you would accept my apology."

The queen rose and walked toward me. "You believe in God?" she whispered.

I smiled. "I do now."

"I'm so happy to hear that. What an answered prayer."

My head jerked back. "You prayed for me?"

"Of course. I could see something was not right in your heart. I'm glad God changed it."

"He really did."

She studied me for a moment. "I forgive you."

A breath I did not know I had been holding released. "E seun, Your Majesty."

"It is truly my pleasure. What does your future hold now?"

Good question. Hopefully a life with Iris. "There is a certain woman . . ."

The queen grinned. "She's the best, isn't she?"

"The very best."

"Are you going to see her now?"

I nodded.

"Then I won't keep you. I'll be praying for you two."

I bowed. "Thank you, Your Majesty."

Her guard opened the door, and I slipped out.

It was easy to find Iris and lead her to Kamso's car. I could not wait to show her the special place I had in mind. One that was kind of an unspoken secret in Etikun, a place locals did not share with tourists. We wanted it kept pure and free of crowds. The location would be the perfect place for me to pour out my heart to Iris. I prayed she still believed I was worth the effort.

I wanted her to take a gamble with me, even though my life was still in shambles. But where I had once believed I had nothing to offer, now I saw endless opportunities. Love was worth so much more than people realized. Love made Bàbá give me up for a better situation than he could offer. Love made him put my needs and those of my mother above his own.

The Etikun elders had spoken to the tribal members and shared how instrumental I had been in ensuring a vote for the royal council was taken. Though they did not talk about Dayo's letter, those who had been there understood. Although people were never going to consider me popular, the elders' backing had stopped most of the dirty looks from my fellow countrymen. I welcomed a life outside the spotlight. Something simple yet honest.

Would that be enough for Iris? Could she love someone like me? Someone who had fallen from grace but had been covered by the blood of Jesus?

All these thoughts occupied my mind so completely, it took a moment to realize Iris had not spoken. She was strangely quiet. By now, she would normally be talking my ear off and asking me all sorts of questions.

I glanced at her. "You are quiet."

"Is it unnerving?" She laughed.

"Not unnerving, but I miss your voice."

"Ekon . . ." She paused. "What should I talk about?"

"I thought you would be excited about the fashion show."

"It was great, wasn't it?"

I could practically hear her grin. There was no point in glancing at her, since nightfall made it almost impossible to see one another. "It was."

"And your jewelry." She sighed. "I loved it."

"I am glad."

"A bunch of people asked me about it. I handed out cards like you requested."

"Thank you." *This woman!*

"Of course."

I turned off the road, right before the small shack that marked the way.

"Where *are* we going?"

I chuckled. "It is a secret."

"What do you mean?"

"It is only for locals to know. Then again, you are the proud owner of an Ọlọran business and have successfully orchestrated Ọlọrọ Ilé's first fashion show. I believe that now makes you a local."

"So I can't tell anyone else?"

"Like I said, locals know of the spot. Maybe someone outside of the region does, but only because they used to live here. Oh, and you cannot tell your brother." She had sent me a bunch of happy GIFs when he arrived earlier this week.

"What about Bri?"

Hmm . . . "Though she *is* the queen, if Tomori has not shown her already, then that is his fault."

She laughed as I parked the car.

"Do not move. I will open your door."

My hands were slightly clammy as I rounded the back of the car. What should I say? How should I say it? *Lord, please give me the words. Please help her receive them with an open heart. I really do not want her to reject me.*

This was purely selfish of me but the truth nonetheless. I had rejected her in a vulnerable moment. She could do the same to me. Yet I really did not believe she would out of spite, more so because her heart had moved on. I would not know until I put myself out there.

I offered my hand, holding Iris's lightly as she got out. "Do you want to take off your heels?"

She looked down at the thick grass. "It would probably be best, but what about bugs?" Her nose scrunched, the moonlight kissing her skin.

"They scatter when they feel the vibrations of your feet."

"Ew, don't say that."

I bit back amusement. "You would rather they stay where they are?"

"I'd rather there be no bugs."

"It is a tropical island."

She rolled her eyes. "I'll leave my heels on."

"Okay, then."

We walked slowly, the night stars twinkling. A trickling sound reached my ears. I smiled as we reached the spot and spied the small waterfall flowing down the hill. Moonlight shimmered across the ripples. If the setting did not help my cause, then it had been helpless from the start.

"I love this," Iris breathed out.

"It is no Victoria Falls, but I find the sound relaxing."

"It really is."

I pointed to a couple of large rocks. "Shall we sit?"

She nodded.

I stared out at the water, searching for how to begin. "Iris . . ."

"Yes?"

I met her gaze, thankful the moon gave me some light. "I am sorry."

Her brow furrowed. "For what?"

"Everything." I rubbed my chin. "I was a mess when I met

you. But somehow, you saw something in me that I did not even know existed. You believed in me when no one else did. You made me hope and search for a God who actually cared about the things that mattered to me. Who believed I was worth something."

"Of course you're worth something."

I smiled. That was such an Iris statement to make. It was one of the things I loved about her. "I did not believe that for the longest time."

"Is that why—" She stopped. "Is that why you didn't want anything to happen between us?"

I nodded. "One of the reasons. I also had nothing to offer you."

"Why did you think that? It's not true."

My heart sped up. "I had no title. No penthouse. No cars. No respect from my fellow countrymen. How could I saddle you with the likes of me?"

"That's why you pushed me away after our kiss?"

"Yes." I could not regret it, for it had given me time to grow, but if I had lost her in the process . . .

"So it wasn't because you didn't like the kiss?"

"That was not even in the realm of possibility."

Her head dipped shyly. "And now?" she asked softly.

"Now . . ." I gently tipped her chin up. "I hope love is enough to offer you. If I offer my heart, Iris"—I gulped—"would that be enough? Would it matter that I still do not have a car? That I live in a modest home? Will never have a title and most likely not earn the respect of all my countrymen? Am I a gamble?"

Iris's eyes widened. "*Are* you offering me your heart?"

This was it. The moment where I needed to take a leap of faith. To go where God had been prodding me in my quiet moments with Him. This woman was who I wanted to spend the rest of my life with. If she was by my side, I knew that no matter what came my way, I would not even blink, because she would be the biggest blessing of my life.

I knelt before her, drawing her hands in mine. "Iris Blakely, my heart is yours if you want it. I love you, ododo mi."

"What does that mean?"

I blinked. Not the response I was going for. "Ododo mi?"

She nodded.

"'My flower.'"

"Oh, Ekon . . ." She threw her arms around my neck.

I barely braced myself in time to keep us from falling backward. She rained kisses all over my face, and I placed my hands gently on her cheeks to stop her movements. "That is a yes?"

"That's a million yeses. I will gladly take your heart and trade it for mine."

Relief pooled in me, and I laid my forehead against hers. "Truly?"

"Did you really have a doubt?"

"I botched that first kiss pretty badly. If I could have done it better, learned a few lessons earlier . . ."

She shook her head. "That kiss was perfection, but yeah, the conversation after was bad. But Ekon, *I* didn't handle it well. I'm sorry for not listening to what you were trying to say and for not letting you know that none of that mattered. I'm pretty sure my heart became yours the moment I laid eyes on you."

I grinned. "That kiss was perfection, huh?"

"That's all you caught?"

I brushed my thumb across her bottom lip. "I need to rewrite history. Is that okay?"

"More than okay."

We stood, and I placed my hands around the curve of her waist. "I love you, Iris."

"And I love you, Ekon."

I placed my lips ever so gently against hers. My heart thrummed in my ears. I had been dreaming of kissing her since long before the first time I had done so. I took my time until she clutched my shirt, begging me to deepen the kiss as we communicated our feelings for a few minutes longer.

Feeling the heat between us grow, I pulled away. "I should drive you home."

Her eyes held a dreamy gaze as she peered up at me. "Okay."

I caressed her chin. "Can I see you tomorrow?"

"You can see me every day. I'll pencil it in my planner if I have to."

I laughed. "Believe me, you have not seen the end of me."

"Nor you me."

I kissed her cheek. "Let us go."

Before I got behind the wheel, I grabbed the jewel case in the back and passed it to her. "Have your fill looking at them."

Iris oohed and ahhed before I turned off the dome light and drove toward her apartment.

"You're going to have so many calls about your jewelry. I just know it."

"I hope so."

"And I just love your business name."

The name of Bukun Designs had come to me at a Bible study meeting. The others had agreed it was the perfect name, since it meant *blessed*.

As we drove, I dropped my other bombshell on Iris. "I almost forgot to tell you—I met my biological father."

"You what?" She clapped her hands together. "Tell me everything."

I laughed, the carefree feeling that had filled me since he embraced me coming to the forefront. I told her about his house in the hills. How he had run to me.

"Oh my goodness, it's like the prodigal son from the Bible."

I paused. "You are right." There was a similar tale in our history, but I had never seen the parallels until now.

"Have you seen him since then?"

"Yes. He came to my house, and I have gone to his a few more times. He said I could come back for harvest."

She sniffed. "I'm so happy for you."

I squeezed her hand. "If you had told me that life would get better after I was sentenced by the council, I would have laughed."

"And now?"

"Now I see endless possibilities."

She squeezed my hand. "I've always seen those with you, Ekon. Always."

"Now I see them as well."

I truly did. I had needed a new perspective, and God had granted me one. I had gone from believing nobles were above others to knowing that true nobility came from the heart. True nobility did not rise above but lifted those around them.

God had been there as I was stripped of all I had ever known, but sometimes we had to remove the lies in order to see the truth. I was just glad Iris had the patience she did. Now she could celebrate my victory with me. I could not help but imagine the endless promises before us.

EPILOGUE

Iris

EIGHT YEARS LATER

Bàbá!" Lily shrieked as she spotted Ekon coming up the hill.

I rubbed my swollen belly as she rushed off the porch and down the dirt path. Her little legs pumped with the effort, but Ekon would run toward her as soon as he saw her twin afro puffs, the bright yellow bows gleaming in the sunlight.

When we'd talked about having kids, Ekon had promised me they would always know they were loved. Considering how much he showed me every single day, I'd eagerly jumped at the idea of kids, knowing he'd be a good father.

I'd been right. Ekon was a wonderful bàbá to Lily. Which was great, because God had surprised us this go-around with twins. I was bigger at seven months than I'd been full-term with Lily. Her pregnancy had been a breeze, but the boys kept me sucking on ginger candies. I had an inkling that life with them would be an adventure.

Ekon noticed Lily and jogged forward, scooping her up. Her giggles filled the air. I smiled at the two of them, their evening ritual such a bright part of my day.

We'd built a great life here in these hills, thanks to Ekon's dad. He'd initially offered Ekon's grandparents' place to us as a wedding gift, but my husband wasn't called to farming. It turned out my father-in-law had another spot available on the Nnadi land. He'd given it to Ekon, encouraging him to build a house there. We'd arranged for Ekon's home to be moved from its old location to the spot here, where we could be sure our kids would always know we were watching for them to come home.

In the meantime, Lily loved being able to run through the fields to her grandpa's house. Which was helpful, since I'd been relegated to house rest—working had been too much for me with these twins. But I loved the moments it afforded me, like spending evenings with Lily as we watched the path for Ekon to return.

He'd built an inlet for cars farther down the path, choosing not to widen the road to allow cars all the way up to the house, instead forcing all visitors to walk and be greeted. My brother grumbled every time he came over, but the palace guards loved it because they knew no one could sneak up on us if Bri and Tomori chose to visit with my godchildren.

I rose as Ekon and Lily neared the front porch.

"Do not get up, ododo mi. You need to conserve your energy."

"My butt was falling asleep anyway."

Ekon smirked. I took a step forward, meeting him near the stairs, where he would stop climbing so we'd be the perfect height to kiss. It was one of my favorite parts of the day. However, my belly was so huge that I had to turn sideways.

I pulled back. "How was your day?"

"Fantastic. I got another order for the Iris. It is currently my most popular necklace."

"What about the Lily?" Lily asked.

"I sold two Lilies today."

Her big brown eyes widened as a smile curved her lips. She was calm just like her father, but then she had moments where she flashed brightly, just like me. It would be scary if it weren't so precious. Ekon told us all the time that he was blessed with two precious flowers and had chosen to design necklaces after us. They continued to be his best sellers.

Meanwhile, Oka had taken over running Aṣọ, with me peeking in here and there. It had never been my desire to run the business forever. I was all too happy running after Lily instead. Someone had to make sure she didn't get into *too* much trouble.

She would be going to school soon, just in time for me to chase after twins. I rested my head against Ekon's shoulder.

"Does that mean the Lily is the best?" she asked.

I chuckled.

"It means I have the best two flowers ever," Ekon answered.

"I love you, Bàbá."

"I love you too, my lily."

We walked inside, hand in hand. I squeezed Ekon's, thankful for this man who'd laid his heart on the line all those years ago. Thankful that I had listened to God to wait and grow in Him. Patience was a lesson I'd never wanted to learn, but if I hadn't, I would have missed the reward. Getting to know Ekon, falling in love with him, and building a life with him was so very worth all the heartache of that waiting period. It had allowed me to focus on a business, build other relationships, and deepen my faith in God.

And when Ekon made me stark raving mad—because he liked a calm and cool approach, letting logic lead in the heat of the moment instead of emotion, like I did—my heart still beat with love for him. Life with him was maddening and wonderful all at the same time.

I wouldn't trade all the arguments, all the ups and downs, all the makeups and times of forgiveness for anything. Every day we chose to love one another. Every day that we remembered love was patient and kind, we were rewarded.

I wasn't a princess like Brielle, and Ekon no longer lived the life of a royal, but I had won the heart of a prince. Love had transformed us. Love from God and love from each other. Our life wouldn't be smooth sailing—*hello, twins!*—but I knew doing life with Ekon was worth any possible tears.

Author's Note

Dear Reader,

Thank you so much for taking the time to read *To Win a Prince*. I wrote this story through a difficult time in my life. I knew I would need to write the story in a crunch, and before I even started writing, I prayed. I prayed that God would let the words flow and that it would be a blessing to whomever read it. Y'all, the first draft was written in six weeks, and God amazed me during that time. It's my prayer that you have fallen in love with Iris and Ekon's journey.

If you read *In Search of a Prince*, then you know that Ọlọrọ Ilé is a fictional location dreamed up in my imagination. You'll also already know that the Oninan language is taken from many words of the Yoruba language spoken by many Nigerians. I changed the name of the language because I wanted to be able to use creative license when necessary to go along with the history of the island country I had fictionalized.

Though I asked a reader from Nigeria to read the book for authenticity's sake, please know that it was only one person's experience. If I have written anything that rings false or untrue, please forgive. My wish was to honor an African setting and its people and take us on a journey where God's glory reigns.

Blessings,
Toni

Acknowledgments

I cannot believe I've gotten to this stage in the writing process. *To Win a Prince*'s publication seemed fast in some areas and slow in others. But throughout the whole process, I met so many people who contributed to its success. In no particular order, I would like to thank the following people.

Rachel McMillian, thank you so much for representing me. But more importantly, thank you for your encouragement when I needed it. You've been a blessing, and I'm so thankful God brought us together.

To my awesome critique partners, Andrea Boyd, Sarah Monzon, and Jaycee Weaver. Ladies, you bring me so much joy! Thank you for all your encouragement, writing smarts, and for being my friends. Love you!

This acknowledgment page could not skip two very important people. Carrie Schmidt, thank you for loving Iris and Ekon from the get-go. I appreciated all your insight and encouragement. Ebos Aifuobhokan, words cannot express my gratitude. You've been such a huge blessing as I wrote this book and the last. Praying many blessings for you.

I also want to thank the entire Bethany House Publishers team. You guys are amazing, and I'm so thankful I get to work with you. Every one of you has helped me in some way, and

I know I don't even get to meet half of you who contributed. Please know you have my biggest thanks.

Last but not least, I have to thank my husband and kids. I'm so sorry I made you put up with Deadline Mommy, but I'm also thankful you put up with me. I love y'all so much. "Bethany House!"

Toni Shiloh is a wife, mom, and multi-published Christian contemporary romance author. She writes to bring God glory and to learn more about His goodness. Her novel *Grace Restored* was a 2019 Holt Medallion finalist, *Risking Love* was a 2020 Selah Award finalist, *The Truth About Fame* a 2021 Holt Medallion finalist, and *The Price of Dreams* a 2021 Maggie Award finalist. A member of American Christian Fiction Writers (ACFW), Toni loves connecting with readers and authors alike via social media. You can learn more about her writing at tonishiloh.com.

Sign Up for Toni's Newsletter

Keep up to date with Toni's latest news on book releases and events by signing up for her email list at tonishiloh.com.

More from Toni Shiloh

Brielle Adebayo's simple life unravels when she discovers she is a princess in the African kingdom of Ọlọrọ Ilé and must immediately assume her royal position. Brielle comes to love the island's culture and studies the language with her handsome tutor. But when her political rivals force her to make a difficult choice, a wrong decision could change her life.

In Search of a Prince

You May Also Like . . .

When their father's death leaves them impoverished, the Summers sisters open their home to guests to provide for their ailing mother. But instead of the elderly invalids they expect, they find themselves hosting eligible gentleman. Sarah must choose between her growing attraction to a mysterious widower, and Viola struggles to heal her deep-hidden scars.

The Sisters of Sea View by Julie Klassen
On Devonshire Shores #1
julieklassen.com

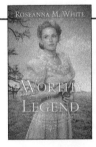

After uncovering a diary that leads to a secret artifact, Lady Emily Scofield and Bram Sinclair must piece together the mystifying legends while dodging a team of archeologists. In a race against time, they must decide what makes a hero. Is it fighting valiantly to claim the treasure or sacrificing everything in the name of selfless love?

Worthy of Legend by Roseanna M. White
The Secrets of the Isles #3
roseannamwhite.com

After years of being her diva mother's understudy, it's time for Delia Vittoria to take her place on stage. Attempting to make amends for a grave mistake, Kit Quincy is suddenly pulled into Delia's plot to win the great opera war and act as her patron and an enigmatic phantom. But when a second phantom appears, more than Delia's career is threatened.

His Delightful Lady Delia by Grace Hitchcock
American Royalty #3
gracehitchcock.com

BETHANYHOUSE

More from Bethany House

Olive Kentworth takes on an architect project with her male cousin posing as the builder and uses her job as a nanny to hide her involvement, but little does she know her charges' father is famous architect and competitor Maxfield Scott. As the architectural one-upmanship heats up, will Olive and Maxfield miss out on building something for their future?

Engaging Deception by Regina Jennings
THE JOPLIN CHRONICLES #3
reginajennings.com

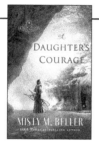

Charlotte Durand sets out on an expedition in search of a skilled artisan who can repair a treasured chalice—but her hike becomes much more daunting when a treacherous snowstorm sets in. When Damien Levette finds Charlotte stranded, they must work together to survive the peril of the mountains against all odds.

A Daughter's Courage by Misty M. Beller
BRIDES OF LAURENT #3
mistymbeller.com

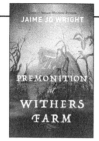

In 1910, rural healer Perliett VanHilton is targeted by a superstitious killer and must rely on the local doctor and an intriguing newcomer for help. Over a century later, Molly Wasziak is pulled into a web of deception surrounding an old farmhouse. Will these women's voices be heard, or will time silence their truths forever?

The Premonition at Withers Farm by Jaime Jo Wright
jaimewrightbooks.com

BETHANY HOUSE

CPSIA information can be obtained
at www.ICGtesting.com
Printed in the USA
LVHW100135161122
733228LV00002B/43